THE
Viscount's
Promise

**THE TWICE
SHY SERIES**

CHRISTINA
BRITTON

everafter ROMANCE

EverAfter Romance
A division of Diversion Publishing Corp.
443 Park Ave, Suite 1004
New York, NY 10016
www.EverAfterRomance.com

For more information, email info@everafterromance.com

First EverAfter Romance edition October 2018.
Paperback ISBN: 978-1-63576-462-8
eBook ISBN: 978-1-63576-461-1

LSIDB/1810

Dedicated with love to Robert and Vickie Jetté,
the best grandparents a girl could have ever been blessed with.
I miss you, Papa and Nani, more than words could ever express.

Chapter 1

"I want you to watch over Emily during the wedding celebrations, Morley."

Malcolm Arborn, Viscount Morley, nearly spit his brandy across the carpet. He turned to his friend, hoping his abhorrence showed on his face. For good measure, he said clearly and distinctly, with more than a touch of horror, "If you think I am going to play nanny to your sister, you are mad."

Caleb Masters, Marquess of Willbridge, didn't so much as flicker an eyelid at the pronouncement. Which was to be expected. Being acquainted as long as they had—hell, they were more than acquainted, they were closer than brothers—liberties were bound to be taken with the friendship, no matter how detestable they might be to the other party.

Though he supposed, with Willbridge marrying in just over a week's time—and, for all reasons, *love*—their friendship would slip away like so much mist with the coming light of day. A sour taste settled on his tongue, a sensation that had been with him since he had learned of his friend's engagement days ago. Malcolm tightened his fingers around the crystal glass in his hand, taking a healthy swig of his brandy in an attempt to eradicate it. Yet the bitterness remained.

"Emily is two and twenty, hardly in need of a nanny," Willbridge said, bringing Malcolm back to the topic at hand. "But she has been protected far too much in the past decade by my mother—a mistake I intend to rectify. I have hopes that the coming wedding and subsequent house party will help to bring her out of her shell."

"And what is my part in all this?"

Willbridge frowned. "Despite my intentions, I do worry what the strain of such a situation will do to her. I need someone to watch over her where I cannot, to make certain it does not become too much for her."

Malcolm let out a bark of laughter. "And I am that remedy? Do you know me at all?"

"I know you very well," Willbridge replied softly, regarding him closely. "Which is why I believe you are ideal for this."

"What, squiring your sister around? Making sure she isn't left without a partner at balls? Or does it go beyond that, and she needs me to tell her when to curtsy, what frock to wear, how to greet this pompous ass or that snobbish dame?"

Malcolm knew he sounded petulant and bitter. If he hadn't been able to hear it in his own voice, Willbridge's raised brows would have told him all. Furious over his loss of temper, he rose and walked across his study to the window. Grosvenor Square lay spread out before him, busy and humming with humanity. It was why he had chosen this room as his private sanctum when he had succeeded to the title after his brother's unexpected demise. He needed this noise, this confusion, this barrage of life. The last thing he desired, after all, was peace and quiet, time to think and remember and...feel.

"I can see where you would come to that assumption," Willbridge replied, his voice cold. "But no, my sister is not an imbecile. She has been fully educated on class and social niceties."

Malcolm downed the rest of his brandy in one quick swallow, letting it burn all the way to his stomach, leaving a blessed numbness behind. "Damn it, I'm sorry," he muttered. "I never meant to disparage her." He shifted his gaze, caught the image of Willbridge in the window as he nodded in acceptance of the apology. Malcolm let out a slow breath. "But that does not explain why you wish me to watch over your sister."

There was a beat of silence, then a rustle as Willbridge stood and walked to his side. "You would remember Emily as a shy but happy child, I assume?"

Indeed he did. Malcolm smiled slightly. She had been sweet, with huge gray eyes and a timid smile that spoke volumes of her awe of him—until the day of the accident.

Malcolm's smile faded. Emily had been badly injured in the same tragedy that had taken her twin brother's life. Malcolm had been there that day, had witnessed it. Never would he forget the feel of her slight, coltish body in his arms, blood pouring from the gash that had cut open her cheek. He had not seen her since, the heartache from the tragedy having caused a nearly insurmountable rift in the family. Until Willbridge's intended, Imogen, had come along and healed the breach.

Now Willbridge and Imogen were planning their marriage at the family's country estate in a week's time—an unwelcome prospect as it was. Willbridge's request, however, added another level to Malcolm's distaste for the situation.

He realized belatedly that Willbridge was awaiting an answer. "Yes, I remember her." He cleared his throat, shooting a careful glance at his friend. "Did her wound heal well?"

Willbridge's lips tightened. "No, it did not. And she has suffered dreadfully for it, I'm afraid. She has retreated into herself in the most disturbing way, and my family allows it."

Malcolm felt a frisson of something travel up his spine. He thought on it for a moment until he saw it for what it was: unease. This situation was quickly getting out of control. Best to be blunt. "I do pity her for it," he stated baldly. "But I cannot see what this has to do with me."

Heaving a troubled sigh, Willbridge met his eyes. "I would ask you to watch out for Emily, perhaps make things easier for her. Stick close to her and see she is not in any distress." He paused, his gaze sober. "I would have your promise, Morley."

A hot knife of displeasure speared beneath Malcolm's skin. He kept his voice neutral as he said, "You know I do not give promises lightly, Willbridge."

"Yes, I know."

A look passed between them. Willbridge was fully aware what

he was about. Having been the victim of so many broken promises in the past, Malcolm would do everything in his power to see a vow through once he gave one. It was his one claim to honor, something he would uphold unto death.

"And you think to weasel a promise from me for this?" Malcolm growled. "Don't you think such a job would be better suited to another female? A relative, perhaps? You must have them in abundance and would have no trouble finding one who would leap to do your bidding."

"That I do. But there is no one I trust as much as I trust you, Morley."

Malcolm's lips twisted even as the compliment warmed him. He banished the better feelings, not wanting them to cloud his judgment. "Not even your esteemed fiancée?"

"You know as well as I that Imogen is something altogether different," his friend murmured, his eyes softening.

"Yes, so I have heard."

Willbridge ignored his surly tone. "You will find out the same for yourself one day, when you let a woman in again."

"Please," Malcolm scoffed, turning back for the window even as his stomach twisted. "We both know that is not likely to happen. Love is not for me."

"I believed the same thing of myself, Morley," his friend said quietly, placing a hand on his shoulder.

Malcolm tensed but did not shrug off his touch. "Enough of sentiment," he said instead. "We will have plenty of that in the week to come. Why don't you spend your valuable time before you return to Willowhaven letting me know why you think I will prove a proper companion to your sister?"

Willbridge removed his hand. "Emily is incredibly sensitive to her looks. Any female I ask to shadow her would only make her feel her...difference all the more."

"Meaning?"

"You ask me to spell it out?" Willbridge let out a frustrated breath. "She is scarred in a very visible way. It has affected every aspect of her life. But she is a lovely young woman who should have every chance in life that any other woman has. Having you by her side would not only detract from this great obstacle in her life, but may give her the confidence she needs to set out and carve a life of her own. And it is quite possible that your attentions, however innocent, might facilitate the interest of a candidate for her hand. She goes to London next Season for our sister Daphne's debut. I would help prepare her in any way I can for that."

It took several moments for the meaning of that to sink in. When it finally did, Malcolm blanched. "You would have me pretend to court your sister?"

Willbridge paled at that. "Gad, no! Although," he amended, his expression turning apologetic as he slid a glance Malcolm's way, "it certainly couldn't hurt that she might think she could garner a man's regard on her own, even if as a friend. Which means that under no circumstances can she know I have asked this favor of you. Learning of our collusion in the matter might very well send her even further back into herself."

Malcolm glowered at his friend. "This is a delicate thing you ask of me, Willbridge. I am to stay close to your sister, feign an interest—however innocuous it may be—and yet keep her in the dark as to my intentions. I also assume I am to ensure no talk erupts over my attentions, but hope they are just enough to make other men see her as a possible life's mate." At Willbridge's nod, Malcolm let loose a frustrated breath. "I do believe your guilt for not having been there to help guide her in the past decade has blinded you to all that can go wrong with this blasted scheme."

Willbridge's shoulders slumped. "I know it sounds foolish, Morley. But I can think of no other way. I truly am doing my best to rectify matters. I'm hoping that in the next weeks she can find a confidence to carry with her into the future. She has had scant practice with men. I would have her see that she is every bit as worthy of attention as any other young woman."

And to do that, you would use one of your closest friends, Malcolm thought acidly. But really, could he blame the man? In the space of a few weeks, Willbridge had gone from a troubled but unencumbered rake to a content family man. It was a state incomprehensible to Malcolm, for what did emotional entanglements provide but the possibility of being betrayed by those you cared for?

"Why not ask Tristan? He's a jovial enough fellow." Sir Tristan Crosby was their mutual friend, the third corner to their fraternal triangle, and the only person in this world who Malcolm cared for besides Willbridge.

"Next to you, he is my dearest friend," Willbridge replied. "However, I have given it much thought, and I do believe his high spirits would prove detrimental to Emily. She is a quiet soul, and he is...not."

Which was putting it mildly, Malcolm thought grudgingly. If Lady Emily was as painfully shy as Willbridge implied, Tristan's bounding love for life might do her more harm than good. Even so, it was every man for himself. "You never know, he might be what she needs."

"I had considered that," Willbridge said slowly, and for a moment hope and relief flared in Malcolm's breast. "But I have come to know my sister since our reconciliation, and such a personality would overwhelm her. She needs someone more levelheaded and restrained. Someone like you."

Malcolm opened his mouth to once more denounce the idea. It was then Willbridge went in for the kill.

"Please, Morley. I trust you with my life. I would not ask you to promise something of this magnitude otherwise."

Nothing he could have said would have swayed Malcolm more. Knowing he was effectively backed into the proverbial corner, he went to his desk, slamming his empty glass down on the polished surface. Taking up the bottle of brandy he had left there, he filled his rummer to the brim and downed the whole lot—a bit of liquid courage, he supposed—before swinging about to face his friend. "Fine," he spat, "I will do it. I swear it."

He could not help feeling, however, as a relieved smile spread over Willbridge's face, that he had signed a deal with the devil himself.

. . .

Lady Emily Masters bent her head determinedly over her embroidery in an attempt to distance herself from the surrounding chaos. With her brother's wedding less than a week away, his future in-laws had already descended upon Willowhaven *en masse*. And Emily was quickly learning how swiftly and completely the peace of her home could be decimated.

It turned out to take no more than two, three minutes at the most.

It's only for a few weeks, she told herself stoutly. Just then a shout went up across the room as two of the youngest visitors got into a bit of friendly banter. Emily tensed, her fingers tightening around her needle. Who knew that the prospect of three weeks' time could be so daunting?

The cushion beside her dipped, and a gentle hand landed on her arm. Emily looked into the kind, worried face of her brother's intended, Miss Imogen Duncan.

"Are you positive you don't mind the wedding being held here?" Imogen asked for what must have been the hundredth time that evening, casting a doubtful eye toward her mother, Lady Tarryton. That lady was waxing poetic to Emily's mother about the grandeur of the house. Imogen pressed her lips together before turning back to Emily. "We did consider having a quick ceremony in London, but thought this would be easiest on everyone involved."

Meaning, Emily thought, *they worried how I would fare in the capital*. She would not deny that when the engagement between her brother Caleb and Imogen was announced, the idea of having to go to London had torn through her with a terror that had left her nearly incoherent. Only when the plan to have the ceremony at Willowhaven had been broached had she relaxed. Even that, however, had its drawbacks, as she was learning now. Weddings meant guests, and guests meant strangers infiltrating her home, polluting all of the places she felt most comfortable and safe. But without doubt this option, as abhorrent as it was proving to be, was the lesser of two evils. She would have to content herself with that. A daunting task, she was coming to learn, now that Imogen's family had arrived.

"Of course I'm certain," she replied, hoping beyond hope that she sounded sincere. And truly, what else could she say? That she wished that Caleb and Imogen had eloped so she would not be forced into social situations with people she did not know; so she would not have to show her face to those who would stare in horror or, even worse, look on her with pity? No matter the truth of that, she was not so uncaring as to voice it. This marriage was nothing but wonderful, and she wished to celebrate it in the best way possible. That her mode of celebration was much more private than everyone else's did not matter, not when it came to the happiness of two people she loved so very much.

Imogen must have read her thoughts, for she looked at her dubiously. "I know my family can be...trying."

"Not all of them," Emily blurted, before gasping in horror at her gaffe. "Oh, I am so sorry, Imogen."

Far from appearing offended, Imogen merely gave her a rueful smile. "My mother is very intense, I know."

Which was putting it mildly. Lady Tarryton had been blessedly awed when setting foot in Willowhaven and thus silent. But as she grew more comfortable, she became more and more vocal. With everyone but Emily.

That should have relieved Emily. The woman frightened her silly, after all, yet she knew too well why the viscountess was leery of making conversation. Her eyes said it all. No doubt the woman had been forewarned about Emily's scar. Her horrified and yet fascinated gaze seemed to be drawn again and again to it...as she was doing right now. Emily flushed hot and turned the ruined side of her face toward the wall.

"I do like your sister very much," Emily said, trying to make up for her slight to Imogen's mother. "Mariah truly is sweet. I can see why you love her so much."

Imogen flushed with pleasure, transferring her gaze to the

opposite corner of the room, where her sister sat in close conversation with Daphne, Emily's younger sister. The two were fast friends mere hours after their introduction.

As her friend looked contentedly upon the sweet duo, Emily's gaze slid away to study the rest of the Duncan family. There were a great many of them present, she thought weakly, and this invasion was only the beginning. As soon as tomorrow, all manner of family from both sides would be descending upon Willowhaven. Heart beating like mad in her ears, she said as calmly as she could manage, "Who else is expected to arrive?"

Her attempt at nonchalance didn't fool Imogen one bit. For, nearly as shy with strangers as Emily was, she understood fully how this affected her. "We did try to keep the guest list down to the necessary people," she said soothingly. "There is your cousin Sir Frederick Knowles and his family, my mother's brother Sir William Gubler and his son, Lord and Lady Tabble and their grown children, who are cousins on my father's side..."

The names went on and on, a seemingly endless litany of people. Emily's mouth went dry as she attempted to keep track of the rapidly growing list. This was the necessary people? Was Imogen related to half of England?

After what seemed forever, Imogen finished with, "And my sister Lady Sumner and her husband, as well as your cousin Sir Alexander Mottram and his family, though neither will be staying here at Willowhaven, their homes being so close."

With each name rattled off, Emily's panic grew until it nearly choked her. What was that, nearly two score of guests? But no, she thought in an attempt to calm herself, more than a quarter of those mentioned she already knew. It could not be as bad as she assumed. No matter her reasoning, however, her heart pounded in her chest so violently Emily thought it would break through her rib cage.

That was when Imogen dropped the final shoe.

"Oh, and Sir Tristan Crosby and Lord Morley, of course. They are your brother's particular friends and will stand up with him."

The rush of emotion and memory Lord Morley's name evoked

caused the edges of Emily's vision to go hazy. She dragged in a deep breath, clearing the light-headedness that had momentarily overtaken her. That, however, did nothing to banish the picture of him in her mind.

Lord Morley. Emily recalled her infatuation with him as a child, how she had thought he was the most handsome man she had ever seen. He used to often visit Willowhaven on holidays with her brother. She had always been a bit awed in his presence. How could she not? Not only was he devilishly good looking, with his dark eyes and black hair, but he was kind as well. He'd always had a smile for her, a gentle word, or even at times a present of ribbons or candy. How could she not love him with all of her twelve-year-old heart?

Then had come The Tragedy.

As Caleb approached and claimed his fiancée's attention, Emily dropped her embroidery back into her sewing basket and reached with shaking fingers for the glass of lemonade on the small table beside her. Instead of drinking it down, however, she pressed the cool glass to her damaged cheek. It had all been a horrible accident: the fall down the cliff that had not only ruined her face, but had taken her twin brother's life. The events leading up to The Tragedy were crystal clear in her mind. She could not forget them if she tried. And she had tried. To forget those last horrible minutes with her brother, who had been everything to her, would have been almost a release. But what had come after, when she was out of her mind from grief and pain, was as murky to her as the silt-filled water at the bottom of the fishing pond. From that day, until the day she had woken from the fever that had nearly taken her life, everything was shadows, mere impressions. Everything, that was, but for Lord Morley.

He had been the one who had carried her back home. She could still see his solemn face above her, feel his arms like bands under her, hear the deep timbre of his voice in her ear as he tried calming her. But that memory was the crux of it, wasn't it? As the years passed, that impression, her one clear recollection of that horrific time, had given him the attributes of a hero. One of the knights of old who would slay dragons and save damsels. He was the pinnacle of manhood, the one to whom she compared each and every male.

But with her brother marrying, Lord Morley would come again to Willowhaven in support of his good friend and force Emily to come face-to-face with what *had* to be a figment of her overactive imagination.

It had been ten years since she had last seen him. At that time, she had been a twelve-year-old girl in the midst of unspeakable horror. He had been her savior, larger than life. He could not be as glorious as she had made him out to be.

That, however, did not ease her mind one bit. Her nerves, already pulled taut to their very breaking point, gave a warning twinge. She could not long keep her composure, she knew. Mayhap she could escape for a short while. Rising on shaking legs, she made for the door.

Just then the butler appeared, blocking her exit. His announcement, ringing through the cheerful cacophony, had her skidding to a horrified halt in the very center of the vast room.

"Lord Morley and Sir Tristan Crosby."

Chapter 2

The air seemed to be sucked from the room. There was no place to run, nowhere to hide. Before she could draw breath, he was there, filling the doorway. And Emily was struck completely dumb.

Her memories, as wonderful as they were, didn't do him justice. In the decade that had passed since the horrible day of The Tragedy, the Fates had been kind to Lord Morley. How was it possible he could be more handsome than before, when he had seemed perfect to her in every way? Her heart stuttered before starting up again in a pounding gallop. He was like a dream made real, so tall and broad shouldered he practically filled the doorway. His face, more chiseled, without the softness of youth, would have been at home on the most dashing pirate. His dark eyes settled almost instantly on her. And there they stayed.

Emily felt her face go hot. Her hand flew up, instinctively covering her ruined cheek. She willed her feet to move, but they seemed to have grown into the floor.

Just then Caleb approached him. "So you have both arrived, and a day earlier than anticipated," he said, the smile evident in his voice. The sound of it, so normal, broke the spell Emily was under. She scurried back into a quiet corner and dropped into a tall wingback chair. Her gaze, however, did not leave the three men.

There was no doubt Caleb and his friends cared for one another; the ease between them that Emily remembered from a decade ago was even more pronounced now. Caleb guided his friends around the room, introducing them to some, reintroducing them to others. Throughout their meandering journey, Emily kept her gaze fastened to Lord Morley. She drank in the sight of him, recognizing that, for the first time in her life, she was looking at him with the mature eyes of a woman. Her body beat out a foreign rhythm of awakening quite unlike anything she had ever felt.

She was in desperate trouble, indeed.

Just then the trio came to her isolated corner.

"Emily," Caleb said, "you remember Sir Tristan and Lord Morley, don't you?"

She had enough sense to look to Sir Tristan first. Which may not have been the best thing to do, after all. As cheerful as the man was, it showed all the more when he caught sight of her scar. His smile faltered noticeably before he forced it back into place and slid his eyes back to hers. The jolly look was gone, however. "It is a pleasure, Lady Emily," he said quietly.

Swallowing hard, Emily fought the overwhelming urge to press her hand to her cheek again. "Sir Tristan," she managed. Then, almost reluctantly, she turned to Lord Morley.

Oh, wasn't that a blunder of the worst sort, for there went her stomach, right up into her chest. And wouldn't her heart go galloping madly away again? But worst of all was her tongue. It tied itself into a right difficult knot, holding hostage all the things she wanted to say, like, *Thank you for being so kind to me all those years ago,* and, *I am glad you have come for my brother's wedding.* And, *You are looking particularly handsome today; may we please marry and have scads of babies?*

Then again, perhaps it was a good thing she was unable to speak.

"Lady Emily." His voice, branded in her brain, was even deeper than it had been, moving almost physically through her in the most unnerving way. And she was simply sitting there, staring at him like a simpleton, unable to even nod her head in greeting. *My word, it should be a crime for a man to have such long lashes. And that thick, luxurious hair.* It fell about in deliciously tousled inky waves. Her fingers itched in her gloves to touch it.

He looked at her oddly, not a hint of a smile on his face. In his favor, his gaze did not linger on her scar. It was obvious, however, that the man was not at all happy to be here. And now she was staring at him in the most dumbfounded way. He must think she had damaged her brain along with her face in that accident. Taking firm mental hold of her errant tongue, she concentrated with all her might. To her relief, words finally emerged from her paralyzed throat.

"Lord Morley, it is a pleasure."

There, six whole words. One whole sentence. So what if they sounded like they came from a terrified cat? She had done it.

A commotion from across the room caught their attention. Caleb, who had seemed unusually alert and desperate to avert disaster with the entire Duncan clan present, quickly excused himself. Sir Tristan followed in his wake.

To Emily's surprise, Lord Morley did not follow. His dark, almost black eyes stayed fixed to her, not even acknowledging his friends' leave-taking.

Her tongue seemed to pirouette, managing an impressive double knot. She flushed and tilted her head ever so slightly, trying to camouflage her scar as best she could. He said nothing, continuing to stare in that unnerving way.

Casting about for something, anything coherent to say, Emily hit upon his recent travels. "Your trip, I pray, was comfortable?"

He grunted and shrugged. "I suppose. If one counts a day and a half of riding in a coach as *comfortable*."

Emily blinked. His tone went right beyond brusque and straight on to surly. "Ah. I am sorry for that."

"Yes, well. Duty and all that."

Had he always been so...irritable? Emily frowned. Her memory could not be that faulty. She cast a covert glance toward the door, wishing she could simply slink away to escape this bizarre exchange. Clearing her throat, she plowed on. "It is good of you to come in support of my brother when you dislike travel so much, then."

He reached down and adjusted his cuff. "Oh, it is not travel I dislike so much as weddings."

What in the world was going on here, and who was this man who had taken the place of Lord Morley? "And my brother is aware of your dislike?"

Here he gave a short bark of laughter. It was better than the bored disdain he had shown thus far, but as the sound of it could only be described as rude, she was not inclined to look well on it. "Of course he is aware," he said. "I have been very vocal in that regard."

Really, the man was reprehensible. There was no possible way that this was the same person who had come to their home when she was young and captured her affections with his kindness.

But when she looked up into his face, at features she had dreamt of so often over the years, she was forced to acknowledge with a sinking heart it was the very same gentleman. Something in her shriveled in that moment. Never mind her thoughts on the Fates being kind to Lord Morley. Here was proof that, while they had been more than generous with his face and form, they had been severely remiss when it came to his temperament.

She raised her chin, refusing to back down from his open hostility. "It is a wonder that you came at all, with your dislike so obvious."

"I didn't have much of a choice, did I?"

"I think you must have. All of us have free choice."

His lip curled. "You obviously do not know me very well, then."

"No, I do not," she declared, rising. Never mind how wrong it was to leave a guest in the lurch, Emily did not think she could take another minute more in his presence. Not without either bursting into tears or snapping his head off. With a shallow curtsy, holding her head up with as much dignity as she could muster, she marched from the room.

· · ·

Malcolm watched as Lady Emily left him, her indignation palpable in the unbending line of her spine. Guilt crept over him like a trickle of ice water down his back. He shrugged it off. Perhaps he should not have been so hard on her. She was an unwitting player in this debacle, after all. Yet, if not for her shyness, he would not be forced to play nursemaid, to be held prisoner by the damnable promise Willbridge had goaded from him. Besides, did she truly need his help? That bit of spirit as she'd walked away from him, her affront at his attitude abundantly clear, had shown that the girl could take care of herself.

In the next instant, his guilt returned tenfold. When he had first entered the room, her expression had said something quite different. She had looked like a rabbit caught in a snare. In that moment he had felt a peculiar connection to her, a recognition of sorts. Her large gray eyes had been filled with a caution and underlying hurt he could understand all too well.

He shook his head, banishing the charitable thoughts. He would not allow sentiment to get in the way of his duty to his friend. Lady Emily may have been hurt, may have had some difficulties in life. But who hadn't? They had both lost people they'd cared about, but at least she was still surrounded by family that loved her.

He would do as he'd promised and watch over her as Willbridge had requested, gaining her a bit of confidence if he could manage it. But under no circumstances would he grow friendly with the chit.

He frowned. No, not a chit any longer but a woman grown.

"Well, I must say," Tristan drawled as he sauntered close, "you certainly wasted no time in scaring the girl off."

Malcolm accepted the glass of lemonade his friend held out to him with a nod of thanks. "What, am I to handle her with kid gloves?"

"I don't know, perhaps you should have." Tristan frowned. "Things cannot have been easy on her. That scar of hers is hard to look at, isn't it?"

Malcolm, in the process of taking a long draft of his beverage, nearly choked. "The scar?"

"I always knew it wouldn't heal well. I wasn't prepared for how angry it looks, however. The poor thing."

A peculiar hot feeling worked its way up Malcolm's spine as he stared at his friend. It took him a moment to realize it was anger. "It's a scar, not a reason to pity her. She's lovely regardless."

"And that's the worst part of it," Tristan mumbled. "She would be so much lovelier without that scar. As it is, she won't be able to snag a husband. What's left to her, then? Living on Willbridge's charity?"

The hot feeling running along Malcolm's spine burst into a snaking flame. "What the hell put that idea in your head?"

His friend finally seemed to see the error in his crass comments. "Damn, that truly was insensitive of me. It wouldn't do for us to speak aloud such things. Willbridge will have my head if he hears me disparage the girl in such a way."

"Only because it isn't remotely true," Malcolm countered hotly. Just then Lady Willbridge, Caleb's mother, called to them. He dutifully followed Tristan to accept a plate piled high with sandwiches and pastries from the newly arrived tray of food. All the while, however, he thought on his friend's words.

Malcolm knew Tristan was a man of society, but he was not cruel. Which was why his friend's comments as to Lady Emily's scar had bothered him to such a degree. Yes, it was a dominant part of her features, as it ran from her left temple to the corner of her mouth in that jagged line. It did not, however, make her disgusting to look upon. In fact, he would say if pressed that she was incredibly pretty: with those soulful eyes of hers, that fair skin colored with a faint blush, a smattering of freckles across the bridge of her nose.

Not that anyone would concentrate on those assets, for even if one discounted her scar, the way she dressed and held herself overshadowed it all. It seemed she had perfected the art of blending into the woodwork. She wore a drab, unadorned brown dress, hunching her shoulders to provide further camouflage and make herself appear smaller. Even the way she had dressed her hair, pulling it back in a tight bun so that not even a tendril was allowed to escape, was done with the intention of staying out of sight. That last bit was an exercise in futility, for the color alone brought attention to it. The same copper as her brother's, her hair fairly shone with all manner of reds and oranges and golds. A brilliant flame atop a plain wax candle. He wondered fleetingly if there was perhaps a bit of a fire inside her as well: hidden, maybe dormant, but like a volcano ready to burst forth with the right atmosphere and circumstances.

Blessedly Tristan once again saved him from his atypical mental poetry. Truly, what in blazes was wrong with him today?

His friend pulled him to an empty corner of the room, one thankfully free of the younger guests, siblings of Miss Imogen Duncan who had regrettably taken over the space. "Egad, do you think they'll relegate the children to the nursery after this?" his friend muttered. "I hate to think of them running amok through this entire affair. It will play havoc with my plans for seducing whatever willing widow or matron may be present."

Malcolm, in the midst of taking a healthy bite of a still warm scone, smiled around the crumbling bits before swallowing and saying, with complete and rueful honesty, "Somehow I doubt you'll allow that to stop you."

Tristan gave a short laugh before sobering. "You must think me a veritable arse, the way I talked about Lady Emily."

Malcolm allowed his lips to turn up in a sardonic smirk. "Well, that goes without saying, for I always think you're an arse."

"And I give you leave to, with my blessing," his friend replied with a chuckle. At the sound of light, feminine laughter, however, their attention quickly shifted to the group of young women that had stationed themselves around Imogen. They were a pretty picture, Imogen flushed and glowing with her future happiness, her sister Miss Mariah Duncan and Caleb's sister Lady Daphne bookending her like beautiful, flawless Sèvres bisque figurines.

"Though you can't help but admit," Tristan continued, "that the unfairness of Lady Emily's situation is even more underlined by her sister. That one," he said, inclining his head in Lady Daphne's direction, "will take London by storm next Season, mark my words."

Malcolm raised a brow, his gaze sharpening on the girl in question. He had not paid her much mind on his arrival. He had been much too intent on beginning the arduous task of shadowing Lady Emily to focus on anyone else. But Tristan's words made him look at the younger girl in a new light. The late afternoon sun, filtering in through the sheer drapes behind her, hit her then. She lit up like an angel, her strawberry blonde hair a halo of soft curls about her face, her skin luminous in the bright light. He had a feeling his friend was correct. Lady Daphne had all the makings of a diamond of the first water. Willbridge would have his hands full keeping the men at bay.

Just then she looked up from whatever wedding frippery the ladies were poring over and spied them. Her faint smile widened, her hand coming up in a waggle of fingers. Beside him Tristan heaved a sigh. Malcolm glanced at his friend, surprised to see a dreamy grin on his face.

"Damn me, 'tis Venus come to life."

Malcolm blinked several times. "That's Willbridge's sister," he hissed.

Tristan shrugged, his eyes following Lady Daphne as she left Imogen's side and made her way to her mother's. Just before she reached the marchioness, however, the girl turned to look back over her shoulder, her lips quirking when she saw Tristan staring.

"No harm in an innocent flirtation, man," Tristan said. "I've no intention of letting anything come of it."

His friend's glib words, however, did nothing to alleviate the unease that had settled in Malcolm's gut. He considered Lady Daphne before he turned back to his friend. Tristan was still gazing after her, his expression rapt. Malcolm determined in that moment to keep a careful watch on the situation. For if this continued, he would lose another friend this year, be it to the parson's mousetrap or to a bullet from Willbridge's dueling pistol.

• • •

Despite Emily's optimism, time did not improve Lord Morley.

All through that long, long evening he was like a bear with a thorn in its paw. Yet, to her consternation, he only seemed cantankerous in her presence. No one else appeared to bring about his churlish behavior. In fact, Emily had seen him smiling and laughing with several members of their party. When he found his way to her side, however—which he seemed to do with disconcerting frequency—he was more often than not glowering and snapping. Compounding her frustration over his bewildering behavior was the lingering grief that had settled on her since learning the truth of his character. And why shouldn't she feel grief? The very last of her dreams had been dashed, then stomped on, then ground with force into the dirt.

As much as it pained her to admit it, the heroic vision of Lord Morley that she'd kept wrapped safely in her heart had been the last vestige of her childhood hopes. Everything else had been shattered the day her brother Jonathan had died and she'd found herself scarred. All but Lord Morley. Surely, she had thought over the years when low spirits threatened to overwhelm her, the world could not be such a bad place if there was someone like that in it. Now even that was gone. Life, somehow, seemed a bit duller with the realization that her dream had no more substance than mist.

Things did not look any brighter the next day. She had hoped to find some peace at her pianoforte, with Lord Morley having shadowed her with his irritable self all the morning long, but he waylaid her before she could even begin. Now she was doing her best to lose him in the vastness of the house. Even so, he was fast on her heels. Truly, why would the man not leave her alone? It was clear he had no liking for her. So intent was she on escaping that she did not hear the gentle roar of voices in front of her. Until, too late, she was confronted with a sight that sent her heart fairly leaping into her throat.

She uncomprehendingly surveyed the crowd of people in the front hall. It took her a moment to realize what it was she was witnessing. The guests had started to arrive in earnest. Emily took a deep breath, trying without luck to ease the tightness in her chest. She had known that her brother's wedding would attract a great number of people. He was a marquess, after all, and well liked to boot. But, even with Imogen's seemingly unending list of guests, she had not expected something of this magnitude. The white marble floor, with its small black diamond inserts that she used to hop across as a child, was nearly hidden beneath the crush of bodies. James I, at his generations-old place of honor in all his gilt-edged glory, seemed to look down on the commotion with royal offense.

At the end of that horrifying gauntlet of people stood the great stone arch she was headed for and the polished wooden staircase beyond it. Taunting her. That was where she needed to go, the exit that led to the upper floor and her room. Her salvation from the surly man who was, for some baffling reason known only to their Maker, pursuing her. She heard the sound of his approach again, closer this time. Gathering her courage, Emily took a fortifying breath and plunged into the mass of people.

With a talent that only the extremely shy possessed, she threaded through the fine ladies and gentlemen. She kept her face averted, a swirl of bright skirts and gleaming boots filling her vision. Her heart pounded in her chest, sounding in her ears like a maddening drum. She realized in that instant, surrounded by strangers, that she may have made a grievous mistake in her attempt to escape Lord Morley. Wasn't one surly gentleman much easier to bear than this horrifying unknown she had unthinkingly thrown herself into? *Please*, she begged, *please don't let anyone notice me.*

To her surprise, they didn't seem to. They all talked and laughed as their bags were brought in, apparently much too immersed in themselves to notice the slight, terrified woman in their midst. She dodged around a portly gentleman and with a quick peek saw her exit. Relief began to pound through her. A couple more people to maneuver about, a few more feet...

The lady she meant to sidestep shifted suddenly. Emily rammed into her face-first. Right into the woman's generous bosom.

"My word!" the woman screeched. Emily gasped and extricated herself, glancing up as she did so.

It was her fatal mistake.

An immediate change came over the lady. Emily's heart dropped. She had seen this reaction before, a hundred times it seemed. Like a moth to a flame, their gazes shifted unerringly to the ruined side of her face. More often than not, they would flinch as if they'd been struck. Then came the jaw dropping, the eyebrows lifting. Emily never could tell if it was done in horror or pity. She typically never stayed around long enough to find out.

But there was no escaping now. Her run-in with the lady had garnered attention. People were closing in on all sides, no doubt to verify they were both unharmed. To Emily, it felt as if she were being buried alive.

She cast about wildly, seeing not concerned faces about her, but strangers who would gape and stare at her. Her chest felt tight, her gaze going black at the edges...

"Lady Emily, I am having a dreadful time finding the way to my room. I don't suppose you can guide me to the correct hallway?"

The deep voice at her side yanked her back into the now. The band about her chest seemed to loosen and she dragged in a slow breath. Turning, feeling a fatalistic doom, she looked up into Lord Morley's somber face.

Chapter 3

It took several seconds for Emily's heartbeat to reduce to something less than a rapid patter. She stared back at Lord Morley with what must have been patent disbelief. He was saving her? He was being kind? Drat it, she had just determined to keep far away from him, had come to terms with her fresh dislike of him, and he went and did something like this.

He looked back at her, his gaze steady, no emotion in those dark, bottomless eyes. Belatedly she realized that he had winged his arm out for her to take. Fingers trembling, she placed her hand gingerly on the woolen sleeve of his slate gray coat. They began to move through the crowd, which parted for them like the Red Sea for Moses. Emily didn't notice how silent the hall had become until they began their winding way up the heavily carved staircase. The people behind her erupted in talk, the sound a dull roar. Emily winced.

Once they made the upper floor, Lord Morley instantly dropped his arm from beneath her touch. She stood there stupidly for a moment, her hand suspended like a marionette's before she let it fall to her side.

A thick silence filled the air of the upper hallway, making the atmosphere cloying. Emily cleared her throat, forcing herself to meet his gaze. As she had feared, he was staring at her from beneath lowered eyebrows.

"I must thank you for saving me," she managed. Because *something* had to be said.

"You should not have tried to get through that crowd," he growled.

Instantly all of Emily's generous thoughts for Lord Morley's gallant actions vanished. She straightened from her typical protective posture. "I beg your pardon, my lord?"

He scowled at her. "You very nearly fainted. It was not an intelligent thing to do."

Which even she in her offended state could not deny. Much as it galled her, it had been foolish. Far be it for her to admit such a thing to him, however. "I did not almost faint," she muttered, more to be contrary than anything else. But her gaze slid to the floor at the lie, her face flushing with heat. She pressed her hand to her cheek, knowing full well what blushing did to her scar. The rush of blood made it stand out all the more, bringing it into painful relief. She would not have him look down on her any more than he already did.

"Tell me," he said, "how do you hope to get through this wedding if you cannot even walk through a room full of people?"

The burn of tears started up behind her eyes. How indeed? It had been something she'd been struggling with for days. She raised her chin, her eyes settling on his cravat, unable to look in his eyes, for they must be filled to the brim with disdain. "Are you quite through, my lord?"

"Not even close."

So surprised was she by his answer—but more for the quiet, almost gentle manner it was spoken—that Emily's gaze flew to meet his own. There she was dealt a double blow, for it was not disdain, or disgust, or even anger in his eyes. It was frustration and...worry? Why? He had made it abundantly clear in the past day that he did not care for her.

Something in her began to ache unbearably. Before she could study it closer to determine its meaning, he gave a shallow bow and marched back down the stairs. Emily stared after him, not at all certain what had happened. That he could do something so kind one minute, then follow it up with such meanness, and then throw her off again with that gentle tone, had her thinking he was perhaps a bit mad.

Frustration welled up in her. She turned, striding through the Long Gallery that stretched the whole front of the house. Her small heels clicked on the polished wood floor, echoing through the vastness of the space, bouncing off the paneled walls and the multitude of Masters portraits that lined them. What manner of man was he, that he could play hot and cold with such dizzying regularity? And why did he choose to concentrate his efforts on her? Didn't he know she was having a hard enough time without his breathing down her neck?

She turned down the hall that housed the guest bedrooms—in that moment currently bustling with servants as they brought chests and bags to rooms—to the family apartments beyond. Why did he bother to seek her out? If he had been any nicer in his manners, she would have thought he was pursuing her.

At that she gave a short, barking laugh. A footman passing her by, his arms loaded with hat boxes, jumped at the sound, nearly dropping his load. Emily ducked around him, appalled that she had let thoughts of Lord Morley affect her to such a degree. Though she was quite determined to put him from her mind; however, she found she could not. He confounded her. But, though she could not make heads or tails of his mercurial moods, there was one thing she was certain of. Lord Morley was not at all the man she had thought him to be. The slow burn of shame heated her skin. That she could have held him in such high regard for so long, putting him up on a pedestal above other men, mortified her to her very soul.

So submerged in thought was she that she had turned into the family quarters and passed by her bedroom without realizing it. She blinked, looking up and scanning the corridor. It was quiet here, the bustle of preparations having faded behind her. But when she would have turned back for her room, a muffled sound carried to her from Imogen's room.

If anyone in this blasted world could comprehend her fear of mingling with the crowd below, it was Imogen. Without a second's thought, she knocked lightly on the door.

There was a squeak of surprise before a voice called out, "I swear, I was just about to come down."

Was it her, or was there a slightly panicked quality to Imogen's tone? Concerned, Emily slipped inside. Imogen sat at her dressing table, her shoulders a tense line, her arms braced as if she were planning to spring from the bench. In one hand was a white handkerchief that appeared to have been shredded. At the sight of Emily, her breath left her in a rush of relief.

"Oh, Emily, I'm so glad it's you." Imogen slumped down in her seat, the wild look melting a bit from her wide turquoise eyes. "I couldn't bear to go down right away. Yet the more time I take to shore up my defenses, the harder it is to enter the fray."

"Perhaps you needn't go down at all," Emily suggested without much hope.

"I'm sure Caleb wouldn't mind in the least. He couldn't be sweeter or more supportive of my shortcomings." Here she grimaced. "But I am the bride, and as future Marchioness of Willbridge it is my duty to learn to be a proper hostess, to make Caleb proud."

Emily sat beside Imogen and took up her hand. Her friend's fingers were cold to the touch. "You could never do anything," she said with real feeling, "that could ever lose my brother's pride in you."

Imogen blinked back tears behind her wire-framed spectacles and gave an audible sniff. "Oh, aren't you lovely," she whispered.

They sat there for a time in companionable silence, holding hands as the seconds ticked by. Gradually, however, Emily could feel the tension return to Imogen. Her friend's mind had wandered, she knew, fretting about the inevitable appearance she had to make below stairs. "If it upsets you so much to have such a large party here for the wedding, why do you allow it?" she asked softly. It had not seemed that the situation had been forced on her, after all. Emily had seen that, much to her surprise, Imogen could hold her own with her mother, the irascible Lady Tarryton.

The smile Imogen gave her was rueful. "If my mother had had her way, we would be planning a London wedding the likes of which you have never seen, complete with the great majority of the *ton* at St. George's and a lavish reception with the Prince Regent himself present. If Caleb had managed to get his way, we would have eloped." She laughed, but Emily could see from the slightly wistful expression in her eyes that Imogen would have much preferred her affianced husband's suggestion, as well.

"So we compromised," she continued. She lifted her shoulders in a shrug. "It seemed a small enough price to pay to give my mother some happiness in the affair. I do love her dearly, despite her abrasive ways."

Just then Daphne sailed into the room. "My goodness, have you seen the crowd of guests below?" She smiled broadly. "This is going to be a glorious party."

Imogen looked like she was going to be sick. Emily suspected it mirrored her own expression quite well.

Daphne was too embroiled in her own excitement to notice. She craned her neck to see past them, considering her reflection in the looking glass before giving a nod of satisfaction. Not a single hair was out of place, her diaphanous muslin gown showing off her neat figure to perfection. Daphne had been born with the great good luck of not only possessing beauty in abundance, but a warm and open personality that thrived on human interaction. This whole affair would be like the very nectar of the gods to her.

"Is Caleb asking after me?" Imogen ventured.

"Of course he is." Daphne looked at once amused and dreamy. "When is he not? My brother is so in love with you I'm surprised he hasn't tethered you to his side."

Imogen's face softened at that. Emily had a feeling that her future sister wouldn't have minded that one bit.

Daphne heaved a great, happy sigh. "Though I was annoyed that you didn't marry in London—for I would have loved to have visited the capital in advance of my come-out—I do believe that having the wedding here will do nicely. As Mama has said to me, a small house party is just what is needed to give me the proper social polish for when I make my debut next Season."

Small house party? If the crowd Emily had plunged through was what Daphne deemed small, then what would they be subject to in London?

The sick feeling that had been present in a small way all through the morning blossomed into something much, much worse.

Miss Mariah Duncan appeared in the doorway. "Daphne, another carriage has pulled up. I do believe it is Sir Frederick Knowles and his family." Her blue eyes were wide, alight with her excitement.

"There are more people?" The appalled words fell from Emily's mouth without warning. Mariah's lovely face clouded with understanding. She had been Imogen's staunchest protector and would understand the panic in Emily's voice. Still, it galled Emily to see the pity in her eyes.

"It truly isn't so many," the girl soothed. "This is a small party by *ton* standards."

Instead of allaying Emily's anxiety, however, Mariah's words served to increase it to a paralyzing degree. How large were the parties in London, that this was tiny in comparison?

Imogen rose, a determined expression tightening her face. "Well, I suppose I have done my hiding for the day. I'd best get downstairs. I won't have them all think I'm cowed." She turned to Emily. "Will you stay here, dear?"

Emily somehow managed a nod. It must have been enough, for Imogen gave her a smile and walked from the room with the two younger women.

Leaving Emily alone with her panicked thoughts.

She was thankful that they had left her in that moment, for her control over her emotions was rapidly deteriorating. London. Why had she forgotten Daphne's debut in London next spring? Emily had never had a Season, had never wanted one. But Daphne was different. She was beautiful and vivacious and had been looking forward to her debut for as long as Emily could remember.

Emily couldn't begin to contemplate what going to London would be like. Being here at a house party with nearly two score of people, most of whom she didn't know, was bad enough. She thought of that episode in the front hall, the feeling of terror that had nearly sent her into a swoon, and knew it would be worse—so much worse—in town.

There would be hundreds, if not thousands, of people in London. Every ball no doubt packed to the rafters with the noble elite and their desire for perfection. Then there were the dinner parties, the musicales, trips to the theatre and Almack's, rides in the park. The list went on and on, endless opportunities to be surrounded by people who would gawk at her, giving her those looks of pity and horror. Making her panic until she couldn't breathe, couldn't think...

Spots began to swim in her vision. Emily let out a shaky breath she hadn't even realized she'd been holding.

Tears burned her eyes and she blinked them back furiously. Look at her. Just contemplating going to London, and she'd nearly been overtaken. How much worse would it be to actually be there? In the middle of her own private hell.

No. She couldn't go. She wouldn't go. She would rather die.

Well, she conceded, perhaps not quite so extreme. Even so, the desire to remain far, far away from that illustrious city was strong. She would not have even considered going had Daphne not begged her. Surely her sister would not insist on it now. She must see how horrifying such a situation would be for Emily and release her from her promise.

She set her jaw, determined to beg off from the trip. As soon as she was able, she would search out Daphne and put an end to this mad scheme of a trip once and for all.

• • •

"Your sister very nearly fainted in the front hall."

Malcolm had not meant the words to come out so accusatory, but his frustration over seeing Lady Emily in such distress had left a bad taste in his mouth. Truly, her fear of being around people went well past mere shyness and straight on to debilitating.

Willbridge looked at him sharply. "Is she well?"

"Yes, though it was a near thing. Truly, why didn't you tell me the extent of her problem? This changes everything."

Willbridge glanced about the billiard room, at the congregation of men who had escaped from the forced company of the women. Several of the guests peered at them, their curiosity palpable. With a quick jerk of his head, Willbridge indicated they should leave. Pressing his lips together in frustration, Malcolm nodded and followed his friend from the room. Men were as bad as women with gossip, he knew.

They made their way to the sunken garden at the west side of the house. Willbridge strode to the bubbling fountain at the center, no doubt in an attempt to disguise their voices should anyone happen by. What they had to discuss would not ruin the girl but would certainly bring unwanted attention to her.

For a long moment Willbridge looked at the water falling into the stone pool. When he spoke, his voice was gruff. "I have told you she has retreated into herself, that she is painfully shy. Even I, however, did not expect that, when confronted with so many people, she would faint."

Willbridge was being truthful, that much was plain. His distress was palpable. Instantly Malcolm regretted confronting his friend in such a manner and placed a hand on his shoulder. "But she did not. I was there and managed to get her away before she could be overcome."

A muscle worked in his friend's jaw before, with a sigh, he dragged a hand over his face. "And I thank God you were there, Morley," he murmured. "More than you know."

Well, hell, Malcolm thought. Here he had been about to beg to be released from his promise to watch over the girl, and now this. He let his hand drop back to his side, looking out over the sunken garden and seeing not a bit of it.

Lady Emily's plight touched him in ways he had not thought possible. She had been truly terrified there in the front hall. And, much to his surprise, as he had looked into her eyes and seen the extent of her fear, something in him long thought dead had been awakened. A deep, primal protectiveness had come roaring to life.

That would not do at all.

He prided himself on his ability to stay aloof. Caring was messy, leaving heartbreak behind more often than not. The only reason he had allowed the closeness to continue with Willbridge and Tristan was their history with him. When everyone else in his life had broken promises and betrayed him, those two alone had stood strong.

Even so, there was always something there between them—a wall that not even they could scale.

It had become clear to him that no matter the history you shared with someone, they inevitably let you down. First with his parents, who had died when Malcolm was so young. Then his uncle, who had taken in Malcolm and his brother when they had been orphaned. He had treated them no better than stones in his shoe.

But it had been that final betrayal that had left the deepest scar. His love for Lydia had been so great he had opened himself up to trusting again. And his reward had been unimaginable pain.

Now there was Lady Emily, whose uncertainty and sadness pulled at his heart. When he had witnessed her in such distress in the midst of the crowd, it had not been Willbridge or the blasted promise Malcolm had given him that had been foremost in his mind. He had thought only of her, had wanted to shelter her from everyone and get her to safety. It had taken all his willpower not to go charging through the sea of people like an enraged bull.

The feelings that had cropped up in him at the sight of Lady Emily in distress had made him positively furious with himself. So much so that, once again, he had taken his anger out on her.

He should not have. It was badly done of him. But she had not cowered from him, he realized. He pursed his lips as he thought of it. No, the moment he had shown the least bit of meanness to her— and to his shame that had been nearly every word he had spoken to her thus far—she had shown surprising backbone. She had not railed at him as he deserved. And he truly did deserve it for being such an arse to her. But she had held her own. He wondered if there was more to her than anyone, herself included, realized. Perhaps Willbridge was right, in that the stifling protectiveness her family had shown her over the past decade had done more harm than good. Never mind watching over her, seeing she wasn't in distress, giving her attention to bolster her confidence. No, mayhap the girl needed a push, something to fight against. Let her see that she could handle things herself, that she was strong and able.

This could prove interesting, a scientific study of sorts. A bit like grooming one of his horses to ensure the proper temperament for the job they were to do. Surely his emotions would not be involved if he went about it in such a way.

No, he would make sure they were not involved. His sanity depended upon it.

• • •

Emily had not taken into account the very real problem of getting her sister alone in a house that held nearly two score people. Especially when said sister seemed determined to make friends with every person present.

All through the day, Daphne was like the busy sedge warblers that flitted about the bushes along the bank of the River Spratt. She mingled with natural talent, jumping from guest to guest with dizzying speed. Now nearing dinner, everyone having retired to their rooms to prepare for the evening ahead, Emily finally ran her to ground.

After quickly donning a nondescript slate blue dress and twisting her hair into a serviceable bun, she hurried down the hall to her sister's room and rapped sharply on the door.

"Come in," Daphne sang out, her voice muffled through the thick wooden panel.

Emily slipped inside. Daphne, seated at her dressing table with a veritable jumble of jewelry before her, beamed when she saw her. She dropped the pearl necklace she had been holding up for inspection and spun in her seat. "Dearest, I'm so happy you're here. I could use your clear head right now." She rose and kissed Emily on the cheek before taking her hand and leading her to the seating area before the hearth.

The space might have been welcoming, but the delicate white-framed chairs with their embroidered pink cushions were nigh invisible, buried as they were under a mountain of discarded clothing. Daphne busied herself for a moment, throwing shawls, bonnets, and pelisses aside before, with a sigh, she sank down onto one of the seats.

Emily followed suit, squeaking in surprise as she came down on something hard. Reaching beneath her skirts, she pulled out a well-worn gothic novel. She handed it to Daphne, who took it excitedly. "I had wondered where that had got off to. Brilliant, I may finish it tonight."

Emily stopped an exasperated sigh from escaping. Her sister was a vibrant, energetic soul. That trait was reflected in a not-so-complementary way by her tendency to create havoc in her inner sanctum. Their mother had given up trying to change her ages ago. As long as the mess was confined to Daphne's bedchamber, the marchioness turned a blind eye to it.

"You have been incredibly busy today; I've scarcely seen you at all," Emily said.

"It's glorious having so many people here. I cannot remember a time Willowhaven was so lively."

That managed to decimate Emily's happy mood in an instant. Ah, yes. There was a reason she had searched Daphne out, and it was not to exchange pleasantries.

But as she strove to calm herself enough to beg off the trip to London next spring, Daphne grew quiet as well. Soon the ticking clock on the mantle was the only sound in the room. Unused to such a hush while in her sister's presence, Emily pushed aside her encroaching anxiety and peered closely at her.

Daphne appeared happy, excited even. Even so, there was something not quite right. Her color was high, her eyes too bright.

And, even more noticeably, her slender hands were almost manic as they smoothed the pristine pale green silk of her gown.

Leaning forward, Emily laid a hand over hers. "Daphne, are you well?"

"Of course, I'm fine. Absolutely fine. Why wouldn't I be?" She laughed as if it was ridiculous to think otherwise.

Emily knew her sister well, however, and heard the strain in the seemingly carefree sound. "Daphne, you know I will get it out of you eventually. You may as well tell me."

Daphne's smile fell from her face as she eyed Emily ruefully. "You always were much too observant for your own good." She let out a breath and slumped back. "Very well. I am a touch... overwhelmed."

Emily blinked. "Overwhelmed."

"Not that I don't love the house party and all it brings," her sister hastened to assure her. "This is what I have waited for. So many elegant people, with their fashion and manners, full of all the latest news from London." She sighed in ecstasy. "It's like a dream."

"But?"

Daphne cast her a rueful glance. "But it is exhausting! Goodness, I never realized what it would be like. And this but a fraction of the people we will meet?"

A twinge of unease started up in Emily's spine. And not just at the reminder of the crowds they would face in London. "Er, Daphne—"

"I mean, can you imagine? There will be hundreds of new faces in the capital. No, thousands! And while I've always longed to throw myself into the fray, so to speak, it has grown somewhat daunting. We have had no exposure to something of this caliber. I feel a veritable country bumpkin amidst such refinement as we have seen. It is one thing to attend the local assemblies with people we have known all our lives. It is quite another to be at the center of such an elegant affair."

Daphne was growing impassioned. Emily had certainly never expected this reaction from her sociable sister. She suddenly felt if she did not voice her intentions this minute, the moment would be lost forever. "About that—"

"I can see it will be no easy thing, ingratiating myself with so many people. Oh, I've no doubt it will be amazing once I've settled. But in the beginning, it is sure to be nerve-wracking. I am so glad you'll be there with me."

A ringing started up in Emily's ears, her stomach going sour. She could almost see her plans floating out of her grasp and straight out the open window. "You are?"

Daphne turned wide, innocent eyes on her. "Of course. Oh, my sweet sister, you have always been my rock, though you may not know it." She let out a relieved breath, her face relaxing in a smile. "Already I'm feeling better; your level head has that much of an effect on me. And so, you see, I could not go to London without you."

"You can't?"

"Certainly not." It was Daphne's turn to place her hand comfortingly over Emily's. "Oh, I know it isn't to your liking. But you'll see, we'll have a gay time. Walks in the park, trips to museums. Perhaps we may even visit the menagerie at the Tower. You would like that, wouldn't you?"

Emily could only nod. And as Daphne went on in her typical enthusiastic fashion, waxing poetic about the joys of London life now that her anxiety had been relieved, Emily felt as if the shackles that bound her had increased tenfold.

But no, all could not be lost. There must be a way out. Her mind whirled dizzily, looking for an answer to her problems and finding none. She blew out a frustrated breath. There must be a solution, some brilliant realization that would hit her like the proverbial thunderbolt. She would have to keep her eyes and ears open for it.

Chapter 4

She could do this. Emily straightened her shoulders and attempted to ignore her roiling stomach as she looked out over the group that had gathered in the large drawing room. She could get through this. The great majority of these people were related to her, or to Imogen, which meant they would soon be indirectly related to her as well. It would be for little more than a fortnight. This was her home, where she felt comfortable and loved and protected. Her family would not let anything unpleasant happen to her.

And, miracle of miracles, Lord Morley was presently absent.

Not that she had been looking for him. Absolutely not. It was mere self-preservation that even had her considering him at all. She certainly didn't need his scowling face directed her way right now. She would make the most of this reprieve from his company. Gathering her courage, she prepared to, if not stride, at least walk with a fair amount of confidence into the room.

"Ah, Lady Emily, how are you?"

The silky voice at her elbow had her back tensing, her feet faltering. She knew that voice well. While always pleasant and even, it carried subtle thorns—like reaching out to pick blackberries and grabbing the barbed runners instead. With dread Emily turned to regard the source.

"Lord Randall." She had known him since she was a child. A local baron, he was renowned for his insistence on perfection in every aspect of his life. From his house, to his wife, to his sons, everything had to be just so, showcasing his status. Never mind his own person, which was always trim and fit and dressed in the latest fashions, his graying hair brushed and tamed, his face unlined though he must be fifty if he was a day. Most would think him handsome, she supposed. All Emily could see was the pity in his eyes when he looked on her. More often than not it was accompanied by a healthy hint of disgust. Apparently having to look upon a scarred face went against every one of his delicate sensibilities.

"I imagine," he said, his gaze scouring the ruined side of her face with a morbid fascination, "that this must be very difficult for you. I know it cannot be easy, having so many strange eyes upon you."

Coldness seeped under Emily's skin. It was not the first time Lord Randall had called attention to her scar in so blunt a manner, nor would it be the last. He must honestly believe he was doing her a service by not skirting about it as everyone else did. At least, that was what she told herself when forced into his presence, which happened much more often than she would like. That did not lessen the cruel shock of it, however.

"It was kind of your mother to invite me to the festivities for your brother's wedding," he went on. "It really is too bad my older boys could not be here. They would have loved this. Such a mix of elegant persons. Many are related to your family?"

She barely managed a nod. How could she extricate herself? Surely he could not have anything of import to discuss with her. But it seemed he was not done with her.

"Your sister, I hear, is soon to make her debut in London."

Emily's heart went right up into her throat at the reminder. She nodded again, her voice apparently having decided to go into temporary hiding.

Lord Randall cast an interested look at Daphne, who stood in the corner of the room surrounded by a gay contingent of young people. As Emily watched, her sister gave a trilling laugh. Truly, she had never looked better. She was positively glowing, in her element. It seemed their talk truly had done wonders for her. Emily returned her gaze to Lord Randall. The man pursed his lips and narrowed his eyes thoughtfully as he looked on Daphne. A shiver of disgust worked its way up Emily's spine.

"It must be difficult for you, constantly being compared to such a gem," he mused.

Stunned at such direct cruelty, all she could think to say was, "I love my sister." A moment later she wanted to curse her coward's tongue. Why did she never have the courage to put the man in his place? The right words would come to her later, she knew, their delay making them impotent and useless.

He tilted his head, regarding her scar again. "I'm sure you do," he said, his voice sweet as honey, and as sticky and cloying. Emily fought the urge to shudder as the sound of it washed over her. "It is perfectly natural, though, to compare yourself. No one would blame you for being envious of her."

Emily's mouth fell open before she closed it with an audible snap. "I am not envious," she managed.

The pity in his eyes as he looked down on her was undercut by the malice there. "You cannot be that sheltered, my lady." He gave a small chuckle and shook his head. "No one is that good. There is always a bit of envy and competition in all of us. But have no fear," he said, giving her a conspiratorial wink, "your secret is safe with me. Now," he said, straightening and returning his gaze to the room, "you truly shouldn't strain yourself to mingle when the atmosphere is undoubtedly unfavorable to you, my dear. I see a quiet corner over there that should suit you well."

At the superior condescension in his eyes, spurred on by his conceited cheek, Emily felt her paralyzed mind break free of its moorings. She was so tired of being pitied and seen as less than a woman. Without acknowledging the man's words, she made to turn away, to escape his stifling presence. A voice behind her, however, cut in before she had a chance.

"I believe the lady is more than capable of handling a gathering in her family's own home."

Just stifling a gasp, Emily spun toward Lord Morley. Truly, of all the people to approach in that moment, he was the last she wanted.

But Lord Randall would not be pleased that he had been put

in his place. She chanced a glance at the man. He was looking at Lord Morley as if he were a piece of offal that had dared to soil his good boots.

Lord Morley, for his part, merely smiled back. It was anything but pleasant. Emily shivered at the positively feral look to it. "I'm sorry," he said, looking over the man with barely concealed animosity, "I don't think I've had the pleasure."

Emily knew that was her cue to make the proper introductions. But she was tired of being intimidated by these men. Clamping her mouth closed mutinously, she stepped back.

Lord Randall's lip curled as he cut her a disgusted look. He inclined his head to Lord Morley as if bestowing a great honor. "I am Douglas Vanguard, Lord Randall," he drawled.

"And how do you know the bride and groom?" Lord Morley questioned.

The man's chest puffed up considerably. "I have been a family friend of Lord Willbridge for many a year. I live a half hour's ride away. My estate, Handel House, is reputed to have the finest horseflesh in Northamptonshire."

"Hmm," Lord Morley intoned. "Strange I have not heard of you then, as I am on intimate footing with all the best breeders. But forgive me, I have not introduced myself. I am Malcolm Arborn, Viscount Morley. My own estate is Fairfax Hall. Perhaps you're acquainted with its reputation? I have been assured over the past years that we have some of the finest horseflesh in the country."

To Emily's surprise, Lord Randall's lily-white complexion— which, having probably never seen a day's labor, stood in sharp contrast to the tan, rugged handsomeness of Lord Morley's—paled. The condescension in his eyes faded into a sickening regret and he cleared his throat. "Indeed, I have heard of you, my lord." His eyes quickly lost their slightly nauseated cast and took on a crafty interest. "Perhaps, while you're in the area, you might deign to visit my own humble stables. You will not be disappointed, I assure you."

"Mayhap," was all Malcolm said. But the doubt that colored the one word spoke volumes.

The two men stared at each other, Lord Morley with smug condescension and Lord Randall with not a small bit of frustration. Ignored in this game of cock-of-the-roost, Emily's disbelief at the bizarre exchange transformed first to offended righteousness, then outright anger. And not a low simmering anger, but an inferno. How dare these two men, who had given her so much grief, treat her like a nonentity? In that moment she suddenly, and finally, had enough.

"If you will both excuse me? I do believe there is an empty corner of the room where I can be ignored in a much more polite manner."

With that she grabbed up her skirts and stalked off.

• • •

Hours later Malcolm was still awed by the glorious display Lady Emily had made in putting himself and Lord Randall in their places.

Yes, he'd acted a complete brute. His intentions, however, had been good. Actually, he would say he'd been damn near a saint, for when he'd entered the drawing room and seen that popinjay Randall talking to her in so rude and condescending a manner, his first instinct had been to take the man by his ridiculously high collar and throw him bodily from the house. Truly, what did the man think he was doing, talking to a lady of the house, indeed any lady at all, in such a manner?

But no, Malcolm had controlled the impulse. After all, what talent had he propagated over the years but the ability to tightly rein in the messier of his emotions? Should he have acknowledged Lady Emily? Yes. There was no doubt as to that. In his defense, however, it had been for her that he'd interrupted in the first place. And he would do it again, in a heartbeat.

Especially if it would wring that same response from her.

For what must have been the hundredth time, he found himself looking her way. She was seated beside her sister, her face tilted away from the main body of the party. Hiding her scar, he knew without being told. It was well after dinner now. The requisite card tables had been dragged out, the typical debutantes fiddling with the pianoforte keys. Much of the male contingent had moved to the billiard room, to smoke and drink and immerse themselves in bawdy talk, though most of the younger generation had hung back to drool over the young ladies. Willbridge and his bride-to-be had disappeared long ago to goodness knew where. And Lord Randall, the pompous bastard, had blessedly departed for home.

He should leave now, he knew, to join the men or retire to his room. Lady Emily was fine, if a bit pale. And Willbridge could not have meant for him to never leave the girl's side. His friend may want to pique the interest of other gentlemen in her, but he certainly had no desire to have his sister be the subject of less-than-desirable gossip should people notice Malcolm's attentions toward her.

Even so, he could not make himself go. So he stayed where he was, leaning against the marble mantle, on occasion lifting his glass of brandy to his lips for a sip he did not taste.

Apparently, however, having an idle gentleman in her purview was not something Lady Tarryton was going to allow.

"Lord Morley," Imogen's mother called from her place of honor in the midst of several of the more prominent matrons of the group, "you look lonely there by yourself. Surely we can tempt you to come join us?"

"Thank you, my lady," he replied with a forced smile, "but I assure you I quite enjoy my solitary post. Especially as it gives me such a glorious view of the present company."

As he'd known she would, the woman tittered, a sound that grated on his ear. His attempt at distracting her through compliments, however, failed. She gave him an assessing look. "How could you possibly prefer to observe the ladies present when there is more joy to be had from conversing with them? Mariah," she called to her younger daughter, who sat in the very heart of the group of young people, "make room for Lord Morley. He will be joining you in a thrice."

"I'm sure we would love to have him join us, but we really

must respect Lord Morley's wish for solitude, Mama," the girl said, flashing him an apologetic smile. Lady Emily, he saw, didn't look his way. Her profile, however, turned stony, and said volumes as to her wish that he remain right where he was.

"How can any sane man wish to be alone when there are such pretty girls to converse with?" Lady Tarryton scoffed. Malcolm could see in that instant that the woman would stop at nothing to ensure he paid homage to her daughter. It had been no secret in the past months that the viscountess had been fairly manic in her desire to get Miss Mariah before as many titled, unmarried gentlemen as possible. Malcolm himself had called upon the girl in her drawing room several times and had seen firsthand how ruthless her mother could be. With her eldest marrying Willbridge—a catch he knew the woman had wanted for Miss Mariah and not Imogen—she would be doubling her efforts to find a grand match for the younger girl.

And as Malcolm was the highest rank out of the eligible gentlemen present, he supposed he was to be the recipient of her efforts now. Her *wasted* efforts, if he had anything to say about it. While he liked Miss Mariah well enough, he was not about to be entrapped in marriage to her. Or to anyone else, for that matter. Let the bloody title die with him, for all he cared.

Regardless, he could not let the woman make a scene. He owed that much to Willbridge, at least, though his watching over Lady Emily was going a long way toward paying off any debt he may have incurred with the man.

Pushing away from the mantle, he sauntered toward the group. Everyone welcomed him jovially enough. All but for Lady Emily, who tensed visibly as he approached, keeping her gaze averted. In a moment of mischief he ignored the empty spot Lady Tarryton waved him toward, instead squeezing himself in between Lady Emily and one of the Miss Knowleses (he hadn't a clue which one; all three looked as alike as anything). He knew he needn't have sat *quite* so close to Lady Emily. There was plenty of room on the sofa, after all. But some devil had perched on his shoulder after seeing that she could be pushed to standing up for herself, and he had a morbid desire to find out if he could do it again.

Lady Daphne, who was sitting in a chair on her sister's other side, leaned over Lady Emily and gifted him with a smile. "You are just in time, my lord. We were discussing what to do tomorrow for entertainment. I know my mother and Lady Tarryton have scheduled fishing for some of the older gentlemen, and lawn games for the guests left behind. There are those of us, however, who are inclined toward something a bit farther afield."

He opened his mouth to speak, but Lady Emily's voice was there first. "I'm sure your plans for the younger partygoers would not interest Lord Morley," she said, sounding as if someone had wrapped their fingers about her throat and squeezed.

He leaned in a bit toward her. "My goodness, Lady Emily," he murmured, "how old do you believe me to be?"

She shivered slightly, the skin of her cheek flushing scarlet. As he watched, bemused, she ducked her chin into her chest and scooted as far from him as she could manage. Which was not far at all, considering she had already been fairly draped over the arm of the sofa in her attempt to put some distance between them.

"You and Sir Tristan will be joining our party instead, will you not?" Lady Daphne asked, gifting him with a smile. "Please say you will."

Goodness, he could see now what Tristan had been talking about. When that girl gave you the full force of her smile, it was blinding. And here she was unpracticed, without artifice. Malcolm wondered, with no little fear, what she would be capable of once she realized the true extent of her power.

"I will certainly consider it, Lady Daphne," he said with honesty, for he couldn't promise a thing to her. Not until he found out where Lady Emily would be on the morrow. He had a job to do, after all.

As the rest of the group discussed possible plans, he turned to Lady Emily. To his shock, she was looking at him with a surprisingly direct gaze.

It felt as if a fist had been planted in his gut. He could not have torn his eyes from her if he had tried. As he watched, her lovely pewter eyes widened, her mouth opening in a small oval. The charged moment, while mere seconds long, felt an eternity to Malcolm. Then she flushed and returned her eyes to her lap, and the spell was blessedly broken.

Shaken, he drew in an uneven breath. What in the name of heaven had that been about? But he had meant to ask her something, hadn't he? He shook his head to clear it, felt the answer fall into place. Ah, yes, he'd been about to question her on her plans for the following day.

He leaned in toward her, saw her suck in a quick breath. When he looked down, he saw her hands grasped desperately on to one another. The skin above her gloves, he noticed with fascination, had pimpled. Clearing his throat, he attempted to focus once more on the matter at hand. "And do you plan on joining your sister's outing on the morrow, my lady?"

She darted a glance toward him, her eyes clouded with confusion and wariness. She may as well have yelled "Why do you care?" But she merely inclined her head stiffly. "Where Daphne goes, I go."

He smiled. "Then I shall go as well." There, let her make of that what she would.

Her expression as she turned away said she'd rather he take a flying leap off the nearest bridge. Malcolm's smile widened as he turned back to the group. She surprised him more and more at every turn. Shadowing Lady Emily might be more entertaining than he'd imagined it would.

Chapter 5

Emily set out the following morning for the rose garden on the east side of the property. The irony that she was taking a preliminary walk to prepare herself for the brisk walk to the village later in the day did not escape her. But her spirits were too agitated to remain indoors a moment longer.

Already breakfast had come and gone. The majority of the older men had left hours earlier for the quiet morning of fishing that had been planned for them. Emily's mother, along with Lady Tarryton, was currently holding court on the side lawn a short distance away, watching over the games of archery and lawn bowling that had already commenced. The younger people were in their rooms, preparing for the trip into the village, where they planned on buying the local shops out of all manner of ribbons and flowers to go with their wedding finery.

Emily would go. Yes, she would go, and join in with the younger people, and play chaperone to her sister as her mother had requested of her. But she was not happy about it.

Nor was she happy to be burdened with the company of one other member of their little expedition. Truly, what was Lord Morley playing at? If his attentions to her after his arrival had seemed suspect, his blatant annoyance of her the evening before was downright baffling. Why did he insist on pressing his company on her? Couldn't he see she had no wish to be in his presence? She had made no secret of it, certainly, though her hostility had only seemed to amuse him.

Her steps became more agitated, quickening around a bend in

the path. Immersed in her frustrations, she came too close to a rose bush, her skirts catching on the thorny branches and tugging her to a stop. Blowing out an aggravated breath, she twisted, the better to extract herself with as little damage to her gown as possible.

A movement out of the corner of her eye caught her attention. She cut her gaze toward it. A low, dark shape lurked in the shadows of the tall hedges that lined the garden. That it was an animal was clear. But what kind? It kept its head low to the ground, the glint of one eye the only discernible feature.

Centered with disturbing intensity on her.

A frisson of fear worked its way down her spine. Her fingers, which had stilled on the material of her dress, began to work frantically to free it from the thorns. She kept her eyes fast on the beast. It was larger than a fox. But how much larger was a mystery. Emily's mind whirled, trying to think what feral animal might be lurking in the wilds of Northamptonshire. Bears were long gone from Britain, and the creature before her was too small for a stag. Were there still wolves in the area? No, surely not, for hadn't she read somewhere that most of the wolves had been eradicated in the time of the Tudors? That did not mean, however, that they were completely gone, did it? Panic was beginning to set in. And her skirt, no matter how she tugged on it, would not come loose. She opened her mouth to call out for help. Someone would have to hear and come to her aid. At that moment, however, the animal gave a pathetic whine that stopped her cold.

She knew that sound well; she had grown up around Willowhaven's kennel of hunting dogs, and the noises of canines were deeply ingrained into her memory. Many an afternoon in her youth had been spent visiting the new litters of pups that often graced their pack. All fear gone now, she dropped her fingers from her skirt, holding her hand out with slow and careful movements. The whine had indicated it was not of a malicious mind. With luck she could beguile it from its hiding place. "Come along, then," she called out softly, making her voice singsong and pleasant. "You've no need to fear me. I won't harm you."

The animal raised its head a fraction. There was a rustle of movement, and it appeared by the shifting shadows that it was coming closer. Emily's heart began to pound. Where had the dog come from? Why was it out here in Willowhaven's garden? That could all wait, however. For now she must coax the beast from its bower. She clicked her tongue at it in encouragement, heartened at what she thought was the shadow of its tail wagging slowly behind it. A bit more, she thought, straining her arm toward it.

Just then the animal stopped, the shimmering glint of its eye indicating a shift in attention. Before she could so much as blink, it turned and bolted. Emily had just enough time to see a long tail and dark flanks before it ducked back through the hedge and was gone.

Disappointment crashed through her. What could have spooked it? A moment later and she had her answer as a familiar voice broke into her troubled thoughts.

"Why does it not surprise me one bit that you've managed to ensnare yourself in a rose bush?"

Emily spun about. There was a loud rending sound as her skirt ripped free of the thorns. Right then she couldn't have cared less. "Drew!" She launched herself forward, straight into her brother's arms.

Lord Andrew Masters, younger than her by a mere year, was one of her very favorite people in the world. Possessing the incredible good looks and ease with people that the other Masters children seemed to have in abundance—and she alone lacked—he had the amazing ability to charm himself out of almost every scrape. She had not seen him for a good long while; now that he was home again after such a lengthy absence, she intended to make the best of it. A small twinge of worry for the beast in the bushes snagged at her, but she endeavored to put it from her mind for now. She could not very well go chasing after the animal, anyway. She would have to wait and watch and hope that it would come close again for her to do it some good.

Drew dropped her back to her feet. Emily looked up into his face, so carefree and handsome. His eyes twinkled merrily. "You all almost had the wedding without me. Could you not have waited to locate me before you went ahead and planned something so momentous?"

Emily laughed, her mood suddenly much improved with her brother's appearance. He had been gadding about in such a havey-cavey fashion since he had left university, they had feared their letters would never catch up to him. Thankfully it seemed at long last they had. Nothing else could have made the joyous occasion of Caleb's wedding even more of a blessing.

"We're lucky they are having any kind of a wedding at all, for I have it on good authority that Caleb was very keen on eloping. Have you seen Mama?"

Her brother appeared affronted at the mere thought. "What's this? You expect me to visit with Mother before I come to see my favorite sister? Blasphemy."

"She will have your head, you know," Emily said, only half teasing. "She has been nearly frantic with worry over your absence. And I take it you have not seen Caleb either?"

"No, that I have not, though you can be assured, I am most eager to see him again after so long." He took hold of Emily's hand, tucking it in the crook of his arm, before setting off down the path. "And so our Caleb is back in the arms of his family. Tell me how this all came about."

Emily smiled. "We have his intended to thank for it, I think. Imogen has had the most fantastic effect on him. Actually, on us all. I could not love her more if she were our natural sister."

Her brother chuckled. "I cannot wait to meet this paragon."

They walked on in silence for a time, the only sounds the laughter from the adjoining lawn as the archery and lawn bowling went on, with the occasional roar of excitement rising up over the border of hedges. A bird passed overhead, calling sweetly, and a warm breeze rifled a few strands of Emily's hair that had managed to escape from her bun. For the first time in days she felt herself again, able to relax a bit and forget some of the chaos that had invaded her home.

Drew leaned toward her. "Tell me, how are you holding up

under such an abundance of guests?" The words were light enough, but Emily could hear the underlying concern in them.

She gave a small sigh, glad she did not have to keep up pretenses with him. "Not well. But you expected as much, I think."

His eyes clouded with worry. "Could they have not chosen a different location?"

Emily gave a strained chuckle. "Where would you have the wedding, then? London? For I'll tell you now, that would not be the better choice."

"No, I suppose not," he muttered. When he spoke again, his voice had taken on a jovial cast. "But you may rest easy now, for your favorite brother is here at long last, and will protect you from all manner of evil."

"You do not know how much that relieves my mind," she replied with feeling. Perhaps now, she thought, Lord Morley would not feel the need to corner her at every turn. Mayhap she could escape him. The thought gladdened her, making her steps light as she walked on beside her brother. Yes, this was a happy thing indeed.

• • •

Later that afternoon, as the party of young people made their way to the local village, Emily learned that the words of young men could easily be broken when they were confronted with a bevy of beauties.

Emily watched in consternation as Drew offered his arm to Miss Mariah Duncan. He flashed her a rakish smile, making the younger girl blush prettily, before helping her around an exposed root in the road.

"You must be happy that your brother is back in time for the wedding."

The low voice in her ear made Emily yelp in surprise. She turned, scowling at Lord Morley. The man had been nowhere to be seen when they had left Willowhaven for Ketterby. Now, however, it seemed he had caught up with them.

Of all the rotten luck.

"Do you enjoy sneaking up on people, my lord?"

Instead of looking contrite, the man merely smiled benignly. "Very much so."

She hoped against hope that he would move past her and join the main body of their group. Instead he matched his pace to hers. She cut him a glare. "I had thought you would miss our outing. Didn't you have anything better to do?"

He chuckled. The sound went right through her in the most disconcerting way. "Why, Lady Emily, one would think you do not care for my company."

"Is it so very obvious, then?" she muttered, and immediately felt mortification flush her cheeks as he looked in surprise at her. She closed her eyes. "I am truly sorry, my lord. That was not well done of me."

"Please," he murmured, "don't curb your tongue on my account."

Her eyes flew open and she looked at him in no little surprise. Had that been amusement coloring his words? But no, he looked somber enough as he gazed toward the rest of their party...who were rapidly pulling ahead. Belatedly, Emily realized how far behind they had fallen from the group. Picking up her pace, she once more hoped the man would take the hint and leave her be. But he merely sped up beside her, his long-legged stride easily keeping pace with her.

"Regardless of how I may feel about you," she said, because she really must say something about her rudeness, "it was not kind of me to say such a thing."

He let out a short, sharp bark of laughter. "If you think your opinion matters in the least to me, you are mistaken, I assure you."

Emily blinked several times. There had been no couching his words at all. They shot at her like arrows and hit just as painfully. She stopped abruptly, angry tears burning behind her eyes, and turned fully to face him. The past days had been hard enough without the man's blatant cruelty. "Why do you insist on harassing me, my lord?"

"Oh, is that what I'm doing? Goodness, how positively brutish of me," he murmured.

The sarcastic drawl that accompanied his words sent a bolt of indignation zinging down her spine. "You mock me, sir," she bit out. "I will have you know that, as weak as you may think me, I am not. I will not allow you to treat me in such a manner."

He lifted one eyebrow in a faintly mocking way. "Won't you?"

Emily surprised herself by letting out a faint growl of frustration. She should not let him get to her, should turn and walk the other way and ignore him for the remainder of his stay. But looking at the condescension in his eyes, she couldn't let his slight pass. "No," she stated firmly, lifting her chin a fraction, "I will not."

He looked at her, his eyes dark and intent. She knew what he was doing. He was trying to prove his superiority, to force her to look away first. Crossing her arms belligerently, she stared right back.

He gave a small shrug and continued along the path. The small thrill of victory she had from him backing down from their juvenile staring competition was short lived, however, as he called back to her, "Hmm, funny that."

She should ignore him, should not feed his ego by demanding he explain. But, standing there alone on the small dirt road, watching him walk away from her, she found she could not let it go. Picking up her skirts in both hands, she ran after him. "What did you mean by that?" she demanded when she came abreast of him.

"You say you will not allow yourself to be treated as a weak person, that you will not allow yourself to be bullied. And yet you permit everyone to treat you as if you're made of glass. How do you expect those of a meaner nature to treat you when you present yourself as such to the world?"

Even through her fury she felt the heat of mortification flush her cheeks. Was that true? Did she allow everyone around her to coddle her in such a way? But she would not let him see he had affected her. She glared up at him. "People like you, my lord?"

His lip quirked sardonically and he gave a little mocking bow of his head in her direction. "As you wish."

"You play with me. But I am stronger than I look."

"So you say. But as I have not seen proof that such a statement is at all true, you will excuse my doubts."

Done with the conversation, she stopped in the path, thinking he would go on ahead and leave her in peace. To her consternation, he stopped as well and looked at her expectantly. She let out a frustrated breath. "Why are you doing this? Why can't you leave me alone? I know you don't like me."

To his credit, he honestly looked surprised at her words. "What put that notion in your head?"

So he thought to play with her, did he? "Please," she scoffed. "You have made no secret of it. Your disdain is clear in every word you speak to me."

He gave a short laugh. "Disdain? Hardly. You must have a very active imagination, my lady."

She clenched her hands at her sides, barely managing to keep herself from striking out at him. The sudden desire for violence shocked her. Never had anyone brought about such a reaction in her. "Do me the credit of respecting my intelligence," she snapped. "Ever since you arrived you have been at me, belittling me with your meanness. You may think you are superior to me, but anyone who torments others as you do is no better than the vilest creature crawling in the dirt at my feet."

He actually had the gall to smile. It stunned her momentarily... until he started up a slow, maddening clap, making her humiliation complete.

She was about to turn and stalk back to the house, anything to get away from him. Until he spoke, stopping her in her tracks.

"Well done, Lady Emily. I always knew you had more backbone than you let on."

She frowned at the admiration—admiration?—lighting up his face. "What are you blathering about?"

He regarded her with narrowed eyes. "You are a spirited woman, Lady Emily. And yet you continue to hide behind this very pale copy of yourself. Why?"

"Do you mean to tell me you have done this on purpose?" The mere idea was preposterous. The smile he gifted her with, however, was answer enough. He had pushed and prodded her until she had blown up in his face in the most embarrassing manner. And he had been trying for just that result?

"You are mad," she whispered.

He shrugged away her words. "Perhaps. But you have to admit, my method is working."

She searched his face, at an utter loss. "But *why?*"

His expression sobered. "Because you deserve more in life than to be the forgotten sister in the corner."

Just like that, her anger melted away. In its place was confusion, and a deep ache that settled heavy in her chest. That was quite the nicest thing anyone had ever said to her. And from the man who had been making her life hell for the past days.

He must have seen her bewilderment, for he smiled and offered his arm. She looked at it blankly for a moment before placing her fingers on it. They began to trace the steps of the others slowly, almost leisurely. And suddenly Emily was glad for it. She was much too shaken at the moment to be any good in company.

"I have stunned you," he murmured.

She gave him a disbelieving glance. "Did you expect anything less?"

"No, I suppose not. It was not well done of me, to prod you in such a manner."

That was an understatement if there ever was one. "I don't understand you," she muttered.

He chuckled, but the sound had more of bitterness than mirth to it. "Not many do."

Emily chewed on her lip. To her surprise, she found that she was becoming curious about this enigma of a man whose arm she was holding.

But small talk had never been her forte. As a matter of fact, she had always been at a loss with any type of talk at all. She eyed the group ahead of them, narrowing her eyes, trying to understand the dynamics. They all mingled and conversed and laughed with seeming ease. Truly, how did one do it?

She cleared her throat, blinked a few times, hoping for some divine lightning bolt to hit her in the head and give her instantaneous insight. But it seemed she was on her own for now.

Finally she said, lamely, "So, you are here for Caleb's wedding."

Immediately she had the urge to dive into the nearest bit of foliage and hide for the next year at least. Especially when he turned his head to look down at her for a long, silent moment. She could not see his expression, as she was still looking determinedly ahead. But she could well imagine it. She flushed and was desperately thankful that her ruined cheek was not facing him at the moment.

"Yes," he answered slowly. "So I am."

"What I meant was," she stammered, "it is good of you to come. For his wedding, that is."

"I wouldn't say it is good of me," he mumbled. "But I could not say no, could I?"

She shot him a confused look. "Couldn't you?" When he merely looked at her as if she were daft, she continued, "I mean, it is not as if you are related to either the bride or the groom. There was nothing forcing you to come. I know if I had a choice, I would not be here."

"Is such a scene so abhorrent to you that you would miss your brother's wedding if given the chance?"

He seemed genuinely curious. So much so that she did what she normally wouldn't and answered him with complete candor, "Yes, it truly is."

His eyes changed as he considered her. But where she expected pity or compassion, perhaps a sliding of his gaze to her scar, she saw instead an undefined emotion, as if he were trying to work her out, to understand her. Unnerved by the intensity there, she turned back to the path before them. "But you have not answered my question. Why could you not decline the invitation if you are not glad to be here?"

He was silent for a time. Bird calls could be heard over their heads, and the chitter of squirrels as they rushed through the underbrush and clambered up the trunks of the trees was almost loud in the strange, intimate cocoon of silence that seemed to envelop them. Belatedly she realized the sounds of the rest of the party had faded. Suddenly nervous to be so alone with him, she was about to suggest they walk a bit quicker to catch up to the rest when he spoke.

"You know that Willbridge and I have been friends since our first days at Eton," he said. His voice, usually so gruff and deep, seemed almost hesitant.

Emily got the distinct impression that he was about to impart something precious to her. Not wanting to break the spell by speaking, she merely nodded. She watched his profile closely, at how a muscle seemed to tick in his jaw, at the way his throat worked as he swallowed hard.

"The truth is," he said, so quiet she had to lean closer to hear him, "Willbridge is my dearest, oldest friend." He turned to look at her then, and his dark eyes fairly blazed with emotion. She sucked in a sharp breath at the intensity of it. "There are not many I care about. Your brother is one of two people in this entire forsaken world that I trust with my life. I would do anything for him."

It was only when he returned his gaze to the path that Emily could draw breath again. Fighting off her roiling emotions at having been witness to such feelings, she said, low and gentle, "I would think, if you cared for him as you say you do, you would be glad to witness him marrying someone he loves so dearly."

He mumbled something that sounded suspiciously like, "Not in the least." Shocked, she blinked several times. She could not have heard him right. She opened her mouth to question him on it. Just then, however, they rounded a bend in the path, and Ketterby came into view. The rest of the party stood in a loose group past the bridge. Daphne peered back along the dirt road, a small frown on her face. When she caught sight of Emily and Lord Morley emerging from the tree line, she smiled broadly and waved.

Disappointment crashed over Emily. She had been so close to something important, something that would have given her greater insight into this mystery that was Lord Morley. As for him, there was an immediate change that came over his person at the sight of the others. He straightened, angling his body away from her. It was as if a physical wall had come up between them.

Which was for the best, she knew. The man had sent her emotions bouncing about in the most maddening manner since his arrival. As he pulled away from her to make his way to Sir Tristan's side, she determinedly went to her sister's. She had no wish to have that sad childhood infatuation that had so defined her in the past take her over again. She would not be able to come back from it this time. That she knew.

Chapter 6

Daphne's voice calling her name snagged Emily's wandering thoughts. She looked up from the book she had been blindly perusing for the past half hour, blinking in incomprehension. Her mind, it seemed, could not grasp onto anything with firmness this evening.

No, that was not right at all. Her inattentiveness had started well before this evening. A vision of Lord Morley's face, alive with emotion as it had been earlier that afternoon on the way to Ketterby, swam in her mind. She shook her head to dispel it.

"I'm sorry?" she asked, not having heard a thing her sister had said.

Daphne was already out of earshot. She and the rest of the young women had risen from their seats and were milling about the outer perimeter of the room, talking quietly to one another, their excited giggles carrying to where Emily sat. The rest of the room was in a vague kind of chaos, with the men moving furniture and rolling back the carpet. Ah, she saw it now. They wished to dance. And she was to play for them. With a small sigh, she placed her unread book aside—truly, she hadn't even the faintest idea what it was she'd been pretending to read anyway—and made her way to the pianoforte.

Music was to Emily as rain and sun were to flowers. She spent hours each morning practicing in the music room, reveling in the release of emotion it provided that other avenues of her life did not. As she was not keen to dance in public, she was always called upon to play when they had any type of party that included dancing. She typically preferred it that way.

For some reason, tonight was different. Her feet dragged as she skirted the group that had gathered in the middle of the room. Her eyes were drawn to the couples pairing off, and a strange sort of longing filled her. She had the sudden urge to join them, to feel the freedom of the dance, to let her body move in the intricate steps. Without meaning to, her gaze shifted and came to rest upon Lord Morley where he stood against the mantle. He regarded her solemnly, his eyes dark and intense. Flushing, she ducked her head and kept on until she made it to the grand instrument and sat herself down before the keys. She scanned through the collection of music sheets always kept nearby, but she could not seem to concentrate on the offerings before her. Instead she felt Lord Morley's eyes like a brand, heating her skin in the most disconcerting way. Frowning, she let out an irritated puff of breath. Never mind the fleeting moment of communion they had shared that afternoon. Never mind his supposed good intentions in trying to get her to stand up for herself by baiting her mercilessly. She could not have him intrude on her thoughts a moment longer. Determined, Emily pulled out a promising score, put her fingers to the keys, and began.

For the next hour, she played. The joy she typically found in the music, however, failed to touch her. As much as she tried to concentrate on the way the notes flowed through her, she was painfully aware of Lord Morley the whole while. He did not dance. That she knew with disconcerting certainty. Instead she could see him out of the corner of her eye as he moved about the room. He joined Sir Tristan at one point, found his way to her mother's side, then moved to the window and stared out it for a good long while. But never did he dance. And she found herself wondering, much to her horror, that if she were free, would he ask her?

But, more importantly, would she say yes? She rather thought that she would.

• • •

Malcolm looked out into the moonlit garden, not seeing a bit of it.

Instead he shifted his gaze in the glass and watched Lady Emily as she labored over the keys.

Truly, didn't any of the other women present think to relieve her? She'd been playing nonstop for an hour, and not once had she been approached. He supposed this was something she often did. It seemed like her, to hide away at the instrument while those about her made merry. And perhaps she had no enjoyment in the dance. As much as he thought the situation unfair, what business was it of his?

He had been deeply shaken at the urge he'd felt to pour his heart out to her earlier that day. What was it about Lady Emily that chipped away so thoroughly at his defenses? She did not accomplish it with pushiness or aggression, but with quiet questions and a gentle, commiserating glance. He had been relieved when they had been reunited with the group at the bridge, though disappointed as well, that he had to part from her. Disturbed at these unwelcome emotions, he had gone to Tristan's side and had not left it for the entirety of the trip. He told himself it was because of his friend's apparently growing interest in Lady Daphne, which was becoming more obvious with each passing day. But he knew better. It was not worry that Tristan might find himself at the wrong end of a bullet, but a desire to put distance between himself and Lady Emily that had him so pointedly ignoring her and placing all of his attentions elsewhere.

He was a coward, plain and simple.

Even so, regardless of how she had affected him that afternoon, he still had a job to do. That did not include cowering in the corner and leaving her to her devices. Just then, there was a pause between songs. But instead of looking through the music sheets beside her as he expected, Lady Emily gazed at the dancers as they laughed and paired up with new partners in expectation of the next dance. A frown marred her brow. Was it him, or did she seem eager to step down from her position as entertainer?

He had the sudden urge to rush to her rescue. But that would be peculiar, would it not? He was nothing to her; surely one of her relatives should go to her aide? Upon closer inspection, however, Malcolm saw that was not going to happen anytime soon. Her mother had been drawn into conversation with Lady Tarryton and would no doubt be stuck there for some time if the latter woman's expression was any indication. Young Lord Drew was flirting in an outrageous way with Miss Mariah. Caleb and Imogen were nowhere to be seen, no doubt having taken advantage of the dancing to sneak off. And Lady Daphne...

She was deep in conversation with Tristan.

Damnation, he should have been paying closer attention. The best thing for all involved would be to keep Tristan far away from Willbridge's sister. But perhaps he could accomplish two things at once. Striding forward, Malcolm insinuated himself between Lady Daphne and his friend. She looked up at him in surprise. Tristan merely scowled.

Malcolm leaned in close to the girl. "It seems to me that Lady Emily may need to be rescued from the pianoforte," he murmured.

Lady Daphne's attention immediately shifted to her sister in the corner of the room. "Rescued?"

"Yes," he pushed. "She does look as if she is done. Perhaps she's fatigued. I don't suppose you could possibly relieve her?"

That seemed to do the trick. Her eyes flashed with excitement at the prospect. Malcolm figured that, if it was as he suspected, and Lady Emily regularly took to the instrument to hide from guests, her sister didn't often get to perform in public. Perhaps this was the chance she'd wanted for so long.

In the next moment, however, he realized his mistake, for Lady Daphne said with a coy smile, "I would be delighted to relieve my sister. But I am not as proficient as her on the pianoforte. Perhaps, Sir Tristan, you would do me the honor of turning the pages for me?"

To Malcolm's disgust, Tristan's face fairly lit up. "Certainly," he said, gallantly offering his arm and walking her off in the direction of the instrument.

Well, hell, Malcolm thought as he watched them go.

• • •

Emily walked away from the pianoforte in a daze, leaving Daphne and Sir Tristan happily talking over song selections. Never had anyone offered to relieve her from the instrument, especially during such a lively party as this. She was certainly not one to look a gift horse in the mouth. Hurrying her steps, almost afraid that Daphne would turn about and call her back, Emily failed to look where she was going. She soon found her face full of snowy white cravat.

She really did need to start paying better attention to her surroundings.

It was then a familiar scent assailed her, a heady mix of leather and black tea and some indiscernible spice that had been branded on her brain since meeting Lord Morley again two days ago. It filled her, making her light-headed. She swayed a bit. His hand was on her upper arm in an instant, steadying her.

"I had feared you were exhausting yourself at the pianoforte," he mumbled. "I see I was proven right in sending your sister to you."

She shot him a stunned look. "Do you mean it was all your idea?"

His ebony brow quirked up. "Does it surprise you that I can be kind?"

"Yes," she answered with all truthfulness.

"Good. Best to keep you on your toes." A small smile softened the harsh line of his lips. To her consternation she was captivated by the small movement. She realized in that instant that she had not seen him smile except in the most sardonic ways in the past days. It transformed his face, made him even more handsome if that were possible. For a moment, just a moment, she remembered why she had become so enamored of him years ago.

But that would not do. Regardless of the small connection they had shared that afternoon, the fact remained that he had no designs on her. She certainly had no designs on him. Bobbing a quick curtsy of thanks, she made to walk around him.

Apparently he wasn't quite through with her.

"Come and sit with me?"

He looked as surprised as she felt that he had made the suggestion. But he held out his arm to her, and what else could she do but take it? It would have been rude not to, she told herself. It had nothing whatsoever to do with how wonderful said arm felt under her fingers, or how she could stay close to him a bit longer to take in more of that captivating smell of his. She realized, however, as he guided her to a quiet corner—which was no easy feat in a room with nearly two score people—that now she had to actually sit and try to converse with him. Would he be kind and considerate, or rude and surly? Truly, there was no way to know with this man. His moods were as mercurial as a feral cat's. And as she had already determined that she had no wish to like him again, it would not do to provide him with any chances to get in her good graces.

Right away she knew that things would not be in her favor, for wouldn't he go and position her with the left side of her face to the wall? She frowned. "So now you will go and be wonderful and undermine my very reasonable dislike of you?"

"No, I would never be so unkind as to do that," he said with a small smile as he lowered himself beside her.

To her surprise, laughter bubbled up in her chest. He gave her a quick glance of mocking surprise. "And here I thought you had no sense of humor at all."

She did not know what possessed her, but in the next moment she raised an eyebrow and said in the most serious manner possible, "I am sitting here with you, aren't I? If that is not a good joke, I don't know what is."

He eyed her in approval. "Nicely done, Lady Emily," he murmured. "We may make something of you yet."

Once again her tongue took on a mischievous mind of its own. "Oh, don't go getting optimistic, my lord. It isn't like you at all."

He looked at her for several long moments, his face slack, not a hint of humor lighting it, and Emily thought perhaps she had gone too far. Then he threw back his head, and the most wonderful laugh burst forth from him. It shook his entire body, lit up his face, completely transformed him. Several people turned in surprise to look their way.

Emily found herself smiling, a large grin that lifted her cheeks, pulling at her scar. For once she didn't mind the unpleasant sensation. He had a wonderful laugh. It was positively infectious.

His laughter died down, and he looked at her in approval. "You know, you really must smile more often. It is very becoming."

Instantly her joy fled. He thought to patronize her with false praise? "I am not a fool, my lord. You hardly need to condescend to me in such a way."

"You think I am talking down to you?"

"I know you are."

He rolled his eyes and sat back, crossing one booted foot over the opposite knee. "I should have known you would be like any other female, looking to drag more compliments out of a fellow."

Affront immediately straightened Emily's spine. "I assure you, I am not at all like that."

"Please," he scoffed. "You must know you're lovely. Look in a mirror and you will see the truth of that."

At his words her indignity of the moment dimmed to an aching sadness. "I *have* looked in a mirror," she all but whispered.

"You are referring to your scar," he said with typical bluntness.

Her mind immediately went blank. Most people were not usually so forthright with her about it. She didn't quite know how to handle this new situation. Avoidance and uncomfortable silences she had dealt with aplenty. She had even dealt with her fair share of couched rudeness, such as those from Lord Randall. But never this.

"I get the feeling," he went on, apparently oblivious to her distress, "that you think it is much worse than it actually is."

"I beg your pardon?"

"Your scar," he clarified blithely, as if she were not perfectly aware what he was referring to. He waved vaguely at her face, as if to bring home the point. "It's truly not bad at all. I do think that, if you did not show so much sensitivity to it, people would ignore it. As it is, the emphasis you give it makes people more aware of it."

Anger ran through her, molten, heating her veins. "How dare you pretend to know what I have been through!"

"No, I don't know what you've been through," he agreed, completely unfazed by her reaction. "But I do know that self-pity will do you no good at all. You may as well raise your head high. To hell with what everyone thinks."

Her mouth fell open, not at the use of his profanity, which was shocking enough, but at his crass attitude toward something that gave her daily pain. "I do not pity myself," she countered hotly. "Nor do I intentionally bring attention to it."

"Well, now, I never said you intentionally did. But *unintentionally*, you certainly do. Pressing your cheek when you flush, tilting your head in that ridiculous way. But worst of all, that slouched, eyes-to-the-ground defeated look you constantly wear."

So shocked was she at his words that when he lowered his foot and leaned forward she did not even have the sense to recoil. In the next moment he extended his hand and gently traced her scar.

Emily could not have moved if she tried. His fingers were warm, feather light. A whisper of sensation on her skin. People generally didn't even look on her scar; she could not remember the last time anyone had touched it. It sent a shiver of awareness through her, a longing.

It stole the very breath from her lungs.

Then his hand was gone. Emily simply sat there, at a complete loss what to do or say.

His lips—those wonderfully chiseled lips that could look so cold and cruel one minute and so boldly seductive the next—curved in a small smile. "See," he murmured. "Not disgusting at all." He held his fingers up and waggled them. "And not a wart to be seen."

He was mad. Absolutely and completely mad. "Well," was all she could think to say. Because, really, how was one supposed to respond after such a thing?

"Do you typically take on the duty of playing for the dancers?"

She blinked myopically at the abrupt change in subject. "Yes."

"Why?"

Though her brain was beginning to function again, she still could not make sense of his new and unexpected line of questioning. "I am good at it, and it allows the others to dance. I have no wish to join them, so what is the point of having one of the other young ladies perform?"

But he was shaking his head. "You do want to dance."

"No, I do not." Truly, her head was beginning to ache from this bizarre and twisted conversation.

"Yes, you do," he insisted. He pointed to her leg, which was bouncing in time to the music. "You give yourself away."

Flushing, she pressed down on the traitorous appendage with both hands.

"So why don't you dance?"

She shrugged. What would he say if she told him no one ever asked her? Not once in all the impromptu dances they'd held with their cousins and other local families had she been asked.

He leaned forward again. In his eyes was a new light. "So dance now," he said, "with me."

Belatedly she recalled the unexpected thought she'd had while at the pianoforte, wondering what she would do if he asked her to dance. She had believed her first instinct would be to say yes. Yet now, in the moment, she wanted nothing more than to politely decline and run from the room as fast as she could.

But at the sight of the challenge in his nearly black eyes, a gleam of excitement called to her. He was pushing her on purpose again, she realized. Trying to drag her from the protective shell she typically wrapped herself in. Was he being kind in trying to draw her out? Or did he get some kind of sick pleasure from seeing her squirm? But more importantly, now that she knew, would she retreat and duck back inside herself? Or would she respond to the dare in his expression?

Taking a deep breath, she reached out and, with only the slightest hesitation, placed her trembling fingers in his own.

Chapter 7

Malcolm hadn't thought she would actually take him up on his challenge. Yet she reached out, accepting the gauntlet he had thrown down with a quivering touch of her fingers.

He stood there for a moment, stunned, waiting for her to renege. She merely looked up into his face, her little chin stuck out at a mulish angle that was altogether endearing. Tucking her hand in the crook of his arm, he guided her to the milling couples, pride in her making his chest expand to such a degree he thought he might burst the buttons of his waistcoat.

Granted, she appeared ready to drop on the spot. And she clung to his arm as if she were dangling from the dome of St. Paul's Cathedral. Even so, here she was, walking out into the middle of the drawing room floor. She took her place beside him in the circle that had formed, her eyes darting about with quick, panicked movements. Her breath came hard and fast, her curtsy to him as the music started up stiff. He worried for a moment he had pushed her too hard. Perhaps he had read her wrong, and she truly hadn't wanted to dance.

Then they joined hands with the other couples and began Le Grand Rond. And it was as if someone had dipped her in magic. He had gotten the distinct impression that she did not often have the chance to dance. One would never know it from the way she moved. Her steps were light, her touch delicate, each movement done with absolute precision. But it was her face that sent him reeling. There, the transformation was stunning. She looked positively radiant. Her eyes, normally so shuttered, fairly glowed, their pale gray depths lively and carefree. No longer did she look as if she were hiding from the world. No, she was grace personified.

It was when they joined hands and faced one another, however, that the breath left his body entirely. For it was then she smiled. And not a small, polite smile, but one that encompassed her entire face. The slight pull of her scar tilted it slightly to one side, giving it an endearing and captivating crookedness. Her joy blinded him to anything else.

Her happiness had made her beautiful.

No, that wasn't right. She had already been beautiful. Now she was stunning.

The music was a distant buzz in his ears now. His entire attention was centered on her face, hoping for one more smile. Surely his reaction had been from mere surprise. He could not be affected by something as simple as a smile from a slip of a girl, and Willbridge's sister at that. He was hardened to such things, after all. But there it was again, that faintly crooked smile that seemed to make time stop.

Before he was aware of the fact, the music came to a close. Something seemed to drain from her at its loss. She looked suddenly a bit less colorful, the joy in her gone like a puff of smoke. As if waking from a dream, he inhaled deeply and broke his gaze from her, troubled by the ache that had started up in his chest. He immediately caught sight of Willbridge and Imogen inside the terrace doors.

Only once had he seen his friend even come close to crying, and that had been at the death of his brother Jonathan all those years ago. The glint of tears shone in Willbridge's eyes now, though much happier in origin. Close by, Willbridge's mother looked on her daughter with equally moist eyes, one hand held before her mouth. Imogen, at Willbridge's side, was fairly beaming.

Alarm shot through him. If they bombarded Lady Emily with compliments and praise, all her progress would be for nothing. She would revert right back into her protective shell again. *Let them pass it off as if it were the most normal thing in the world*, he pleaded silently. And for a moment it seemed as if his request had been answered. They all kept to their places, and Lady Emily turned to him to thank him, her smile not full of the ecstatic happiness it had been earlier but still there, still lovely to look at.

But then Lady Daphne burst on the scene and all Malcolm's hopes were dashed to pieces.

"Oh, Emily, how wonderful you dance. I vow I could not believe my eyes when I saw you on the floor. Why have you never danced when we've had our dinner parties with our cousins? You must next time; they will be so very surprised. Though I think perhaps we can ask Mother or Imogen to play, as I would hate to miss dancing myself. I vow, you shined. Everyone had their eyes on you. You caused quite a stir."

With each sentence spoken by her voluble sister, Lady Emily seemed to shrink more and more into herself. By the end of Lady Daphne's monologue, Lady Emily's face appeared almost as pale as the gray of her gown. Malcolm could only watch helplessly. And matters grew worse as the other young couples surrounded them. Every fiber of his being urged him to step close to Emily, to pull her into his embrace and shield her from the bombardment of attention. Before he could make an utter fool of himself, however, Imogen came forward, putting her arms about Lady Emily and giving her a supportive squeeze. Her eyes met Malcolm's, and he could see that Lady Daphne's loud proclamations had troubled her as much as they had him.

But Lady Emily had the support she needed. He could leave her in capable hands. Dancing with her had been a spur-of-the-moment thing. He could see now that he could think clearly that it had been a mistake of the first order. Once again she had managed to touch something deep inside of him that he did not want revived, something he wanted to keep dead and buried.

He pulled back, intending to put some much-needed distance between himself and Lady Emily. In that moment, however, the lady herself did just that. Pulling from Imogen's hold, she turned and walked from the room without looking back.

• • •

Malcolm lay awake staring out the window of his bedroom two mornings later, his eyes dry and itchy from lack of sleep. Disgusted with himself, he blew out a breath and turned over. The covers bunched up about his legs. He kicked out at them, then sat up and pounded on his pillow, turning it to the cool side before lying back down. But he was no more comfortable than when he'd started.

What had he expected last night when he had retired? To awaken in the morning, fully rested and ready to take on the day? He snorted into the gloom of predawn. One of his dearest friends was to be married in mere hours, an event Malcolm had been dreading since its announcement nearly a fortnight ago. Sleep had never been in the cards for him.

The most galling thing, though, was that Willbridge's wedding was not the cause for his sleeplessness. No, that blame landed squarely on Lady Emily Masters's slender shoulders. He'd had an unhealthy interest in her since his arrival that had nothing whatsoever to do with the promise he had made to Willbridge and everything to do with the woman herself.

But why? Why, damn it?

He had to stop thinking of her. He shifted again, flipping to his other side. *Yes, that was it.* He would put her from his mind. No more would he contemplate Lady Emily's smiling face from two nights before. He would forget the slight unevenness of her rosy lips, the way her eyes lit up, how her soul had seemed to glow from within her like a river of gold when they'd danced...

Groaning, he forced his gaze to the window. The sky, he saw, was changing, from the deepest indigo to a flat gray. Blowing out a disgusted breath, Malcolm threw off the covers and swung his bare feet over the side of the bed. All day yesterday she had been busy with wedding preparations and he had hardly seen her. He thought the break from watching over her would have helped him forget the unwelcome reaction he'd had to her. But to his disgust, it had seemed to make it sharper.

What he needed was a brisk walk to clear his head. He would have a hard enough time getting through this damn day without being disoriented from lack of sleep. Throwing on clothes haphazardly, he strode from the room, letting the faint morning light lead the way. He moved past the closed doors of bedrooms where people still slumbered peacefully, his footsteps muffled by the thick rug that ran the length of the hall.

Which door led to Lady Emily's bedroom?

The thought flashed through his head with startling clarity. He reeled, his steps faltering, before he tucked his chin against his chest and plowed on.

The house was already awake, with the servants rushing about on silent feet, preparing for the important day ahead. They didn't give him a second glance. And why should they? He was merely a mad English lord running through the house as if the hounds of hell were nipping at his heels. Soon he would be outside in the cool morning air. Then he could leave everything behind and calm his mind.

He was at the side door that led to the gardens, the handle tight in his grip, when he heard it—the faintest music, moving through the air with a wrenching melancholy. It wrapped about him like the soft arms of a lover. His hand fell back to his side, his head tilting to better hear the tune. Who could possibly be up so very early? An image of Lady Emily flashed through his mind, but he quickly dismissed it. It could not be her. The music she had played in the drawing room two nights ago had been lovely, but it had not possessed this haunting quality. No, this was something altogether different. As if a glowing golden string had attached itself to him, he unconsciously followed the sound. There was no choice but to go where the music originated.

The polished wood door to the music room was cracked open, but there he stopped, not wanting to disturb whoever was within. The music, though still soft, was louder here, washing over and through him. Such emotion emanated from the plaintive notes. Such feelings, long thought forgotten, welled up within him. He caught his breath at it, overwhelmed with the need to learn the source.

He moved closer, angling his head to see as much of the room through the crack between the door and the jam as he could. But the pianoforte was on the other side of the room, well beyond view. Blowing out a frustrated breath, he placed one hand on the panel and pushed as gently as he could. The door was blessedly silent, the hinges well oiled. Not so the floor. As he took a step forward, following the door as it swung slowly inward, a floorboard gave a distinctive creak.

Malcolm stilled, not wanting to startle whoever was playing, listening with the breath frozen in his chest for any indication that he had been overheard. But no, the music played on. Breathing a small sigh of relief, he renewed his efforts. A small push more, a few inches, and he could clear his head through the opening and take a peek.

Without warning, Malcolm was rammed from behind. He lurched forward and slammed into the door, barely hearing it crash against the wall as he went tumbling to the floor. Behind him he could hear a small, feminine cry of dismay. The music halted with a discordant jumble of notes.

He closed his eyes, praying this was all just a dream and he was safe in his bed. But a small voice, trembling with fear, made him see the futility of such a wish.

"I'm so very sorry, sir. Please forgive me, sir. I never meant to topple you. Only my arms was full of linens, you see, for the wedding breakfast, and I didn't see you over the tops of them."

Malcolm resolutely opened his eyes and glanced up. A young maid was standing in the doorway, wringing her hands, looking for all the world as if she were about to burst into tears. At her feet lay a good quantity of fine white cloth.

"Please think nothing of it," he said, hauling himself to his feet. "It was my fault entirely, I assure you. I should not have been lurking in corridors." He retrieved the linens, placing them back in the maid's arms.

Stammering her thanks, the girl beat a hasty retreat. And now, Malcolm thought as he straightened his shoulders, it was time to face the music. So to speak, considering the music itself had stopped at his not-so-graceful entrance.

Turning, he plastered an apologetic smile on his face in preparation for some well-needed groveling...and lost his ability to speak as he gazed upon the startled face of Lady Emily Masters.

. . .

Surprised was not the word Emily would have used when Lord Morley tumbled through the music room door. A more apt word would have been *stunned*, or even *flabbergasted*. But even those did not do justice to what she felt, for it had been that man, and that man alone, who had been on her mind while she sat on that narrow bench and poured her heart into the music.

To say she had thought about him since their dance two nights ago would have been an understatement. He had been one of the few things she'd thought about. How it had felt to glide about the floor as if on a cloud, the music moving through her like something alive. The feel of his hand in hers, his eyes shining on her face as they passed in a turn.

That she had been called to help her mother with the preparations for the wedding the day before had been a blessing. Though the dance with him had been one of the most wonderful things she had ever experienced, her family's reaction to it had told her all she needed to know: that the world of dancing and laughing and making merry was not her world. More importantly, *he* was not part of her world. And he never would be.

She had often wondered how different life would have been if that accident from so long ago had not occurred, if she had not lost her brother and been disfigured by a horrible whim of fate. She had always been shy, but with her twin brother, Jonathan, she had been more of the person she most wished to be; his mischievous ways and high spirits used to draw some of the same out in her. Even so, she had always been a private person, craving peace and solitude at times the way others might crave food. It was a necessity of life for her.

Since that fateful day, however, she had not only needed isolation, she had used it like a shield. She could not be hurt, after all, if there were no one around to hurt her. And in the beginning, people did hurt her. Their reaction to her face always left her feeling ashamed, so that keeping to herself, pushing others away, was more than a simple defense mechanism. It became who she was.

Since Lord Morley's arrival and his constant haranguing of her, though, a desire had risen in her for more. He had woken something she had thought to never feel.

Now he stood before her looking absolutely stunned. There was none of the typical haughtiness he usually adopted in her presence. No, he looked almost vulnerable. Emily's heart twisted in her chest.

He opened his mouth silently several times before he blurted, seemingly without thought, "It's you."

Emily flinched at his unguarded words. Feeling the heat creep into her face, she went to press her hand to her cheek. Recalling his observations of her quirks from the night of the dance, she barely managed to stop herself. "Yes," she said. An obvious statement, but then so was his.

"You were the one playing."

So that was why he had been outside the room? He had heard her playing? And here she had thought that an early start would give her the privacy she had needed for such an intimate thing as to lay her heart out in music. She rose to go. To her surprise, he took a step toward her, his hands out in front of him.

"Please don't leave on my account," he said, the words rapid and a bit breathless. "Won't you keep playing?"

"I'm done for the morning," she mumbled. She made to hurry around him, desperate to escape. His hand caught at her arm, making her gasp as the heat from his fingers seemed to brand her skin. His reaction was just as strong, his hand jerking from her as if he'd laid it on a hot coal. He cleared his throat loudly.

"I would love to hear you play if you have the time for one more song."

She shot him a quick, disbelieving glance, and immediately regretted it. They were close, closer even than they had been during the dance. Her mouth went dry.

"You want me to play for you?"

"Yes, please."

"You have heard me play before," she reminded him.

"Yes, but that was different."

She frowned. "How?"

He looked flummoxed for a moment, as if he hadn't expected the question and didn't have the least idea how to answer it. Finally, he shrugged. "There was something more to your playing this morning. I cannot explain it."

His eyes were fervent and wondering as he looked down at her. Had he truly heard the emotions she had poured into her music, the bit of her soul she had bared in her playing? It touched her deeply that he sensed it, for he had been the one to inspire it in the first place.

Something warm unfurled in her chest. In that moment she would not have denied him anything.

"Very well," she whispered.

On shaky legs she returned to her place at the pianoforte. He sat halfway across the length of the room, as if he were trying to maintain some space between them. And yet Emily could feel his gaze on her like a physical touch. Taking a deep breath, she laid her fingers on the keys and, closing her eyes, began to play.

She could have chosen a piece of incredible difficulty to lay every bit of her skill out in front of him. Instead her fingers glided over the keys, finding and weaving through a soft, plaintive melody. It was slow and deep, reflecting her heart and what Malcolm was pulling from it.

For he was dragging emotions from her she never thought to feel.

Every strike of the hammers on the strings vibrated through her, from her fingertips to her very core. Tears pressed against her closed lids. Did he hear it? Could he feel what she was putting into the song?

All too soon the last note died away. The echo of it was slower to leave her, flowing through her body, swirling about her heart. She was almost bereft when that, too, died away. But with the loss of it, she became aware of something else missing as well. There was not a sound in the room. Had he left? With great will she opened her eyes, quickly blinking away her tears, and looked in the direction he had been sitting.

He was there still, his dark eyes intent on her, his expression rapt. That look was like a spark to dry tinder; suddenly it was as if the music had started up again, the magic of it touching her very soul.

"Thank you," he said, his voice hushed and fervent. He smiled, and a bit of the scar that had grown, protective and tough, around Emily's heart fell away. As she watched him go, she clutched her arms about her waist, more frightened than she had ever been.

Chapter 8

Despite the prestigious guests that had traveled far and wide to Willowhaven to celebrate the marriage of Caleb Masters, Marquess of Willbridge, to Miss Imogen Duncan, the wedding itself was a simple affair. There were no great swathes of silk and satin, no enormous bouquets of hothouse flowers, nor elaborate cakes shipped exclusively from Gunter's. The bride wore a simple pale blue gown that she and her sisters had fashioned themselves and a crown of apple blossoms in her light brown hair. The village church was ancient and small, barely able to hold the guests that crowded within its stone walls. Ordinary folk mingled with the nobility on the polished benches. It was not uncommon on that morning to see a viscount and the innkeeper rubbing elbows.

Yet never had anything sounded so beautiful to the guests' ears as when the couple's voices echoed about the chapel, strong and clear in the surety of their vows. By the time the groom turned to his bride and took her in his arms, sealing their promises to one another with a tender kiss, not a dry eye could be seen. It was then that quiet happiness turned to raucous joy, and the celebration, quick in the actual planning but long awaited by both families, commenced.

As the revelers made their way from the church and down the lane headed for Willowhaven, Malcolm hung back. He was happy for his friend. He truly was. But there was a horrible tightness that had begun to fill his chest as the ceremony progressed. Now that it was over, that tightness had turned into a steel band that made it difficult to even breathe. The group walked on, leaving him behind. He was glad for it. He did not want anyone, especially Willbridge and Tristan, to witness his loss of control over his emotions.

Willbridge's copper head, growing farther away with every second, drew his eye like a punishment. Malcolm leaned against a tree for support. Black dots swam in his vision, and he shook his head to dispel them. Swirling in his mind were many such scenes from his past: his mother and father driving away, promising their swift return; his uncle turning his back after one of his many tirades; Lydia, as she walked away from him for good in order to marry another. And now one more scene added to that, the loss of one of the two men in this world he had believed would never abandon him.

What a damn fool he had been.

He forced himself to relax, to bring back up the veneer of sophisticated boredom that he used as a shield. Taking several deep, cleansing breaths of the morning air, he pushed away from the tree and started out in the direction of the group. Already they were nearly out of sight, though the sounds of their laughter and conversation still reached him, bouncing through the dense trees.

What the devil was the matter with him? So Willbridge had gone and done what they had believed impossible, had fallen in love with a respectable woman and married her. There was no turning back the clock. He would soldier on, as he did when anyone of import left him.

He lengthened his strides. Best if he caught up with the others. No good could come from all this isolation, all this quiet.

He was eating up the distance quickly, making progress, when something at the side of the lane caught his eye. A figure, hunched over. He nearly groaned when he caught sight of that telltale shock of copper hair in a stray sunbeam. Lady Emily Masters.

His every instinct urged him to hurry past as quickly as his legs could take him. The episode in the music room that morning had done nothing for him but erode the wall of armor he was trying to build up against her. Sitting and listening to the music she had played, saturated with what must have been the very raw emotions that were in her heart, had only made him more aware of her, more transfixed by her.

As much as he dreaded having to speak to her in that moment, however, his sense of honor would not let him slink by. Perhaps she had been hurt, had twisted an ankle. Heaving a sigh, he strode to her side.

"Lady Emily, are you unwell? Have you injured yourself?"

To his surprise, she let out an unladylike growl. She glared up at him. "You have scared it away."

Malcolm blinked several times, before saying the only thing possible in such an odd situation. "I'm sorry."

She let out a frustrated breath and rose. Malcolm automatically reached out to help, but she shook him off impatiently. Once on her feet, she turned back to the copse of trees, craning her neck to see into its depths. Not finding whatever it was she was searching for, her shoulders slumped and she turned back to face him.

"It's gone now. I don't know when I will see it again."

"And I have managed to scare it away." When she nodded morosely, he asked, "And what is this creature that I have terrified into decamping, perhaps forever?"

"A dog. I think."

"You think." She nodded again. He cleared his throat, certain she must be losing her mind. "What, if you don't mind me asking, is the importance of a creature that may or may not be a dog that you have only seen apparently skulking about in the forest?"

She seemed to recall herself and, without answering, began heading toward the house. Malcolm followed. He wasn't sure why, but he did. It seemed important, for some unholy reason, that he not let her out of his sight. For a long moment he thought she would not respond. Finally her light voice carried to him.

"I have seen the animal once before. Two days ago, before our visit to Ketterby. It was on the outskirts of the rose garden at the time."

"Yes?" he prompted.

His interest—for he was strangely captivated by this bizarre tale—seemed to embolden her to continue. "It stayed to the shadows, and so I could not determine what it was. But it sounded like a dog, and when it fled, it had the tail of a dog. And today, that same creature was by the side of the road, again in shadows. I attempted to draw it out, but..."

"But I came along," he finished when she gave him a frustrated look. "You know me well enough now, I think, that I do not soften my words." She gave an unladylike snort, and he might have smiled had he felt more himself. "What the hell are you planning on doing with the creature if you catch it?"

She shrugged, not at all disturbed this time by his profanity. He couldn't tell if it was because she was used to his bluntness or if she was so concerned over the dog that she hadn't heard it. "I'm not certain. If it is indeed a dog, and in need of a home, I suppose I shall take it in."

As simple as that. She was planning on locating a possibly feral creature and welcoming it into her home. "Most people would leave the animal to its fate," he said. He rubbed a hand over his face, wiping away the fine sheen of perspiration his attack at the church had produced. Perhaps he was not as completely over it as he had thought.

"I am not most people," she all but whispered. She shot a tentative look at him, as if daring him to deny it. Suddenly she went still and narrowed her eyes, studying his face. "Lord Morley, is something wrong?"

He raised one eyebrow at her, though within him he could feel the band once again tightening about his chest. Her soft question, tinged with concern, was bringing back to the fore why he had been forced to stay behind at the church. She was entirely too observant. He tried for nonchalance when he answered her. "Not at all. Why do you ask?"

"Only that you seem a bit pale and drawn."

"My, but you truly know how to compliment a man," he drawled. If he could work her into another bout of temper, he thought. Perhaps then he could feel some normalcy. He could not be overtaken again by his errant emotions, for he did not think he had the strength to fight off that horrible panic a second time.

As expected, she blushed crimson, averting her face—and thus, her too-keen eyes. "Still rude, I see," she muttered.

"Did you truly expect any different?"

She flashed him a glare, and his chest lightened considerably at the bit of fire within her pale gray gaze. There was something about her that distracted him from his cares. He didn't know why—and didn't much care what the reason was, if truth be told. All that mattered was she was the perfect antidote to his volatile emotions. Funny, he thought, that he now needed this girl's company. He should be alarmed, he knew. But all he could feel was something akin to gratitude. He offered her his arm. "Shall we return, my lady? They'll be expecting us."

She looked at him a moment as if he were a snake about to bite. Finally she blew out an agitated puff of breath and placed her hand on his sleeve.

They started off for the manor house. The wedding party was long gone, the woods about them quiet except for the rustle of leaves and the sound of their footsteps on the path. He breathed in deeply, enjoying the fresh air that was already losing the cool bite of morning and promising a warm afternoon. Beside him Lady Emily walked on in silence. Where he often would have felt the need to speak into the void, with her he didn't have that urge. He smiled slightly. What a freeing thing that was, to be able to drop his social façade and relax.

He expected her to maintain her silence through the whole of their journey as well. After all, she wasn't exactly the most voluble person he knew. She surprised him, however, by asking, "Your country seat is Fairfax Hall?"

He glanced down at her. She was staring straight ahead. Her scarred cheek was facing him this time, and he studied it a moment, remembering the feel of it under his finger two nights ago. The scar had been raised though smooth. He had the urge to reach out again, to touch her cheek, but stopped himself. "Er, yes.

Fairfax Hall. In Oxfordshire." He tilted his head, curious, trying to understand how her mind worked that she would bring that up. "You have heard of it?"

"You mentioned it when you met Lord Randall," she said, almost distractedly. "Do you go there often?"

Ah, yes, the infamous meeting with Lord Randall. The pompous bastard. He had seen him in the chapel and made a mental note to make sure the man didn't corner Lady Emily again. "I return there as much as I can manage," he said in reply to her question.

"So you spend most of your time in London."

"Yes." He frowned slightly. "Forgive me, my lady, but I get the feeling you're working up to something. I think it best for both of us if you simply get to the point."

She looked up at him, her gaze direct, an undercurrent of disquiet in her eyes. "I am to go to London next Season for Daphne's debut. I've heard a bit of what it may be like, but I would have it of you, if you've a mind to inform me. Since you are so familiar with it, that is."

Instantly he understood. She feared the trip. Wasn't that one of the reasons he had been asked by her brother to help her through this house party, to prepare her for her coming trip to London? After witnessing her level of shyness, however, he secretly thought that Willbridge had set them up for a nearly impossible task. Even after all the headway he'd managed in provoking her to stand up for herself, she was still far from being ready for London.

"I do believe you already know what to expect," he said, almost gently. "I'm not at all certain that anything I might tell you would ease your mind on the subject." It was quite possibly the kindest tone he had ever taken with her. But now was not the time, he expected, to push her.

She gave a soft sigh. At that small, forlorn sound, he felt a tug on his heart. It was not due to any affection for the girl, he told himself. He would feel compassion for anyone in such a situation. Even so, the unfamiliar drag on his emotions made him uneasy.

"I admit I had hoped it wasn't as bad as I have come to expect."

"I suppose 'bad' is a matter for interpretation," he drawled.

She peered up at him, seemed to study him. He had the distinct and uncomfortable feeling that he was no better than an insect under glass to her.

"You enjoy London, do you not?"

The way she said it, with the slight curl of her upper lip and delicate flaring of her nostrils, sounded more like an accusation than a query.

He had the insane urge to defend his choice to live in the city. Instead he said neutrally, "I like it well enough."

"Why?"

He blinked. "Why?"

She nodded, her gaze on his face growing intent. "Yes, why? Why do you like it?"

He certainly hadn't expected to explain it to her. "I don't know. I've never thought of it before."

"Well, you must have a reason. People do not like things simply for the sake of liking them."

"Don't they?"

"Not if they are at all intelligent."

He chuckled and looked back toward the path. "You have much to learn about the *ton,* then."

"And you, sir, are skirting around the question."

"There really is no fooling you, is there?"

"No, there isn't."

Was that humor in her voice? The sound of it, so unexpected when their entire relationship thus far had been based on his aggravating her, caused a particularly lighthearted feeling to go stealing through his chest. He grinned. "Very well, you stubborn baggage. Give me a moment to consider it though, will you?"

Her light chuckle surprised him even more than the almost playful tone of her voice had. His brain went momentarily blank at the sound of it. It was no simpering giggle, but warm and a bit raspy. It did the strangest things to him, made him feel alive in places he had no business being alive in. Not with her, at any rate. Shaking his head, he forced his mind to the subject at hand.

Why did he like London? Truthfully, he had never thought on it before. It was the place he had settled after the whole debacle with Lydia. He had needed the noise and distraction and stimulation that the capital could provide. And Willbridge and Tristan had been there as well. He supposed he had enjoyed it at first. There was always something to do. He was never without companionship, never without a ball or soirée or dinner party to attend. He was popular among the young bucks, even more so among the bored wives and widows that littered each event like ripe fallen apples, ready for the taking.

But over the past several years, it had begun to seem a bit too hard, a touch too jaded. The colors were too bright and gaudy, the laughter too forced, the gossip more pointed and cruel. As he thought long and hard about it, he realized that he didn't enjoy it any longer. It was a habit now, plain and simple.

He looked down at the woman at his side. She was gazing up at him in curiosity, without artifice. He thought of the members of the *ton* and their unending appetite to destroy anything pure and sweet. They would eat her up and spit her out.

But that was not his decision to make, was it? No, his job was to help prepare her as well as he could for her time in London.

His mind worked frantically. There must be something positive about London that he could give her. What would a woman like her enjoy? Finally he thought of one thing that could draw her like nothing else. "Tell me, Lady Emily, have you ever been to an opera?"

The change over her was instantaneous. Her eyes widened, her lips parted in wonder. "You have been to the opera?"

Inwardly he smiled. Outwardly he presented her a properly sober, awed look. "Many, many times. And each time better than the last. Nowhere else in England will you be able to feed your love of music better than in London."

"Is that right?" She was hanging on his every word, an interested light sparking in her eyes.

He nodded. "Think of it—everywhere you go there are musicians playing for your pleasure. Balls, musicales, the theatre, the opera. You will be surrounded by talent, immersed in lyrical beauty."

Excitement washed over her face. Truly, why hadn't anyone thought to come at it from this angle before? But in the next instant her eyes dulled, her shoulders drooping. "But that is neither here nor there. I will still be surrounded by all those strange people. Nothing will change that."

"No," he murmured, "you're right in that." He watched her for a time as she looked back along the path. A small muscle ticked in her jaw as she fought whatever demons she had residing in her. When she spoke again, he had to lean in to hear her, it was so faint.

"You must think me silly, I suppose, to want to remain behind when they go to London. Any other woman would be happy to go."

He shrugged. "You are not most women, my lady."

She gave a small, humorless laugh. "I don't know if that is a compliment or an insult."

He smiled slightly at her small, dark attempt at humor. "Take it as you like," he murmured.

She didn't smile back. Her mind, he knew, was too strained by what the future held. It really was unfair that she was forced to do something that was so repugnant to her. Without meaning to, he blurted, "Why couldn't you stay behind?"

He shouldn't have asked it. He knew that immediately. Yet he pushed aside the twinge of guilt. She was suffering; why was she being forced to go?

When her eyes met his, the quiet despair in them tugged at his heart. "My sister has expressed a particular wish for me to join her. I could not possibly say no."

"Why not?"

Emily stopped on the path. Malcolm stopped as well.

"I cannot disappoint my sister," she replied with simplicity. "Despite our very great differences, I love her dearly. She has told me she wants me with her; I will go with her."

Much as Imogen had done for her own sister Miss Mariah—

no, she was Miss Duncan now that her elder sisters were married off—earlier in the year. Though he was without such a close familial relationship, he could understand it. For he had once had that closeness with his own brother. His heart seized at the memory. And, though that was long gone, he had Tristan and Willbridge. He would suffer through much to ensure their happiness. Look at his presence here, after all.

"That is a great sacrifice you make for your sister," he said solemnly.

She shrugged and started for the house again. He thought they would continue on in silence once more. But suddenly, from under her breath, he heard her mumble, "Perhaps I will not have to make the sacrifice, after all."

He glanced sharply at her, about to question her on it. Just then the house loomed into view. Lady Daphne hurried out toward them. She paused when she caught sight of them together, her eyebrows raised in question.

"I was worried you might have twisted your ankle," she explained as she came closer. "But I see you are well, after all. Imogen needs us."

Emily hurried after her sister. But before she had taken a dozen steps, she turned back to him. A small smile lifted her lips. "Thank you, my lord, for your escort. I truly enjoyed it."

Before he could so much as blink, she turned and hurried away to her sister's side, leaving Malcolm staring after her. Something had changed between them during that short walk, but he didn't have it in him to regret it even one bit.

Chapter 9

"Where in the world did you go off to with Lady Emily?"

Malcolm tore his gaze from where the lady in question stood in the far corner of the room, chatting quietly with Imogen. Tristan stood at his elbow, a drink of what looked suspiciously like brandy clasped in his hand. "Where in the world did you get *that*?" he demanded. "I was under the impression that there was to be exclusively champagne and insipid punch at this affair."

Tristan grinned and indicated the pocket in the tail of his coat, where no doubt a flask was concealed. "Never think I am without resources. I thought you knew me better than that. But I won't have you skirting around my question. You were a long time returning from the church, and I've been told by the best possible source that you were in company with Lady Emily, and Lady Emily alone."

Damn, but his friend was much too perceptive today. Malcolm raised an eyebrow. "You are no better than Lady Tarryton. Are you turning into a gossip in your old age?"

But Tristan merely chuckled low and leaned in closer. "You forget, Morley, I know you almost as well as I know myself. You are attempting to deflect me, m'boy. But I will not be waylaid, so have out with it, man."

Malcolm gave Tristan a long, searching look. Despite the alcohol that he nursed, the man looked disgustingly sober. No, there would be no distracting him. Blowing out a breath, he pressed his lips together in annoyance. He supposed it had been a matter of time before Tristan began noticing that he was paying more than the normal, polite attention to Lady Emily. Malcolm had never been one to cater to the unmarried young women in social events, after all. He supposed he should be grateful it had taken his friend this long.

"Fine," he grumbled. "There's still time before we're to eat. Walk with me and I'll tell you all." He turned for the glass double doors, not waiting for Tristan's acquiescence.

The courtyard was open and blessedly empty, aside from several tall, meticulously trimmed topiaries bordering the sanded paths. They walked slowly, Malcolm all the while attempting to put into words what his purpose was in sticking so close to Lady Emily. He didn't think Willbridge would want him telling Tristan what the reason was. The request had been made in confidence, after all. Though what other reason could he give to explain his sudden interest in the girl?

But while Tristan had been patient in allowing Malcolm to lead him from the ballroom, he was not so patient that he was going to let the tense silence go on for longer than necessary.

"You don't have to beat about the bush, you know. I've seen the way you've stayed close to her side. You think I could be blind to such a thing?" Suddenly the man's eyes widened in horror. "Never tell me you're courting the chit!"

Instead of quickly and loudly disabusing his friend of the notion—for hadn't the thought of it been repugnant to him when he'd first discussed the thing with Willbridge?—a slither of hot anger worked its way up his back. "Would that be so terrible?" he asked stiffly.

"Yes!" his friend nearly shouted. "You cannot possibly be thinking of marrying the girl."

"Quiet, you idiot, or someone will hear you," Malcolm hissed. He pushed Tristan behind a meticulously trained bush, partially obscuring them from the ballroom's many windows. "What could possibly be wrong with someone wishing to court Lady Emily? She is sweet, and lovely, and would make any man a fine wife."

Tristan looked at him as if he'd grown another head. For his own part, Malcolm was nearly as stunned at the vehemence of his own reaction. What the devil was wrong with him? If anyone heard, they would assume he truly did want to marry her.

"What the hell is going on, Morley?"

Malcolm's anger dissipated as quickly as it had come. He sighed and reached up to rub the back of his neck. "Forgive me. This whole thing has me on edge."

Tristan eyed him for a moment before downing the rest of his drink. "Perhaps you'd best explain from the beginning."

"Yes, you're right," he mumbled. "It was foolish for Willbridge to expect me to keep this from you. I'm sure he never meant that, for you would see right through any pretense, anyway." He took a steadying breath before forging on. "The truth of the matter is, Willbridge asked me to stay close to Lady Emily."

Tristan blinked several times in incomprehension. "Willbridge asked you to pay court to his sister?"

"No, not that. He asked me to stick close to her, to watch over her."

His friend looked at him blankly for a long moment. "I don't understand."

Malcolm growled low. "You have met the girl, I presume?"

"Yes." The answer was slow and confused. Then it was as if the sun came out, so much did comprehension change his expression. "Ah, I see now. It's that scar."

What could he say to that? Without a doubt it was because of the scar. Everything she had suffered, every slight, every lack of confidence, was all due to that scar. "Yes."

"So you have to play nursemaid to the girl?"

Again, what could he say but the truth? "Yes."

Tristan let out a low whistle. "That hardly seems a fair thing for Willbridge to ask of you."

"So I thought. But it's not as much of a chore as I'd first thought it would be."

His friend chuckled. "Please. A man like you, having to act as chaperone to an awkward girl who has trouble talking even to those she's closest to? It's not a job I envy you for. I'm glad he didn't ask it of me."

Anger pounded at Malcolm's temples. "Don't talk of her that way," he intoned darkly.

Tristan shot him a dismissing look. "Please, don't tell me you didn't wish him to the devil when he first asked it of you."

"That was before I knew her."

"Have you gotten to know her very well, then?"

The faint suggestion had Malcolm seeing red. He seized Tristan's cravat. His friend's eyes bulged in shock.

"I would have you speaking better of the girl," he said quietly. Tristan must have heard the menace in his voice, for he held his hands up in the air, glass and all.

"You're right, I'm sorry," he rasped around the pressure of Malcolm's fisted fingers pressing into his windpipe. Once released, Tristan stepped back and rubbed at his neck, his blue eyes wary as he regarded his friend.

It was that look that made Malcolm realize how excessive his reaction to Tristan's taunts had been. Not that the man hadn't deserved it. Even so, for Malcolm to lose control like that was worrisome indeed. He cleared his throat. "Damn it," he said gruffly, "but this day is getting to me."

"It was a quick affair," Tristan soothed. "As much as we teased him about his interest in Imogen, I'm sure neither of us thought he would ever get ensnared."

Malcolm sensed the tentative truce for what it was. He attempted a smile. "No, you are right in that."

"Though I don't believe I've ever seen the man so happy in his life," Tristan went on quietly. "We certainly cannot look too harshly on her for that, can we?"

"I suppose not," Malcolm admitted with reluctance. But enough of this sentimental claptrap. "We'd best return," he said gruffly. "There's food to eat, a cake to cut, and dancing to commence."

Tristan smiled slyly, his eyes once more twinkling with their typical lighthearted mirth. "And you've a job to do in watching over Lady Emily, haven't you, old man?"

"Indeed." As they rounded the topiary and made their way to the ballroom and the throng within, however, Malcolm wondered why the prospect didn't seem as dour a thing as it had just days ago.

. . .

Emily had been having a lovely conversation with her new sister—an idea that warmed her soul in the most wonderful way. But Imogen was the bride and in much demand at the moment. All too soon, Emily found herself alone again in a corner of the ballroom. Which was as she typically preferred it. So why did her solitary state have her feeling agitated? A foreign urge rose up in her to leave her corner, to seek out company. But it was not any company she wished for in that moment. No, it was Lord Morley's.

That thought brought her up short. It was not as if the man had made her life easy since his arrival. Yet in the past days something in her had shifted. A realization hit that had her reeling.

She was coming to care for Lord Morley.

The breath left her in a rush. Oh my. How in the world had something like this happened? She was meant to live out her life alone. She had always known no man would be interested in her. She would never be a wife or mother, would never have a home of her own. For who could ever look past the imperfection of her features or her painful shyness?

But Lord Morley had, she realized. He had never once, in all the days they had known each other, looked on her with disgust. From the very beginning he had pushed and prodded and tormented her until she found herself forgetting about her scar, facing him down, and standing up for herself.

For the first time in a decade, she felt like a woman and not a thing to be pitied. It was wonderfully freeing.

All thanks to Lord Morley.

Her heart light and hopeful, she scanned the ballroom and its mass of people. His dark head, however, was not visible amidst the revelers. Frowning, she began to move through the crowd, for once heedless of the volume of people. Still she could not find him. Frustrated—for why was it the one time she wished to find him he was nowhere to be seen?—she stepped to the wide bank of windows that looked out onto the courtyard. Suddenly she caught sight of him, partially hidden behind a topiary. Smiling, she slipped out the open doors and headed his way.

The voices should have alerted her to the fact that he wasn't alone. Yet so intent was she on reaching him that she was nearly upon them before she realized. It was the words themselves, however, that stopped her cold.

"The truth of the matter is, Willbridge asked me to stay close to Lady Emily."

Emily's blood turned to ice in her veins, her heart seizing painfully in her chest. What was he talking about? Caleb asked Lord Morley to do what?

His companion spoke up then, a voice Emily belatedly realized was Sir Tristan's. "Willbridge asked you to pay court to his sister?"

"No, not that. He asked me to stick close to her, to watch over her."

"I don't understand."

There was a low growl from Lord Morley. "You have met the girl, I presume?"

"Yes." There was a pause. And then, "Ah, I see now. It's that scar."

A great roaring filled Emily's ears. She didn't want to hear Lord Morley's answer, didn't want proof of this great betrayal. *Move*, she told her feet. At long last they obeyed, backing her up, away from that damning conversation that was breaking her heart. But she was not quick enough. Before she was out of earshot, she heard it, the one word that could destroy her.

"Yes."

Cruel fate, however, was not quite done with her. As she turned, with every intention of racing back for the ballroom, one more bit reached her ears.

"So you have to play nursemaid to the girl?"

"Yes."

She could not move away fast enough. *Please*, she begged, *please don't let them see me. Please let me escape with a small bit of my shredded pride intact.*

Blessedly, it seemed that her prayers were heard. But though she made it back to the ballroom, she found she could not stand to be there. She needed solitude to calm her mind and, more importantly, to heal her heart. She would not let her foolish, traitorous emotions for the man break her.

For Lord Morley did not deserve her tears. Not even one.

Chapter 10

Malcolm parted ways with Tristan at the ballroom doors, glad to be done with their disturbing conversation. More than that, though, he was looking forward to seeing Lady Emily again. Their conversation on the way from the church had been eye-opening. He had seen a side to her that he hadn't expected, and she had brought him down, however unknowingly, from the ledge he had been on.

He had not even realized such latent panic had been within him, but when faced with Willbridge's marriage that morning it had reared up, overwhelming him. Would it have cropped up sooner had his attentions and energy not been so focused on Lady Emily these past days? Perhaps. All he knew was she calmed him.

He wanted more of that, more of her.

His steps became more hurried, anticipation to see her again starting up like an itch under his skin. It had nothing to do with his promise to Willbridge. No, he simply wanted to be with *her*.

He pushed through the crowd, searching for that telltale shock of bright copper hair. To his consternation she was nowhere to be found. The room was quite empty of her presence, almost glaringly so.

Frowning, he moved toward the door that led into the hall. Guests were pouring into the room now, and he felt like a fish swimming upriver as he pushed against them. All the while frustration mounted, liberally laced with concern. Where in the devil was she? Despite her deep dislike of crowds, she would never miss celebrating Caleb and Imogen.

He made it into the hall and glanced down each side, determined to pick a direction and search, when he saw it, the flash of copper hair ducking inside the music room door. Relief filled him. Striding down the quickly emptying hall, he made the room and, without knocking, pushed the door wide and slipped inside.

It was dark here, this part of the house not having been opened to guests. By the shaft of light coming in from the hallway, he saw her at the pianoforte bench. She sat still, her head bowed, an air of despondency hovering around her like a dense fog. Alarmed, he closed the door quietly behind him and hurried forward. Had she been injured? Had anyone—that bastard Lord Randall, perhaps—given her any kind of grief?

He stopped beside her, but if she was aware of his presence she made no indication of it. Dropping down on his haunches, he peered at her through the gloom. "Lady Emily? Are you well?"

She turned her face from him. "Leave me alone," she whispered brokenly.

Something had definitely occurred to put her in such a state. His mind swam with all manner of things. "Please tell me, has anyone hurt you?"

She cut a glance to him. The expression in her eyes sent a chill straight through his bones. "You could say that," she said. Her voice, normally so quiet and sweet, was tight with some unnamed emotion.

A surge of protectiveness for this girl washed away all instinct to keep his emotions out of the equation. Whoever it was that had hurt her, he would see to it that they wished they had never been born. "Tell me who," he urged gruffly, "and I swear, I will make them pay."

"You will have to look in the mirror, then," she bit out.

He blinked in incomprehension. "What are you talking about?" He hadn't seen her since their return from the church. How in blazes could he have been the one to hurt her?

But as he looked at the condemnation that clouded her eyes, he knew. She had heard his conversation with Tristan.

He felt the blood drain from his face. Light-headed, he sat back on his heels. "Oh," was all he could think to say.

Her lips twisted, pulling her scar tight. "I see you comprehend me now."

"You must understand—" he began, but she cut a hand through the air. He closed his mouth with a snap.

She rose abruptly. Heart pounding in his ears, a cold sweat filming his skin, he scrambled to his feet. Pushing past him, she strode across the room. He had the sick feeling that it was more to put distance between them than anything else. "I see it now," she rasped, "the reason you followed me about. Poor, pathetic Lady Emily, who cannot manage herself in a crowd, who must be coddled and protected. How you must have laughed about it."

"I never laughed, I swear it," he said. He stepped closer to her. "Yes, your brother asked me to look after you. He is worried for you. But after I came to know you better, it became more than that."

She spun to face him, and even in the shadows he could see the furious light in her eyes. "Oh, how you compliment me. Do you mean to tell me that had you not been forced into my presence, you would have sought me out? That you would have wanted to stay by my side, to make conversation with me?"

He knew he should lie, to tell her that he would have. But the words could not pass his lips. He had hurt this girl enough; she did not need his dishonesty. He had enough sin on his soul.

She saw his pause and let out a short bark of laughter. He flinched at the raw, pained sound of it. "I see I'm right. No need to explain, my lord. I know I'm a pariah, that my face would have kept you far away, even if my shyness had not."

Anger filled him at her self-deprecating words. "Damn it, that's enough. Your scar has nothing at all to do with it."

"Doesn't it? You forget, my lord, I have had years of seeing how it affects others."

She went to turn away from him, to leave him standing there in the middle of the room with nothing settled, these angry words hanging about his head like phantoms. Without thinking, he reached out and grabbed her arm. She gasped in outrage, spinning back to face him, looking at his hand as if it were a slimy creature that had attached itself to her.

"Unhand me, sir," she ground out, "or I swear I will scream."

"You will not," he bit out. "You will stay here and listen to me. You think your scar is what drives people away? I tell you, it's not. It is you, and you alone. I was being truthful when I told you earlier that you push people away. You are so concerned with how people may view you, so obsessed with protecting yourself from possible unpleasantness, that you will not open yourself to giving a person a chance to get to know you." The words spilling from his mouth had the faint taste of bitterness to them. She stared mutely at him in shock, unknowingly giving him the chance he needed to have his say, for once she regained her senses it would be lost forever.

"It was not your brother that had me baiting you and pushing you these past days. That was me and me alone. You cannot continue to live your life in such a way, holed up from hurt. You are a lovely person, Lady Emily. Stop letting your fear lead you."

Her face flushed as she stood mute under his barrage. When he fell silent, exhausted from the rush of words that had poured from him, she raised her hand slowly, balled her fingers into a fist, and struck him in the chest. Hard.

"You do not tell me how to behave." Hit. "You do not know what I have lived through." Hit. "You do not know what I see in people's eyes." Hit.

Again and again she pummeled his chest. Her small fists may as well have been flies for all the damage they did. But it was the devastation in her eyes that broke his heart. He stood speechless under the onslaught. Let her have this release. She'd had fair little of such things in the past decade, it seemed. It was when the sobs started ripping through her body that he knew he had to put a stop to it.

He wrapped his arms about her and pulled her tight to his chest. She struggled against his hold before, with a wrenching sob, she collapsed in his arms.

Her slender body shuddered with the force of her tears. Never, in all his life, had Malcolm felt like a worm as much as he did in that heartbreaking moment. And the crux of it was, there was nothing he could do to repair it. He would never lay the blame for this at Willbridge's feet. At least love and good intentions had prompted his request. Malcolm had been the one to go into it with anger, to get more involved than he should have, to bully her into changing, to delve deeper into her emotions in an attempt to change her from the person she was. If he had not, if he had kept his distance, she would not now be hurting.

Not knowing what else to do, he rubbed her back, hoping to bring her some sort of comfort in all this horribleness. To his relief, her sobs subsided, her body stilled. She could have pulled away. Yet she remained in his arms. Against his better judgment he continued to hold her. He knew it was a dangerous thing to do. If anyone were to walk in with the door closed, the two of them alone and in an embrace, he would be seeing the parson's noose before the day was out. But, he found, much to his surprise, that he liked holding her.

He frowned, tensing, his arms going a bit tighter around her. She pressed into him, so soft, so feminine, a delicious fragrance, like vanilla and roses, drifting up to him. His mouth watered, and he lowered his head, dragging in a deep breath. His senses awakened like the sky clearing after a cleansing rain, his skin tingling. At that moment, she raised her head to look at him.

The rest of the world fell away.

Her eyes were large and luminous in the faint light, her lashes darkened with tears. The porcelain of her skin was faintly flushed, her lips plump from crying. He had never seen anything so alluring in his life. What would it be like, he wondered, if he were to bend his head, to kiss those lips, to feel her sigh and go pliant in his arms...?

In an instant his mind recoiled. This was Willbridge's sister. What in hell was he thinking? Abruptly dropping his arms from around her, he stumbled back, putting as much distance between them as he could manage. Finding a chair, he ducked behind it, grabbing onto the back with both hands like a shield. She stood where she was, looking more bereft than any one person should. He ached to rush to her, to drag her into his arms, to console her in any and every way he could. In response to the nearly overwhelming need, he gripped the chair back even tighter, forcing his feet to remain where they were.

Her arms wrapped about her middle. In the next moment she lowered them and straightened, her face hardening. "And so I am proved right," she whispered. "Don't worry, my lord. You need not burden yourself with me again. In fact, I expect you to stay far away from me in the future. Good day."

With that, she raised her chin and walked regally from the room. Never had Malcolm seen such a magnificent sight.

Never had he hated himself quite so much.

• • •

"Willbridge, a word if you have time?"

Malcolm had not wanted to ruin his friend's wedding celebrations by burdening him with the whole debacle with Lady Emily. Imogen had disappeared to change into her traveling clothes, however, and soon the newlyweds would be off for a fortnight while the house party continued without them. This discussion could not wait a moment more.

A wide smile spread over Willbridge's already beaming countenance. "Morley. I'm so glad you've found me. I thought I would have to leave without talking to you at all. Let's get out of this crowd and spend a minute in blessed peace."

Malcolm nodded, and as one they wound through the revelers that had congregated in the front hall to see the happy couple off on their wedding trip. They made their way to the library, a room thankfully free of humanity at the moment.

Willbridge closed the door and turned to him. "Morley, I cannot thank you enough for what you have done for my sister this last week."

Malcolm's heart dropped. Damn it, the man had gotten the

jump on him. He had intended to speak first; what he had to say was hard enough without having to muddle through whatever his thoroughly besotted friend had to say. After the confrontation with Lady Emily, there was only one thing he felt he could do: have Willbridge release him from his promise so he could leave Willowhaven and never return.

There were many things in Malcolm's life he was guilty of. What he had done to Lady Emily, inadvertently or not, left those all in the dust.

To make matters worse—so much worse—he had developed a new awareness of her. She had become more than Willbridge's sister, more than the young lady that he was supposed to watch over. Now every time he looked at her, he saw a lovely and very desirable woman.

The curve of her hip under the pale green of her gown, the gentle swell of her breast beneath her bodice, the little divot above her upper lip, all had him aching to feel again that feminine softness that had been hinted at in their embrace. His fingers itched to trail along her cheek, down the slender column of her throat. But more than anything, he wanted to bend his head, to kiss those lips...

The blood drained from his face. Yes, he needed to get away from her, as quickly as possible, before he did something he would regret.

"I'm glad I could be of help," he said. "Your sister is a lovely young woman. I do think, however—"

"You don't understand the change that's come over her." Willbridge seemed completely oblivious to the tension that was coiling like a snake ready to strike in Malcolm's breast. His eyes looked to be turned inward, toward some less than pleasant memory. "I mean, you actually got her to dance two nights ago. I cannot begin to tell you how that made me feel. I was seeing my sister for the first time with the hope of a normal future."

The man was making this harder by the minute. Malcolm once again opened his mouth to speak, to tell his friend he had to leave

Willowhaven immediately, that Lady Emily knew what they had been about. But Willbridge, it seemed, was not quite done.

"I admit I had my doubts. Especially as you were so against the idea. I very nearly relented and told you to forget the entire thing."

Malcolm began to sweat. "Willbridge—"

"You have no idea how your presence here eases my mind. I don't think I could leave on our wedding trip with any comfort if you weren't here in my stead. I vow, this house party that my mother and Lady Tarryton are so adamant on throwing had me nervous as hell when they told me of it. But after seeing how Emily has responded to you over the past days, I know I'm leaving her in good hands." He smiled broadly. "But enough about all that. You wished to speak to me of something?"

Malcolm felt vaguely sick. The guilt he'd been feeling over Lady Emily doubled in the space of a second. If he told Willbridge now, his friend would either suffer for worrying over his sister throughout the duration of his wedding trip, or he would insist on staying back and thereby ruin his first days as a married man.

A small devil perched on his shoulders. So what if the entire thing was ruined? It was Willbridge's family, after all. It certainly wasn't Malcolm's responsibility, damn it. If his friend wished so desperately to play the family man, shouldn't he be the one to deal with all of the problems that went along with it?

In the next moment he pushed the selfish thoughts aside. He would not do that to him. No matter whose responsibility it was, he cared for Willbridge and his happiness too much to be a bastard about it now. The whole mess was his own fault, after all. He should have had the strength to say no from the get-go, instead of crumbling under pressure and being forced into that damnable promise. He had known it was a bad idea from the start. Now he would have to deal with the consequences.

Willbridge was smiling at him, waiting patiently. Malcolm managed a sickly one in return. "I have not had a chance to congratulate you on your marriage." There was a sudden thickness in his throat and he cleared it loudly. "Imogen is a wonderful woman. I know she'll make you happy."

To his surprise—and horror—Willbridge began blinking rapidly. Was the man going to cry? His friend *ahemed* gruffly several times, adjusted his cravat, and generally avoided Malcolm's eye. After what seemed an inordinately long time, he pulled himself together enough to look up and say, with feeling, "Thank you, Morley. Coming from you, that means a great deal."

"Think nothing of it," Malcolm mumbled, wanting nothing more than to escape this debacle of an exchange.

"Now that we've got that out of the way," his friend said, "I wonder if I might talk with you about something that's been troubling me." He paused, as if searching for the words. "Have you noticed anything between Tristan and Daphne?"

What could he say to that? "Yes," he answered truthfully.

Willbridge frowned. "I admit, I'd hoped it was all in my head."

Malcolm was suddenly incredibly grateful he had never been burdened with sisters. His friend looked a decade older in the space of a heartbeat. "I'm sure there's nothing there," he said. There was little conviction behind the words, however.

Willbridge tried for a smile. It did not reach his eyes. "You're a blasted terrible liar, Morley." The smile fell from his face as he took out his pocket watch. "But there is no time to prevaricate," he muttered. "Admit it, man. Tristan has an interest in her."

"Mayhap," was all Malcolm would say.

Willbridge nodded. "Though it pains me to do it, I must ask another favor of you, my friend."

Damn it all to hell.

"It is not that I don't think the match would be a good one on all sides," Willbridge continued. "Though Daphne is my youngest sister..." Here his face twisted with a mix of disgust and displeasure and exhausted affection. He cleared his throat. "If they truly loved one another, I would have to support them. Tristan is a good fellow, and with his fortune I know he can provide for Daphne." Here he looked Malcolm straight in the eye. "But you and I both know, though we love the man, Tristan is a flighty fellow at best. There is no way in hell he's ready to take on a wife. Especially one of Daphne's temperament."

Which was all too true. Malcolm's stomach dropped. "You want me to look after them while you're gone." It was not a question. He could see the intent in his friend's eyes, the muted kind of panic.

"I'm asking too much of you." Willbridge raked a hand through his hair. "If there was anyone else I could trust to do the damn thing right, I would infinitely prefer it."

As would I, Malcolm thought.

"This is a delicate thing, though," his friend continued. "My mother would be more than happy to promote the match immediately, and if I talked to Tristan or Daphne, there is no telling what fool notion it might put into their heads."

Willbridge was growing more agitated by the minute.

Malcolm held up a hand. "I'll do it."

Relief filled his friend's eyes. "You are certain? I truly do hate to do this to you, Morley."

Malcolm shrugged, even as he felt the last rays of hope for escaping this place extinguish. "I am already in Lady Emily's company most of the time. Lady Daphne is never far from her. It won't be much more trouble."

Willbridge grasped his hand, shaking it heartily. Malcolm felt as if he had signed a deal with the devil himself.

"I owe you," Willbridge said. "Damn it, but I'll owe you for a lifetime after this." He grinned, looking to the door. "I'd best get back," he murmured. "I've a wife to collect, after all."

Malcolm watched his friend leave. It was ironic, really. He had come into this room hoping for release from his promise. And had somehow managed to embroil himself in another.

He was an idiot, in every sense of the word.

Chapter 11

After emerging from the music room, Emily was more determined than ever to find a way—any way—to make sure the coming trip to London never happened.

The question was, how? Her mind in a fog from the encounter with Lord Morley, she lacked the energy to work it out properly. Through the long evening after Caleb and Imogen's departure, she huddled in her corner, watching the gaiety about her with a confused sorrow. A new desire had begun to stir in her breast, to live a normal life, to attract the love of a man, to become a wife and mother. Pointless, she knew, though that knowledge could not eradicate it.

Perhaps it was this awakened yearning, and her certainty that she would never see it realized herself, that made her so achingly aware of the young couples making eyes at one another, so full of naïve hope for the future. They were all no doubt affected by the romance that a wedding brought. Especially this particular wedding, with a couple who loved each other to distraction. There would be more than one engagement announced at the end of the fortnight.

It had been as she'd watched a young man escort a blushing lady for a stroll in the gardens that her mind cleared enough for realization to strike. If these other young women could find their future husbands in such a setting, why couldn't Daphne? After all, wasn't the whole point of the London trip to find a husband for her? And if Daphne were to become engaged in the next two weeks, there would be no London trip. And Emily would be able to stay here at Willowhaven and away from men like Lord Morley and his ilk.

Lord Morley. She shuddered just thinking his name. Never had she felt such burning shame as when she thought of the scene with him in the music room. His disgust for her could not have been more obvious. The horror in his eyes had been clear, his violent recoil from her saying more than words what he thought of her disfigurement.

And, to make her humiliation complete, she found she still wished for him to kiss her.

Stupid, stupid girl. Her cheeks burned in shame. She had thought perhaps they had begun to be friends. Her heart, apparently, had hoped for even more. Well, she refused to be duped liked that again, to be made to feel a fool. Her heart had been broken enough for a thousand lifetimes.

The breakfast room was still empty save for a lone footman by the time she emerged from the music room later the next morning. She had hoped that Daphne and some of the young, unattached men of the party would be present. She did not have much time to find out who her sister might have developed an interest in, after all. But it seemed everyone was still sleeping off the effects of the previous night's drinking and dancing. No doubt the great majority of them wouldn't peel their eyes open before noon. Tamping down her impatience, she determined to eat heartily. Best to prepare for the coming course of action.

She had settled into a seat at one end of the long mahogany table, her back to the door, when she heard someone enter. Her heart stuttered in her chest, a tingling awareness breezing over her skin. It could not possibly be Lord Morley, she thought in desperation. Fate could not be so cruel. She knew deep down, however, it could be no one else.

He stopped inside the doorway. For a moment she thought he would turn right around and head back out. She prayed he would. The last thing she wanted on this earth was to come face-to-face with him.

His guilt must be a small burden indeed, if not nonexistent, for he came into the room and moved past her. When he was within view, he dipped his head in a sober manner.

"Lady Emily."

For the first time in her life, Emily had the urge to give the cut direct. But her good breeding would not allow it, no matter how desperately she wished. Despicably polite creature that she was, she lifted her chin a fraction and gritted, "My lord."

He looked surprised at the acknowledgement. Something like gratitude or relief flared briefly in his eyes. Before she could understand it, he turned from her and began to fill his plate at the sideboard.

Emily attempted to return her attention to her meal. But the toast suddenly seemed dry as sawdust, the eggs bland, the chocolate too sweet. Disgusted, she pushed the plate aside and reached for the *Times*. Yet after scanning over the freshly ironed pages, she could find nothing to hold her interest. In desperation she began an article on the completion of some canal in Newport Pagnall but was in the middle before she even knew she had started. Just then, Lord Morley sat directly across from her, and there was no hope for it after that. Truly, the table held a dozen people or better. Must he choose the one seat where she could not help but meet his eyes? Carefully folding the paper, knowing a losing battle when she saw one, she made a move to rise.

"Please don't."

Lord Morley's voice, softer and gentler than she had ever heard it, stopped her halfway out of her seat. She should not acknowledge him, just turn and leave without a word. Looking his way had never done her any good. But her traitorous eyes would not heed a direct order and shot a glance at him anyway.

That he appeared completely miserable should have had her gloating in triumph. Instead she felt a lowering sadness. Without meaning to, she sank back into her chair. The footman, who had rushed forward to assist her, stepped back and took up his post at the sideboard once again.

When Lord Morley stayed silent, she quirked her eyebrow at him in question. He flushed—actually flushed—and swallowed hard. "I would not have you leave on my account," he said.

"I see no reason to stay, my lord. I think we said everything we had to say to one another yesterday."

"I would apologize again for my part in hurting you. Though I expect it will not make a bit of difference."

She merely stared at him, refusing to be baited into offering forgiveness. So he felt sorry for himself, did he? Well, good. Let him regret what he had done. Let him wallow in his guilt, positively drown in it.

The silence between them stretched and grew. Lord Morley seemed to be at a loss in the face of her stubborn silence. When it appeared no more was forthcoming, she planted her hands on the table and began to rise, the footman rushing forward again to help.

"You never told your brother about what you overheard."

Again she dropped into her seat. The footman once again scurried back to his spot. "No."

"Why?"

She blinked several times. "Why should I have? It would have ruined his wedding trip." At the renewed guilt on his face, disbelief filled her. "Never tell me you told him."

"No," he was quick to answer. Then a lowering of the eyes. "I had planned on it but did not."

Relief washed over her. She would not have Caleb and Imogen's first days married sullied by this. Yes, Caleb had been the one to ask Lord Morley to shadow her. And yes, she was furious with him as well. He should not have meddled, or, barring that, at least had the decency to ask her wishes in the matter. But she also knew he had done what he had out of worry and love for her, even if it was a high-handed way of taking care of things. No, the bulk of her ire was centered on Lord Morley. He didn't have to take it as far as he had, did not have to pretend to an affection he did not feel.

Did not have to make her care for him.

She truly had believed he liked her for who she was, regardless of her faults. But then to overhear him disparaging her scar, when he had begun to make her feel that perhaps it was inconsequential? That stung more than anything, was salt in a wound. Rubbed in with a bit of lemon juice, perhaps.

"So you do not blame him for what happened?" Lord Morley seemed genuinely hopeful.

"No, I very much blame him. I, however, realize he did what he did out of love for me, whereas your intentions are questionable at best."

He dipped his head in acknowledgement. At least he had the good sense not to defend himself from such accusations.

She made to rise again.

"He asked me to stay, you know."

From behind her, Emily thought she heard the footman groan in frustration. But he headed back to the sideboard, and she, for the third time, lowered herself back into her chair.

"I wanted you to know that. I would have left, to lessen your pain in the matter. But he wanted me to stay. He secured my promise in the matter."

So he was still to look after her, was he? She narrowed her eyes, indignation creeping along her skin, a slow burning fire. "If you think I will allow you to follow me about again, you are much mistaken, sir."

"I cannot break my promise to him."

She gaped at him. "You would go against my wishes in the matter? It is my life, after all."

He had the audacity to shrug. "I cannot break my promise," he repeated.

Fury boiled up in her. "I have had quite enough from you, my lord, and I do not give a fig about your promise. Know this, I will not permit you to play nursemaid to me any longer. I expect you to stay far away from me. Is that understood?"

He looked surprised. As well he should. She felt power course through her. Never had she been able to work up the courage to stick up for herself in such a manner. It was freeing.

...And a bit frightening, if truth be told. It was as if she were a phoenix, had burned down to ash, down to nothing with the revelations of the previous day. Now here she was, reborn from that ash, a new person, but in the same skin. The overwhelming need to be alone in that moment filled her. She needed time to process this, to come to terms with it. Pushing back from the table, not giving the poor beleaguered footman time to help, she dipped her head to Lord Morley in a cold manner and swept from the room, her heart pounding all the while like a drum in her chest. What else was she capable of, she wondered. Mayhap it was time to find out.

• • •

The partygoers were decidedly lacking in any kind of celebratory spirit throughout the remainder of the day, no doubt due to over-imbibing the day before. Emily was glad for it. Her mood was too volatile at the moment to put any effort into gallivanting about the countryside after her sister.

That did not mean that she was in any way comfortable. Lord Morley, despite his apologies that morning and her very vocal orders for him to stay away from her, had decided to forego the pleasures of the older gentlemen and had remained behind with the women, to relax in quiet pursuits in the drawing room and basically waste the day away. Thankfully Sir Tristan, too, had decided to laze the day away with the ladies, and Lord Morley stayed close to his side. That did not mean, though, that she was any less aware of him.

But she would not allow his presence to detract her from today's purpose of beginning the search for a husband for her sister. She watched Daphne closely. Thus far she had not shown any marked attention to any of the young men present. And there were a fair few, thank goodness, no doubt thinking that being in the vicinity of the young, unattached ladies was a sight better than sitting around with the older men, playing cards and drinking. Emily could only be thankful for it. It gave her much to study as the afternoon wore on.

There were, she realized, a goodly amount of baronets and

barons, or heirs to such, in the room. Mr. Ignatius Knowles, heir to her cousin Sir Frederick Knowles, she could easily rule out. That moment he was showing marked attention to Miss Catherine Forster. Yesterday he had been seen giving Miss Mariah Duncan the same interest. And during the trip into Ketterby she was sure she had seen him flirting with Miss Rebecca Sanders, the vicar's eldest daughter. No, he would never do.

Mr. Edward Forster, heir to Lord Tabble and related to Imogen on her father's side, was handsome and well off. But he was also dumb as a post. She had overheard him saying to her brother Drew that he thought a pelisse was a kind of edible confection. And so she could safely exclude him. While he might make a sweet enough husband, even Emily, as desperate as she was, did not wish stupid children on Daphne.

Mr. Daniel Gubler, heir to Sir William Gubler on Imogen's mother's side, was too young. Not much past twenty, the man spent most of his time trying to impress his older counterparts. He also had an unhealthy obsession with his wardrobe. This morning he had his collar so high and starched he could not turn his head.

Lastly (for she certainly did not count Lord Morley in with the group of hopefuls, no matter his elevated status as a viscount) was Sir Tristan Crosby. She studied him for a moment over her embroidery. Thus far she had not been able to determine anything horrible enough to discount him from the running. Despite that devastating conversation she had heard between him and Lord Morley the day before, she knew him to be a jolly fellow, yet mature enough to not be an embarrassment to himself. He showed marked interest in Daphne, that was certain. From the moment he had arrived, she had seen his eyes wander to her sister much more than was proper. He had danced with her several times the other evening, as well as during the wedding festivities the night before. And hadn't he stayed close to Daphne when she had moved to the pianoforte, turning pages for her? Today he seemed stuck to her side like a barnacle on the hull of a ship. So it seemed the attraction was there, on his part at least.

Though the question remained, how did Daphne feel about him?

This was much harder to figure. Her sister had an open, friendly personality. So much so that it could prove difficult in determining where a deeper affection might lie. But Emily was confident that, with close observation, some small tell would become apparent.

She almost missed it when it did show itself. If she had blinked she would have. As it was, the small smile and sideways glance that Daphne sent Sir Tristan's way would have been innocuous to most. Not to Emily. And so Sir Tristan's regard was reciprocated in kind. Emily smiled, looking back to her embroidery hoop. Such a stroke of luck would make her job all the easier.

"You are looking much like the cat that licked the cream, Sister."

Emily nearly jumped out of her skin at the sound of Drew's voice in her ear. Her embroidery hoop fell to the ground, making a mess of the delicate silk thread she had been working into the fabric. She retrieved it from the floor and frowned at her brother. "Why can you never approach me in the normal way, instead of scaring me half to death whenever you deign to grace me with your presence?"

Instead of being properly shamed, however, he merely chuckled. "Ah, still cross with me, I see."

She glared meaningfully at him before bending her head to the thread in her lap. She worked at the tangle before her. "You know I have every right to be cross. You promised to stay close to me, but at the first sign of a pretty face you abandoned me. I have hardly seen you for the past three days, so intent are you on flirting with every available girl in the place."

"Can you blame me? There is so much here to distract. But," he continued when she would have given him a scathing retort, "I promise to be on my best behavior. *If* you tell me who you were watching so diligently a moment ago."

She let out a disgusted scoff. "I should have known you were not coming over here for me and me alone."

He placed a hand to his chest as if mortally offended. "You

wound me. Why, you act as if I don't care for your well-being at all." When she shot him a disbelieving look, he said, "No, truly, I do care. It's why I came over, after all. I thought you may have formed a *tendre* for one of our esteemed guests. It is my job to look after you, you know. Regardless of how uncaring my actions these past days have made me appear."

Had the tone of the conversation suddenly turned serious? Emily's gaze sharpened on her brother. Sure enough, though his carefree smile was firmly in place, the glint of amusement was gone from his eyes. He was looking at her closely. Too closely for Emily's peace of mind. She flushed and immediately averted her face. "I don't have the faintest idea what you're talking about," she muttered. She gave a particularly vicious tug on the thread in her agitation, managing to tangle it beyond salvation. Growling low in her throat, she tossed the whole blasted thing aside. She would work it out later, when her mind wasn't in such an uproar.

"Your reaction tells me you do." He lowered his voice and leaned in a bit closer. "Emily, I've seen the attention Lord Morley has paid you."

She pressed a cool hand to her cheek, so hot did her face flush. "You mistake the meaning of his attentions, Drew," she managed. *As did I.* "I swear, there is nothing untoward about it." *Though I wish with all my might there were.*

The thought came unbidden, shocking Emily and making her thoroughly disgusted with herself. Truly, even after learning the true nature of his "friendship" she thought of him in that way? There was something horribly wrong with her. There must be, to want the man after everything that had occurred.

Drew was frowning at her. "I don't understand."

Did they really need to dredge this up? Hadn't she been through enough in the past day, without having her brother aware of how pathetic she was, that a veritable stranger had been asked to play nursemaid to her? But Drew needed some answer. He was liable to think the very worst if she did not provide him with something. Best to play it down, however. There was no reason he had to know the full extent of her humiliation. "He was simply doing a favor for Caleb, watching out for me."

"Is that all it was?"

Emily had the sudden urge to punch her brother right in his face. Which was a ridiculous reaction, as she hadn't wanted him to think it was important in the first place. But wouldn't it be nice to have someone to commiserate with over the whole affair?

"Yes," she grumbled instead, "that's all it was."

"Too bad, that," he said thoughtfully, sending a glance in Lord Morley's direction.

"What?" she very nearly screeched. Several members of the party stopped what they were doing to look their way—including Lord Morley, who was gazing at her with hooded black eyes. Emily flushed and, turning the ruined side of her face to the wall, said in a much quieter voice, "What are you talking about? What exactly is 'too bad' about his having no designs upon me?"

Drew shrugged, leaning back and crossing one foot over his knee. "He'd be a fine catch for any woman. I certainly wouldn't mind him as a brother."

Emily's jaw dropped before she could rein in her reaction. Scowling, she said, "Well, you may put the idea from your mind, for it won't happen. Not now, not ever."

"Goodness, what has gotten into you?" When Emily turned her frown on him, he held up both hands in a defensive posture. "Very well, I'll leave it be. Consider it forgotten. Only," he said a bit more softly, planting his feet on the floor and leaning toward her, "it would do much for my peace of mind to see you settled, before I talk Caleb into buying my commission and I head off to the Continent."

A muted grief filled her at the reminder, obliterating the last of her ire. She had always known he was meant for the army. Goodness knows he had talked of it often enough on his holidays home. It had only been Caleb's insistence that Drew finish university before enlisting that had Drew still in England at all.

She reached across the space that divided them and took his hand in hers. "Have no fear for me," she murmured kindly.

"You know I'll always worry about you," he said gruffly. He sat for a time, looking more down than she had seen him in a good long while. Soon, however, he shook it off and was smiling mischievously at her. "But if not Lord Morley, perhaps another has caught your eye? Shall I guess, then?" He chuckled as she rolled her eyes, then cast his gaze over the assembled men. "Knowles is too much of a flirt to interest you. And Forster is an idiot. You're much too smart for the likes of him."

Despite herself, Emily laughed. Drew was, as ever, a balm for her soul.

"I know!" he suddenly exclaimed, turning to her with shining eyes. "It is Sir Tristan, is it not?"

"You are ridiculous," she pronounced, trying—and failing—to fight back her grin. Suddenly she stilled. Mayhap her brother would be able to verify whether Sir Tristan was a good catch for Daphne. Not that he had to know that she meant the baronet for their sister, but it certainly couldn't hurt to learn all she could about the man before she went and married him off to her.

"I remember him coming around often when we were children but admit I don't know the first thing about him. Have you heard anything?"

If Drew was at all suspicious of her line of questioning, he didn't show it. "He's a capital fellow," he said. "Right fun to be around. Never knew a man who could make merry like him. I admit, I wish I could have a chance to gad about London with him before I go off to fight."

Emily frowned. "Does he shirk his duties for pleasure, then?" That certainly wouldn't do for Daphne.

"Not that I'm aware," Drew said, his attention wandering to his cuff. "He's got a tidy property in Kent, and another sprawling estate in the north by the border. Rich as they come, from what I've heard. Sir Tristan lives much of the time in London, but I haven't heard of any scandal attached to him. No, he's a right jolly fellow, is all. Probably having a bit of fun before he settles." He speared her with a teasing look. "You sure you're not interested? I could help things along."

"Not in the slightest," Emily pronounced primly. At least, she silently corrected, sending a covert look across the room to where Sir Tristan and Daphne were laughing together, not for herself at any rate.

Yes, she thought with a small, private smile, he would do nicely for Daphne indeed.

Chapter 12

By the next afternoon, Emily was just beginning to comprehend the full extent of the monumental feat she had set out for herself in trying to marry off her sister in the space of a fortnight.

She leaned back against the trunk of a willow tree that grew close to the riverbank. Its drooping branches reached out over the small river—more of a brook, really—affording Emily a private place to observe Daphne as she swung her battledore at the descending shuttlecock. The racket hit the feathered cork with a resounding smack, sending it back up into the sky. Daphne squealed in delight. Sir Tristan, standing with Lord Morley on the small stone bridge that spanned the brook, cheered her loudly. She didn't even glance his way.

It was not as if Daphne had been completely uninterested in the man. If that was true, Emily would have been hard pressed to continue with her plans. She didn't want to go to London, but she would not subject her sister to an unhappy union in order to achieve that end. Thankfully there had been several small tells—a sideways glance, a blush, a quick and surreptitious pinch to the cheeks when she thought no one was looking—that proved Daphne's interest was still in play.

But there was also this strange aloofness she showed the man, when he was so obviously trying to claim her attention. Worrying at her lip with her teeth, Emily attempted to make sense of the situation. There were not many chances the Masters girls had to meet new gentlemen. They had been extremely sheltered up till that point. As were most young women of good breeding, she supposed. Still, it did not lead to proper confidence in dealings with the more masculine sex.

Mayhap that was the problem, Emily conceded. Her sister was young, only seventeen years of age. It could very well be that Daphne's lack of interactions meant that she was unable to translate her more tender feelings properly. Perhaps she was even confused by them.

Well, far be it for Emily to let her sister remain befuddled. She would be glad to help in any way she could. The problem with that, however, was *how* she could accomplish it, while spending as little time in Lord Morley's company as she could manage, for that man had been chained to Sir Tristan's side since the wedding.

It was to be expected, she supposed. The two were close friends; they would surely be in each other's company often. That closeness, however, would make getting Daphne and Sir Tristan alone a near impossibility.

Just then Daphne broke away from the game. She dropped her battledore to the blankets that had been laid out for a picnic, her face becomingly flushed, several curling strands of hair falling from her chignon. The other girls called out, begging for her to return to the game. She laughed and flapped her hands to ward off their entreaties. "I am done for the time being," she called to them, letting out a relieved breath as she flopped down. "I shall join you again after I've caught my breath."

Emily was certainly not going to question this apparent gift from the heavens. She had been struggling to think of a way to get Daphne alone all through the morning; her sister had become the center of the small group of young women and was rarely without a friend at her side, day or night. Emily hurried from her bower, knowing she had to grasp at this chance to promote a match with Sir Tristan, yet not having the faintest idea how to go about it. It was only when she came near and spied the overflowing picnic baskets that an idea popped into her head. If her sister's insecurities regarding London were still as strong as they had been, it would work like a charm. She dropped beside the containers of food, making a great show of rifling through them. A frown creased her forehead. "Oh dear," she muttered.

As hoped, Daphne peered over at her, suddenly alert. She had been the one to painstakingly put this picnic together; she would be sensitive to any problems that might arise.

"What is it?" she demanded.

"I thought for certain you would have strawberries. But I see none. And what is a picnic without strawberries?"

Emily had no idea if strawberries were *de rigueur* for picnics. She was not exactly what one would call up-to-date on all the necessaries for these types of things. But neither did Daphne, a fact that Emily was counting on.

Daphne bolted upright, hurrying to Emily and the baskets. "Do you think it's very important?" she fretted, looking within the confines of the wicker basket.

"Oh, certainly."

Daphne stilled in her frantic perusal and turned to Emily, narrowing her eyes in suspicion. "How would you know?"

Well, Emily certainly hadn't expected to be questioned on her pronouncement. She had hoped that if she declared such a thing with enough force that Daphne would take her word for it. Mind whirling, she cast about for a reason that would sound believable. As luck would have it, Miss Mariah Duncan's light laugh carried to them and provided Emily with the perfect excuse.

"I overheard the others talking about it," she lied, hoping her face didn't betray the massive fib she was spewing. "Apparently it's all the rage in London."

To Emily's relief, that seemed to do the trick nicely. Daphne's mouth formed a small circle of dismay. She looked at Emily wildly. "What shall we do?"

A little stab of guilt shot through Emily at causing her sister anxiety. *It's all for the greater good*, she thought stoutly. Now was not the time for a conscience. Not if she wanted to keep from London next year.

"Isn't there a clearing not far from here where we can find some berries?"

Daphne's face fairly lit from within, her relief was so great. "Of course. You know," she whispered, "perhaps we should make a game of it, gather everyone together to help in the picking, give out prizes for the most berries harvested."

Which was actually a grand idea, Emily thought, her heart dropping. But not at all helpful in what she was trying to do, which was to get Daphne and Sir Tristan alone together. And so she did something reprehensible.

She gave her sister a horrified look.

"What?" Daphne demanded. "Is that not proper?"

"To have our guests pick their own fruit? We couldn't do that. But perhaps we can sneak away? Maybe bring one of the gentlemen with us to help?"

Without waiting for an answer, Emily rose and set off for the stone bridge, Daphne following behind.

Here, however, was where her biggest difficulty lay. How would she ever be able to get up the nerve to talk Sir Tristan into accompanying them? Yes, she had managed to talk to Lord Morley, even to have full conversations with him. That did not mean, however, that she was any more adept at approaching other men. But she had come this far. She would not back down now.

Sir Tristan was leaning idly against the stone railing. At their approach, he straightened. Lord Morley, at his side, did likewise. Emily's heart leapt as his attention shifted to her. It seemed that, despite his appalling behavior toward her, he still affected her much more than he rightly should.

"Ladies," Sir Tristan said with a smile and a bow, "how may we be of service to you?"

It was now or never. Taking a deep breath, forcing her thoughts from the man's friend, Emily blurted, "Sir Tristan, it seems we do not have strawberries for the picnic. Perhaps you can accompany us to pick some before the food is served?"

The man blinked in surprise before smiling broadly, his entire attention shifting to Daphne, who stood anxiously at Emily's side. "I would love to help." He offered his arm. Daphne accepted it with gratitude and they started across the bridge.

Emily made to follow. To her consternation, Lord Morley fell in beside her. She stopped, and he stopped as well. Ahead of them, Daphne and Sir Tristan had paused and were waiting on them. Nearly growling in frustration, Emily kept her gaze forward along the dirt path and said, "I'm sure you don't need to bother, my lord. It is only picking berries, after all. Hardly an endeavor requiring an army of people."

There was a short, charged silence, before he replied in his deep voice, "I insist. I would help where I can." The slight edge to his voice told her he would brook no arguments.

Emily, however, had come too far to give up quite so easily. Even if her skin was beginning to tingle in the most disconcerting manner at his closeness.

"I would be most obliged if you would stay here in our stead." It was a weak argument at best. But then, so was his.

Like a fox scenting prey, Lord Morley narrowed his dark eyes on her before turning. "Knowles, Tristan and I will be escorting Lady Emily and her sister to gather some strawberries. Be so kind as to mind the party while we're gone. We won't be long."

When Mr. Ignatius Knowles, who was in a lively dispute with some of the other gentlemen, gave him a grin and jaunty salute, Lord Morley turned back to her with a satisfied smile. "There," he drawled, "now there is no need for me to stay behind."

He held out his arm, his eyes throwing a challenge at her. Emily cast her gaze over the assembled group. Where the devil was her brother when she needed him? It was then she saw him, on the opposite side of the clearing, his eyes fairly devouring Miss Mariah Duncan. She frowned. Her brother's interest in the girl was proving her downfall. Briefly she considered giving Lord Morley a scathing set-down. But something of that nature could only draw attention to them and bring Sir Tristan and Daphne back. Which would completely undermine her efforts to get the two of them alone. She looked up into the suspicious dark eyes of Lord Morley and wondered briefly if he knew her purpose for getting his friend alone with her sister. It would certainly explain his insistence in going off with her, when he was fully aware she no longer welcomed his company. But how could he? Even if he did, what could he say against the match? His friend was a baronet, and Daphne a marquess's daughter. It would be a good alliance.

He waited patiently, a small smile curving his lips. Blowing out an exasperated breath, she gritted her teeth and accepted his proffered arm. Daphne and Sir Tristan started off again ahead of them, the rumble of their voices and light laughter carrying back to Emily. At least they were conversing. Emily knew, however, that if their affections were to be fully realized, they needed time alone. And with Lord Morley's eagle eyes on their backs, there was no chance of that happening. As they trekked across the meadow, where her half-boots kicked up the warm scent of summer, to the cool shade of the copse beyond, her mind galloped ahead. How, she wondered, could she ensure that Daphne would have time alone with Sir Tristan?

Even as her mind raced, her steps slowed. Truly, she couldn't have walked slower if she had been in a pool of honey. It was a surprise that Lord Morley didn't forcibly take her arm and pull her along at a more normal pace. The only indication he gave of his aggravation was the tightening of his mouth and a small muscle working in his jaw, which she saw when she chanced to glance up at him from under her lashes. The very idea gave her a selfish little thrill. So he was annoyed, was he? Good. Emily would take any chance she could to further her cause. Even if that meant enraging Lord Morley. No, *especially* if that meant enraging Lord Morley.

Daphne and Sir Tristan suddenly ducked out of view, no doubt having found the small glen that she knew held wild strawberry plants in abundance. Not knowing what else to do, knowing she had to prevent Lord Morley from taking a step further, Emily stopped dead in the path. The problem now, unfortunately, was that her arm was linked securely with Lord Morley's. Unaware of her intentions, he kept moving, pulling her right off her feet.

She didn't go down, thank goodness, though there was a slight twinge in her ankle as she caught herself. It was nothing that she hadn't felt a hundred times before when walking the grounds surrounding Willowhaven, and so she knew instantly that it was not serious. It did, however, plant quite the most diabolical idea into her brain. The question was, did she have the ability to pull something like this off? There was one way to find out.

Emily let out a squeak of pain and released Lord Morley's arm, dropping down to the ground and gripping her ankle with both hands. In an instant, Lord Morley was at her side.

"Lady Emily, are you all right?"

He sounded surprisingly distressed. She was a better actress than she'd first surmised.

"A bit of a twist, I'm afraid," she said, keeping her face averted. She might be able to pull this off, but if she looked in his eyes he was sure to see the lie in them.

"Will you allow me to ascertain the damage?"

Emily stilled. Oh dear, to have this man's hands on her ankle. The remembrance of that episode in the music room seared through her mind. How it had felt to be in his arms, the desperation that had come over her to have him bend his head to hers and take her lips with his own. She gripped her skirts with both hands and yanked them down protectively over the body part in question. "I don't think that's necessary, my lord."

"I believe it's important to determine as swiftly as possible that there is no break. Won't you allow me to probe the injury for damage?"

Face flaming, Emily closed her eyes and sent up a silent prayer. When she had managed to get hold of her embarrassment, she said, "I'm certain it's not as bad as all that. I do believe I just need to rest it for a moment."

"Can I help you to your feet? Mayhap we can check to see how bad the damage might be by putting some weight on it."

Goodness, but the man was pushy. She opened her eyes and chanced a glance at him. He was still crouched in front of her, worry clouding his eyes. He was ridiculously handsome this close, with that deliciously chiseled mouth, the aquiline nose, those devastating dark eyes. For a long moment she stared, utterly transfixed. She felt herself melting a bit, leaning in toward him.

Until his eyes flickered away from her, back up along the path where Daphne and Sir Tristan had disappeared. An indication of his eagerness to escape her. In a flash she recalled his reaction to her the last time they had been this close, his horror over her scar.

The devastation that rejection had given her.

Clearing her throat loudly, she leaned back away from him. Lord Morley, too, moved in that moment, lurching to his feet. She did not miss the surreptitious step back he took, though he seemed to make pains to have it appear as natural as possible. He reached his hand out to help her up. She could not have placed her fingers in his in that moment for anything, so hurt was she. Stupid, stupid girl, to forget so easily his true feelings regarding her appearance.

"No, thank you," she managed. "I'm fine on my own."

She heard his frustration at her stubbornness in his softly expelled breath. His next words were much more akin to the gruff meanness he had shown her upon their first few meetings. "Don't be a fool. Take my hand and let me help you up."

"Oh, and I'm sure *that* attitude will make me want to accept your help."

From his silence, she expected he was as surprised as she by the venom in her voice. Truly, no one frustrated her like this man.

"Damnation, woman. You are the most stubborn creature I have ever had the displeasure to encounter. Why your brother thought you needed looking after I haven't a clue."

She smiled, syrupy sweet, up at him. "You may be pleased to know, you are the only one who brings about such a side in me."

A reluctant admiration flared in his eyes. "Truly now? Well, I'll have *you* know—"

But whatever he had been about to say trailed off into nothing.

His gaze, which had been planted firmly and disconcertingly on her face, shifted off to her left. She thought for a moment he was ogling her scar again, and felt the return of her hurt and fury, when he spoke.

"Lady Emily." Lord Morley's voice, while calm and soothing, was filled with a peculiar tension. "Stand and move to my side."

She raised her eyebrows in disbelief. "What in the name of all that is good has come over you?"

"Do as I say." Tension was threaded through his body like veins in marble, his entire body taut. He held his hand out to her again. "I beg of you."

"You are acting most peculiar, my lord. I will do nothing of the sort."

"Dammit, come here now."

The sudden sharpness of his tone shocked her. It was quickly followed by a sound that turned her blood to ice.

A low, menacing growl vibrated the very air around her. A dog, she immediately knew, and not a happy one at that. Briefly she considered taking Lord Morley's proffered hand and allowing him to pull her to safety. Horrified curiosity won out. She turned her head.

Yes, it was a dog. And not a pleasant-looking one. Its fur was filthy and matted with so much dirt she could not determine its color. The ears were so covered in bramble that their length was a mystery. One eye was completely missing. Even under the mass of dirty fur, she could tell the animal was gaunt. She should have been frightened. The creature was so close it could have lunged for her in a moment, had its jaw around her throat before she had time to even scream.

Yet she wasn't afraid. This was the dog she had seen around the estate, the dog she had worried over. The dog that had made friendly overtures toward her.

"Hello there," she crooned, making her voice as soft and calming as she could while still perched on her derriere in the dirt.

At the sound of her voice, the beast shifted its gaze, which had been centered furiously on Lord Morley, to her.

There was a choking sound from his direction. "What in the hell are you doing?"

"Trust me," she sang pleasantly, her eyes still glued to the dog. The animal tilted its head. Those matted ears, which had been lying flat against its skull, perked forward.

"I have been looking for you, you know," she chided gently. "I have been worried sick."

"Lady Emily." Lord Morley's voice was hoarse in his anxiety. She thought she sensed movement from his direction. The dog's one eye slid back to Lord Morley, a low rumbling coming from its chest.

"I really must insist, my lord, that you remain still," she crooned, keeping her voice pleasant. Really, if the man continued in this vein she may very well lose her one chance with the creature. To her relief, however, Lord Morley did stop, though the tension coming off of him was so thick she could have cut it.

Putting him from her mind, she centered her full concentration on the poor beast before her. "Now, my beauty," she said to the dog, "come here, and make friends with me. I have had sore few of them and truly think we could do each other some good." She held out one hand, slowly so as not to startle it. "Come along. That's a good dog, come here."

The creature studied her for a long moment, its big brown eye blinking slowly. It seemed to tense, and for a moment she feared it would bolt. To her immense relief, however, it crept toward her, its moist nose skimming over her fingers. Then, to her shock and delight, she felt a warm tongue lathe her hand once, twice, before it pushed its matted head under her arm. Its long tail, up until then stuck straight out behind it, began a slow wag. Emily had the insane urge to burst into tears from the joy that this wretched creature was putting its trust in her.

Just then voices could be heard. Emily had but a second to compose herself before Daphne and Sir Tristan, laughing and talking gaily, strode into view. The baronet held his hat before him, filled to the brim with berries. Funny, that she had forgotten completely about them in the furor of finding the dog.

"Ah, there you are," Daphne called. "I had wondered where you had gotten off to. As you see, we found the meadow, and there were ever so many berries..." Her voice faltered as she took in Emily's position on the ground. Frowning, she hurried forward. Until the dog in Emily's arms lifted its great dirty head and peered at her. She let out a small squeak and skidded to a halt, sending up a cloud of dust. Sir Tristan was at her side in an instant.

"Emily, what in the world is that thing?"

Her sister's strident voice made the dog press into Emily's side. A small, pathetic whine drifted up to her. Heedless of the filth coating the creature, Emily put her arms about it protectively. "It is a dog, and unless I can find who it belongs to, it is now mine."

"You cannot be serious," Lord Morley scoffed. "The creature may be feral. It could be violent."

She glared up at him and motioned to the creature in her arms, which was doing its best to bury its head in her skirts. "Does this look feral or violent to you?"

"It was going to attack me," he gritted out.

"Only because it looked as if *you* were attacking *me*. If you recall, you were showing a decided lack of kindness right before the dog showed itself. But enough of this. I need to get it home and cleaned up. And it looks as if it could use a good meal, as well." So saying, she extricated herself from the dog and scrambled to her feet, pointedly ignoring Lord Morley's helping hand.

Daphne seemed to have recovered and, after giving the dog a cautious look, said, "But you will miss the picnic."

"There will be others. At this time I have more important things to do. Come, let us head back to the group, and I'll be on my way."

She turned and started off, clicking her tongue at the dog. Without a bit of hesitation, the creature trotted along at her side, its flank pressed into her skirts.

Immediately, Lord Morley was at her side. "I really must protest, Lady Emily," he said low. "I cannot allow you to put yourself in danger with the creature."

She stopped abruptly and spun to face him. "You have no place in *allowing* me to do anything. Good day, sir."

So saying, she turned from him and strode for the house, her new friend glued to her side.

Chapter 13

"I must say, my dear," Emily's mother said two days later as they sat near the vast side lawn and watched the archery competition, "I had my doubts about that dog. But you have both surprised me."

Emily smiled and reached down to pat the silky head of her new friend. To her surprise and delight, the creature had been a veritable angel during his extensive and detailed grooming. With the help of two maids and a footman, she had managed to scrub and brush and trim him into something altogether beautiful to behold. As it turned out, the filthy creature that had firmly burrowed its way into her heart was, when clean, a creamy white setter, its coat sprinkled all over in pale orange specks. They'd had to cut much of his fur short, due to the mats and brambles that choked it. Even so, he was a handsome thing, if painfully thin, and seemingly healthy and whole but for the missing eye.

"What will you name him?" her mother asked now.

Instantly Emily's spirits sank. "I'd rather not name him, Mama. Not yet."

Her mother gave her a surprised glance from under her parasol. "Why ever not, dear?"

"He may have an owner that's missing him. If so, I have a responsibility to reunite them, don't I?" No matter how it broke her heart to do so. For already, after just two days, she loved him desperately.

"I don't know," her mother murmured. "He may have been abandoned. You may not have an owner to find."

"Abandoned? Who could abandon such an animal?"

"Many would rather destroy an animal, especially a working animal, that has an issue like a missing eye. How can he properly do his job, after all? They would not want, or perhaps aren't able, to take on the expense of such a creature if he cannot properly do what he was bred to do."

Emily straightened, letting her own parasol drop to the ground. The dog, sensing the tension in her, sat up and looked expectantly at her. "Then they are a beast," she cried. "How can anyone abandon an animal for such a thing?"

Her mother heaved a heavy sigh. "I understand your feelings on the matter. But please do yourself a favor? Don't spend too long looking. I truly do feel that the two of you are good for one another."

The ache of tears sprung up behind Emily's eyes. Sniffing loudly, she reached for the dog, who leaned into her hand, heaving a happy sigh. "Very well," she managed around the sudden lump in her throat.

"No more than a day," her mother said in mock sternness, before she smiled, effectively ruining the effect of the order. "And, if at the end of that day, you have not found someone to claim that creature, you will give him a proper name. Agreed?"

"Yes." Emily smiled in return. "I'll set out this very afternoon, if you can spare me. I'm sure he could not have come from far. I'll ask about the local farms and houses, and if I cannot locate his original owner I'll give him a right proper name and set him up like a king."

Her mother laughed, her own hand reaching across the space between them to stroke the dog's head. He gave a contented groan. "I can spare you. Lady Tarryton has most of the event in hand. I vow, I have not had to lift a finger through this whole affair."

Emily directed her gaze to the woman in question, who was overseeing the placement of a light repast off to the side of the archers. "I had worried," Emily said, "that she was overstepping her bounds. Imogen voiced a fear of it before she left for her wedding trip. Several times, in fact."

Her mother waved a hand in the air. "What have I to complain about? She has taken most of the strain of the house party onto her own shoulders, leaving me quite free to enjoy our company. I suppose I should rein her in. She has fairly terrified the help."

"I know she terrifies me," Emily muttered.

"Shall I tell you a secret?" Her mother leaned in close and dropped her voice to a whisper. "She terrifies me, as well."

Emily laughed. Her mother's eyes danced with mischief. "And so, you see," she went on, "it is more self-preservation than anything else that I let her have her head." She chuckled, then sobered. "But if you are insistent on trying to find the owner, please don't go at it alone. I would have you bring some support with you, if at all possible." As Emily nodded and lifted her glass of lemonade to her lips, Lady Willbridge arched one brow and said, much too calmly, "Like that Lord Morley. He could help, you know."

An immediate choking fit assailed Emily. The dog regarded her, his head tilting to one side. Her mother merely looked to the archers. Really, Emily thought not a little meanly, the dog showed more concern over her distress.

As she worked to gain control of her breathing, Emily managed to keep her gaze from straying to the group collected on the lawn. She had spent enough time that morning not looking in that direction, knowing that Lord Morley was of the party trying their hand at bow and arrow. "I don't have the faintest idea why you would suggest him." She had hoped to sound unconcerned. She must have failed miserably if the small lift of her mother's lips was any indication.

"You children, you all think your mother is blind. I have seen the way he's paid you particular attention."

Mortification made Emily's cheeks burn. "No, Mama," she choked. "You have it quite wrong, I assure you."

The older woman gave her a long look. There was entirely too much knowledge in her eyes. Emily felt stripped bare and had the insane desire to bolt. Providence, however, took pity on her, as Daphne approached them with Sir Tristan. She was laughing at something he said while unlacing her bracer.

"Daphne," Emily blurted, eager to deflect her mother's attention from her nonexistent love life, "I'll be heading out in a short while to canvass the houses and farms nearby in an attempt to locate the dog's owner. I don't suppose you and Sir Tristan would care to join me?" Really, this was too perfect. She could do her duty and search for the dog's owner and have a chance to get Daphne and Sir Tristan off alone again. Her efforts thus far had been well rewarded. The two had been fairly inseparable since the trip to pick berries. No thanks to Lord Morley's constant hovering about them.

"Are you really going to get rid of this lovely fellow?" Her sister tossed her bracer aside and dropped down on her haunches beside the dog, who wagged his tail as Daphne ruffled his ears.

"Only if necessary. I have promised Mama to put a day into the search for his rightful owner and not a moment more."

"Well," Daphne said, "I can't say I shall be happy in the search, but I shall join you nonetheless." She craned her neck to peer up at Sir Tristan. "And you? Will you come along?"

"Oh, certainly. I would not leave you ladies to the wilds of Ketterby."

"What is this about the wilds of Ketterby?" Lord Morley's deliciously deep voice interrupted.

Emily's heart dropped into her toes. Of all the luck.

Sir Tristan helped Daphne to her feet. "I've promised to accompany these lovely ladies on the search for the owner of this pup here."

"Is that so?" Lord Morley's eyes flickered to her for a moment. "Well, I do hope your little party can accommodate one more."

"Oh, certainly," Sir Tristan replied. "Though I should leave it up to the ladies." He dipped his head in their direction.

Emily opened her mouth, more than ready to refuse Lord Morley's offering, when Daphne spoke. "But of course. The more the merrier. You know," she said, rising, "perhaps we could make a large party of it. Send groups off in different directions. We can cover more ground that way, don't you think, Mama?"

"Oh, certainly," that woman replied. "How clever. Perhaps you can even bring Imogen's siblings into it as well. They have not been able to join in much with the festivities. I'm afraid Lady Tarryton does not seem as if she cares to have them underfoot. This could be just the thing to make them feel included."

Daphne clapped her hands together in delight. "What a capital idea. I shall go in directly to change and inform their nanny. Sir Tristan, I leave the gathering of the rest to you." So saying, she spun about and ran inside, the pink ribbons of her gown trailing behind her.

Emily sat, stunned, as Sir Tristan hurried off to do Daphne's bidding. What should have been a simple thing of her own making had quickly been yanked from her hands and made into a complicated—and crowded—undertaking. Belatedly she recalled Lord Morley's presence. He looked down at her with shadowed eyes. Flustered, she abruptly stood. The dog did likewise, and she was distinctly grateful for his warm presence against her leg.

"Excuse me," she murmured. "I'd best get ready, as well. Mama. Lord Morley." Dipping a quick curtsy, grabbing up her discarded parasol, she hurried away as fast as she could manage with that dark gaze burning her back.

•   •   •

She was up to something.

Malcolm watched Lady Emily send Lady Daphne and Tristan off ahead to the farmhouse up the hill in an obvious attempt to get them alone. Bending down to the young boy at his side, he whispered in his ear, "Go on now, you know what you need to do." With a wide grin young Bingham Duncan sped off, insinuating himself between the other couple. Malcolm smiled.

It truly had been a stroke of luck that Lady Willbridge had suggested they bring along Imogen's siblings. And even better luck that his little group had been blessed with the eleven-year-old boy. The fellow was eager to get in his good graces, it seemed, having been mostly ignored by his elder brothers for much of his life. And so Malcolm had come up with a brilliant plan. It was a secret, their own little game, to see how often the boy could insinuate himself between Tristan and Lady Daphne. Blessedly, Bingham had not thought the request odd at all, too in awe of Malcolm to think of questioning it.

Lady Emily glared at him. "What do you think you're about with that boy?"

What do you think you're about, pushing Tristan and your sister together? he wanted to ask. He'd best not get her back up. Instead, he said, "Thus far we have not had any luck in locating the owner of that beastie by your side. You must be relieved."

The distraction worked. She turned to look down at the dog walking between them. Her face softened considerably. He secretly hoped she would not have to give up the animal. No matter how at odds they were, she did not need that grief in her life. Even he could see how the creature doted on her, and how much more relaxed she was with him by her side.

"The other three groups may have had luck," she replied. Even as she said it, her gloved fingers entwined in the dog's closely shorn fur, as if she could hold him to her side by sheer force.

"Well, for your sake, I hope we do not find them." The words came from him unbidden, gruff. He cleared his throat, looking away as she glanced at him in surprise.

"Please don't tell me you intend to be nice. You really don't have to, you know. You must no longer feel beholden to watch over me. I have officially released you from your promise, even though you have not broken it officially with my brother."

Her words sent a shaft of anger through him. "Do you think that I cannot wish for your company without being forced?"

"No," she answered immediately, without a hint of self-pity in her tone.

He walked on beside her in troubled silence. Her confidence in herself had not improved a bit. Had he done the girl no good at all? He watched as Lady Daphne and Sir Tristan, young Bingham between them, headed up the lane to the farmhouse. Forcing his thoughts away from Lady Emily and her low opinion of herself, he concentrated instead on this growing affection between his friend and Lady Emily's young sister.

Tristan had been fairly inseparable from Lady Daphne since the day of the picnic. Malcolm feared that, if it continued on as it had been, his friend would be engaged by the end of this fortnight, either by choice or by force.

Not for the first time he wondered at Lady Emily's involvement in the rapidly evolving relationship. She seemed to push the two together every chance she got, pairing them off and making certain that they were in each others' orbit. Was she playing matchmaker? He rather thought she was.

But why? That was the burning question. What could possibly be the reason she would have for wanting to get her sister married off so swiftly? The answer to that did not take much searching. London. She had that trip to the capital looming over her head. But would she really go so far as to see her sister married off to prevent it?

He blew out a breath. Of course she would. She would easily be blinded in her desperation, would go to any length to save herself from something so dreaded. It had ruled the rest of her life; why wouldn't it rule this as well?

He had to put a stop to it.

"I know what you're about," he murmured.

She stumbled to a halt at the foot of the lane and eyed him cautiously. "I don't have a clue what you mean."

He gave a low chuckle. "Please, Lady Emily. I can see you're attempting to play matchmaker between my friend and your sister."

She stuck her chin out mulishly and turned her gaze toward the other couple and young Bingham. He did likewise. They were at the door to the small stone house, talking to a large woman in a bright blue gown. As they watched, Daphne motioned toward them. The woman shook her head and retreated, and the trio headed back their way. Malcolm heard Lady Emily give a small sigh of relief before she turned to him.

"You cannot prove it, my lord," she said with surprising spunk. Despite himself, he felt a deep-seated satisfaction at her stubbornness.

"No," he replied with a smile. "But I can stop it."

Just then the others rejoined them. As they all continued on to the next dwelling, he thought he heard Lady Emily say, very softly, "Not if I can help it."

Chapter 14

The dog was hers.

By some miracle each and every group that had been out searching came back with the same news: the owner of the animal was nowhere to be found. Emily looked down at the sweet creature sitting patiently at her feet, her heart swelling almost painfully. She had done it, had kept her promise to look for the dog's home. Now the ordeal was over. She need never part from him. The realization that they belonged to one another filled her with such joy she nearly lost her composure then and there. She mumbled a thank-you to the assembled guests before quickly retreating to the seclusion of her room. When she reappeared the next morning, her heart was light and free, the newly christened Bach at her side.

The day was a warm one, the sky heavy with clouds, the air damp with threatening rain. Lady Tarryton had declared the partygoers could not possibly attend outdoor events with such a storm looming, and so inside provisions were made for their amusement. Even so, there was a general air of restlessness permeating the house all the day long. The weather was making everyone surly, the electricity of the coming storm charging the very air with biting discontent. Even Emily, in her happiness over the dog, was not immune. Especially as a certain viscount continued to interfere in regard to her plans for Daphne and Sir Tristan.

No, it was more than interfering now. Ever since his observations of her matchmaking attempts the day before, it had turned into an all-out war, albeit a silent one. No matter where she turned, there he was, glowering and subtly thwarting all her efforts. It was enough to set her teeth on edge, even more so for the fact that his increasing physical proximity sent the most disturbing shiver of awareness through her. She was entirely too affected by him. Which made her intentions to ignore him and put him from her mind difficult, to say the least.

Perhaps he meant to frighten her into decamping. His frowns certainly seemed to say as much. Instead of sending her scurrying, he managed to make her all the more determined. She would not let some troublesome lord ruin her plans. Too much was at stake.

Later that evening, she moved across the room with Daphne in yet another attempt to maneuver her sister into Sir Tristan's vicinity. Lord Morley followed in her wake, like a small and annoying insect that insisted on buzzing about you no matter how you swatted at it to discourage it. Or, in his case, a large brute of an insect. She was turning to Daphne to suggest that Sir Tristan might like to view the orangery before they went in to dinner when Lord Morley sidled up disturbingly close behind her. As had become the norm when he was near, a tingling started up at the back of her neck, moving along her skin, causing it to pimple with awareness.

It was that reaction, accompanied by the small burst of anticipation, that heated her blood, that had her snapping like a worn pianoforte string. Abandoning her attempts to manipulate Daphne, she spun to face him. "Do you mind, my lord? I am attempting to have a conversation with my sister."

"I do believe, Lady Emily, that I am allowed to stand wherever I wish." To her outrage, he took a step closer. His arm brushed hers, sending a shaft of fire through her. Glaring daggers at him, she took a step to the side, not even attempting to mask the distaste that twisted her features.

"You do not have to stand so close," she hissed. "This drawing room is not small. You could just as easily stand, say, over there." She pointed to a lonely corner the full breadth of the room away. To her annoyance, he ignored her completely, instead staring intently ahead. By the time Emily returned her attention to her sister, Daphne had moved off. And not with Sir Tristan as she'd hoped.

Blowing out a small, frustrated breath, she followed. She found her sister close to their mother, and again opened her mouth to speak, only to find that once more Lord Morley had followed on her heels. Annoyed beyond bearing, she motioned for him to move to the side with her. After a slight pause he complied, then proceeded to look at her with that infuriating haughty disdain of his.

"Stop following me about," Emily snapped. "I told you, I don't need looking after any longer."

"I am not following you around," he gritted, his voice pitched low so the others wouldn't hear.

"You must think me an imbecile. Everywhere I turn, every move I make, you're there. I want your promise, as a gentleman, that you will keep your distance from me. Knowing how much it pains me to have you near, you cannot deny me such a wish."

He gave an inelegant snort and made to move away. But she was well and done with him and intended to finish this here and now. She grabbed at his jacket sleeve.

"Sir," she ground out, "I have asked you a question and would like the respect of an answer. I think you owe me that much, at least, after your initial subterfuge."

Her reminder of his promise to her brother seemed to do the trick. He turned a glare on her that would have melted stone. "You wish for an answer? Fine," he spat. Casting a quick glance around, no doubt to ascertain whether they were unobserved, he took hold of her arm and propelled her out of the room and down the hall.

At the library he yanked her unceremoniously inside and closed the door. It took a moment for her eyes to adjust to the gloom. A fire had been lit in the hearth, but it was a small thing, hardly bright enough to travel to the farthest reaches where they presently stood. Even so, she could see the glint of anger in his eyes when he turned the full potency of it on her. Her breath hitched in her throat at the disturbing nearness of him, and of the sudden realization of how intimate this meeting was. But this was no time for faintheartedness. She could not take a minute more of his unwanted presence and would end it now.

"So you wish me to promise to stay far away from you, do you?"

"Yes." She raised her chin a fraction to hide the thrill that shot through her from the dark timbre of his voice.

"I do not follow you about on purpose, I assure you," he bit out.

"Well," she declared, clapping her hands together in front of her, "that settles it, then. You will kindly keep yourself away from me for the remainder of the house party."

"I cannot do that, and you know it," he growled, his frown casting darker shadows over his face.

"You can have no possible reason to be in my vicinity."

The look he gave her was ripe with disbelief. "Oh, don't I?" he drawled.

Emily felt her face heat. "No, not a one."

He blew out a breath and raked a hand through his hair, sending the inky locks into disarray. "Despite the glaring fact that you cannot free me from a promise that was never given to you, there is one other reason I might have for staying close to you. As I have told you before, I know of your attempts to play matchmaker with Tristan and your sister. And I saw it for myself tonight. You are not subtle, my lady."

As if she would own up to it. Her insistence on her innocence in the matter may very well be the one thing keeping her plan from falling apart before her very eyes. "You are delusional," she said as lightly as she could manage.

"I am not delusional. And I tell you here and now, you will not succeed. There is no way in hell I will allow you to marry Lady Daphne off to Tristan."

His insistence that she would fail rekindled her frustration and panic over the matter. For a moment she forgot the need for subterfuge. "Why are you so determined to keep it from happening?"

"It's none of your business," he mumbled.

"Come along. You must have a reason." A sudden, horrifying thought came to her. He had been incredibly stubborn in regard to keeping Daphne and Sir Tristan from each other the day before. He had declared to her that he would not allow her to play matchmaker with them, with much more force than he should have had a right to feel. Did the man care for her sister?

Goodness, did Lord Morley have designs on Daphne himself?

A sick feeling settled in her stomach. It was possible. Daphne was young and beautiful and sweet. With her outgoing, vivacious personality and her pedigree, she could claim any man as her own. She was certain to be much in demand if she went to London next Season. Why wouldn't Lord Morley want her?

An image of them together made bile rise up in her throat. To see Daphne marrying him, having his children…The grief that welled up in her nearly had her knees giving out from under her.

"Ah," she choked. "You wish to court her yourself. I see it now."

Instant horror filled his features. "What in blazes gave you that idea?"

She managed a shrug, even as she pressed a fist into her stomach. "It makes sense, my lord. You don't wish her to make a match of it with your friend. She is young and beautiful. You really could not do better than her."

He gave her an odd, almost pained look, and seemed about to reach out for her. Then he frowned and took a step back. "Of course I don't want her for myself. You are not even remotely close on that account."

She blinked uncomprehendingly at him, his words not sinking in through the tangle her brain had become. "Then what is it? What is your interest in my sister if not romantically?"

"I have no interest in her at all," he growled.

"You expect me to believe that?"

"Yes."

She searched his face for any hint of insincerity. Cursing herself for the relief that bloomed in her chest when she saw none, she said, much more harshly than intended, "I do not understand your insistence in keeping them apart then. If they hold affection for one another, why not let them form an attachment? They make a lovely couple, and the connection is not a bad one, on either side."

"I have said it before and I will say it again, it is no business of yours." He stepped closer, looming over her in an obvious attempt to force her to a retreat. "But hear me and hear me well. Tristan shall not marry your sister."

Emily glared up at him. "You may have your reasons, my lord. But so do I. And so you had best get used to the idea. For, despite your wishes, it will happen."

She turned for the door. He reached out and gripped her arms with both hands, stopping not only her forward movement but also her breath and, seemingly, her heart as well. Her eyes flew to his face as his gloved fingers burned through the sheer sleeves of her gown. She was suddenly transported to that day in the music room, when she had been so sure he had been about to kiss her. She had wanted it so desperately she had fairly ached with the need of it, even long after he had left her.

His eyes skimmed over her face, and in the dark recesses of her mind she remembered his horror when he had pushed her away. But it was a mere echo. All she could feel in that moment was the firmness of his chest pressing into her breasts, his hands on her arms, and the pool of heat that was quickly settling in the very core of her. Their breaths rasped in the quiet of the library, accompanied by the sharp crackle of the fire. Somewhere off in the distance, the sounds of revelry could still be heard, faintly. It was another world. The only real thing was here and now.

"Emily," he groaned. It was a pained sound, ripped from the very depths of his soul. Her body responded instantly to her name on his lips, molten longing making her breath short, her knees weak with wanting him. Her fingers came up of their own accord and gripped onto his evening coat, crushing the fine material. It was the first time her name, and just her name, had passed his lips. She knew now why societal dictates were so strict on proper decorum, why the use of first names alone was so taboo. Never had she felt so open and raw, so bared to another. It was as if every wall that had been built up between them had been ripped away with that one tortured word.

He bent a bit closer, his face mere inches from hers. Yet he seemed to be doing battle with himself. He fairly shook under her fists. Every inch of him trembled. Her own body—her untutored and innocent body—was responding to it. She pressed a bit closer to him, saw the flare in his eyes. It was not the faint firelight, she knew. No, it was something more primal, something he was fighting with everything in him.

And she was tired of fighting. She was so damned tired of being alone, of being without. The devastating knowledge that she might never, ever have this intimacy with a man again struck her then. Dragging in a deep breath, her senses filled with him, with that wonderfully mouthwatering scent of black tea and leather and soap, underlined with the sweet spice of the brandy he had consumed. She wanted him. More than anything in her life, she wanted this man. With that realization, that the one person who had brought her so much heartache and grief could be the one man her heart and body wanted above all others, she shuddered.

He seemed to regain control of his errant emotions. She could feel it in him, the gradual pulling away. Her heart fairly broke with it. If he left her in that moment, when she wanted him with such raw need, she knew it would destroy her. Of its own accord, her heart spoke in that moment, a mere whisper of a sound that came out like a prayer in the stillness of the room.

"Malcolm."

His breath escaped him in a long, ragged rush. Then his mouth was on hers, hot and insistent. And there was no time to think. There was only him, and her. She gripped on tight, never wanting to let him go.

Chapter 15

Had she said anything else he could have pulled away from her with a small portion of his sanity intact. But his name in her sweet voice, when she had never before let it pass her lips, was like a drug to his inflamed senses. Nothing would do in that moment but to claim her mouth with his own.

She was like the nectar of the gods. Her mouth opened beneath his, all hot eagerness. He needed no further encouragement. Plunging his tongue between her parted lips, he reveled in her taste, breathed in her very essence. The scent of her, intoxicating and mouthwatering, drifted up to him and seeped into his lungs, driving him wild. He released her arms, moved his hands to her back, pressing her body flush to his. Her delicate spine arched under his touch, making the contact of their bodies that much more potent.

Now that her arms were free, her hands seemed everywhere at once. They roamed over his back, his arms, his shoulders with a sweet abandon that made him groan aloud into her mouth. She shivered, seeming to grow bolder at the proof of his desire. Her fingers delved into his hair, gripping tight. A tingling flashed over his skin, making him hard. Furiously hard. Some primal instinct had him grasping her hips, pulling her closer to press himself into the softness of her belly. Did she feel the effect she had on him? Did she understand what she did to him?

As if she heard the silent questions, she tore her lips free for the briefest moment. "Malcolm." His name rode her breath, the desperate sound of it hitting him like a punch to the gut. Then her mouth was back on his, fumbling in its exuberance, made all the sweeter for its untrained ardor. Such unrestrained passion he never expected from her. That she, who held herself back with such care from others, shared such a piece of herself with him was glorious.

He wanted to tell her how beautiful she was to him, how desirable. That he had never wanted another with such a total loss of control. Instead he took her face in his hands, deepened the kiss, fearful of the emotions that were coursing through him. If possible, she became even more impassioned. And, forgive him, but he took everything she gave and more. His hands moved from her face, skimmed down the long length of her neck, caressed the swell of her breasts.

She gasped into his mouth and arched her back. Her breasts, small yet high and full, pressed into his palm. The warmth of them, their softness, undid him. He needed more.

But he should not be doing this. She was his best friend's sister, an innocent. And, more importantly, someone he respected and was coming to care for too damn much.

He yanked his lips free. That small burst of willpower, however, was all he could manage. His arms tightened about her, his forehead pressing against her own. Her eyes glinted up at him in the dim light, and he closed his lids against the passion-laced questions lurking in their depths.

"Tell me to stop," he begged, his voice a hoarse whisper of sound. "Please."

There was a pause. And then her hand, so small against his face, her fingers curving around his cheek. In the next moment her lips were on his, and the last of his will crumbled. With a groan he ripped off his gloves and dropped them to the floor. Then, hooking one arm about her slender waist, he brought his free hand up and found the neckline of her gown. His fingers dipped below the fabric, trailing over the top curves of her breasts, feeling the velvet soft skin tremble at his caress. Still that was not enough. Without a second's thought he pulled the bodice low, tugging her shift down with it. She gripped his hair tighter, her tongue twining with his own, a silent plea. And then she was in his hand, her sweet breast filling his palm, and there was no more room to think.

She gasped at the contact and ripped her mouth free of his, her head falling back, one word escaping her lips, low and throaty and full of need.

"Yes."

Like a starving man, his mouth moved to the arch of her throat, working his way down toward the delectable fruit that filled his palm. Lathing her flesh with his tongue, he let the anticipation build until it could no longer be denied.

When he finally reached her breast and drew her puckered nipple into his mouth, he thought he would burst right then and there from the exquisite pleasure of it. A soft cry escaped her lips, her hands frantic as she grasped his head to her breast. She seemed to sway in his arms and he gripped her tight, one hand pressed between her shoulder blades, the other over the supple roundness of her backside. The soft little gasps that were coming from her, the way she pressed up against him in supplication, made him wilder. He felt if he did not claim her this moment, he would expire on the spot.

He lifted his head, needing to look upon her in that moment, to see with his eyes that she was as affected as he, to hear from her lips that she wanted this. She was achingly lovely, her face flushed in the faint light, her lips moist and parted, her eyes closed. As if sensing his gaze, she opened her eyes then and returned it.

It was the expression on her face that stopped him from dragging her to the ground and taking her right then. Beneath her passion was such trust, such wonder, her bow lips lifted in a shy smile. He knew then that there was something much more than mere physical need driving her. She cared for him. He saw it in the way her gaze caressed his features as if memorizing them, in the gentle touch of her fingers against the nape of his neck.

More importantly, he felt it in his heart, that answering call for something more. It beat hard and strong, a force that demanded an answer, a primal drumming that could only be quieted by her.

Everything in him froze. He was not ready for this, had not

meant for any of this to happen. He had given his heart before; he could not give it again. Stepping back, he steadied her and went to work righting her clothes.

"Malcolm?"

Her voice was uncertain and faint. Even so, his name on her lips had the same effect on him as before, reawakening that blinding need for her, undermining his better intentions. He drew in a deep, shuddering breath to rein himself in and met her gaze. There was a glazed confusion in her pewter eyes. Chest aching, his body screaming in protest, he nonetheless smiled comfortingly at her and, because he could not resist touching her again, cupped her ruined cheek in his palm. She stiffened for a moment before she tilted her head with a small sigh, relaxing into his touch.

Her features, normally so guarded and tense, relaxed. She closed her eyes, her long lashes brushing her cheeks, the faint line that always seemed between her brows smoothing. Her lips, still swollen from his kisses, lifted up at the corners in a small smile. In that moment, as he stood gazing down at her, he had the mad idea that he shouldn't fight this pull. It had been a losing battle thus far, had seemed to grow harder to fight as time passed. He imagined sleeping beside her each night, waking beside her each morning, facing that hidden spark of hers in endless conversations, endless bouts of passion. Suddenly the idea of surrendering a bit of himself to her, an idea that had seemed so abhorrent a moment ago, held a wonderful appeal. Two damaged souls, coming together. Perhaps learning to heal with the other's help. She opened her eyes then, looked up at him with such happiness in her expression, and the words very nearly ripped from his lips proclaiming his intentions to court her.

At the last minute, however, he halted his overeager tongue. This was all too new. He needed to think it over, consider it, come to terms with it. Pulling back from her, he murmured, "We should return before we're missed."

Disappointment flitted across her face, but she nodded and took hold of his proffered arm. There was time, he thought as he led her from the dim library and began heading back toward the drawing room.

The sound of voices reached them as they came closer to the party of guests. Malcolm's steps faltered. The noise of it, the company of others, seemed too intrusive after the life-altering intimacy he'd shared with Emily. Something had changed between them irrevocably. She had touched something deep in him, in a place he had not allowed to be trespassed upon for too long now.

He glanced down at the woman at his side. Though she hurt, she was willing to give of herself in such a way. Perhaps, he thought as he felt the insistent pull toward her, it was time to let some light into that part of his soul.

• • •

Malcolm half expected the unfamiliar feelings that had awakened in him at Emily's hands to vanish overnight. Mayhap it had been the electricity and anticipation of the storm that had broken over the house in the night. Perhaps the general air of romance from the wedding had finally worked its way under his skin. As he settled in for a restless night, he thought that the bright light of day must do something to wash away those troubling thoughts and return him to some semblance of normalcy. Surely the foreign urgings of his heart were no more substantial than smoke.

As he opened his eyes to find the sky blue and cloudless, washed fresh from the rain that had bathed the countryside mere hours before, he looked deep into his heart and found it unchanged.

Why was he not panicking at this sudden about-face of his most firmly held beliefs? He should be packing his bags and heading back to London to immerse himself in all kinds of debauchery and vice, to cleanse himself of the mad wishes swirling about in his head. The firm and steady beating of his heart, however, made that all fade to the merest echo.

His intentions toward Emily felt so easy and natural. The lack of panic, however, was itself beginning to panic him. He took a deep, cleansing breath. He had made no promises, nothing was set in stone. It was not as if he were going down to propose to the girl that very minute, after all. And there was no guarantee that she would accept him if he did. There was plenty of time to study these burgeoning emotions, to determine where they would lead, to see if she felt the same.

He took his time readying himself for the day. The desperate urgings in his breast to see Emily had to be tamed, after all. His valet was called, his wardrobe gone over with care, each piece picked with precision. His cravat he insisted on having retied twice, his jacket changed out. Even after the man left him, Malcolm fiddled with his cuffs and combed his hair again. When every inch of him had been gone over thrice, he took a deep breath and strode from the room, trying his damnedest to keep his steps slow and solemn but failing miserably.

He made for the ground floor, heading straight for the breakfast room, when the faint strains of something light and happy reached his ears. As before, he was drawn to the sound, a veritable puppet on a string, his path veering off from its set course. He knew where that sweet music would lead him, what he would find at the end of that melodic trail. Anticipation heated his blood, his steps quickening almost against his will.

Once at the music room door, he listened raptly to the rise and fall of notes from within. Silently he moved forward, pressing on the wooden panel, letting the door swing inward. The sight of her, seated on the pianoforte bench, her head bent industriously over the keys, had him sucking in his breath. He had always thought her attractive, beautiful even. How had he not seen how stunning a creature she truly was? A shaft of light from the open drapes caressed her, illuminating the porcelain curve of her cheek and the fiery brilliance of her hair. The latter had been softened; while usually pulled back into an uncompromising bun, today several curls had been worked free to frame her face. He ached to go to her, to take one of those curls, to press it to his lips...

A soft woof dragged him back to the present. Belatedly he spied

Bach on the floor beside her. The dog looked at him with curiosity, its long ears perched forward, its tail thumping rhythmically against the polished parquet floor. At the animal's notice, Emily gasped softly and pulled her fingers back against her chest. The abandoned instrument hummed with the last notes before falling silent altogether.

Malcolm swallowed hard as her gray eyes met his. "Good morning," he managed.

A hesitant smile lifted her lips. "And to you as well, my lord."

"I had thought," he murmured softly, coming into the room, "that perhaps we were done with the 'my lords' and 'my ladys.'"

Malcolm watched, entranced, as a rosy blush stained her cheek. She looked away, and he knew without being told that, had he not brought the small tell to her attention before, she would be pressing her hand to her scarred cheek.

"Are we done with that, then?" she asked, a bit breathlessly.

He drew closer to her. Bach sniffed his boot, and he reached down to scratch the animal behind the ear. "I do believe we have," he said quietly.

Her gaze skimmed up to meet his, her eyes soft and luminous. "Very well, Malcolm," she whispered.

When she continued to sit there, her fingers gripped tight in her lap, he said, "I didn't mean to intrude. I can leave if you wish, so you might resume your practice."

"You are not intruding," she said.

"What was that you were playing?"

"A Haydn piano sonata."

"It was much more cheerful than what I've heard you play on previous occasions."

She shrugged, her fingers caressing the ivory keys gently. "I'm in a much more cheerful frame of mind, I suppose," she murmured.

A spurt of pleasure filled him until he thought he would burst. "Will you play it again for me?"

She dipped her head in acknowledgement, raising her hands over the keys, and began to play.

The notes filled the room in a light, trilling cadence. His gaze fell to her fingers on the keys. How graceful they were, long and slender, hitting the ivories with rapidity one minute, slowing with quiet elegance the next, all the while dancing across the instrument with unerring precision. He felt each note vibrate through his body, sensed the music swirl through the air and wrap about his heart. Every uncertainty he'd woken with was quickly and completely snuffed out as her song worked its magic on him. As *she* worked her magic on him.

How could he fail to be drawn completely under her spell? Her face was rapt, emotion saturating every line and curve. She had closed her eyes, her body swaying to the music, an extension of the instrument under her hands.

Needing to touch her again, he moved closer and let his fingers caress the graceful arch of her back.

Emily sucked in her breath, the sound sharp, her fingers stumbling over one another for a moment.

He pulled his hand back. "I'm sorry."

"Don't be," she managed, the words hoarse. She cleared her throat. "I mean, I don't mind it."

He took that for the invitation it was, returning his fingers to her back, moving up to settle on the nape of her neck. They stayed that way for some time, his hand light on her satiny skin, stray copper tendrils falling over his fingers, her music at once calming and exciting his senses.

He had never been so contented in his life.

After some minutes, the song came to a close. The notes died away slowly, the vibration of them lingering in the air. She dragged in a deep breath and looked up at him. "Shall we go into breakfast?"

"I've no wish to pull you from your practice," he murmured.

Her lips quirked in an amused smile. "I've had several hours' practice already. I do think it's time to give my fingers a rest."

He helped her from the bench, offering his arm and guiding her from the room, Bach following at her side. "At what time did you awake this morning?"

"I'm not certain. Five, perhaps? Maybe six?"

He blanched. "Do you always practice so blasted early?"

She laughed. "Not always, no. It is just since the house party began that I've kept such hours. I typically don't get to my practice until after breakfast."

"You must be anxious for us all to leave so you can return to your schedule then."

Her voice drifted up to him as they made the breakfast room door. "Not all of you."

Those quiet words warmed him in the most wonderful way. What he wouldn't give to pull her aside, to take her in his arms and kiss her senseless as he had been longing to do all morning. Just then, however, they were set upon by Lady Daphne and her contingent of females, who had apparently shaken off their malaise of yesterday and were ready to tackle the glorious new day.

"Emily, I was just coming to look for you," she exclaimed. "And you as well, Lord Morley. We are all dying to get out of doors and revel in the sunshine after the dismal confinement of yesterday. We've decided on a ride across the fields. Say you'll both come."

"Certainly," Emily answered. Her eyes swung up to search his face. "And you, Lord Morley? Will you join our group as well?"

"I wouldn't miss it," he murmured. Her eyes flared with happiness. As he continued to gaze at her, however, her happiness turned to something much more, a hot desire he felt clear to his toes. He forcibly dragged his attention away from the sight of it, knowing if he didn't, he would embarrass himself in the worst way.

Blessedly, it seemed Lady Daphne had missed the small exchange. She clapped her hands. "Splendid. We shall see you within the hour at the stables." So saying, she spun about, the other young ladies following in her wake like sheep after their shepherd.

They were left standing alone in the deserted hallway, Emily's small hand still tucked in the crook of his arm. The heat of her seeped into his side, scattering his senses like leaves in a gust of wind. They had been about to do something, but for the life of him, he couldn't remember what.

Ah, yes. Breakfast.

"Perhaps we'd best eat now," he said, "for I've a feeling we will need it to survive your sister's exuberance."

She laughed lightly. As he guided her into the room, the warm smell of eggs and ham drifting to him, he thought he would need the sustenance to withstand the pull of Emily even more. All the while, however, he knew that nothing on this earth could help him in that particular matter.

Chapter 16

It was when Emily emerged from her room later that morning, freshly changed into her riding habit, that she knew without a doubt things had changed between herself and Malcolm. She had expected to see him at the stables with the others, yet here he was in the picture gallery, staring up at the portrait of some long dead Masters ancestor. His gaze swung to her as she approached, a smile softening the harsh, beautiful lines of his face.

He had been waiting for her.

It warmed her, that look, bringing to mind why her feelings had taken such a drastic turn from this time yesterday. How much a heart could change in a mere twenty-four hours, how completely life could alter from one day to the next. Nay, from one *moment* to the next. One bright and shining moment that would forever stay etched upon her soul.

Never in her life had she dreamed such a thing could exist. She had known that some found pleasure in kisses, in caresses. Why, she had seen for herself firsthand the small stolen touches and looks Caleb and Imogen had shared when they thought no one was looking. Even so, the idea of such intimacy and the pleasure that could be derived from it had been as easy for her to comprehend as grasping at a waterfall. Certainly not something she ever expected to feel herself.

Not until Malcolm had taken her in his arms.

She moved to stand before him, trying with all her might to keep her steps slow and dignified. It would not do for her to grab her skirts up above her knees and dash across the gleaming floor until she could touch him again. He could not possibly feel the same way for her, after all. She would only make a fool of herself, would make him look at her in pity.

But it was not pity in his expression as she came near. No, nothing like pity at all. There was warmth and—dare she say it?—affection lighting the depths of his dark eyes.

He held out a hand to her. With but a moment's hesitation, she placed her own in his. Even through their kidskin gloves she felt the heat and strength in his grip. She recalled in a flash those hands on her skin, baring her, touching her in a way she had thought never to be touched.

His expression was full, as if he were remembering, too. As if there were too many things he wished to say. But when he spoke, it was to ask, "Shall we meet with the others, then?"

As she nodded and turned with him to walk to the stables, she wondered at the disappointment that settled under her skin. It had been present in small waves throughout the morning, and she took advantage of the companionable silence between them to look inside herself, to turn over her peculiar reaction.

Things had changed so drastically between Malcolm and herself. She had felt drawn to him before, but it had become so much stronger since their kiss. It was like a delicate thread that had been transformed into an unbreakable chain. It tugged on her, dragging her attention to wherever he was, making her want to touch him, to step back into that strong embrace and feel again his arms about her and his lips on hers.

In a flash she knew what her disappointment stemmed from. She wanted him to kiss her again. With everything in her she wanted to feel that incredible sensation of being in his arms, as if she were the most precious thing in the world.

She shook her head, banishing the silly, fanciful thoughts. Malcolm could not have thought it more than a simple kiss. Men like him did not want women like her, awkward and scarred and too fearful to live life.

He glanced down at her then, a small smile on his lips, and she felt her doubts melt under his perusal. Perhaps there was something more there, after all.

Soon they were at the stables, and there was no more time to think of Malcolm and kisses. Daphne took the small group quickly in hand, directing everyone in the mounting of the waiting horses, setting them off across the back lawn and the rolling hills of Willowhaven. Everyone was in high spirits, no doubt happy to be out of doors after being forced inside for so long.

Emily hung back, keeping her mare behind the group, unable to bear the thought of being within that rambunctious party. To her surprise and secret pleasure, Malcolm brought his mount aside hers. With the same quiet ease that had been with them all morning long, they rode on together, letting the others pull ahead. As they started up a gentle rise, the rest of the group kicked their horses off and as one made a mad gallop over the crest.

She squinted, frowning. "I suppose we should hurry on after them. I am the chaperone, after all," she murmured.

"I suppose we should," he replied. Yet he didn't urge on his mount. The animal tossed its head, prancing a bit, before Malcolm expertly brought it under control. Emily would have felt sorry for the poor beast—he obviously wished to stretch his legs and run with the others—if she weren't so happy to have his rider at her side.

"Then again," she mused, "I suppose there are enough of them that they cannot possibly get into trouble."

"I completely agree."

There was a companionable moment of silence. A breeze caressed her, and Emily lifted her face to it, breathing in deeply of the smell of wet earth and fresh, clean air. Her chest felt lighter than it had in longer than she cared to remember.

"This is odd," Malcolm mumbled.

Emily glanced at him in question.

"I'm not at all used to this."

"This?"

"The silence. I'm not used to it."

Her heart fell a bit. Here she had been enjoying the peace of the morning, and he had been made uncomfortable by it. "I apologize. I'm not the most voluble person, as you might have guessed. I'm sure you would be more comfortable if we hurried to rejoin the others."

"No, that's not what I meant at all," he said as she made to kick her mare on.

"Then perhaps you'd best elaborate," she said through suddenly stiff lips, forcing her hands to relax on the reins.

She watched as he blew out a breath, no doubt looking for the right words to say.

"I meant," he said haltingly, "that I am not used to *enjoying* the silence."

"Oh," was all she could think to say. Warmth spread through her chest.

He apparently thought his explanation needed further elaboration. "I spend much of my time in London, as you know. I typically surround myself with all manner of noise and excitement and stimulation. I've never found quiet comfortable. Yet here, with you,.... I...am." His voice trailed off and he frowned, as if he could not quite believe what he was admitting.

"Why?" A second later she blushed furiously, overcome by her own boldness in questioning him on something that no doubt had very personal roots.

He blinked. "I'm sorry?"

She considered waving it off and changing the subject, then shrugged. In for a penny, in for a pound. "Why have you never found silence comfortable?"

At first she thought he would either ignore her question and change the subject or kick his mount on to escape her. A wave of pain seemed to roll through his dark eyes.

"There are things," he said, his voice a hoarse rasp, "that I would rather not think about too clearly. And silence, more often than not, gives one room to think far too much."

She nodded, her heart twisting for him. "I'm sorry I pried," she said quietly. "I know something of pain and so can understand a bit of where you might be coming from." She paused, not at all sure she could be as daring as she wished. In the next instant she threw caution to the wind. Nudging her mare closer to him, she leaned toward him and laid her gloved hand over his. "But know you have my ear to bend, should you wish it."

He looked down at her hand for a long moment. As she was about to draw it back, convinced she had crossed some invisible line, he turned his hand under hers and gripped her fingers tight. Raising it to his lips, he kissed her knuckles. She sucked in her breath as the firmness of his mouth lingered a touch too long. Heat pooled low in her belly.

"Malcolm," she whispered.

His eyes raised to her, and even in her innocent state she could see the same hunger in his eyes that had been present when he had kissed her senseless in the library. Her eyes focused on his lips and she swayed in her saddle.

Suddenly, out of the corner of her eye, a small brown blur darted past. Before she could regain her senses enough to tighten her grip on the reins, her mare reared up, her panicked cry rending the quiet afternoon air. Emily's world tilted. Her leg lost its grip on the pommel, and she saw with horror the ground rising to meet her.

At once she was caught up. Malcolm's strong arms banded around her waist, lifting her as if she weighed no more than a sheet of music. He pulled her across his lap, securing her tight to his chest. Her hat tumbled to the ground and was promptly trampled beneath the hoof of her horse as it galloped away.

For a long moment they sat there, breathing heavily. Her hands gripped tight to his coat, her face pressing into his shoulder. She was achingly aware of the strength of his thighs beneath her and the mad beat of her heart within her ears.

"Are you well?"

His voice rasped in her ear. She closed her eyes against the waves of pleasure that coursed through her, pounding through her blood in the most maddening way, weakening limbs already shaky from the fear of her near fall.

"Yes."

"What happened? Why did she spook?"

Emily fought for composure. But his voice, his warm breath fanning against the side of her face, the feel of his arms about her all had her senses scattering like the small stoneware marbles she had seen the children in the village use. With effort, she gathered her wits enough to answer with a semblance of coherency. "A rabbit. She saw a rabbit."

"Should we go after her?"

Was that reluctance in his voice? His hands, did they tighten the smallest bit on her waist? No, it must be wishful thinking. She shook her head, feeling the tendrils of her hair rasp against his coat. "She will head for home. It is what she was trained to do. Violet is a sweet horse, but she is uncommonly skittish of rabbits." She gave a shaky laugh, more from nerves than anything humorous in the situation, for it truly was absurd. "It is my own fault. I would not have fallen had I been paying attention."

There was a pause. Then his voice, so soft, drifted to her. "Remind me to thank that rabbit."

Her breath caught in her throat. She could not have heard him right. It must have been the longing of her heart that had her thinking he said such a thing. But then, suddenly, his lips moved, feathering across her temple. Emily closed her eyes, holding herself utterly still. The steel of his arms softened, his hands splaying against her back, dragging her even closer until not an ounce of space separated them. He rubbed his cheek against her hair, his lips brushing down the side of her face.

Across her ruined cheek.

She froze. His muscles tensed, no doubt at the change in her. He would pull back now, she thought with the ache of sadness souring her gut. In the next moment, however, he did the most incredible thing.

He pressed his mouth, warm and open, against her scar.

Tears burned Emily's eyes. For, if the swelling of her battered heart was anything to go by, she knew, then and there, that she was in a fair way to falling in love with Malcolm. And not the silly infatuation that had sustained her for so many years, but a real and abiding love. She moved her gloved hands to cradle the strong line of his jaw and met his lips with her own. He responded instantly, his tongue plunging into the recesses of her hungry mouth. One hand splayed over the small of her back, the other moving up to cradle the back of her head, holding her still for his onslaught.

As before, she was overwhelmed with the force of her body's reaction to him. This time, however, she knew what to expect, and welcomed it eagerly. She ran her hands over the breadth of his shoulders, marveling at the power in them, before sending her fingers diving into his inky hair, sending his hat tumbling to join hers on the sodden ground. Her tongue met his with a boldness she had been lacking before, giving no quarter, demanding more from him.

He gave her more, digging his fingers into her hip, pressing himself into her. She felt the hard ridge of his manhood through the layers of her riding habit, knew it for what it was. Wild with need, she squirmed in his grip. He growled low, the vibration of it spearing straight to the core of her, filling her with a molten fire that had her trembling.

His mount, which had been standing silent beneath them, nickered softly. In an instant Emily became aware how public a place this was, that anyone could come upon them.

Malcolm seemed to become aware of it as well. After one final soft kiss, he pulled back. His eyes were like obsidian fire as he gazed down at her. He smiled, and Emily's heart turned over in her chest.

She was not a fair way of being in love with him. She *was* in love with him, completely and irrevocably.

The distant echo of pounding reached them then, growing quickly closer. Malcolm raised his head to look over her, steadying her with one hand on her back as he raised the other in greeting. Emily flushed furiously, pressing her face into his shoulder.

"Is my sister well?" she heard Drew shout.

"Yes, though she is badly shaken." Malcolm's voice rumbled in her ear as her brother pulled up alongside them. "Her mare was spooked and reared. Lady Emily would have fallen to the ground had I not caught her."

Drew dismounted and came to her. Emily looked at him with reluctance. It must be glaringly obvious, what had occurred between Malcolm and herself. She could not bear her brother's laughter just then. He would think it a fine lark that the popular, handsome, and eligible Lord Morley was kissing his awkward sister.

But his face was filled with nothing but deep concern.

"I suppose Violet has run off for home as she always does. But you have never tumbled from her back before. Are you all right, Em?"

She nodded. He held his hands up to help her to the ground. For a single second she thought she felt Malcolm's hands flex possessively on her. In the next moment, however, he was helping her into her brother's arms. She slid to the ground, feeling the loss of Malcolm's warmth as a deep ache, just managing to keep her eyes from devouring him as he dismounted beside her.

The rest of the party approached, and chaos reigned for a full ten minutes. Each person required the details of her *harrowing ordeal* from Malcolm's lips, questioned her endlessly over how she fared, asked about the fate of the horse.

It was not that she did not appreciate their concern. In that moment, however, with the taste of Malcolm's kiss lingering on her lips and the overwhelming realization that she was head over heels in love with him ringing through her head, she wanted nothing more than to have a quiet moment to reflect and soak it all in. The small, heated looks Malcolm sent her way did not help either, sending her body into desperate need and muddling her brain in the worst way. Blessedly, the rest of the party seemed to think her distracted state of mind was due to her near fall and did not question it.

They did not seem to think it possible that she could have been involved in something as scandalous and wanton as kissing her rescuer.

She didn't know whether she should feel grateful or insulted.

A new plan for the day was discussed by all and sundry. With her horse gone, the options were discussed loud and long. It was finally determined, with Daphne's clear voice rising above the general buzz of conversation, that they would all ride back for Willowhaven, that Emily would ride up before Drew, and that they would all find other entertainments to get them through the day.

Hearing herself talked of in such a way, as if she were a mere extension of the group that must be dealt with, sent a tingle of outrage down Emily's spine. Turning slowly to face the others, she said, her voice warbling slightly, "I am perfectly capable of walking back to Willowhaven myself. You all go on and finish your ride. I shall be fine."

They all stared at her as if she had opened her mouth and squawked like a chicken. Without waiting for their acquiescence, she turned and marched with purposeful strides back the way they had come.

"But, Emily, you cannot go alone," Daphne called after her, her voice meeker than Emily could remember ever hearing it.

"And why not?" Emily called over her shoulder. "I have ridden and walked over these hills for years and have never lost my way."

Again a stunned kind of silence fell. Emily marched on, picking her way carefully down the gentle rise. Soon the jingle of tackle and the fading sound of horses cantering off reached her ears. She breathed a sigh of relief. They had finally done as she'd wanted and left her in peace.

In a flash, the realization of what she had done hit her. She had stood up for herself at last, had let them all know she was a person in her own right. She smiled, a full-blown smile that pulled at her scar. She had never felt so wonderful. And because she couldn't help herself, she laughed.

"If you have a joke to tell, please share it."

Malcolm's voice so startled her, she jumped and let out an awful squeak. She stopped and spun to face him as he made his way down to where she stood, leading his stallion. "What are you doing here?"

"Seeing you back to the house, if you don't mind my company."

She scowled, some of her pleasure in her burst of courage dimming somewhat. "I can see myself back just fine."

"I know you can," he replied with apparent unconcern. "But I knew your sister would hound you if you did not have an escort, or would team up with your brother, thereby making it much worse on you. I quite liked that little burst of rebellion you showed and didn't wish for them to snuff it out."

Which was horribly presumptuous and wonderfully kind at the same time. So much so that she could not bring herself to be more than mildly annoyed. "It does take away a bit of my victory," she grumbled halfheartedly. "But I suppose you may join me. Though that does not mean," she added hastily, "that I am not fully able to do it alone."

"I know you are," he said with impressive soberness, before ruining the effect by grinning widely. When she glowered at him, he held up a free hand in defense. "No, truly. I have always known you are far more capable than you first appeared, or even what you seemed to believe yourself to be."

"Oh." Overcome and strangely touched, she ducked her head and began walking again. Malcolm quickly fell into step at her side, his horse following placidly behind him, and they walked on for a ways in silence.

Until, once again, he broke that silence.

"I was lying, you know," he murmured.

She shot him a confused sideways glance. "Lying? What about?"

"About joining you because of your sister's insistence that you do not return to Willowhaven alone. I came of my own accord because I wished to walk with you."

She melted. Her insides turned into a puddle of tender aching. "Oh," was all she said again, this time in a whisper.

He reached out and grasped her hand. Her heart leapt in her chest.

"You truly don't mind my presence so much, do you, Emily?"

She gazed down at their clasped hands. "No," she managed.

Then, more strongly, her fingers squeezing his, "No, I don't mind in the least."

He smiled down into her eyes. "Good."

• • •

The remainder of the trip back to Willowhaven was filled with quiet chatter. It did not escape Emily, however, that neither London nor the subject of Daphne and Sir Tristan was mentioned once. Talk veered toward whatever was pleasant, as if they were both afraid to break this fragile peace that had settled between them. He kept her hand in his, releasing it when they came into view of the stables. Emily wasn't sure what to make of this strange place their relationship had taken them. She only knew she was happier than she had been in too long.

Malcolm handed his horse over to a groom, and they moved off together to check that Violet was safely back at the stables. The mare was thankfully suffering no ill effects of her scare. She seemed quite content as a groom brushed her coat, and she accepted the apple Emily offered happily enough.

As Emily and Malcolm walked along the path for home, however, his steps slowed drastically. If she hadn't known better, Emily would have thought he was trying to prolong their time together. A thrill shot through her. She fought to ignore it and failed abysmally.

"What will you do for the remainder of the afternoon?" he asked softly.

"I hardly know," she replied. "It seems I have not had time to myself for ages. I believe I'll check in on my mother first. After that I haven't a clue."

"Perhaps you can take up a new hobby," he suggested, his tone light and teasing, and far from anything she had heard from him before.

She cast a dubious glance up at him. "And what would you suggest?"

"Oh, I don't know. Fencing, maybe? Sword play? I saw some

impressively old weapons hanging in Caleb's study. Mayhap we can take them down and give them a go."

A laugh burst from her lips. "You are being absurd."

"And what is so absurd about it?"

"First off, I haven't the strength to lift those great swords."

He peered down at her, his lips pursed. "Hmm. Yes, you are quite petite. Then we can start you off on something small. A dagger, perhaps? So you can *smite thine enemies* or whatever the saying is."

"And what enemies do you think I have here in Northamptonshire?" she asked as they entered the house, laughter coloring her voice.

"Well, there is that fellow Lord Randall," Malcolm said with a decided twinkle in his dark eyes. "I do believe he could do with some smoting. Or is it smiting?"

Emily chuckled, but her laughter quickly transformed into a gasp of surprise as the man himself exited the drawing room doors just ahead of them.

"It appears the man has come to meet his fate," Malcolm muttered under his breath. "Get out thy dagger, my lady."

"Quiet," she hissed, elbowing him in the side.

"Lord Morley, how fortuitous," Lord Randall called out as he approached. "I have issued an invitation directly to Lady Willbridge and Lady Tarryton but had hoped to extend it in person to you. Oh. Lady Emily," he said, his cool eyes swinging to her. "I didn't see you there."

Emily dipped her head in greeting, more to hide her mortified blush than anything. "Lord Randall," she murmured. Malcolm's arm tensed under her hand and she gave it a warning squeeze.

"As I was saying," Lord Randall went on, "my wife and I have planned an elegant picnic for Monday afternoon. Your hostess has already given her consent to the scheme, and we are quite looking forward to having you all there. But I wished to extend an especial invitation to your lordship."

"And Lady Emily as well, I assume," Malcolm said, his voice chill.

Lord Randall blinked. "Lady Emily?"

"Certainly," Malcolm went on, even as Emily's hand tightened on his arm, desperate for him to stop. "As a daughter of the house, surely you would like to extend your especial invitation to her as well."

"It would be my pleasure," Lord Randall pronounced in a horrible monotone that suggested it was not his pleasure at all. He turned to Emily, his eyes narrowing. "Lady Emily, it would be my honor to have you join our party."

"Certainly," Emily stammered. "I thank you for the invitation and look forward to it."

Malcolm smiled at the man. "You may count us both in, Randall."

Lord Randall could not have looked more nonplussed if he tried. While his lips lifted in a smile, his eyes showed profound confusion. "Very good, my lord. I shall see you in three days' time. And you as well, Lady Emily," he added as an afterthought before, bowing smartly, he strode off.

Emily waited for a moment, listening to the sound of his boots on the polished floor as he departed. Then, her face unbearably hot, she turned to Malcolm. "That was unnecessary," she said, her voice tight and pained in her throat.

"It was not," he declared firmly. "The man has to learn he cannot treat you in such a way."

"He always has," Emily said quietly, her gaze dropping to her toes. "It matters not."

"It matters to me," Malcolm said fiercely. "It matters a great deal."

Stunned, she looked up into his face. His eyes blazed down into hers.

"You matter," he whispered. Then, taking up her hand, he placed a lingering kiss on her knuckles before he spun about, leaving her in the hallway. With a heart that was even more his than it had been before.

Chapter 17

There was something disturbingly sterile about Handel House, Lord Randall's country estate. Malcolm eyed it as the party from Willowhaven made its merry way up the drive Monday morning on the way to the much-lauded picnic. The house was beautiful enough, he supposed, with its brick façade and stone accents. It could be welcoming, a feast for the senses.

If it weren't all so precise.

He frowned. Precise seemed such a pale word, yet he could not think of another to describe the vista laid out before him. Hedges tamed and trimmed just so. The long drive straight as an arrow, lacking any curve or bend. Not a leaf nor stone nor branch out of place. A statue stood dead center to greet any visitors, its copper fittings gleaming and brilliant in the sunlight. Malcolm took in the stone arm holding aloft a deadly-looking spear and the obnoxiously ornate helmet atop the naked centurion's curls. Ares, the god of war. Of course it was, Malcolm thought with a wry twist to his lips. No fanciful creatures for Lord Randall. And there was the man himself, stationed like a reigning monarch in the front portico.

Malcolm pulled his stallion up and turned to gaze upon the carriages trundling up the drive behind him. The men from Willowhaven had taken to horseback for the half hour drive to Handel House. Most of the women, however, had come by carriage. It was the front equipage he eyed now, the one carrying the dowager marchioness and Lady Tarryton.

And Emily.

His heart warmed at the thought of her. Every hour, every

minute he was with her and the warning bells pealing off in his head sounded more and more distant.

As if she could sense his thoughts, her face appeared in the carriage window. She smiled when she saw him, gave a small wave, and ducked back within. Malcolm frowned, for she had looked uncommonly pale. He knew the strain of this visit had to be difficult on her. Lord Randall seemed to go out of his way to make Emily feel small.

Malcolm pressed his lips tight. The man would soon learn that Emily was not a nobody. Especially as Malcolm had decided to make her his viscountess.

The thought had come to him in the small hours of the morning, an idea that had been marinating for the better part of the past four days. Marry Emily. He was a fool not to. She was sweet, and kind, and lovely. He wanted her desperately. And she touched his damaged soul in a way he had not thought possible. Most of all, he cared for her as he had not cared for another in too long.

He could marry her, bring her out from the darkness she had been hiding in for so long.

He watched her carriage pass, caught sight of her again in the window. And all doubt instantly flew like a bird to the sky. His gaze softened as she looked his way.

Then and there, he decided. He would propose that very night.

Happiness filled him until he thought he would burst. Hurrying his horse after her, he dismounted and handed his reins off to a waiting groom, then stood by impatiently as a footman handed her down. In an instant he was at her side, offering his arm.

"Hello," he murmured.

She looked up at him bemusedly. "Hello."

"Did you have a pleasant ride?"

Her mouth twisted. "As pleasant as possible, I suppose," she replied, cutting her gaze to Lady Tarryton, who was taking in the landscape with rapturous—and vociferous—praise.

"I can imagine," he mumbled. "Can you not change carriages on the way back?"

"None of the other ladies wished to ride with her," she explained.

He stared at her. "And so you are the sacrificial lamb?"

She sputtered on a laugh. "You are the worst sort of influence," she scolded, "for I should not be laughing. Or complaining. I should sit meekly and take life's problems with a smile."

"Like a lamb," he said, causing another bout of laughter from her.

"Do lambs smile as the wolf stalks them, then?" she queried archly.

"Of course they do."

"And how would you know?"

"That is quite simple. I am the wolf. Though," he said, his voice lowering, "I admit I'm sorely tempted to turn in my claws for something a bit more...domestic."

Emily's eyes fairly glowed as she gazed up at him. "Are you?"

"I am," he murmured.

She smiled. It took everything in him not to drop to one knee right there and claim her hand on the spot.

Lord Randall spoke, his voice booming out with joviality over the assembled. "I thank you all for coming to my humble home," he said, with a self-deprecating smile that fooled Malcolm not one bit.

"Pompous arse," he said under his breath.

"Malcolm," Emily admonished, laughter in her voice.

"Please excuse the absence of my wife. An old school friend of hers has come for a short visit. They will both be down momentarily, and then we may proceed."

There was the buzz of polite murmurs as Lord Randall finished. The man stepped down into the waiting throng, bowing and smiling benignly on those assembled. When he came to where Malcolm stood with Emily, he stopped.

"I think, my lord, that you will be most pleased to see who we are entertaining, for you know her well."

Malcolm frowned as the man smiled mysteriously and moved on.

"What the devil was that about?" he muttered.

"Do you have an acquaintance in common with Lord Randall, then?" Emily asked.

"No doubt, if he has spent any time in London. I know a great many people, many of them female. But I cannot think who might have gone to school with Lady Randall. With two grown sons, she must be close to fifty if she's a day."

"You are thinking of Lord Randall's first wife. She died some time ago. He is remarried now. His new wife is not above seven and twenty, I would say."

An unexplainable foreboding settled like a weight in his stomach. He had the sudden and inexplicable desire to take Emily's hand and flee. There was no reason for such a reaction, he told himself. And yet he could not seem to shake it.

A commotion arose by the portico. With fatalistic doom, Malcolm turned.

And spied Lydia's sweetly smiling face staring back at him.

A kick to the gut could not have knocked the air so completely from him. She looked the same as she had all those years ago when he had loved her and she had broken his heart. Her figure was tall and lithe, grace personified in the gentle arch of her spine and the long curve of her neck. Hair piled high in a golden array of ringlets he had once wanted to see tumbled down about her shoulder. Face heart-shaped, skin the palest porcelain, full lips he had kissed ardently. And those eyes. They were the clearest blue, angelically innocent.

Or so he had thought. Before she had betrayed him. A treachery made all the worse for who she had betrayed him with.

As if through a tunnel he watched as Lord Randall hurried up the front steps to his wife's side. The party had gone silent as they stared in mild curiosity at the newcomer. All but one. Tristan was looking at Malcolm with a combination of shock and horror.

"Our guest has arrived," Lord Randall announced, "and in grand fashion. Though she is known to at least one of you." Here he looked at Lord Morley with a proud smile. "May I introduce Lady Morley, wife to our dear Lord Morley's late brother."

The group exploded into conversation. Tristan was at his side in an instant.

"Are you all right?" Tristan whispered.

Malcolm watched Lydia as she descended the front steps with Lord and Lady Randall. "Yes," he answered curtly.

His friend gripped his shoulder. It was meant to be comforting, he knew. Instead it made him feel as if he wanted to jump right out of his skin.

"We can leave," Tristan insisted, his voice low and fierce. "I don't give a good damn what anyone might say about it. I'd rather it be remarked on than for you to have to suffer through her presence."

"My lord? Is anything amiss?"

Emily. He had forgotten her for a moment. She looked up at him with wide, confused eyes. Malcolm wanted to simultaneously drag her into his arms and run from here as fast as he could.

Damn it. For one blessed moment he had forgotten Lydia, had forgotten why he needed to shield his heart.

Had believed that maybe, just maybe, he could open it up again. To Emily.

He wanted to weep. He wanted to curse. Instead he stood mute, gazing down at Emily as a horrible numbness spread through him.

Lord Randall approached, Lydia in tow. "My lord," he said with a self-satisfied smile, "you must be surprised by our little deception."

"Deception," Malcolm repeated dumbly, his eyes shifting of their own accord to Lydia.

Lord Randall chuckled in delight. "You were right, my dear," he said to Lydia. "He is completely flummoxed." He returned his attention to Malcolm. "Lady Morley was quite insistent that we surprise you with her presence. And after witnessing your reaction myself, I must say it was a splendid idea. Never have I seen someone so surprised."

"It has been an age, after all, and this is a family reunion of sorts. Isn't that right, Malcolm?" Lydia said with a small smile. He would have thought it affectionate at one time, when he didn't know her character quite so well. Now he knew the woman wasn't capable of softer feelings.

"And, Sir Tristan," she said, transferring her gaze to his friend. "So lovely to see you again."

"Lady Morley," Tristan said stiffly.

Her eyes glinted with a teasing light. "I am glad to see the two of you are still such fast friends after all these years. Though I was surprised to learn that the third corner of your fraternal triangle had set sail on the tide of holy matrimony. Lord Willbridge has become domestic, has he?"

"Just over a sennight now," Lord Randall confirmed when no one else offered the information. "My wife and I were witness to the happy event ourselves."

"How wonderful. I wish him well, then." Just then Lydia seemed to notice their little group contained another. Her gaze shifted to Emily at his side.

Her face took on an immediate change. She blinked and jerked back slightly, her nostrils flaring as she looked Emily over in disbelief. She quickly schooled her features, her brow furrowing delicately as she smiled quizzically at her. "And who is this young lady?"

It all happened so quickly, he might have missed it had he not been watching Lydia so closely. He hoped that Emily had not seen it. Yet when he looked down at her, his stomach fell. There was a faint flush to her cheeks, her chin tucked into her chest, her head tilted to better disguise her scarred cheek. Yes, she had seen Lydia's reaction.

He had the sudden and violent urge to shield her.

"This is Lord Willbridge's sister, Lady Emily Masters," Lord Randall replied once more into the yawning silence. "Lady Emily, Lady Morley."

As the two women acknowledged one another, Lord Randall turned to Malcolm. "My lord, as you and your sister have much catching up to do, why don't you escort Lady Morley to the picnic."

"No."

The one word, said with such force, had every eye turning their way.

Tristan spoke up then. "He has promised Lady Emily his escort."

"Lady Emily?" Lord Randall's voice was colored with amused relief. "You wouldn't mind releasing Lord Morley from his promise, would you, my dear? After all, he has not seen his sister in an age. And she is only here for the day. It would be a lovely chance for them to reconnect."

A spurt of rage broke through the numbing cloud Malcolm had found himself in since clapping eyes on Lydia. A scathing retort rose in his throat. Emily's hasty response cut him off.

"Certainly, Lord Morley. Please feel free to see to your sister."

He frowned. "I would not dream of breaking a promise."

"There was no promise given," she replied, smiling slightly, though it did not reach her eyes. "And I cannot hold you to an assumption. Please," she continued, quietly but insistently, when he made to stand firm on escorting her once again, "I would not hear of you refusing Lady Morley your company."

She was being polite. That was her, unfailingly kind, always looking to cause the least ripples in the pond. That thing in him that had awakened with her and had gone into hiding with Lydia's presence stirred again.

He should fight the suggestion of escorting Lydia, should insist on accompanying Emily. Eventually he would win out over her innate politeness. But he would not draw unwanted attention to Emily, something she abhorred above all else. And so instead he placed a hand at her back, leaned in toward her. "I will see you at the picnic, then?"

The smile reached her eyes then. "Oh yes."

He reluctantly turned to Lydia, offering her his arm. "It appears you have an escort, madam."

She smiled brightly, slipping her hand into the crook of his elbow. But it was the too-knowing glint in her eyes, the thoughtful look she sent Emily's way, that turned his blood to ice. Suddenly desperate to get Lydia as far from Emily as possible, he turned and led her away.

Chapter 18

"How have you been, Malcolm?"

They headed the party that was tramping across the manicured lawn to the picnic grounds, as per Lord Randall's directions. Malcolm kept his gaze on the great sea of white tents in the distance and fought to keep his features even as distaste roiled through him. He would not lose his composure, would not allow Lydia to see how she affected him.

That did not mean, however, that he would not let her know what he thought of this little deception she had perpetrated.

"Are you truly going to pretend that this is simply a casual meeting, Lydia? You must know that I would rather be anywhere but here right now."

Her light laugh grated on him. "Of course, which is the reason for my little ruse, you silly man," she said. "Though you mustn't think I came here for the express purpose of seeing you. No, this trip was planned long ago. This chance meeting is simply a bonus."

"A bonus." He glared down at her serene profile. "I would hardly call it that."

"To me, it is."

The purr in her voice, instead of softening him to her, made his skin crawl. Especially as he was painfully aware that at one time he had lived for such a tone from her.

"What are you about?" he demanded. "You must be fully aware that any further communication between us is abhorrent to me. I told you as much after Bertram died. There can be nothing more we have to say to each other. You inherited a more than substantial property and allowance upon my brother's death and can need nothing further of me. Anything you do require can be handled through my solicitor."

Her rosy lips turned down into a little moue. "Can I not merely wish to see you, Malcolm? We used to be so much to one another at one time, after all."

"Yes, we did," he bit out. "Before you cuckolded me with my own brother. Before I found out that every word you spoke to me was a lie to reel in a bigger fish."

The shift in her expression was immediate. Though her smile stayed fixed, her eyes went cold as ice. "All that is water under the bridge, Malcolm," she stated with disturbing calm. "Can we not get past that?"

Get past it? Malcolm pressed his lips together to stop the searing retort that fought to break free. If it were as easy as that, he would, in a heartbeat.

"Lady Emily is an...interesting creature."

The abrupt change of subject caught Malcolm off guard. "Do not call her a creature as if she were an animal in a menagerie," he snapped. The reaction had been instinctual—and much too revealing, he saw, as she turned her sly gaze up to him. Once again his blood congealed, fairly frozen in his veins. Something settled in the muscles of his back, and it took a moment for Malcolm to name it: dread.

"She is much to you, then." It was not a question. She always had been too clever for her own good.

Take care, a voice in his head warned, *or she will target Emily with her cruelties.* "She is the sister of my closest friend, and so it would seem odd if she weren't."

She arched one perfectly manicured brow. "You are implying she is like a sister to you?"

"Of course she is."

"And nothing more?"

He sent up a silent apology for the lie he was about to tell. "No, nothing more."

She nodded slowly and looked away. Did she believe him? He prayed she did, for there was no telling what havoc she might create in that devious mind of hers.

Out of the corner of his eye, he caught sight of Emily's flaming hair as she walked along on Tristan's arm. She was so different from Lydia, so innocent and pure and good. She would never betray him.

But wasn't that what he had thought of Lydia when he had first begun to fall under her spell?

He recalled it now, those cornflower blue eyes that had seemed so open and honest. Her innocence that had him wanting to at once protect her and claim her for his own. For months he had courted her, stealing kisses from her honeyed lips, sending her ridiculous poems declaring his unswerving love. When he had told his brother of his intention to marry her, Bertram had shown such reluctance to give his consent to the match. Malcolm had been too young, he'd declared, too unsettled in life to take on the responsibilities of a wife. Surely, Malcolm had thought, his brother could not fail to allow it once he got to know Lydia, a paragon of goodness and beauty.

How little he had understood human nature, he thought, bitterness settling like acid in his gut even after all these years.

He had worn that betrayal like a suit of armor since then, keeping people at bay, keeping his heart untouched. Emily's sweetness and purity, however, had begun to wear away at his defenses. Hell, he had been damn near close to proposing to her.

The thought nearly had him stumbling. What the devil was he thinking? Would he allow Lydia to ruin his future with Emily now? The woman had already poisoned the bond he'd had with his brother, had destroyed forever that most important relationship. He would not give her sway in his life any longer. He would propose to Emily and leave Lydia and her cruelty behind him once and for all.

• • •

Emily wished she could enjoy the day. The picnic was everything Lord Randall had promised and more. Set up on a bluff, it commanded magnificent views of the rolling countryside. Along one side, the River Spratt meandered through. Upon the other, bucolic sheep dotted hillsides blanketed in hues of brilliant emerald, jade, and sage. Great white tents provided shade from the warm afternoon sun, rugs spread out beneath them and covered in all manner of tables and chairs. A small army of footmen were about to see to every comfort imaginable. Off to one side, a young woman played a harp, the gentle strains breaking over the gathered guests and providing a tranquil backdrop.

Emily was blind to it all, for she could not keep her eyes from Malcolm.

His attitude had changed drastically from the friendly, even intimate banter of that morning. Then, she had been sure they had been close to something wonderful. The hope she had felt when she had looked into his smiling eyes and listened to him talk of a wolf trading in his claws for something more domestic had been glorious. Surely, she had thought, this was leading somewhere she had never dreamed possible. Could she be so lucky as to have him care for her?

Yet in the hours since Lady Morley's arrival, he had been a changed man.

Emily eyed that woman now. She was holding court beneath one of the tents, perched on a plush settee as if it were the finest throne. Surrounding her were all manner of gentlemen, many who had been paying court to Daphne and Mariah for the past weeks.

She couldn't blame them their sudden infatuation. Lady Morley was all that was graceful and ethereal. Every movement was a study in beauty, a score by the master composers come to life in flesh and bone. As she watched, the woman gave a husky laugh. She was a creature of contrast, for while there was all that seemed angelic about her, there was also a knowing look in her eyes as well, a surety in her manner that was like temptation in the famed garden itself.

Emily had learned long ago that no good came from comparing herself to others that were more blessed in looks and manners. That hard-won knowledge, however, was suffering temporary amnesia at Lady Morley's presence.

She settled deeper into the wingback chair she had earlier taken refuge in. There was something about Lady Morley that had seemed to deeply disturb Malcolm. Oh, he had attempted to hide it with bland, bored looks and a calm demeanor. Most, she knew, would not have seen a difference in him. Emily, however, was not most people. Her shyness had lent her a sensitivity to others that many lacked. The person in question being Malcolm, she possessed an even greater awareness.

That man was even now in deep discussion with Sir Tristan some distance away, close to the edge of the bluff and away from the bustle of the elegant tents. Just then, Malcolm's gaze cut to where Lady Morley sat. His lips thinned, his brows lowering over already stormy eyes.

Yes, he was definitely affected by the woman's presence.

His conversation with Sir Tristan seemed to make him more agitated. After what appeared to be one final biting remark, Malcolm broke away from his friend and began to stride across the ground toward a copse of trees.

Emily chewed at her lip. Though he had expressed a desire to spend time with her, he had been glaringly absent from her side throughout the picnic. Not that she expected him to be in her pocket. He had other friends, other commitments; yet she couldn't shake the idea that he was keeping away from her on purpose.

She eyed Lady Morley again. To her surprise, she was looking at her in a very direct manner. A trickle of unease worked its way up Emily's spine. The woman held her gaze for the briefest moment, one of her numerous admirers capturing it in short order. But Emily could not shake the feeling that there had been something altogether predatory in that look.

Which was ridiculous, Emily thought. What interest could she hold for a woman such as Lady Morley?

She thought again of Malcolm's reaction to the woman. And was surprised at the spurt of jealousy that soured her stomach. But she was a fool to be jealous of her. There was nothing between the two of them. Lady Morley was his brother's widow. That in itself was a good enough reason for his altered spirits. She must remind him painfully of the brother he lost. Yes, that was it surely.

Well, she knew a thing or two about losing a brother. She gripped the arms of her chair and pushed from her seat, quickly following in the direction she had last seen Malcolm. She would lend an ear if he would let her and hopefully take away some of the pain he was feeling in the process.

• • •

Thus far Malcolm had managed to keep away from Emily throughout the afternoon. After Lydia's interest in her, he had known evasion would be imperative to protect Emily from the other woman's poison. He could not let Lydia see again what Emily was to him.

He had not expected how difficult such a thing would be.

He paced the small clearing he had taken refuge in, a last-ditch attempt to keep from searching Emily out. Tristan had not been helpful in the least. He'd actually had the nerve to demand he not shun Emily. Did the man think he was doing it willingly? That he could see any other option?

Malcolm took up a branch from the ground, swinging it through the air, lopping off several unsuspecting leaves from a nearby bush. The action was oddly satisfying. Taking up the proper fencing position, he lunged forward, spearing the bush with a practiced thrust before slicing this way and that. Leaves flew through the air, a sacrifice to his frustration.

"I did not realize you were such an accomplished swordsman."

The unexpected voice, soft and achingly familiar, jolted him as nothing else could. He straightened, the stick falling to the ground. He could almost hear the bush sigh in relief as its branches settled from his onslaught.

"Emily. How did you find me?"

She blushed, staying where she was on the far side of the clearing. Her fingers gripped one another. A new habit, he knew, since he had called her out on her tendency to press her hand to her cheek.

"I was watching you," she admitted.

He softened at the admission. "Were you?"

She nodded, her eyes luminous in the dappled light.

A thought occurred then. If she was watching him, others could have been as well. Namely one other. And if Lydia were to find him and Emily alone, there was no telling what mischief she could do. He straightened, his gaze sweeping the foliage behind her. "Did anyone follow you?"

She frowned before, with a glimmer of understanding, her face cleared. "No, no one followed me. We are quite safe from discovery." Her lips quirked humorlessly. "You've no need to fear I will be compromised by being found alone with you."

Is that what she thought he feared? Little did she know, he didn't give a damn about that at all. But how could he tell her the truth, that he feared them being found by Lydia?

And so, instead of answering, he went to her, taking her in his arms, capturing her lips with his own. She turned pliant in an instant, sighing into his mouth. Her clever fingers ran up his chest, splayed across his cheeks, threaded back into his hair, as if she were playing him like her pianoforte.

He responded as the instrument would, his body singing with every light touch, every dance of her fingers across his skin. He groaned, his tongue delving into her mouth. Gripping her bottom in both hands, he pressed her up and into the proof of his desire, reveling in the answering shudder her body gave.

He could have stayed like that forever, kissing her into oblivion. All too soon, however, she pulled away, just enough to look him in the eye.

"That was not why I followed you, you know," she said, her body still arched into his.

"I'd say it's a damned brilliant reason," he growled, trying to capture her lips again.

She gave a breathy chuckle, turning her head so his lips landed on her jaw instead. "Malcolm," she admonished, though amusement and something altogether husky and delicious colored the word.

"Emily," he murmured as he ran his lips down the long length of her throat.

She moaned, her head falling back. But she was more determined to have her say than he gave her credit for. Soon her hands were planted firmly on his shoulders and she pushed out of his arms.

"We really should talk, Malcolm."

"Talking is overrated." He reached for her, but his fingers barely brushed the material of her gown as she took a hasty step back. "You are entirely too nimble for my liking just now, madam," he grumbled.

She did not laugh as he thought she might. Instead her eyes had taken on a decidedly serious cast. "We really must talk," she insisted again.

All playfulness immediately left him. He eyed her uneasily. "I don't see what could possibly be so important."

"Don't you?" When he did not answer, she gave a small sigh. "I saw your reaction to Lady Morley, Malcolm."

He nearly blanched. "I'm sure I don't know what you're referring to," he hedged, suddenly unable to meet her eyes.

Her hand was on his arm in an instant. "Malcolm," she said, her voice unbearably gentle. "Do you think I would not see how she affects you?"

"I think," he bit out, pulling away from her touch, "that you have an active imagination."

She followed him as he moved across the clearing, more dogged than he had ever seen her. He could not fail to see the irony in it, for hadn't he been the one who had worked so tirelessly to make certain she was never cowed again?

"You are affected by her," she said, cornering him between two bushes. "And I think I know why."

His lungs suddenly stopped working, his skin going clammy as he pressed back into the foliage. It took him a moment to realize that what he was feeling was panic. Panic that she knew the darkest secret in his soul: that he had once loved Lydia, had wanted her, with every ounce of his being. And, worse than that, even after she had married his brother, even after he had begun to hate her more desperately than he had loved her, he had wanted her still.

Shame filled him then. That Emily, who was all goodness and light, could see this depraved corner of his soul.

Then she spoke. "She reminds you of your brother, does she not?"

He looked at her then, his mouth falling open. "I'm sorry?"

"She must remind you of the brother you lost. I know full well how such memories can affect one. How they drag down on your spirits until the grief is almost as strong as the day of your loss."

Relief saturated him, nearly buckling his knees. She thought this was about losing Bertram?

He stood stupidly for a time, too overcome to form words. She took hold of his hand then, pulling him to a nearby boulder, tugging him down to sit beside her.

"Perhaps it would help to talk of him," she suggested. "I know when I miss Jonathan, talking about him to Daphne or my mother helps considerably. And though I did not know your brother, I can be a friendly ear to bend should you wish it, for with my own loss I can commiserate with whatever you may be feeling regarding yours."

He stared at her. "You wish me to talk of Bertram?"

"If you wish it." She looked at him expectantly, folding her hands patiently in her lap.

Talk of Bertram? He frowned. That was not something he had done since the man had taken Lydia to wife. Ever since he discovered that his brother, the one person who had been there for him through all the heartache and turmoil of life, had cared so little for him that he had betrayed him in the worst possible way.

Emily must have sensed his distaste at the idea. She straightened, turning more fully toward him. "Shall I tell you a story?"

"A story?"

She wasn't at all put off by the brusque reply. Instead she nodded, smiling, that wonderfully crooked smile of hers. "Yes, a story. Granted, it is a true story. But a story all the same."

He eyed her uncertainly. "Very well."

"It is about a brother and sister. Twins, actually. One full of life and joy, the other quite shy."

Her smile softened, her eyes taking on a faraway look. He imagined what she must be seeing just then, her brother Jonathan as he had been, all bounding enthusiasm and that shock of Masters copper hair.

"The boy was forever getting into scrapes, you see," she continued. "And his sister, though much more careful, never failed to follow right along, as she loved him that much.

"One day, the boy decided on a particularly naughty prank. Wouldn't it be grand, he said, to let all of the chickens into the house? He imagined the rooster crowing at the break of dawn, waking his parents and siblings. He laughed at the idea of chickens infiltrating every inch of the house, of them laying eggs in cupboards and causing havoc in the drawing room, of finding them sitting in shoes and hiding under tables. Nothing the girl said could dissuade him, for he was a stubborn creature. And so, in the middle of the night, the two children snuck out to the chicken coop and opened the gate. Little knowing that chickens are not the most biddable creatures. They did not listen even once as the children bade them to follow. Instead the birds were incredibly incensed, and rightly so, having been woken most rudely from a peaceful night's sleep. Those horrid chickens ran hither and thither, right out the gate and into the woods beyond."

Malcolm burst forth in an unexpected laugh. He could imagine it all as she described it. He remembered well Jonathan and his propensity for mischief. Emily, eyes dancing, gave him an answering smile.

"You can imagine the uproar it caused the following morning, when the chicken coop was found empty," she continued. "That was made even worse when it was realized there would be no eggs for their breakfasts. The children's parents, of course, knew where to lay the blame. The boy was known for his pranks, after all, and this had all the flavor of his particular brand of devilment. They railed at him in the most awful way, promising all sorts of dire punishments. They would, they vowed, send him straight into the navy as a cabin boy, never to be heard from again.

"The girl could not know her parents' threats were empty. She only saw life without her best friend by her side. She swore she was the one at fault, that she had visited the chickens the night before, bringing them the vegetables from her dinner so she did not have to eat them, and she had left the gate open by mistake. Her parents believed her, as she was never one to lie. And so her brother was saved from a fate certainly worse than death."

Malcolm chuckled. "And what became of the poor chickens?"

"Most were recovered, thank goodness, though I suspect several met a wily fox in the woods and made a delicious meal for him."

They laughed, the happy sound bouncing about their leafy bower. As their mirth subsided, a thoughtful melancholy washed over him. He took up her hand, rubbing his thumb over her knuckles. "Why did you tell me that story, Emily?"

"Because I wanted you to see that talking of those who have left us can help ease the grief. We will never be completely free of it, especially if we have loved them dearly. But for a time we can look on the happier memories and remember them with joy." She paused. "I have never told another person that story, you know."

"What, no one?"

She shook her head. "It was something Jonathan and I vowed to keep between us."

"Why did you tell me?"

There was no mistaking her heart in her eyes. "I think you must know."

He longed to drag her back into his arms then, to propose to her right then and there. But something held him back. Their life together should not begin while Lydia was around. He would not have their engagement tainted in any way by her.

But he would not wait much longer, he vowed.

She squeezed his hand, jolting him from pleasant thoughts of her in his bed. "Tell me of your brother," she said softly.

He sighed. "What is there to tell? He is dead. There is no bringing him back."

"There is plenty to tell," she urged.

When he stayed silent, she persisted. Stubborn little minx.

"You and he were quite close, weren't you? I remember you talking of him when I was a child."

"Yes, we were close," he admitted almost reluctantly. She looked at him in expectation and he let out a breath. "You are not going to give up, are you?"

She shook her head, laughter dancing in her eyes.

"Fine." He frowned. "Yes, Bertram and I were close. Exceptionally close. Our parents died when I was six and he eight. And so we only had each other."

"Where did you go? Who cared for you?"

"My uncle." The mere memory of that man left a bitter taste in Malcolm's mouth. "Though 'cared for' is not a term I would use."

Emily frowned. "I don't understand."

"My uncle was not a kind man. He was jealous of my father. I suspect he secretly wished my brother and I would follow him to the grave, so he might get his hands on the title and all that came with it. Instead he was forced to take us in, to look on the two creatures that separated him from everything he ever wanted. Needless to say, this did not lead to a loving, nurturing environment."

He glanced at her face then, saw her grief. He should not have unloaded the burden of that part of his past on her, for she was entirely too sensitive and would take it to heart. Desperate to relieve the heaviness of the moment and bring a smile back to her face, he dragged in a deep breath and tried to think of the happy moments of those too-dark years.

"That did not mean, however, that it was completely unbearable. I had Bertram, after all. He was great fun. I recall one time he looted our uncle's attic and found trunks of musty, moth-eaten clothes. He dragged them down to the nursery and we spent an entire week dressing up as our favorite historical figures, acting out scenes of battles and intrigue. When we tired of dressing up, he spent whole afternoons cutting up those garments, fashioning puppets from the cloth to entertain me. Needless to say, Uncle was not happy that our ancestors' clothing had been destroyed in such a manner."

He chuckled. And immediately stilled, shocked. He had not thought of that in years, was surprised at the joy it gave him.

"It sounds wonderfully fun," Emily said.

Malcolm cleared his throat. "Er, yes. Yes, it was." Now that he had allowed one memory through, however, a whole barrage insisted on letting themselves be known. Images flashed with dizzying speed through his mind, of Bertram taking him on hikes through the woods, Bertram teaching him to fish, Bertram reading him stories at night when he woke from nightmares.

He had forgotten, in the years of bitterness, how much Bertram had cared for him. Even though he had been just two years Malcolm's elder, he had taken on all the cares and responsibilities of a parent. He had been forced to grow up much too soon, yet he had done it uncomplainingly.

But he stole Lydia from you, he reminded himself. *He betrayed you in the worst way.* Yet the feeling of betrayal that such a reminder typically brought about in him was muted. He gazed down at Emily bemusedly. Had she done that? Had she woven her quiet magic about him and begun to heal the gaping wound that had festered in his breast for so long?

She smiled. "I'm glad you shared that with me."

"I am, too," he replied. And was surprised to find he actually meant it.

Chapter 19

Emily took particular care with her appearance that evening. Before they had left their quiet bower to rejoin the picnic, Malcolm had hinted quite boldly at their future. A future that was looking brighter by the second. Was it possible that he might propose? Even this very night?

The one thing dimming her joy had been his insistence to keep separate the remainder of the afternoon. It had seemed a strange request when he had made it. But Emily comforted herself with the certainty that he must want to do things properly, seeing as she was sure he would ask her to marry him.

And so, as Emily descended to the drawing room to join the party before dinner, her step was lighter than it had ever been. She fairly floated through the house, a small smile lifting her lips.

Until she stepped through the doors and caught sight of Lady Morley across the room. With Malcolm.

Her feet faltered on the plush carpet. She should not be so affected by the woman's presence here. It was the polite thing to do, after all, to invite her tonight after making her acquaintance that afternoon. That knowledge did not make seeing her any easier, however. She was as stunning as she had been that afternoon. No, even more beautiful, if it could be believed. The candlelight gave her an angelic glow, caressing her alabaster skin, turning her hair to spun gold. As Emily continued to stare, the viscountess spied her. Her full lips turned up in a small, knowing smile before she turned back to Malcolm. He did not look her way; his gaze instead stayed fixed and intent on Lady Morley.

Emily shivered, suddenly chilled to the bone. She tore her gaze away but was immediately confronted with her own image in the bevel-edged mirror across the room. Even from this distance, she could see how pale her cheeks had become, how angry the scar looked, a crimson slash across her cheek. She pressed her lips tight, felt the puckered skin tighten and pull.

Needing to move, to hide, Emily scurried to the side of the room. Why the woman had such an effect on her she didn't know. Mayhap it was the residue of Malcolm's own reaction. Though he did not seem nearly as opposed to being in the woman's presence as he had that afternoon. Which should have been a positive change. Perhaps their talk had done him some good and he had been able to put aside his grief for his brother. As she tucked herself into the corner, however, she could not help thinking that his totally focused attention—and Lady Morley's open flirtatiousness—made her extremely uneasy.

She remembered again her initial suspicion that there was something more between them. And as before, she dismissed it. This was his brother's widow, after all.

The idea was slow to leave her this time.

Just then her mother approached, tearing her from her troubled thoughts. "Emily, dearest, you are looking exceptionally lovely tonight."

"Thank you, Mama," Emily murmured distractedly. "You invited Lady Morley?"

"Actually, Lady Tarryton did." Her mother's lips twisted in amusement. "Not that I mind in the slightest. It was the polite thing to do, seeing as she is in the area until tomorrow, and is so closely related to our dear Lord Morley." She frowned then, peering closely at Emily. "But you look pale. Are you sure you're well?"

"Of course," Emily was quick to assure her.

Her mother's frown deepened. "Are you certain? You look peaked. I know this house party has been hard on you, though you seemed to have improved in the last few days. Perhaps you should take dinner in your room tonight. I would hate for you to grow ill from the strain of all this."

It was a bit of irony—and a testament to how much Lady Morley had affected her—that her mother chose this moment to grant permission to escape. Emily knew she worried for her. And at any other time she would have taken the suggestion without hesitation.

Her gaze drifted to Malcolm, still deep in conversation with Lady Morley. Now, though, the idea of leaving, of hiding away, made her positively panicked.

"I'm well, truly, Mama." She smiled, hoping to put her mother at ease, to distract her from the scent of her very real but completely unfounded fear.

Blessedly, her mother nodded. "Very well, dear heart." Her attention was captured then by something across the room. "I'd best see to our guests. I shall see you later." Cupping Emily's cheek, she moved off.

Emily took a moment to compose herself. If her mother had noticed how upset she was, others would as well. She had her pride, after all. She did not want people looking on her with pity any longer. Not now that things looked so promising with Malcolm and she might even become his wife.

The joy from before was tempered now. Dismayed, she searched him out. To her shock, he was nowhere to be found. And Lady Morley was headed her way.

She started. The woman had no reason to seek her out. Perplexed, her insides pulling as taut as a pianoforte string, she watched with apprehension as the woman approached.

"Lady Emily," the woman said with a smile, "how perfectly lovely to see you again."

Emily dipped into a shallow curtsy. "Lady Morley."

The viscountess positioned herself in front of Emily, effectively trapping her in the corner. Emily fought down the feeling of being buried alive.

"I was so happy to receive the generous invitation to join you all here this evening," Lady Morley said. "I have so longed to see Willowhaven since your dear brother spoke of it to me."

"You know Caleb?" Emily could not help the question.

"Long ago. My goodness, it seems an age since I saw him last. I regret not seeing him for this visit, though I am happy that he has found such joy in his marriage. The new Lady Willbridge, I hear, is a gem among women. Everyone gives her only the highest praise."

She should warm to the woman after such a speech. So why did she feel the need to escape with all haste? Eyeing her warily as one might a growling dog, she said, "Yes, Imogen is all that is lovely."

Lady Morley's smile widened, showing a flash of white teeth. "Wonderful. I hope that his two closest friends are equally blessed in their own marriages. Though," she said with a wicked little smile, "I will admit that the very idea of Malcolm settling so happily turns me positively green with jealousy."

Emily frowned. "You wish your brother an unhappy future?"

"Why, my dear, you refer to him as my brother as if we are blood relations."

"You are his late brother's wife. It is close enough, I would think."

The woman's tinkling laugh stabbed at Emily like poisoned barbs. "Oh, darling, not even close. And thank God for that."

Emily felt sick. "You mean you and Malc—er, Lord Morley? But...that is not even legal."

"You think I mean to marry him? You sweet, innocent thing."

Lady Morley reached out, her slender fingers taking hold of one of the tendrils of hair that Emily had let trail loose in an attempt to capture Malcolm's eye. Emily shivered, disgust wrapping like tentacles about her as the woman tugged on it.

"Though no one can be that naïve," the viscountess continued bemusedly. "Your face is pretty despite your scar. Some man must have overlooked it enough to get you alone for a thorough kissing. You cannot be unaware that there are certain...things...that can be done without the trappings of a wedding ring." She grinned. "Surely there is someone here that has captured your fancy. Shall I help you secure his interest?"

Emily shook her head sharply, dislodging the hand from her

hair. She ignored the woman's suggestion—and the amusement that colored it, as if helping Emily gain a man's attentions was a great joke—and frowned. "I repeat myself. Lord Morley is your husband's brother. You cannot wish for such a thing." A sick feeling settled in her stomach at the mere thought of Malcolm in this woman's arms.

"Do I wish for it? Darling, I've known dear Malcolm for ever so long, well before I married my Bertram. He was a delicious thing even then. Do you think I could have denied him, as young and untutored as I was? And he was ever so persuasive. It surprises me not one bit that he turned out to be the rake he is." She laughed, the sound low and throaty and knowing.

The implication hit Emily with all the force of a slap. She very nearly blanched. But she must be mistaken. The woman could not mean what Emily thought she meant.

In the next moment, however, Lady Morley cast those desperate doubts to the ground. "He loved me quite desperately at one time. But I could not help my feelings for my dear Bertram. It quite broke my heart to refuse Malcolm, especially as he was so impassioned in his pleas that I accept him instead of his brother."

The room spun. Emily laid her hands flat on the wall behind her to steady herself. "Where is Malcolm?" she rasped. In her distress, she was beyond caring that she might give something away to this woman.

"Gone to drink with the other men. But, darling," Lady Morley said, tilting her head as she studied Emily, "you aren't looking at all well. Poor dear, this must all be so much for you. Perhaps you'd best rest before we go into dinner." She smiled, laid a hand on Emily's arm. "I'm ever so glad we had a chance to talk."

With that, she walked off, leaving Emily to her lonely corner.

Unable to hold herself up a moment longer, Emily lurched into the closest chair. She should not have let the woman affect her so much, should not feel this burning jealousy. So Malcolm had loved her once. But their romance had been long ago. The woman may have voiced her desires to start up intimacies again with Malcolm, but that did not mean he would have her. After all, he could not possibly still be in love with Lady Morley. Not after she had married his brother.

Especially not after the way he had kissed Emily that afternoon, as if they were the only two people on earth.

Even so, she could not seem to focus on that beautiful memory. Instead she remembered how he had refused to be near her when the others were around, how he had voiced his insistence to stay separated until they were back on Willowhaven grounds.

How his mood had altered the moment he had seen Lady Morley.

She had believed it had been the reminder of his brother, the grief of losing him. And he had not corrected her. He had let her blather on about remembering the dead and finding joy despite the grief, when all along it had been his unrequited love for Lady Morley that had affected him.

Her body heated with shame. *Of course he had loved Lady Morley.* The woman was everything a man would want. And Emily was...not.

But she was being a fool. She was letting the woman get to her. Yes, Malcolm was a rake. Yes, he had no doubt had many affairs over the years. But she was convinced he cared for her now. He could not have been playing with her all this time.

Though mayhap it had just been the romance of the wedding that had carried him away, a small voice in her head whispered. Maybe, just maybe, seeing Lady Morley again reminded him of what he could have. Instead of settling for her.

No, she reprimanded herself severely, forcing herself to recall the look in his eyes as he'd pulled her close that afternoon. He was not playing with her. And he would prove it this evening. He would walk into the room and smile at her. And she would have no doubt that she meant something to him.

Malcolm entered then, as if she had willed him into being. His sharp gaze scanned the room, stopping briefly on Lady Morley, before finishing a circuit of the room and finding her in her lonely corner. She straightened, a desperate anticipation making her heart pound in her ears.

He nodded, his eyes somber, and proceeded to make his way to Sir Tristan's side without a second glance her way.

The hopes that had bloomed like spring flowers in her breast shriveled then, as if a cold winter wind had robbed them of their very lives. And she wondered numbly if she would ever be warm again.

· · ·

The meal was done, and a good portion of the evening had been whiled away in the typical inane conversations and insipid music from the debutantes by the time Malcolm decided it was time to make a short escape from the drawing room. He could not look one more minute on Emily's lovely face without rushing to her side, to hell with Lydia and her damnable presence.

Yet that woman's pointed stares at Emily, and the cunning glances she sent his way, told him all he needed to know. She had not given up on the idea that Emily meant something to him. His one hope in protecting Emily was to make sure it stayed that, an idea, in Lydia's head. She certainly would not create mischief over a mere assumption.

He hurried a short distance down the hall, slowing as he passed the billiard room. The deep buzz of conversation reached him, and the sharp crack as balls made contact on the baize tabletop. He could enter, immerse himself in conversation and company.

But what he needed was privacy. To set his mind to rights and comfort himself with some of Willbridge's fine whiskey and the knowledge that Lydia would be gone by dawn. And so he went to the one place he was sure he would find what he needed: Willbridge's study.

The room was dark and quiet, the sound of the partygoers a distant hum now. He shrugged out of his coat, then hurried to the hearth and quickly lit a fire. Once he had a merry little blaze snapping away, bathing the room in a faint orange glow, he strode to the cabinet in the corner and helped himself to what was within. The liquor burned all the way down into his gut, warming the chill in his bones. A chill Lydia had created. Damn, but the woman was the very devil, wrapped up in rosy cheeks and golden ringlets.

As if the very thought of her could summon her, she was suddenly there in the doorway. She smiled her slow smile. "I had wondered where you had gone off to," she fairly purred, slinking into the room, closing the door behind her.

"I have told you once already this evening, madam," he growled, his fingers tightening around the cut glass in his hand as she approached. "I want you to stay out of my way."

"Oh, you don't mean it," she pouted.

"I do." To prove the point, he slammed the glass down on Caleb's desk and made to leave.

She stepped in his path, her hands out, effectively blocking him. "No, don't leave."

"We have nothing to say to each other."

"You will not even let me apologize?"

He laughed, the sound harsh and echoing. "You have never apologized in your life."

"Well I am now. I had thought you had gotten over me, you see. I did not know my presence here would affect you as it did."

"You give yourself too much importance. You are nothing to me, madam."

Her cornflower blue eyes, glowing orange in the firelight, widened. She tugged at a strand of her hair, dislodging a pale lock, wrapping it around her fingers. "Oh, now, there's no need to be cruel, Malcolm."

"You have not seen even a portion of what I am capable of," he snapped.

"Oh, stop being such a surly beast. Can't you see I wish to make up?" Her fingers skimmed up his chest, tugging at his waistcoat, tangling in his cravat, sending the careful folds into complete disarray.

Disgust at her touch roiled through him. He glared down at her, fighting the violent urge to push her away. But he had never struck a woman, and he wasn't about to start now. "Remove your hands from my person at once."

"In a moment," she murmured before, with a move as quick as lightning, she pushed up on her toes and pressed her lips to his.

He wrenched away from her, wiping his hand across his mouth. "Enough of your mischief, madam."

"You will not even accept a parting kiss of friendship? Very well, you horrid man." She pouted. "I shall leave you to your lonely splendor."

He watched her go, a sudden exhaustion sapping him. The woman was a menace. He ran his hands through his hair, tugging at the strands in frustration before, with a sigh, he returned to his drink. Finding the glass empty, he poured himself another healthy measure. He would take any help he could to get through tonight. Though surely, he thought as he dropped into a chair before the hearth and took a swig, things could not get any worse than they were.

• • •

Emily was painfully aware of Malcolm's every movement for the entirety of the evening, as she waited in vain for him to acknowledge her beyond the brief nod of greeting. But he never did. Oh, he looked her way often. But never once did he approach or offer her anything in the way of friendly overtures. Certainly nothing close to the affection he had shown her that afternoon. And as the night wore on, she felt herself shrinking back into the shell of a creature she used to be.

More than once, she told herself she was being foolish. It meant nothing. But why else had his attentions shifted so drastically, if not due to a change of feelings on his part?

She busied herself as best she could. She would not be seen mooning after him. But even as she tried to immerse herself in a book, she saw from the corner of her eye as he left the drawing room. Moments later, after a sly look around the room, Lady Morley followed.

Emily sat frozen. Surely it was coincidence. There could be any number of reasons for the two of them to leave the room practically together. But no matter how she tried to give rationale to it, her mind kept spinning back to her conversation with Lady Morley. The woman wanted Malcolm. She had left no doubt as to that. But he did not want her. He *could* not want her.

She kept to her seat, her gaze on the door. They would return at any moment. Yet as the minutes ticked by, the small spark of hope in her breast threatened to go out entirely. Desperate now, she rose and strode for the door. She would see for herself that the very idea of Malcolm and Lady Morley together was foolish. She would prove once and for all that there was nothing between them.

Once in the hall, she found it deserted. Which way had they gone? She stood there, undecided. Frustrated, she very nearly returned to the drawing room when she saw it, a door opening down the hall. Caleb's study, she knew. Suddenly Lady Morley appeared and started back to the drawing room.

There was a flushed look to her face, her hair in disarray. She looked, Emily thought with dread, as if she had just been kissed.

The woman spotted her then. "Oh! Lady Emily. I am so happy I have run into you, for I cannot contain my happiness a moment longer."

Emily shook her head. "Where is Malcolm?" she rasped.

"I have just come from him." She sighed happily. "To think, after so many years, he still cares for me. Oh! But you must promise to keep it a secret. There is a girl here who has the most embarrassing infatuation with him and he doesn't wish to hurt her."

Spots began to swim in Emily's vision. "Is there?"

"Yes. The poor thing told him this sad little story about her brother and a prank and chickens." She laughed. "Can you imagine? Telling a worldly man like Malcolm such a thing? She could not have been more pathetic if she tried. But I'd best be off. Ladies retiring room, you know." With a wink she left.

Emily could not breathe. No, he would not have told the story about Jonathan. Yet no matter how she tried to reason, she knew there was no other way Lady Morley could have known about it. She stared stupidly at the study door. *Turn back*, she told herself in desperation. Her body, traitor that it was, would not listen to the plea. She moved forward, as if drawn by ropes down the hall. Knowing what she would find, not wanting to see, unable to stop. All too soon she was at the door. With a deep breath and trembling fingers, she pushed it open.

Malcolm lounged in a low overstuffed chair, bathed in faint orange light. His head rested on the back of the chair, eyes closed. But it was not his presence itself that had her heart shattering. It was the state of dishabille he was in. His jacket lay draped over a chair, his cravat in messy folds. Even his hair was mussed, falling over his forehead in inky waves. As if someone had run their fingers through it in a moment of passion.

As if Lady Morley had done so.

She barely managed to choke back the sob that threatened. What had she expected, that he would be content with her after being reminded of the stunning creature he had loved so ardently? That she could ever compete with Lady Morley, who was quite simply the most beautiful woman Emily had ever seen?

Even without this physical reminder, she was a fool to think she and Malcolm would have suited in the first place. They came from different worlds. No, it was better she found this out now, before she went and married him and learned the very cruel lesson that life with Malcolm, no matter how she loved him, would have eventually destroyed her.

With one last long look on him, she quietly closed the door and made her way back to the party.

Chapter 20

It was with immense relief that Malcolm watched Lydia, along with Lord and Lady Randall, leave for the evening. The party broke up immediately after, everyone trickling out to find their beds. Finally Emily rose, heading for the door.

He followed on her heels. He was done with waiting. If he did not get her into his arms this instant, he would perish.

The hallway was blessedly empty. She walked ahead of him, head down, oblivious to him following behind. Seeing his opportunity in the form of an empty sitting room looming ahead, he came up behind her and snaked an arm about her waist. She did not have even a moment to show her surprise before he had her in the room, the door closed soundly behind them. And then she was in his arms, her mouth under his. Nothing had ever felt so glorious.

It took him a moment to realize she was not kissing him back. She was, in fact, struggling against him. In an instant, he let her go. She fell back, panting, and stepped into a pool of silvery moonlight.

But it was not her refusal of his embrace that stunned him so. No, it was the haunted look in her eyes. She looked desolate, as if she would never be happy again.

Fear speared through him. "Emily, what is it?"

She merely stared up at him, her expression growing darker. He reached for her hand. It lay limp in his, cold to the touch.

He swallowed. Damn it, he should not have stayed away from her so completely this evening. Of course she would be hurt by it. But he had seen no other way.

"Emily," he began, "about my actions this evening—"

"What is Lady Morley to you?"

His mouth went dry as dust. Her voice, which was usually so sweet, almost musical, sounded harsh in the quiet of the room. "She is my brother's widow," he answered carefully.

Finally emotion flooded her face. It was anger, however, that brought the flush to her cheeks. "Shall I reword the question? Very well, what *was* Lady Morley to you?"

He swallowed hard. "It matters not. Whatever she was to me, she has effectively destroyed it."

"Did you love her?"

What could he do but tell her the truth? "Yes."

She closed her eyes. For a moment he thought she might cry. The next instant, the fury was back, like banked fires in the pale depths of her eyes. "Was it grief for your brother that affected you when you first saw her this afternoon? And please do me the honor of not lying to me."

Again, he could only answer her truthfully. "No."

"You made me look a fool, blathering on about honoring the memory of the dead. When all along it was what she once was to you."

He had never seen her so overcome. Not even when she had learned of the promise he had made to her brother did she lose such control. His heart pounded out a fearful rhythm.

"She is nothing to me now, I swear it."

Her lower lip trembled. She pressed her lips tight and tucked her chin into her chest. "It doesn't matter, I suppose," she mumbled, almost as if to herself. Sounding suddenly defeated.

Panic bloomed, hot and fierce. Taking a step forward, he reached for her.

She threw up her arms, backing away from him.

He could almost hear his heart crack.

"You cannot mean to let her come between us," he rasped.

"It is not only her, my lord. She was merely the catalyst." She dragged in a deep breath, as if girding herself for a difficult task. "I think," she said, the words sounding as if they were being wrung from her, "that perhaps we have been too hasty in our affections, my lord."

He saw then the inevitable loss of her, like a brilliant gold string slipping from his fingers. The grief of it overwhelmed him, made him snap. "You did not think so this afternoon." In an instant he regretted the harsh words. "Damn it, Emily. I'm sorry."

But the dead look had returned to her eyes. "No, you are right. I was free with my affections this afternoon." Her voice strengthened. "But it will not happen again."

The breath left his body completely, so much so that she was nearly to the door before he could find voice to speak. "Emily, you don't mean that. Take the night to think it over, please."

She stopped, her hand on the knob. "There is nothing to consider. It was all done in such haste, neither of us were prepared. It was badly done of me to encourage you. I should have seen from the beginning we were not matched. We are too different, you and I. We could never be happy together."

"We could," he said, desperation making the words come hard and fast. "Our differences don't matter a bit. We could be happy. We *will* be happy together."

An ancient kind of wisdom passed over her face. She gave him a sad smile. "You are fooling yourself. Soon you will be gone to your life in London. And I will remain here with my family. I don't belong in your world. I never have. It would destroy me. And we would soon hate each other because of it."

"No—"

"Yes." Her voice was firm, sure. And utterly weary. "If you ever cared for me, Malcolm, you will leave me in peace. I have made up my mind and will not change it again. It is over."

She walked from the room. In a flash he saw it, the long procession of people who had left him. And at the end of it all, Emily. The one person in the world he had thought would never turn her back on him.

The armor that had so long encased his heart and in the last days had begun to fall away reappeared in that instant. He had been a fool to open himself up again. Would he never learn? He should leave and never return.

But he was still bound by his promises to Willbridge, damn it. Would that he could shed them as easily as others seemed to cast him off. But he would be damned if he would relinquish this one last claim to honor he possessed.

Blowing out the candle, he left the room. He would see this promise through even if it killed him. And then he would leave Willowhaven and hope to never see Lady Emily Masters's sweet face again.

• • •

Emily rose from her bed before dawn the next morning determined to get on with her life as if Malcolm had not come into it and turned it on its end. She rose early and dressed in the pale gray light with the intention of escaping to the music room, as she had every morning since this infernal house party started. But as she walked through the guest wing, Bach following close to her heels, her feet slowed.

There was a disturbing emptiness inside her. She dug deep down, searching for that ever-present urge to create music, the desire to shelter herself in song. It must still be there, awaiting her as it always did, ready to help her through her most trying times. But there was only an echoing silence in her heart. By the time she reached the long gallery, her determination to go on as if her heart had not been shattered was gone as well, falling away like dead leaves in an autumn wind. Her steps faltered and stopped, and she stood in the middle of the vast room, surrounded by all manner of Masters ancestors. Feeling completely alone.

As if sensing her disquiet, Bach pushed his nose into her hand, his warm tongue flicking out to wet her skin. The contact jolted her back to herself. She blinked, dragging in a deep breath. She was stronger than she realized. Isn't that what Malcolm had been telling her?

At the thought of him, she sucked in her breath, the pain of last night returning just as sharp, just as jarring. And along with it, anger that she could allow him to affect her so. How could she have allowed herself to be lulled into caring for the man? She had thought she was smarter than this. Yet here was her heart, aching and twisting in agony over Malcolm's unexpected betrayal.

But no, she could get through this, could go back to her life as it had been before he had come back into it. It did not matter that he had made her feel precious, that his kisses had touched something new and exciting in her, something she had never thought to feel.

That he had made her love him.

She did not realize she had begun to cry until she felt the tell-tale wetness on her cheeks. She swiped it away, desperate to get rid of this proof of her weakness. Somehow thinking if she appeared normal without, she would become calm within.

More fool, she. No matter that she might appear unfazed by her break from Malcolm. It would do nothing to heal the wounds deep inside.

Bach pressed into her side. She laid her hand on his smooth head and looked down into his single mournful eye. "It's for the best," she said, though whether it was more for him or for her she didn't know. "In a matter of days, he will return to London. And we will remain here. Where we are safe. Where no one can hurt us again."

But not for long, she realized with a jolt, for in the happiness and misery of the last days there was one very important thing she had forgotten: the trip for Daphne's coming-out was still very much on.

In the spring, Emily would go to London.

She blanched as the reality of it came crashing down on her. But if she had been unwilling to go before, she refused to go now. Yes, there would be people there who would gape and stare at her. But there was one added reason that horrified her even beyond that.

Malcolm would be there.

As she was wont to do under great stress, her gaze sought out one particular portrait along the paneled gallery wall. The tears she had so quickly suppressed returned. Her brother Jonathan's face smiled down at her, perpetually young, forever twelve years of age. She rubbed at her aching chest absently. He had been the brave one, the one who had truly lived life. He should be the one here today, planning his future, taking chances. Not her, who had become so trampled by circumstances that she could hardly function.

Her eyes skimmed over his beloved face, still faintly round with youth, his gray eyes smiling down at her with that hint of mischief he had never been without. It had always seemed a strange quirk of fate that they had been conceived together, one child full of a zest for all that life held, the other content to watch it all pass her by. Even so, they had been as close as any two siblings could be. Emily had adored him, more than willing to face her fears in order to share in his adventures. With him she had been brave. The person she could have been.

She closed her eyes tight as regret and grief washed over her. All of her courage had seemed to vanish with Jonathan's untimely death. She had thought mayhap in the past days she had begun to feel that part of herself reawaken.

Because of Malcolm, her heart whispered. But no, she would not think of him or she would shatter.

She would return to her original plan to get her sister married off before the trip to London. Yet the final ball, the culmination of the grand, nearly fortnight-long house party, was but three days away. There was no possible way she would be able to wring out a proposal for Daphne by then.

But she was not the same person she had been two weeks ago. Opening her eyes, she gazed up in determination at the smiling face of her brother. Who was to say she could not manage it? She would renew her efforts to pair off Daphne and Sir Tristan, to bring about their engagement. She had been close before; surely it could not take much more effort on her part.

No more distractions. She would do everything in her power to see that the dreaded trip to London never took place.

Chapter 21

Malcolm heaved a sigh. Emily, with incredible cunning and skill, had successfully herded Tristan and Lady Daphne to the river's edge, pairing them off into a small boat. He had done his best to keep his distance from her over the past two days, since she had walked out on him and shown him how little she was willing to fight for what they had. It was as if their sweet interlude had never happened, as if he and Emily had not found a connection of both body and soul.

As if he had not nearly asked her to share her life with him.

He wished he could put this whole farce behind him. If he left, however, and Tristan went ahead and did something idiotic with Lady Daphne, he would never forgive himself. That, or Caleb would kill him, and deservedly so.

Tristan settled the young woman into the skiff. Malcolm was much too far away to separate them now. He could imagine what he would look like, sprinting down the green toward the riverbank like a madman, launching himself into the boat to prevent Tristan from pushing away from shore.

It was apparent that avoiding Emily was not benefitting anyone. She was simply getting into more mischief, causing more trouble. Despite the pain it gave him to even look on her, he could not afford to let her have free rein in her little matchmaking scheme a moment longer.

Straightening his shoulders, he marched down the gentle, grassy slope near where Emily stood, her hands clasped before her, her dog at her side, watching with obvious pleasure as Tristan and Lady Daphne pushed out into the middle of the River Spratt. There were other couples out on the water already, and a tent had been set up for those who had no wish to try their luck in the small crafts. Half the guests of Willowhaven were looking on, watching the proceedings, and so he need have no fear that Tristan would do anything stupid with the girl.

But for every moment Tristan had alone with her, he was one step closer toward a foolish future he could not return from. And with the final ball the next evening, the chance of that happening was becoming more and more likely. Malcolm had to get out there, to distract them from one another. Something had to be done to stop this mess that Emily was creating.

One of the small boats, with Lord Andrew Masters and Miss Mariah Duncan aboard, was pulling up to the bank as Malcolm approached. Miss Duncan, he noted absently, looked sweetly flushed. He touched the brim of his hat as he passed the young couple and made to step into their vacated boat. Lady Tarryton's strident voice, however, brought him up short.

"Lord Morley," she called, hurrying toward him, a dainty parasol held over her head to shield her skin from the warm afternoon sun, "you cannot take that out by yourself."

He closed his eyes and sighed, praying for patience, before opening them again and facing the viscountess. "I cannot?"

She gave him a faintly condescending look. "You will need to take a young lady with you if you're to go on the river. There are rules, after all."

He raised one eyebrow. "I was not aware there are rules to rowing on the river."

His officious tone, however, didn't affect the woman one bit. She smiled at him. "Most assuredly we have rules. If we did not, society itself would fall into chaos."

Malcolm was completely without recourse to that line of thinking. So his not taking a lady out with him on the river was likened to the collapse of civilization as they knew it? He looked at her sure expression and wondered for a fleeting moment if they were in Bedlam. Perhaps, he thought a bit wildly, that infamous institute for the insane was now a lovely country house, and he had been unwittingly tricked into staying there.

She compounded upon that thought a moment later as she looked about at the surrounding females. "Let me see," she murmured, "I do believe we can find a partner for you among the ladies present. Ah, I know: my daughter Mariah. She has just returned from a trip on the river with young Lord Andrew. I'm sure she would love to accompany you."

Damn it, the woman was back at her matchmaking attempts again. A vague sense of being trapped set in as he watched Lady Tarryton turn to her daughter. He wouldn't put it past her to force the girl into a compromising position to attain what she wanted. He had the panicked thought that, if he allowed Miss Duncan into the boat, Lady Tarryton would hold him prisoner like a spider with her prey.

"Ah, I do apologize, my lady," he called, even as she took her daughter aside, "but I have promised to bring another lady out on the river with me."

Lady Tarryton's eyebrows rose, as if to question the rightness of his mind in preferring another to her offspring. "Oh? And who might that be?"

His gaze careened desperately about, searching for anyone else he might drag into this farce. Suddenly he spotted Emily, standing a short distance away. Looking right at him. As his gaze met hers, he stumbled and stopped. She flushed, her formerly pale countenance turning rosy. *Damn, but she was beautiful.* His heart fairly ached from the sight of her.

But he could not lose possession of his hard-won control. The past two days had been difficult enough. With effort, he wrenched his gaze from her.

Lady Tarryton, however, caught the exchange. "You cannot possibly mean Lady Emily, my lord?" she scoffed.

Immediately everyone in the vicinity went still. Miss Duncan, aghast, was attempting to calm an irate Drew. Several others stopped to stare in unabashed disbelief.

Malcolm hardly saw it for the red haze that obscured his vision. Yes, Emily had fairly broken his heart. But that did not mean he wished to see her trampled on by Lady Tarryton, or anyone else, for that matter.

"I'm sorry, my lady," he said, his voice pitched to a deadly calm, "but I don't think you could have possibly meant what you implied by that statement."

To her credit, the viscountess looked appropriately embarrassed. "Certainly not, my lord," she stammered, looking in wild desperation at Emily, who stood frozen a dozen feet away. Her eyes dropped to Bach at her feet, before lighting with relief. "I merely meant," she continued, "that she has her dog with her, and would not wish to leave him ashore."

It was a flimsy excuse at best and only inflamed Malcolm's fury. "Oh, I think the animal is brave enough to join us." He turned to Emily. "What say you, my lady? Do you think that beast of yours is capable of joining us?"

Her silver eyes flared wide in alarm. For a moment he thought she would balk and miss out on the chance to redeem herself in front of this obnoxious woman.

As luck would have it, however, it was Lady Tarryton herself who decided Emily's fate.

"You cannot think to bring that creature on board with you," she fairly screeched. "Why, he is damaged, compromised due to the loss of that eye. He will tip you for sure."

At Lady Tarryton's brash words, Emily straightened to her full height. She stuck her chin out, her eyes going cold as she considered the older woman. "I assure you," she said with quiet precision, "that there is nothing at all the matter with my dog. I do believe, my lady, that you underestimate him." She turned to Malcolm, her bearing conveying all the grace of a queen. "Lord Morley, thank you for inviting us, we should love to join you." With that, she marched past a gaping Lady Tarryton.

Malcolm took hold of her hand and helped her into the small boat, then reached down to heft Bach in beside her, all the while staring in awe at Emily. She was more alluring than ever. His plan to keep watch on Tristan had suddenly taken a dangerous turn, he realized. How much of a struggle would this little fiasco be, to keep them all in the boat and afloat, but to keep his emotions from going overboard as well?

· · ·

Emily settled into the bow of the little skiff, suddenly feeling all the folly of her brash actions. That she should have allowed Lady Tarryton to bully her into going along with this mad scheme was idiocy at its worst. Bach sat at her feet, apparently unaffected by the rocking beneath him, and tilted his head back to look at her steadily. Taking comfort from his calming presence, she dragged in a deep breath of the warm summer air and attempted to relax on the hard wooden bench. Just then, the boat tilted precariously as Malcom joined them. She tensed, fighting the urge to grab at the sides of the craft. Instead she laid a steadying hand on Bach's back and attempted to look unconcerned. This was her pride on the line, after all.

Malcolm pushed away from the shore without a word. The boat swayed, dipping from side to side in the water as it found purchase. Emily held her breath as Malcolm settled on the bench across from her and put the oars in the water. Damn him for getting her into this. He must know she had no wish to be near him, that being in forced proximity with him was the very last place she wished to be. She attempted to keep her eyes on the surrounding countryside. But, traitorous orbs that they were, she found them drawn to Malcolm. He had taken off his fine sage coat and looked wickedly handsome in his shirt and amber waistcoat. It enhanced his physique as he moved his arms in long, sure strokes, plying the oars in the water and moving them along at a smooth, brisk pace.

"This is all your fault, you know."

His voice, so dark and low, made her jump. When his words finally sank in, she scowled at him. "How is this remotely my fault?"

He turned disgusted eyes on her. "Please. Do you think me a fool?"

"Do you truly wish me to answer that?" she muttered under her breath.

To his credit, he chose to ignore that. "If you had not insisted on playing matchmaker—again—we would not be sitting here in this boat together."

Hurt flamed through her chest. "A situation I would much prefer, I assure you."

He looked pained, opening his mouth as if he were about to say something. At the last moment he closed it with an audible snap and drew a deep breath in through his nose. "I have told you why it is a mistake to encourage an attachment between your sister and Tristan. Why do you insist on promoting it?"

She ignored him, pointedly looking out over the water.

He growled in frustration. "You will not win this battle, madam."

"You think not?" she murmured.

"I know you won't. I will guarantee it."

She turned on him, all the grief and frustration of the past days coalescing into a desperate kind of anger. "Why can't you let it be? They care for one another. They would be happy, I'm sure of it. Let them see where their affections may take them."

His black eyes were hard. "Sometimes mutual affection is not enough to guarantee future happiness."

If he had taken a knife and plunged it straight into her heart, giving it a twist for good measure, it would not have given her such pain. No, he was right in that, for weren't they proof? Yes, they had cared for one another. But it had not been enough. *She* had not been enough. She turned to Bach, dragging her fingers through his fur, trying to stave off the tears that threatened. She would not let Malcolm see how his unfeeling words affected her.

Several long minutes passed in blessed silence. Emily began to fidget in her seat. Surely they had made their point as far as Lady Tarryton was concerned and needn't stay out on the water any longer. Clearing her throat, she said as firmly as she could muster, "Please return me to shore. I wish to disembark."

"I'm not ready to head back," he murmured.

Emily shot him a suspicious look. He appeared incredibly focused on something. Following his gaze, she spied Sir Tristan and Daphne a short distance away. They had stopped their boat within a canopy of branches provided by an obliging willow tree and seemed in their own world. She narrowed her eyes. Was it her, or was Malcolm coming up unusually fast on them?

"Malcolm," she said, "perhaps you'd best slow down."

He didn't seem to hear her, instead seeming to pick up speed. The oars were cutting through the water with impressive swiftness. That is, it would have been impressive, if they were not on what she now suspected was a purposeful collision course with the other boat.

Not thinking, only knowing that she had to save them from crashing, Emily launched herself at Malcolm.

Everything happened at once. There was the sound of the clattering of wood, Bach barking furiously, Malcolm's shouts. And then a sloshing as the boat careened to one side. In the next moment, the cold shock of the water hit her as she sank down into the depths of the river.

Chapter 22

Malcolm came up sputtering, the shock of the chill water falling rapidly away to panic as he looked about him and didn't see a familiar copper head bobbing beside him. Bach paddled like mad, his head held high above the surface. Tristan was calling out, but the dog wasn't abiding. Daphne's shrill voice echoed out over the water, calling for her sister.

There was no answer.

"Where is she?" Malcolm cried out.

"She went under and hasn't resurfaced," Tristan called back.

"Get the damn dog in the boat," he yelled before he dove under. The water was like cotton in his ears, the silt that he was stirring up stinging his eyes and making it difficult to see. His lungs burned as he pulled himself deeper, using his hands to scour the water for her. Desperation and a burning fear for Emily made him stay down longer than he should have. When he could not ignore his body's need for air a moment longer, he kicked hard, sputtering and gulping as he reached the surface. His breathing ragged, he turned back for the other boat. "Any sign of her?" he gasped.

He didn't need Tristan to tell him. Lady Daphne's pale face was more potent than any words would have been. His heart skipped and stuttered in his chest. He'd heard of women who had fallen into water fully dressed. Their sodden skirts were like a death trap to them, an anchor weighing them down, tangling in their legs, making it impossible to surface. An image of Emily's sweet face, pale and cold in death, her beautiful pewter eyes closed forever, made his voice hoarse as he shouted for her.

The people on the far shore seemed to have realized what was going on. He could hear their voices carrying, shouts and crying drifting to him over the water's surface. But there was not a hint of Emily's voice. Bach, too, was still splashing about, ignoring Tristan's attempts to get him in the boat. Malcolm couldn't worry about him now. He had to find Emily. If anything were to happen to her—

He left the thought unfinished. He would not consider it. Dragging in another gulping breath, he was about to dive down again into the murky depths when the dog's sudden frantic barks stopped him cold. Bach began a mad paddle for the closest bank. Heart pounding, Malcolm followed, and nearly shouted with relief when he saw movement in the deep shadows.

"I think she's in there," he called to Tristan. "Take Lady Daphne to shore and come back for Lady Emily." Without waiting for Tristan's assent, he was off again, his arms slicing through the water, his feet kicking hard, propelling him forward.

He swam through the shade of the willow tree, heading for the small hidden inlet there. The dog had made the shore, was shaking water from his coat. And there, still in the water and clinging to a low hanging branch, was Emily.

She was drenched, her hair a heavy mass of dark copper that streamed down her back and over her shoulders. Her face was pale, her eyes huge in her face, her lips trembling and tinged blue from the chill of the water.

Never had anyone looked so beautiful.

Bach was dancing about on the bank, letting loose sharp yips as if to say, *Here, you idiot. I've had to go and find her for you.* Malcolm ignored him, heading straight for Emily. Once at her side, he did the only thing he could think to do. He dragged her away from the tree, into his arms, and kissed her.

Though her lips here cold, her mouth was hot and eager. The fear that had been burning in him just below the surface during his desperate search burst to brilliant life, transforming in a blink to a searing passion. Forgotten was the way she had turned from him, breaking his heart in the process. She was alive and in his arms. That was all that mattered. Their bodies entwined beneath the water, her gown billowing about them. He held her to him with one arm, dug through the water with the other until they were in the shallows. Once there, he pressed her into the bank. Her soft body gave to his willingly, the ebb and flow of the water around them making their embrace exquisitely erotic. He ran his hand down her body, the dampened fabric hiding nothing from his questing fingers. Every curve, every dip and valley was given up to him. She clung to him, her fingers digging into his back, her legs rubbing against his in silent entreaty.

Bach's low whine pierced the haze of passion in his brain. Suddenly he was intensely aware of how chill her skin was to the touch; of the tremor of cold, not desire, that shook her thin frame. What the hell was he doing? They needed to get Emily to shore, to dry her off. Instead he was pawing at her in the shallows.

The horrifying realization of how easily he had forgotten how she'd turned on him sliced through him. He had known it was foolish to open himself up to another, but had ignored his better instincts and had done just that with Emily. And he had paid dearly for it. Now here he was, days later, and in a split second of panic he had willingly allowed her to lay waste to his newly erected barriers. Again. Anger consumed him then, dark and dangerous.

"What in hell did you think you were about, tackling me and overturning our boat like that?" he growled. "You could be lifeless at the bottom of the river this very moment. You damned fool woman."

The passion in Emily's eyes faded in an instant. She pushed away from him, dragging herself further up the muddy bank. "What did you expect me to do? You were planning on ramming into Daphne's boat."

"You thought I was going to ram them?" That had to be the most ridiculous thing he'd ever heard.

She opened her mouth, no doubt to spew some scathing retort. Bach came bounding up just then, pushing between them, lathing her wet face with kisses. His tail flew from side to side in a wide arc, his joy in seeing Emily safe making him fairly tremble. She gave the beast a tight hug, pressing her face into his wet fur before pushing him back and bidding him to sit. The dog did so immediately. His one eye, however, remained fixed firmly on her, no doubt intending to make sure that she remained safe now that she was on land.

Turning from him, she pulled the heavy hank of her hair over one shoulder and twisted it viciously, sending rivulets of river water down over her breasts. Breasts, Malcolm noted, that were shown off in exquisite detail by the dampened bodice of her gown. He swallowed hard, unable to tear his eyes from the sight.

But she was talking. "You were headed directly for them. I am perfectly aware of your desire to see them parted. I am not an imbecile. You cannot possibly deny that you were heading for them with the intent to crash into them. I saw how you sped up, your direction. There could have been no other possible outcome had you continued on in that way."

"As you are so well acquainted with my intentions," he drawled, heaving himself to a more comfortable position in the shallows—if one could be at all comfortable sitting in slimy mud with water lapping at your once pristine boots, "tell me, what purpose would I have had in ramming them? It would have not only sent us in the water, but them as well."

"I don't know. I only knew I had to prevent the accident."

He blew out a frustrated breath, running a hand through his hair to sluice the water from it. "For the last time, I was not going to hit them. If you must know, I was merely going to give them a bit of a scare. They were entirely too intimate with one another."

"As I had planned on," she shot back. The dog, hearing the frustration in her voice, moved close to her side and pressed himself against her. She reached for him blindly, grabbing onto him for all she was worth. It was then he saw what was underlying her anger. She was frightened. And desperately unhappy.

His anger dissipated in an instant. "Emily," he said, softly. He reached out a hand for her.

"No." She sliced a hand through the air. "Leave me alone, Malcolm. Please."

It was the please that did it. Said in that broken way, when up until then she had been so gloriously furious, it cracked something deep within him.

She had hurt him dreadfully. But he realized now that he was not the only one affected by the brutal ending of their romance. He had just been too wounded—and too proud—to see it.

Emily was not cruel. Nor was she free with her affections. She would not have given so much of herself had she not felt something for him. Though she may not be deeply grieved by his presence, she must have felt some pain at it.

He stared at her in silence. She pressed her face into the dog's neck, apparently more than willing to have the conversation over and done. Grief settled like a mantle about his shoulders then, making him feel as if he'd sink straight into the damp ground and never emerge.

Just then, he heard a shout. Tristan was headed their way.

"We're here," Malcolm called out. He winced, his voice sounding almost violent in the thick silence that had descended between them. Emily didn't look up, the only indication she had been similarly affected was the slight stiffening of her shoulders and the low whine from the dog's chest. It seemed an eternity before Drew and Tristan arrived, both rowing into the hidden inlet. With effort Malcolm rose, water streaming from his clothes, to help pull the first boat close. It was then that Emily roused herself, silently handing over Bach. Malcolm took hold of him to put him in the boat, but the dog backed away and pressed into Emily's side.

"He won't leave you," Malcolm said.

Without acknowledging him, she accepted her brother's hand, then picked up her sodden skirts with her free hand and heaved herself into the small craft. Bach followed close after, leaping up beside her, setting his slick head in her lap. Malcolm watched numbly as her brother carefully wrapped a blanket about her shoulders, then pushed away from the bank with his oar. He hardly saw Tristan's skiff as it came closer for him to board, his gaze instead firmly on the back of Emily's head as she floated away from him, feeling he was watching a part of himself float away as well.

. . .

To Malcolm's disgust, the party did not break up after the disaster in the water. Lady Tarryton would allow nothing to stop her carefully planned outing. Emily was already being handed up into a cart by the time Malcolm reached the shore. Her face impassive and pale, with her mother by her side and the dog at her feet, she was soon out of sight. Waving off the offer of a second cart, Malcolm accepted a blanket and started for the long walk back to the manor house. He regretted it after less than twenty feet. His fine leather boots had been soaked through and would have to be cut off him. His stockings, too, were sodden, making a horrible squishing sensation between his toes with every step.

But he needed this time away from the others to think. Too much was in turmoil, too many things tossed up in the air like colorful juggling balls. The question was, how many of those would he manage to catch when they all came tumbling down again about his head?

It was during that half hour walk back to Willowhaven that he came to the stark realization that he had to leave, and the sooner the better. His own feelings for Emily and the hurt he felt at her abandonment aside, he had seen firsthand the grief his presence caused her. It was one thing to have to deal with his own emotions on the matter. But now he was fully aware what he was costing Emily. Yes, she had been the one to break things off. Even so, he could not bear to see her in pain.

After changing into something dry, Malcolm went down to wait for the party to return. If he sat about with nothing to do, he would go utterly and completely mad. Finally he saw them and emerged from the overhang that protected the side door, hurrying out to meet them. Many of the group called to him, asking how he fared after his "swim"—most of them apparently unaware how serious the situation had truly been. Lady Tarryton must have been hard at work dispelling the initial panic that had set in when he and Emily had first gone under, he thought scathingly. He managed a vague smile in their direction, some murmured response that he could not remember a minute later but had them laughing. At the end of the group was Tristan, Lady Daphne at his side. *Of course*, Malcolm thought sourly.

They saw him in that moment, rushing forward, the only ones to show the proper gravity to the situation.

"How is my sister?" Lady Daphne asked when they were close enough.

"I hardly know," Malcolm replied with utmost honesty, frustration coursing through him. "Your mother took her upstairs the moment they returned and they have not reappeared."

She frowned, worry clouding her clear blue eyes. "I must go to them." She turned to Tristan. "Thank you for your escort. I shall see you later this evening." Her attention then shifted to Malcolm. To his surprise, she took up his hand, pressing it between the both of hers. "Thank you, my lord, for saving my sister. I shall be indebted to you always." With one long, intent look, her eyes welling with emotion, she released him and was off, picking her skirts up in her hands and disappearing into the house.

Malcolm looked after her, struck dumb. Clearing his throat in embarrassment, he turned back to Tristan. "I must thank you for your help," he muttered, "for coming to get us."

"It was the least I could do," his friend said, then gave him an odd look. "What I want to know, however," he drawled, "is what the devil you were doing that upset your boat. Lady Tarryton would swear it was the dog, but I don't think so."

"I pity Willbridge for his choice in mother-in-law," Malcolm growled. "I would not want to be tied to such a woman."

Tristan's lips quirked. "I hardly think he was considering Lady Tarryton when he proposed to Imogen." He quickly sobered. "Apparently she was not very kind when Lady Emily got back to shore. She claimed she predicted the dog upsetting the boat?" He raised an eyebrow at Malcolm in inquiry.

"Ah, yes, the all-seeing Lady Tarryton," Malcolm bit out. A cold frisson worked its way through Malcolm, an intuition. "Do not tell me she attacked Emily about it."

Tristan blinked at his use of Emily's Christian name. Malcolm cursed himself for his loose tongue, praying his friend would not comment on it. To his relief, Tristan merely asked, "Do you think the woman would let something like that go?"

Malcolm's blood boiled. "I don't give a bloody damn who she is. She cannot talk to Willbridge's sister in such a manner."

"Oh, I wouldn't worry over Lady Emily," Tristan replied.

Malcolm cut a glance to his friend. "What do you mean?"

Humor glinted in Tristan's eyes. "To hear it told, she was no longer the mild creature you and I are used to when Lady Tarryton made her ill-advised remark."

He waited, but his friend merely smiled broadly at him. Malcolm frowned. "I am not in the mood for you to play with me. Have out with it, man. What did Lady Emily do?"

"Well, now, let me see. I have to think about this."

"Tristan," Malcolm growled.

His friend chuckled. "Very well. You are no fun at all. I do believe I was informed that Lady Emily's exact words were, 'You may keep your opinions to yourself, for you have no clue what you are talking about.'"

Malcolm stared long and hard at him. "You must be joking. That does not sound at all like Lady Emily."

"Oh, I assure you, that is exactly what she said. I have it from more than one source. Though I do believe it took Lady Tarryton so much by surprise that she didn't quite understand that she had been thoroughly insulted and put in her place." He laughed. "I would have loved to have seen such a magnificent outburst. I didn't know she had it in her."

Which was all part of the problem, Malcolm thought. No one ever expected such things of her. Not even the lady herself.

"But you are doing a fine job of dancing around my question," Tristan said, breaking Malcolm from his maudlin thoughts. "What in the devil was going on in your boat? I cannot imagine Lady Emily doing something so careless that it would upset you both in the river. Then again, I certainly didn't expect her to give that bat Lady Tarryton such a brilliant let-down, either, so that shows you what I know."

Malcolm flushed. He felt itchy and uncomfortable all of a sudden. Needing movement, he said, "Come and walk with me in the knot garden?"

Tristan raised an eyebrow but nodded. As one, they turned for the small side garden. Malcolm stayed silent for a time, gathering his thoughts. To his relief, Tristan seemed more than happy to wait on him. He certainly could not tell his friend that the whole debacle had happened because of a bit of matchmaking. Such a remark would only bring about more questions, even possibly heighten Tristan's interest in Lady Daphne. There was nothing like opposition to one's desires to make those desires undeniable, Malcolm thought caustically. So what in the hell could he say? Instead, he tried a roundabout reasoning.

"You know that Willbridge had me looking after Lady Emily." Tristan nodded. "Well, Lady Emily discovered my subterfuge. She was not happy about it."

Tristan whistled low. "I can imagine not. No lady wants to be seen as so hopeless that her brother would set a keeper out after her. And so it was due to the two of you fighting that the boat was overturned?"

"Yes." Close enough, anyway, in that the lie did not seem a lie at all.

"Well," Tristan said, "I did not know the girl had such fire in her. I must say, it puts her in a whole new light."

Malcolm froze, stumbling to a halt in the gravel path. Was that interest in Tristan's voice? He could not remember the last time he'd felt the urge to punch his friend, but he was dangerously close to it just then. "What the devil does that mean?" he snapped.

Tristan stopped and looked at Malcolm in alarm. "Nothing at all. What the hell has gotten into you?"

Another loss of control, Malcolm thought with frustration. Damn, but Emily had the worst effect on him. He let out a pent-up breath and ran a hand through his still-damp hair. "If you must know, I'm through with this place. It was the reason I searched you out in the first place. Willbridge is gone off on his wedding trip, my job of looking after Lady Emily compromised. I see no reason for us to continue here. Can we not return to London?"

Tristan frowned. "You seem awfully worked up, man. Is something else bothering you?"

Damn it, he'd let his emotions show through. Drawing up his typical mantle of bored cynicism with effort, he gave his friend a haughty lift of his eyebrow. "We are surrounded by debutantes and are being lorded over by a troublesome viscountess who should not even be playing hostess. What do you think is wrong with me?"

Tristan did not seem mollified. If anything, he appeared even more curious. "You know," he murmured, "I do think something has happened that has spooked you." Then he sobered, his clear blue gaze sharpening. "Was it Lydia?"

The trouble with having a friend with whom you had grown up, who knew you almost as well as you knew yourself, was that they often caught even the slightest tell. Malcolm deepened his frown. "You are delirious. She can no longer have any hold over me; you must know that by now. Now, what say you? Can we leave this hellhole or not?"

Tristan considered him for a long moment in concern before shrugging. "You may go if you like. I, however, have found there is much to recommend Willowhaven to me."

Meaning Lady Daphne. Malcolm very nearly gave voice to the thought in his frustration. At the last minute, he halted his tongue. To bring it out in the open would be sure to sharpen the man's interest in her.

"Besides," his friend went on, "I would not want to miss the ball tomorrow night for anything."

There was enough of a glazed, dreamy look in Tristan's eyes that Malcolm realized there was nothing on this earth he could say to sway his friend. Even so, he could not give up as easy as that without a fight. "You cannot think that a country ball would be more exciting than an evening in London. Come on, man. I know how you thrive on that stuff. You've never been content with something so tame."

"Somehow I doubt the evening will prove tame at all. In fact, it promises to be positively thrilling," Tristan drawled with a sparkle in his eyes.

Well, apparently there was no choice for it now. Malcolm would have to stay for the entirety of the house party whether he wished it or not. For, if he wasn't mistaken, the man was planning something foolish the following evening. What, he wondered, was his idiot friend going to do, and how would Malcolm prevent it?

The greater question, though, was whether he could withstand Emily's pull on him, which no amount of heartbreak seemed to be able to lessen.

Chapter 23

Nothing could hold Emily's attention, it seemed, since the accident. Not the book she had attempted to read, nor the embroidery she'd been trying to work on prior to that. Even her pianoforte held no draw. In one last bid to distract herself from troubled thoughts, she had taken up the music sheets borrowed from Imogen with the intent of copying the pieces into her own music book. Surely the focus needed for something of that nature would draw her in. After just half a page, however, she slammed down her quill with nearly enough force to break it.

Throwing up her hands, knowing she would fail at anything else she tried just as spectacularly, Emily retreated to her chair before the unlit hearth, staring sightlessly ahead. Bach lay at her feet, his warmth against her leg a welcome thing, keeping her from feeling quite so alone.

Again and again her thoughts returned to that scene by the river. Being in Malcolm's arms again, his mouth hot and desperate on hers, had been achingly wonderful. She had been filled with need for him, a fire that had fairly scorched her from the inside out.

Would she have been able to pull away from him had he not done so first? Would she have dragged him back to her had he not lashed out? She would never know.

"Fool, fool woman," she whispered, even as tears stung her eyes.

A knock sounded at her door. She jumped, her heart faltering in her chest, her thoughts immediately veering toward Malcolm. But it would not be him. He would know that he was the last person she wished to see in that moment.

"Come in," she called out, wincing at the hoarseness in her voice. When Daphne entered, slipping into the room and quietly closing the door behind her, Emily knew she should feel relief. She had no wish to see him ever again, after all. The tiny fissure she felt work through her heart, however, told her how traitorous her emotions were on the subject.

Her sister approached and sank into the chair next to Emily, the small smile on her lips doing nothing to disguise her worry. "How are you faring?"

"As well as can be after falling into the River Spratt. And no better than the last two times you were in here asking after me."

"You forget, I've taken many a dunking in the river myself," Daphne said, her eyes twinkling. "I know the toll it can take on one."

Which was nothing but the absolute truth. Daphne was notorious for her inability to sit still in a boat. Emily could not count the number of times her sister had returned to the house looking like a drowned rat. "I pity Drew for all the times he's had to fish you out," Emily teased, before quickly sobering. "Though thank goodness you are a much stronger swimmer than I. Truly, I cannot remember the last time I was so frightened."

"I admit I was lucky that Drew never took me into the deeper parts of the river. For me it was simply a matter of planting my feet and standing."

"Though you kept your seat today," Emily stated with a small smile.

"Yes, I did," Daphne replied with a smile of her own.

They sat in companionable silence for a time. Emily eyed her thoughtfully. "I must say, this is a wonderful novelty, having you here with me while there is so much gaiety below stairs. Truly, I don't think I've seen this much of you since this house party began. I should have fallen into the river long before now."

Daphne bent and scratched Bach's long ear. He gave a happy groan and tilted his head, providing Daphne better access. She laughed. "Yes, you great beast, you will get plenty of love from me for helping to save my sister. You are a hero, you know." She leaned back in her seat and looked intently at Emily. "And Lord Morley as well. We are indebted to him for his part in your rescue."

Emily flushed. She pressed a hand to her cheek before quickly checking the automatic response and dropping it uselessly back to her lap. "If we are doling out medals of valor for heroism, we must not forget Sir Tristan. I'm grateful he came back with help."

As she hoped, Daphne's smile softened. "Yes, he was quite impressive, wasn't he?"

Emily paused. Then, "Sir Tristan seems a good man, Daphne."

"He is."

"You seem to like him very much."

Daphne's eyes glowed. "I do."

Emily smiled widely. "I'm so glad." She cleared her throat. "He would make any woman a fine husband, I'm thinking."

Daphne sighed happily. "I think so, too." She gazed at nothing in particular for a time. Then, quite suddenly, she blinked, dispelling the dreamy expression. "But I have forgotten what I came here for. Mama wants to know if you'll be down for dinner or if you wish for a tray to be sent up?"

Immediately thoughts of Malcolm came rolling over her. She nearly blanched. "Please have a tray sent up. I'm not quite ready to go into company. With the fall into the river and all." Which was complete poppycock, as she had never felt more fit. Physically, at least. Her mind, however, was another matter entirely.

But Daphne nodded her head in understanding. "I do hope you don't catch a cold. That would really be too bad. Especially with tomorrow night."

Emily frowned. "Tomorrow night?"

"The ball, of course." She looked at Emily with wide eyes. "Don't tell me you've forgotten. It's all any of us have been talking about for the better part of a week."

She had absolutely forgotten. Hadn't she been distracted in the last few days by a dark rake with kisses that had melted her reserve, exposing her heart in the most vivid, painful way?

Not that she would have ever looked with any excitement on the evening. There was nothing worse to her mind, after all, than a grand social evening. "No," she replied, "I don't think I'll attend. I need the rest."

"Oh, that truly is too bad. I had so hoped you would be there." Daphne appeared completely crestfallen. "It's the final night of the house party, after all, and everyone leaves the following morning. We shall not meet with most of them again until our trip to London in the spring."

Emily felt as if her heart took a dive out of her chest and straight to the floor. She was incredibly slow today. Of course the ball meant it was the final night of the house party. Which meant the guests would be leaving the following day. All of them.

Malcolm included.

Loss settled hard and heavy in her gut. As much as she wanted to be free of his presence, the thought of him actually leaving, of having to go on without him in her life, was devastating.

But no, she would not dwell on that. There was a much more important, much more crucial matter that must be dealt with. Tomorrow night was her last chance to pair Daphne with Sir Tristan, her last chance to stop the dreaded trip to London. Pushing all thoughts of Malcolm aside, she instead concentrated on the repercussions of the departure of his friend. If she missed the ball, she would have lost her one chance to ensure an engagement between Sir Tristan and Daphne.

Her sister gave the dog one final pat and rose, heading for the door. "Well, I shall go to Mama and tell her that you won't be joining us tomorrow evening, then."

"Wait!"

Emily hadn't realized how loud her voice was until her sister nearly jumped out of her slippers. Even Bach's head snapped up, his one eye flying to her, comically wide in surprise. Daphne placed a hand over her heart. "My goodness, Emily, you nearly scared me to death."

She had to go to that ball. The thought ripped the very breath from her lungs. Daphne stood silently, a question in her eyes. Emily forced herself to breathe. If she didn't say it now, she might lose her nerve. *It's for the greater good*, she told herself bracingly.

Finally she managed to blurt, "I'll be going. To the ball tomorrow, that is. Please tell Mama that I'll go."

Daphne seemed not to hear the latent panic in her voice. She beamed. "Will you really?" At Emily's hesitant nod she clapped her hands together. "Oh, this is wonderful. I'm so happy. You've nothing to worry about, it will be glorious. I'll even help you ready yourself." To Emily's surprise, Daphne rushed forward and gave her a quick hug. "You won't regret it." And with that she was off.

Emily stared after her, dread settling on her shoulders. She looked down at Bach. He looked steadily up at her. As their eyes met, he gave a soft woof, his wet nose pressing into her hand. She ran her fingers over his smooth head and muttered, "What in the world have I done?"

· · ·

The following afternoon and Willowhaven was bustling with activity. As soon as luncheon was over, the guests retired to their rooms to prepare for the upcoming evening of grand, lavish entertainment, Tristan with them. Malcolm should feel nothing but relief. It meant they were nearly done with this fortnight of torture. He could leave Emily and the threat of her behind, could return to his old life and take up where he had left off, as if nothing had happened to upset his careful existence. As he closed himself off in his room, however, he could not help noticing that there was no satisfaction in the thought.

No matter. He yanked off his cravat in sharp jerks. Once he was free of this place he would feel differently. Tomorrow morning, with the rising sun, he would leave Willowhaven and not look back.

The soft sounds of muted conversation came through his door. He might have ignored it. The house was full of people, after all. If one particular voice had not caught his attention.

Willbridge. He was back.

Without a second's thought, Malcolm bounded across the room, yanking open his door. Willbridge and Imogen were passing by and appeared surprised at his abrupt appearance.

"Damn, but it's good to see you, man," Malcolm blurted.

Willbridge's lips quirked. "Missed me, have you?"

"You have no idea." He greeted Imogen before turning back to Willbridge. "I didn't think you were to return until after tomorrow."

"Imogen thought it only right that we come back in time for the final ball," Willbridge explained, giving his wife a tender look that was not lost on Malcolm. "Though do try and keep it under your hat, Morley. I've a mind to see my bride settled in her new apartments before we're set upon by all and sundry, and I don't wish to be disturbed."

"Good, good," he mumbled, earning him a strange look from Willbridge. The couple started off again. In a panic he leaped forward. "Wait. I would speak to you a moment."

Willbridge looked at him in disbelief. "Now?"

"I'm afraid so," Malcolm replied. "It cannot wait another minute."

His friend gave him a scowl and appeared ready to refuse. Imogen, however, peered closely at him. "Lord Morley, are you well?"

"Certainly," he declared. Imogen, however, did not look convinced.

"Caleb," she murmured, "perhaps you had better see what Lord Morley needs."

The change in Willbridge was instantaneous. He smiled, bringing his wife's hand to his lips and kissing it softly. "I'll be along shortly," he said before turning to Malcolm. "Very well, Morley, lead on."

If the outcome hadn't been in his favor, Malcolm might have found the whole situation disgusting in the extreme. He hurried Willbridge into his room and closed the door.

Once inside, however, Malcolm couldn't think how best to

bring up what he needed. After several seconds of uncertainty, he blurted, "I want you to release me from my promises, Willbridge."

His friend frowned, concern darkening his pale gray eyes. Eyes the exact hue of Emily's.

At the pang of grief in his chest, Malcolm's resolve strengthened. The sooner he left this place, the better.

"What is it?" Willbridge asked.

His gaze was too piercing, too seeing. Malcolm's eyes slid away and he stepped past him to peer out the window. "Nothing's wrong. I have things to do in London and would like to return as soon as I'm able. To do that, you need to release me from the promises I made to you. It's as simple as that."

"It doesn't sound simple at all," Willbridge said quietly. "You look rattled. I haven't seen you in such a state since..."

The air was thick with the implications of the unsaid word. *Lydia*. Willbridge would remember the torment he'd been in with Lydia and Bertram's betrayal. That he even remotely resembled the distraught man he used to be was troubling indeed.

"Just release me," Malcolm said.

Willbridge's boots sounded across the floor as he came closer. The tension in Malcolm's body was incredible. Willbridge knew him as well as anyone could; he would be able to see what he was hiding.

When Willbridge's hand settled warm and comforting on his shoulder, Malcolm nearly lost his resolve to remain aloof then and there. Here was a man who had stood by him throughout some of the most difficult times of his life. Now he needed his companionship more than ever before. Yet he could never claim it, for it was this man's sister who was at the center of it all.

Damn it, but Willbridge would hate him if he ever found out.

"You and I have known each other almost all our lives," Willbridge said now, underscoring the treachery Malcolm had unconsciously perpetrated. "You know I have always been there for you. I will be here for you now, if you will let me. What happened while I was gone that has you in such a state? I'll help if I can."

Malcolm felt all the sting of the words. He shrugged out from beneath Willbridge's touch. "I simply wish to leave," he bit out. "Can't you understand that? I've been at the beck and call of your sisters, watching over Tristan as if he were a recalcitrant child, for a fortnight now. I grow weary of doing your job for you, Willbridge."

To Malcolm's frustration, instead of taking offense at the blatantly rude words, Willbridge seemed to grow more concerned. "You think to insult me. You forget, I've seen you do this before, Morley."

"Do what?" Malcolm demanded gruffly.

"You are pushing me away, hoping I let you go so you may wallow in your solitude and self-pity. I've not let you do it before, my friend. I will certainly not let you do it now."

The quiet compassion in Willbridge's voice nearly undid him. In that moment, Malcolm could see it clearly. Willbridge would not let him go easily. He would persist, and goad, and make his life hell.

Unable to breathe, knowing he had to do anything to get out of there, he turned to Willbridge and looked him in the eye.

His friend sucked in his breath sharply. "Morley?" he whispered.

"Let me go," Malcolm begged. "Please."

Willbridge's eyes scoured his face for a long moment. Malcolm stood still under the scrutiny, fighting every urge in him to look away. Finally his friend's shoulders slumped.

"Very well," he said. "I release you from your promises to me."

Relief—and a pain so heavy he thought he might drown in it—filled Malcolm. He nodded, beyond words. Striding to his bag, he opened it to begin a swift packing of his things for the ride back to town. "I'll only take what I can carry," he said, all business now, as he moved about the room. "I can get back faster on horseback. You will send my valet and the rest of my things on tomorrow with Tristan, won't you?"

"Of course," Willbridge said, his voice sober. He moved for the door. As he was about to leave, Malcolm heard him stop.

"I'm sorry, Morley," Willbridge said. "I am so sorry for my selfishness in asking so much of you. It was never my intention to cause you grief. If I could go back in time and change things, I would."

Stunned, Malcolm listened as his friend walked out the door, closing it softly behind him. He stared down at his open bag, frozen. Faced with the devastating knowledge that, even if he could, he would not change the past weeks with Emily for anything.

．．．

Within the hour, Malcolm was off, hurrying through the house to the side door that would lead to the stables and freedom. As before, when he had made to escape the confines of the great house the morning of Willbridge's wedding, his hand was on the handle when he heard it.

Music.

There was no doubt in his mind this time as to the source. He felt in his heart Emily's influence behind the notes, could hear her soul in every strain. And as before, he found his steps taking him against his will down that long hallway to the open door of the music room.

He stood quietly for a time, with maids and footmen rushing to and fro around him in their preparations for the great ball that evening. Even though he was surrounded by busy humanity, he felt alone and adrift, enveloped by the plaintive tune coming from Emily's instrument. There was nothing but sorrow played out under her fingertips today, a swelling grief that let him know, more than any words could, the state of her mind.

The minutes passed, the time ticking mercilessly on toward evening. He must leave soon, he knew, to get as many hours of daylight as possible before darkness made the roads impossible to navigate. Emily's music, however, was like a chain binding him to the spot. As he was about to turn away, there was a movement at the door, and a pale head came into view.

"Bach," Malcolm whispered.

The dog peered at him somberly before padding out into the hall. He stopped a short distance from him, eyeing him with canine worry before letting loose a low whine.

"I know," Malcolm murmured, coming closer to the animal and kneeling down before him. He ran his free hand over Bach's head. "And I am sorry for it. More than you know."

The dog gave a soft woof, nosing his chest.

"Yes, it does hurt," Malcolm agreed. "But that is neither here nor there. For I must leave. Just promise me something, will you? You will look after her for me?" His voice broke, and he cleared his throat. "Look after her and give her all the love she needs."

Bach looked at him with that one brown eye, an eye that seemed to see straight through to his very soul. Unable to take the scrutiny—of an animal, no less—Malcolm rose. Instead of leaving, however, he took the few steps necessary to peer into the music room. One more look, he thought a bit desperately. One more view to warm him for the rest of his days.

She was there, a vision in pale blue, her hair a bright flame, beckoning him. Her face was too pale, he noted, the smudges under her eyes prominent. His heart ached at this proof of her sleepless nights. For one bright, golden moment he was nearly overcome with the need to go to her, to take her in his arms and erase all the grief that tightened her features.

His fingers gripped tight to his satchel, the one solid thing still tethering him to reality. He had made mistakes in the whole debacle, he knew. Yet she hadn't cared for him enough to give him another chance.

But the pain was growing too great. He had to leave, before his heart—and his peace of mind—was lost forever. Turning, he strode off without another glance.

Chapter 24

There were so many people. Emily hadn't thought there were this many people in the world, much less just in this small part of Northamptonshire. This was no mere country dance, but a ball of the finest order.

Leave it to Lady Tarryton to end her two weeks of assumed hostess duties with such a flourish.

Emily stood with her back pressed against the wall inside the ballroom doors as the throng before her twirled and laughed, talked and promenaded. She swallowed hard. There had to be two hundred people here at the very least. Where had they all come from? How was it possible that her family even knew two hundred people? She had the insane urge to find an alcove, to hide and not emerge until the last person had left. Just then, however, she spied Daphne dancing with Mr. Ignatius Knowles. Sir Tristan was in another set. The man kept throwing longing glances Daphne's way. No, she could not hide. She had a job to do. Even so, her feet would not obey her. She stayed frozen in place, like a frightened rabbit faced with a hungry horde, certain she would be ripped to shreds the moment she stepped within their midst.

The music came to a flourishing close. Emily blinked. She had been so immersed in her panic that she hadn't heard a single chord of it. Had it been a quadrille, a cotillion? Truly, she hadn't a clue. She pushed herself away from the wall, forcing her feet to move in her sister's direction. The more she played slave to her fears, the less time she had to accomplish what she had set out to do. She would wring some sort of promise between those two tonight, no matter what it took.

Although, she thought as she stepped forward only to find herself within an unmoving clump of humanity, perhaps she could take a few minutes more to ready herself for the ordeal ahead. Feeling an utter coward, she retreated back toward the open ballroom doors. The sight there, however, stunned her completely. She sprang into movement, launching herself straight into her brother's arms.

"Caleb!" she cried. "You're back. And Imogen," she went on happily, embracing her sister-in-law. "It's so good to see the both of you."

"We've missed you, dearest," Imogen said, pulling back and smiling, her clear turquoise eyes scanning Emily's face. "How have you fared while we were gone?"

An image of Malcolm's face rose up in her mind, the memory of his kisses crashing over her with all the strength of a wave. "Fine," she managed, her smile turning brittle. "Just fine. But we didn't expect you until tomorrow at the earliest."

"We could not miss this final jewel in the crown that is the first house party Willowhaven has seen since I was a boy," Caleb said with a wry smile.

"And what a jewel it is," Imogen murmured, trepidation ripe in her voice as she took in the room. She turned worried eyes up to Caleb. "I did tell you I should have reined her in. What must your mother think of all this?"

Emily could well imagine Imogen's worry. Not only had it been her mother who had overtaken the duties that should have rightly belonged to the dowager marchioness, but Imogen's own shyness in crowds must be overwhelming her. If it was a portion of what Emily was feeling at the moment, she knew it was horrible indeed.

"Don't worry, love," Caleb said soothingly. "My mother would not have allowed it if she had been unwilling to have it happen."

"But you don't know my mother," Imogen fretted.

"No," Emily cut in, "but we do know ours. And Caleb is right in that she's stronger than you think and would not have given in to Lady Tarryton unless she wished to."

Just then, Sir Tristan approached. "Well, look who's arrived," he said in his jovial way, shaking Caleb's hand. "And looking none the worse for having spent nearly a fortnight in the sole company of this lovely woman." He grinned, kissing Imogen on the cheek. "You're looking well, Imogen. I do hope that means this bounder is treating you well."

Imogen blushed. "Very well."

Sir Tristan gave her a saucy wink before turning back to his friend. "Morley will be glad to see you. Though where he's got off to I don't know. I haven't seen him all evening. I was about to go looking for him when I caught sight of you."

Caleb frowned. "But didn't you know? Morley left hours ago."

Emily's blood turned to ice. "Malcolm has left?" she blurted.

"What do you mean he's left?" Sir Tristan demanded, his face showing his shock.

Caleb's frown deepened. "Imogen and I ran into him as we arrived. He took his leave immediately, said he had business in London." His eyes slid to Emily for a second. She clenched her fingers in her skirts to stop their trembling, wondering at the flash of worry in his face.

"That damn stubborn fool," Sir Tristan exploded.

"Why do I get the feeling," Caleb asked slowly, "that something deep is going on here?"

Sir Tristan pressed his lips tight, looking about the crowded room. Several people were staring their way, their expressions blatantly curious. "Perhaps we had best take this to a more private location," he mumbled. "Let me fetch Daphne, and we'll meet you in the library in a thrice."

If Caleb thought anything unusual about his friend's request, he gave no hint of it. He guided Imogen and Emily down the hall to the empty library. The three of them were quietly pensive as they waited, Caleb busying himself by stoking the low fire in the hearth.

Malcolm had left? And without bidding her farewell?

Naturally without saying good-bye, she silently upbraided herself. They had not exactly been on friendly terms the past days. Perhaps it was better this way. They needn't have to deal with one another again, could go on with their lives.

Yet the knowledge that she would never see him again was like a piercing claw, reaching into her chest, finding and squeezing her heart until she was certain another ounce of pain could not be wrung from it.

Within minutes—though what felt like hours—the door opened and Sir Tristan and Daphne slipped inside, approaching their small group.

"Now," Caleb said, still facing the hearth, his voice harsh in the quiet of the vast room, "perhaps someone would care to let me know what is going on here. For after Morley's strange leave-taking and the peculiar reaction I received when the news of his departure was conveyed, I expect something interesting happened in my absence."

Sir Tristan was the one to speak into the tense silence. "First, let me tell you that everything that was done, was done for the right reasons."

Caleb spun about to face his friend, a fatalistic kind of doom darkening his features. "What did you do, Tristan?"

Daphne stepped forward then. "He didn't decide on it alone," she declared. "If anything, it was my idea. He was simply going along with it."

"Your idea," Caleb stated blankly. "Why am I getting a very bad feeling about all of this?"

As was Emily. She gripped tight to the back of the chair she stood behind as if it were the one thing tethering her to the ground.

Daphne looked at her then. Emily felt her entire world tip.

"We did so want Emily and Lord Morley to be happy, you see," Daphne explained, her eyes begging forgiveness.

"Morley?" Caleb asked, even as Emily's heart thumped heavy in her chest. "And Emily? What the devil are you talking about?"

"I am so sorry, Emily," Daphne said, ignoring their brother. "We were convinced there was something between you and Lord

Morley. And your attraction for one another seemed more apparent the more Tristan and I were in each other's company. You seemed so determined to throw Tristan and I together at every turn, and Lord Morley to see that it didn't happen, that we believed feigning a romance was the best way to force you together and make the both of you see that you needed one another."

A thick silence descended. Emily felt she was suffocating under it. "Do you mean to tell me," she said slowly, distinctly, "that you and Sir Tristan were never attracted to one another?"

"Oh, no, we were," Daphne declared. "But once we kissed we both realized there was nothing there."

"You kissed my sister?" Caleb roared.

"It was nothing, really," Daphne said dismissively, waving her brother's rage off with one slender hand.

"Well, now, I wouldn't say it was nothing," Sir Tristan said defensively before he caught sight of Caleb's expression. He backed away several steps. "No, you are so right. It was nothing. Nothing at all."

"You made it all up?" Emily asked, her voice trembling. She stepped out from behind the chair, storming forward until she was directly in front of the couple. Her hands shook so violently she feared what she might do with them and clenched them into tight balls. "How could you do something like that? How could you manipulate us in such an underhanded way?"

"We were not manipulating you," Daphne denied. "We were simply giving you both the opportunity to form an attachment, to throw you both together in the most inflamed situations possible."

Emily's vision went red. "So we were some kind of scientific experiment to you? Throw the damaged spinster together with the handsome rake and see what happens?"

Daphne's eyes widened in horror. "No! Of course not!"

Imogen rushed forward, putting her arm around Emily. "Dearest, you're becoming overset. Daphne would never have done such a thing lightly. She loves you."

The calm reason in her friend's voice finally cut through Emily's anger. The air left her in a rush, taking with it all her indignation. She slumped, leaning into Imogen. "You're right," she rasped. "And how much better am I? Wasn't I doing just that, manipulating them into forming an attachment? Though my reasons were not so noble."

"What do you mean?" Imogen asked quietly.

Emily looked at Daphne, guilt filling her. "I thought I saw a mutual attraction between you and Sir Tristan. But my main reason for attempting to throw you both together was a desire to see you married off, to prevent our trip to London."

Daphne stared at her in shock. "Why didn't you tell me the trip was so abhorrent to you?"

Emily shrugged. "How could I? You were so happy. And you asked me to go. I could not disappoint you by abandoning you when you needed me most."

Her sister came closer and took up her hands. "I knew you wouldn't care for it, but I didn't think it would panic you to such a degree. My goodness, I am a selfish creature indeed, to not know your heart."

She pulled Emily into a hug. Emily stood frozen for a moment, stunned, before she crumbled. Wrapping her arms about her sister's slender waist, she pressed her burning eyes into Daphne's shoulder. "I'm sorry," she whispered.

"It's I who am sorry," Daphne murmured. She pulled back, looking Emily in the eye. "Though I would love to have you there with me, I won't force you. Your happiness means more to me than anything. I could not enjoy my time in London knowing I was making you miserable by forcing you to go."

Emily gave her a watery smile. She waited, expecting relief to lighten the weight on her chest. This was a kind of victory, after all. It was what she had wanted all along, to be able to stay behind at Willowhaven. But it did not give her an ounce of relief. Instead the muted grief in her breast seemed to grow more acute.

"Now that we have that settled," Caleb said, his voice breaking through the silence, "would someone mind telling me what that business was about Emily and Morley forming an attachment?"

Emily felt as if she'd taken a punch to the gut. In a flash she knew what settled so heavy on her soul. Malcolm. Or rather the loss of him and the promise of what they could have had together.

"There was nothing between us," she said. "Daphne and Sir Tristan were quite mistaken."

"I don't think we were," Sir Tristan said thoughtfully. He stepped forward. "You cannot mean to tell me you felt nothing for him."

She couldn't look him in the eye. "It matters not," she replied, bitterness coating her words though she strived to keep them as neutral as she could. "For, if you have not noticed, he has left, like a thief in the night, without even a farewell. I would not say those are the actions of a man who cares."

"Actually, as we are talking of Morley, I would say that is exactly what that man would do if he were falling in love."

She looked at him in disbelief. "Love? You cannot mean that, sir. We are too different, he and I. We will never suit. And besides, his affections are still engaged, with Lady Morley."

"Lady Morley?" He laughed. "You must be joking. He doesn't give a whit about her."

She shook her head sharply. "No, you don't know, you didn't see. He was too gentlemanly to tell me outright, but the second he spied her, his manners toward me changed. He was quite cold, would hardly look at me. Are those the actions of a man in love?"

"If it is Morley we are talking about, then yes," Sir Tristan answered quietly.

Stunned by his blind certainty in Malcolm, she stared mutely at him.

"Please trust me, Lady Emily," he continued, his eyes boring down into hers. "For I know Morley. And I knew Lydia. She is a selfish woman who causes mischief when she feels slighted. And she was ever so jealous of you."

"You must be inebriated, to think such a thing," she whispered.

"I'm sober as a vicar. Yes, Morley was a pigheaded idiot for staying away from you while Lydia was around. And I told him so. But he did it to protect you."

"Me?"

"Yes, you." He smiled gently. "He feared what Lydia might do to you if she saw how he cared for you. And so he did what he could to protect you. It was done in his own fumbling, stupid way. But his heart was in the right place."

She shook her head. He would not stop trying to convince her. She had to lay her full shame at his feet then, so he would know how hopeless this all was. "But they kissed, Sir Tristan. You cannot explain away that."

He did not so much as flinch at her revelation, instead tilting his head. "Did he kiss her? Or did Lydia do the kissing?"

Malcolm's words swirled in her head then: *She is nothing to me now, I swear it.*

But Lady Morley's appearance after leaving Malcolm in the study. And Malcolm's own rumpled appearance. She had seen the proof with her own eyes.

Proof of what? her mind whispered. *You never confronted him, never allowed him to defend himself.*

She felt it then, the crumbling of her defenses. Desperate to hold onto her hurt—for without it she knew she would break—she shook her head. "You may think well of your friend, Sir Tristan, but it is more than his coldness, more than the kiss. He confided something to Lady Morley, something I told him and no one else. There could have been no one she could have learned it from. And so Malcolm betrayed me in the worst way. Can you possibly defend him now?"

But his calm expression did not change. "Yes. For I know how mercenary Lydia is. And I also know that Morley is an honorable man. If you told him something in secret, he would not have told another. I swear it."

Just like that, he laid waste to her every argument. She looked deep into Sir Tristan's eyes, searching for some hint of uncertainty. But the surprisingly warm blue of his eyes stayed steady. He smiled in encouragement.

Her breath escaped her.

"What the devil is going on?" Caleb demanded, his voice explosive, echoing about the far reaches of the cavernous room.

"I do believe," Imogen said, a smile lighting her tone, "that our Emily and Lord Morley have formed an attachment."

"Oh, no," he groaned.

All eyes turned his way. Caleb, Emily noticed, was looking at her in horror.

"No, you mistake the matter," he rasped. "And I can lay the blame at my own feet."

Imogen took a step toward her husband. "What are you talking about, Caleb?"

He cast her a guilty glance before returning it to Emily. "You believed Morley's attentions to Emily meant he cared for her. The reason he stayed close to her, however, had nothing to do with romantic intentions toward Emily, and everything to do with a promise he made to me."

"What promise?" Imogen demanded, her brows lowering.

"Now, you must know," he said, backing up a step, "that my intentions were pure."

"It seems everyone tonight had good intentions, but not a lot of sense," Sir Tristan muttered.

Caleb cast him a furious glare.

"Caleb," Imogen warned.

Unable to stand one moment more of the drama being played out before her, Emily stepped forward. "Caleb had Lord Morley promise to watch over me, much like a nursemaid over a particularly troublesome child." The words came out much more acidic than she had planned.

"You knew about that?" Caleb asked in disbelief.

"You did *what*?" Imogen demanded of her husband.

"Am I that much trouble to you, Caleb," Emily asked in a small voice, "that you must extract the promise of your friend to shadow my footsteps?"

"No." Caleb rushed to her and pulled her into his embrace. "You are infinitely precious to me. I did what I did because I knew this house party would be difficult for you and I wanted to make certain you were protected. Which," he continued, pulling away and eyeing his wife's furious expression, "I suppose sounds weak, now that I think about it."

"It was not weak," Emily said, suddenly weary beyond belief. "I know what you did was out of love for me. Though I would have liked to have been given a choice in the matter."

She made to leave then. What more was there to say? All her shame was out in the open for all to see. She wanted nothing more than to escape to her room and soak away her miseries in a hot bath.

Sir Tristan's voice, however, stopped her.

"No," he declared, frustration lacing his normally cheerful voice. "It was more than that idiotic promise. It was something more. I saw it with my own blasted eyes."

"What the devil are you talking about, Tristan?" Caleb growled. "Don't you see you're upsetting her more?"

"If upsetting her is the only way to make her see that Morley's feelings for her are genuine, then I will." He strode to her and took up her hands. "You don't know him as I do. Morley has been hurt, and dreadfully. More than one person has broken his heart, has betrayed his trust and abandoned him. First with his parents, dying when he was so young. Then his uncle, who took Morley and his brother in. Gad, but he hated them. The man made their lives miserable. But Morley always had Bertram through it all. And then me and Willbridge. But it was his brother who made his life at home bearable, who was his rock when things got bad."

Despite herself, Emily hung on his every word. She pictured Malcolm as a boy, dark and sensitive and hurting. And her heart ached for him. "Then what?" she rasped when he fell silent.

"Morley fell in love."

The words were like a slap to the face. She didn't want to hear this, how Malcolm had loved another.

Sir Tristan seemed oblivious to her distress. "He was head over arse for her—pardon my language—and would have given her the moon if she'd asked. I'd never seen him so happy." He paused, the pain in his eyes sparking to furious life. "Until," he continued in a tight voice, "his brother went and married the girl himself."

"Lady Morley," Emily whispered brokenly.

Sir Tristan nodded grimly. "Yes, Lydia. She broke his heart. They both did, she and Bertram, for as horrible as Lydia's betrayal had been, it was Bertram's that completely destroyed him. He closed himself off after that. From everyone, Caleb and myself included. Oh, I knew he cared for us in his own way. And we stayed the closest of friends. Yet there was a wall put up after that day that no one, not even Caleb nor I, could breech." He looked at her intently. "Until you."

She shook her head, tears blinding her. "He doesn't love me. He might have cared for me, but he doesn't love me. Your affection for him is clouding your better judgment."

"I'm right," he insisted, triumph lighting his eyes. "And you love him as well."

Anger rose up in her, fueled by her despair. "If you know my heart so well, then tell me, what am I supposed to do? We have broken things off. And he must hate me for abandoning him as nearly everyone else in his life has. Would you have me run after him? Believe that things will work out despite our very real differences? Throw myself on his mercy? Declare my love for him?"

"Yes."

That one word, said with such surety, hung in the air between them.

Emily laughed, the sound raw and bitter. "You are mad."

"No," he said with utter calm, "I am completely sane."

She stared at him long and hard. His gaze never wavered, as steady as his conviction in the insane idea she had spewed. He truly meant for her to do such a thing.

"I can't," she choked out. "Why won't you see? I can't go after him. I'm not strong enough."

"You are," he insisted.

Daphne stepped up beside him. "You truly are, Emily," she said.

"No!" she fairly shouted. "It's everything I fought against. To go to London, to draw attention to myself. To court rejection..."

Sir Tristan looked on her with sorrowful eyes. "And yet, if you don't, you both will live out the rest of your lives in the acutest misery. Always wondering what would have happened had you taken a chance on him. A chance on yourself."

Emily looked from one face to another, feeling as if the walls were closing in on her. Her mind froze, and with it all coherent thought. She opened her mouth, willing something, anything, to emerge that could make them see how deluded they were.

A sharp, furious barking started up in the hall. Even with the heavy wooden door muffling it, there was no mistaking the warning note in it.

Emily took her silk skirts up in her hands and ran from the room. The sight that met her in the hall, however, had her skidding to a stunned halt.

Bach had Lord Randall cornered in an alcove. The dog's very fur seemed to stand on end, his tail stuck straight out behind him, his teeth bared.

"Bach!" she cried, rushing forward and taking hold of the dog's collar, pulling him back from the cowering nobleman. Bach's barking ceased, his stance relaxing at her touch, though fierce growls continued to vibrate through him. He kept his eye trained on Lord Randall, who was looking at the dog as if he were seeing a ghost.

"Where did you find that creature?"

Something in the way he said it made Emily look at him with narrowed eyes. "Do you know this dog, then?"

"Of course I do," he spat, straightening away from the wall and tugging at his impeccably cut evening coat. "My youngest tried hiding it in the house, thought to keep the thing as a pet. I put a stop to that. I won't have such a damaged creature in my home."

The hallway was quickly filling with people pouring from the ballroom, no doubt curious as to the cause of the commotion. Emily ignored them, her attention focused solely on the disgusting excuse for a man before her. "Do you mean to tell me," she said, her voice low and fierce, "that you are the one to abandon him? You are the one who threw him out like garbage?"

"Certainly not," he said, curling his lip. "I meant to put the fiend out of its misery and put a bullet in his head. It's a travesty to let a creature such as he live with such an infirmity. But he bolted, and so I was unable to perform my duty."

"Your duty? You call killing an innocent creature your duty? Well, sir, I do not know who you answer to, but I answer to God, and He would never condone such an inhumane act."

There was a general murmur of agreement at that. Lord Randall opened his mouth, no doubt to give her a scathing set-down, when he became aware of their audience. At once he turned a putrid sort of green, for the faces surrounding him were not friendly.

"You are a despicable excuse of a man," Emily went on, quite unable to stop now that she had started. "You have belittled me and tormented me for as long as I can remember, all because I lack the perfection you desire in life. And now I find you would have ended the life of a beautiful creature, all because it does not conform to what you believe beauty to be. Well, let me tell you, my lord, this dog has a pure heart, and a beautiful soul. Something I am sure you could never understand. For though your form and face is handsome, within you is nothing but the vilest monster."

Gasps could be heard, and above the sudden roar of voices emerged a faint clapping. Gripping Bach tight, she pulled him away from the fascinated onlookers, past her gawking siblings and friends, and into the library. Once there, she let go of the dog's collar and held her hands up to her burning cheeks. But it was not horror or distress that caused her skin to heat. No, it was elation that ran through her veins, that had her heart beating out a furious rhythm. She truly was stronger than she had supposed.

With that realization, another wild, amazing idea took shape. Perhaps she *could* go after Malcolm, tell him how she felt and put her heart on the line. Mayhap she could take a chance to see if they could find happiness with each other.

Malcolm. Goodness, but she loved him. Wasn't he worth the leap of faith? Wasn't she?

"Emily?"

Trembling with excitement, she turned to face her siblings and friends.

"Ready the carriage, Brother," she said. "We leave for London within the hour."

Chapter 25

What have I done? Oh dear, oh dear, oh dear, what have I done?

It was not the first time that lamentation had spun dizzyingly about in her head during the lengthy journey to London, which, thanks to a broken carriage axle, had turned into a full two-day trip instead of the mere one-and-a-half she had been promised. Now, surrounded by the hustle and bustle of the great city itself, she found that her doubts were growing so loud she thought her head would burst from the panic of it.

It was one thing to make an exciting exit in the wake of the glorious—and well-deserved—insults she had given Lord Randall. It was quite another to sit in a carriage for the next two days and contemplate the utter idiocy of that rash decision.

As if reading her volatile thoughts, Imogen reached across the carriage and laid a gentle hand on hers. "Emily, are you all right?"

"Fine!" she squawked. Blushing, she managed a pitiful smile. "I'm fine."

"It's late," Caleb murmured, glancing out the carriage window. "We'll retire for the night and visit Morley tomorrow."

"No," Emily burst out. Gad, no. If she had all night to think it over, another night to contemplate what an utter fool she was for putting everything on the line like this with no guarantee that she would have Malcolm's heart at the end of it, she might turn coward and run all the way back to Willowhaven. "That is, can we drive by his home, to at least see if he's in?"

"Of course we can," Caleb said gently. He rapped on the ceiling, giving the driver the new directions when the man opened the trapdoor. "We should be there within the quarter hour," he told Emily when he was through.

She nodded, turning her attention to the passing scenery—not the best idea, given the circumstances.

Goodness, she had never seen so many carriages and people in her life. Even as they moved into the more genteel area of the city—Mayfair, Imogen told her—there was still an incredible amount of movement. It was as if the city never rested, never slept. A constant moving, living entity, bustling with humanity.

She felt ill.

Much too soon, the carriage slowed, then rocked to a stop. Emily sat frozen for a moment, staring out the window, up at the towering ochre town house, glowing golden in the lamplight. This was where Malcolm lived a good portion of the time, she realized. He could even now be within. She only had to exit the carriage, walk up the front steps, knock on that altogether imposing and elegant door.

"Shall we?" Caleb murmured.

"Yes," she replied with far more bravado than she felt.

Her brother descended from the carriage, turning to help her and Imogen down. In a blink they were standing on the top steps. Caleb rapped the knocker sharply.

At once the door swung open to reveal a rotund, jovial butler.

"Why, Lord Willbridge," he said affably. "This is a pleasant surprise. We had heard you had married and would be in the country for some time."

"Alas, there is something in town that needed my immediate attention," Caleb replied. "Though, as you can see, I have had the good sense to bring along my bride, as well as my sister to keep me company. Imogen, Emily, this is Burnell, Morley's esteemed butler. Burnell, may I introduce you to my wife, Lady Willbridge, and my sister, Lady Emily. Burnell," he continued as the man greeted them with a wide smile and deep bow, "I don't suppose Morley is at home this evening? We have some pressing business with him."

The butler's face fell. "Ah, I am heartily sorry, my lord, but Lord Morley has gone out for the evening, and we do not anticipate him back before dawn."

Emily had not expected to be turned away. But obviously he would be out, she berated herself. The man no doubt kept himself busy while in town with all manner of social obligations. He certainly would not have been waiting at home on the off chance that she would travel from the comfort of Northamptonshire to lay her heart at his feet.

"That's too bad," Caleb said. "Well, we shall have to wait until tomorrow, then. Good evening, Burnell." He touched his hat and made to usher Emily and Imogen away.

"Wait," Emily said.

The other three paused and stared at her in surprise. Emily was beyond caring. She could not wait another night to see Malcolm. She could not wait another hour; she would go mad if she did.

She turned to the jolly butler. "Do you by chance know where Lord Morley was off to for the evening?"

"That I do, my lady," he replied. "He is attending Lady Beezleton's annual ball."

"Thank you." With that, she turned and marched back for the carriage.

"Emily," Imogen called, fast on her heels, with Caleb not far behind her, "what are you planning on doing?"

"I am going to locate an appropriate gown, and then I am going to Lady Beezleton's ball."

She felt more than heard them pause behind her as she vaulted up into the carriage. A moment later, her brother and Imogen followed her inside.

"Emily," Caleb said as the door closed behind them, "you cannot mean to go to a London ball. Why, Lady Beezleton throws some of the most lavish affairs of the year."

"I can and I do," she replied. The carriage started off, and she looked her brother full in the eye, praying he would not fight her on this. Knowing it would break whatever fragile hold she had on her determination if he did. "Caleb, if I do not do this now, I will never have the nerve."

Silence reigned for a moment. Then Imogen spoke up, her voice strong and certain. "We really must have the appropriate clothing for such a momentous event. Let's make a detour to my family home. Mariah and I left plenty of ball gowns behind to choose from. Then we may go to Lady Beezleton's ball in style."

As Caleb directed the driver, Emily sat silent in her corner of the carriage, trying not to think of the possible repercussions of her rash decision. No matter what, she could not go another night without knowing her future with the man she loved.

• • •

A mere hour later, they rolled up before a towering mansion, the much-lauded Lady Beezleton's London residence. Emily's jaw nearly dropped at the magnificence of it. Whereas Willowhaven was elegant and sprawling, full of history, there was still something wonderfully welcoming about it. It had been made for comfort, to be lived in.

This place, however, screamed wealth and prestige. It rose above the gathered nobility a full three stories, its columns and cornices giving it all the splendor of ancient Rome. What must be thousands of candles—pure beeswax, no doubt, and not a tallow one in sight—made the pale stone edifice seem to glow from within, a beacon of pleasure and elegance in the dark, dank London night.

The carriage rocked to a halt and a footman made to open the door. Caleb stilled it with a hand and turned to Emily.

"Are you certain?" he asked, low and intense.

She nodded before she could think better of it. After one more long, searching look, Caleb opened the door.

They made their way up the wide stone staircase and through the towering double doors into the entrance hall, falling into the long receiving line. Emily gripped tight to Caleb's sleeve, painfully aware of the tension in his arm. Imogen, too, cast worried glances her way, but she was unable to utter a single word or dredge up even the smallest of smiles to ease their minds. Knowing her scar would bring them unwanted attention, she attempted to keep her gaze on the inlaid marble floor. Yet she couldn't help but snatch small glances to the left and right, taking in the magnificence of her surroundings. Which was not the best of ideas. Her brief glimpses of the impeccably dressed people and rich decor surrounding them had her heart pattering in trepidation. A servant came forward for her wrap and Emily reluctantly handed it over. Cool evening air immediately hit her exposed skin, and she fought the instinct to cover her décolletage. She had never been so bared before. The low-cut gown seemed as thin and inconsequential as a whisper, framing her bosom and leaving most of her chest and shoulders bare. Imogen had assured her it was the latest fashion when she had first helped Emily into it, hurriedly pinning and securing the excess material in the hem and bodice of the pale blue silk. And, being Mariah's gown, it must be the height of fashion, for she was the most elegant young woman Emily had ever met. Even so, she could not help thinking this was a mistake. Surely these people would see her for the fraud she was, would denounce her on the spot, and chase her from the house.

To her amazement, she sailed right through the crowd. Keeping her face averted as much as possible without stumbling into anyone, gripping tight to her brother's arm, she waited for that first sight of her ruined cheek. Dreading it. Finally, coming to the front of the receiving line, it happened.

Caleb directed them to a tall, robust matron with a large bejeweled turban on her steel curls. "Lady Beezleton," he said with a flourishing bow and easy grin, "you are looking wonderful this evening."

She lifted her lorgnette, peering at Caleb with obvious pleasure. "Lord Willbridge, I did not think you were in town at present. I'd heard you'd married. Lord Tarryton's eldest, I believe."

Caleb directed his attention to Imogen, pulling her against his side. A protective gesture, as Imogen looked like she would rather sink through the floor than be where she was. "Yes. Please let me introduce my wife, Imogen, Lady Willbridge. Imogen, you of course know Lady Beezleton? And this young lady," he said, tilting his head in Emily's direction, "is my sister, Lady Emily Masters."

The woman directed her haughty gaze in Emily's direction. Immediately the woman froze, her eyes widening in that all-too-familiar expression. Emily felt her hand creep to her cheek, began the inevitable slide of her eyes to the ground.

Instead she stopped, lowering her hand and raising her head, looking the woman straight in the eye.

The matron met her gaze. Then, to Emily's surprise, she dipped her head in acknowledgement and smiled.

"Lady Emily, it is a pleasure."

Emily stood stunned for a moment. Caleb nudged her with the arm she was gripping. Belatedly, she dipped into a jerking curtsy. "My lady."

If the woman noticed the delay in propriety, she made no notice of it. "Please enjoy yourselves this evening," she said affably. As Caleb made to guide Imogen and Emily past Lady Beezleton, she stopped him. "Oh, and Lord Willbridge. I'm in your debt, you know. Many a hostess would give her right arm to have been the one to entice you and your lovely wife for your debut as a married couple into society." She chuckled. "The Duchess of Morledge will be green with envy."

He chuckled, said something that made the woman beam with pleasure, and they were on their way.

Emily was dumbfounded. What had happened? Where was the disgust and horror she had come to expect? Perhaps it had been a fluke. Perhaps the woman had a strong stomach. Or horrendous eyesight.

The only way to test that theory, however, was to see how others reacted. And to do that, she must leave her bubble of comfort and actually look at people. In the eye.

It wasn't the most palatable of plans. In truth, it had her stomach roiling in the worst way. It went against every instinct she had lived by for the past decade. Yet as Caleb was stopped time and again by acquaintances—either her brother was incredibly popular, or his marriage to Imogen truly was the event of the Season as Lady Beezleton had implied—she raised her head high, making certain she met the gazes of those she was introduced to, and took careful stock of their reactions to her.

As expected, most were taken aback, or gave her a quick and surprised second glance. Following that was the hard stare, confusion puckering their brows as they studied her scar. And then...

Nothing.

They acknowledged her with a smile and a bow, and that was that. Not one person looked horrified. Certainly there was a subdued kind of pity in more than one person's face, but it was a type that was easily handled and dismissed. It was in that moment that Emily realized the irony of the situation. Malcolm had been right. She had been so busy protecting herself from what she believed others might think of her that she had not given anyone a chance to know her.

It was humbling and dismaying. And freeing.

Caleb must have sensed the change in her demeanor. He bent his head toward her as they extracted themselves from another group of well-wishers and said in her ear, "Emily, is something amiss?"

"Not at all," she said with complete honesty. She smiled widely up at him. "Everything is brilliant."

He blinked and stared down at her as if he had never seen her before. "That's...good."

They came upon the ballroom doors. Caleb gave their name to the butler stationed there, and they were announced. Just one step within the vast room and Caleb was immediately hailed by several friends.

But Emily was done with being waylaid. She had come here for a purpose, and that did not include meeting half of London. There was only one man in the entire city she cared for in that moment.

Malcolm.

Anticipation tingled along her skin. He was here somewhere. She would find him, and let him know what he meant to her.

Giving her brother and Imogen a quick glance to verify their attention was diverted, she slipped away into the mass of people. She had a sudden flash of that long-ago day at Willowhaven when she had plunged into the crowd to get away from Malcolm and his surly hovering. Then he had saved her from her panic. Now she boldly dove into the crowd again, to find her way to him.

Perhaps to save *him* this time.

Chapter 26

Malcolm had tried.

For hours he had tried to blend back into this world, to put the last three weeks behind him and return to what he had been before. He looked out over the mass of bodies, and just managed to hold back the growl that clamored and clawed in his chest. Nothing had been the same since his return to London.

He knew, deep in his soul, it never would be again.

Emily had changed the very essence of him. The dissolute, unfeeling rake—that persona he had claimed for so many years— was no longer within him. There was not a hint of it left. His heart no longer lay dead and cold in his chest. Instead it beat with fierce life. Telling him he was a fool. That he should go back for her, claim her, live the remainder of his days with her arms cradling him and her kiss on his lips.

Letting loose a low curse, ignoring the passing debutantes who gasped and tittered at him behind their fans, he snatched up a glass of champagne from the tray of a passing footman. He downed it in one swallow, returning it to the tray as quickly as he had taken it, and strode to the open doors leading to the dark garden. Breathing in deeply of the cool evening air, he fought to put his mad desire for Emily from his mind.

Had he learned nothing? He was better off alone. Even if he followed his desires and returned to Emily, even if he took her for his own, there would always be something between them. In his heart he would know that, no matter how happy he was in the moment, it could not last. It never did. Hadn't Emily already proved that she would rather be alone than take a chance on what they could have?

The crowd felt suddenly too dense, the conversation too loud, the laughter too grating. Desperate for escape, he turned back to the ballroom, determined to leave this farce of an evening and lick his wounds in the privacy of his own home.

"Malcolm."

Foolish hope leapt in his breast. For one bright, shining moment he thought it might be Emily. But no, she was safely back at Willowhaven. She would never come to London, at least not willingly.

Even so, he turned, a silent prayer on his lips that died a swift death when he saw who it was.

"Lydia."

She smiled up at him, those cerulean eyes of hers as wide and innocent as when he'd fallen in love with her. Though now he looked clearly into their depths and could see that a flat emptiness lurked there.

"I didn't expect you back in London so soon," she said.

"Yet here I am."

"Yes, you are." Her smile widened. "And alone. I admit I had expected you to have a...companion with you when next I saw you."

His every muscle tensed. Emily flashed in his mind, quickly banished. "Did you?"

"Oh, yes. Though I am ever so glad you're unattached. Did things not work out, then, with your little friend?"

"What do you want, Lydia?" he gritted.

"I'm just so glad to see you again after so many years. I admit, I had not thought of you when I decided to move to London. But then I saw you in Northamptonshire. It was such a pleasant surprise. I had forgotten how...virile you are."

She moved closer, her fingers skimming up his arm. He fought the urge to slap her hand away, instead stepping back so it fell back to her side.

She smirked. "You needn't act so coy, Malcolm."

"I assure you, I am not acting coy," he bit out.

"Come now, we are no longer at that stuffy house party. This is London. The rules are quite different here. It is expected that widowed women take lovers." To punctuate her words, she stepped closer to him, surreptitiously running her hand along his sleeve.

Malcolm stared hard at her. "You cannot possibly be serious."

"I assure you, I am."

The purr of her voice, meant to inflame his interest no doubt, only managed to spark his disgust. "Entering into such a relationship with you, madam, is the very last thing I wish in the world. As I told you in Northamptonshire, if I never see you again, I will be too happy. What I wish is for you to disappear from my life. Forever."

She stared up at him, stunned, before her expression dissolved into humor. "You cannot mean to tell me you don't want me, Malcolm." She chuckled, a throaty sound that at one time would have sent him into a frenzy of passion. "Not after our past. I have never had anyone want me with such desperation. That could not have faded."

He leaned in close to her, letting his lips brush her ear, fiercely pleased at the utter lack of response his body had for her. She gave a breathy little gasp, the laugh falling from her lips as quickly as it had started. Proving that she was not so immune.

"I do mean it, Lydia," he murmured. "You are nothing to me now. If you were to strip naked and perform the most erotic dance possible, I would feel not an ounce of desire for you."

"You lie," she shot back, though her voice lacked snap. She leaned into him. Her eyelashes fluttered against the flawless pink porcelain of her cheeks.

Yet they were flawed in his eyes, as they lacked the scar that had become desperately dear to him.

The unexpected reminder of Emily so stunned him that he froze. Would he never forget her? He saw it now, the long years stretched ahead of him, haunted by the memory of her.

Exhaustion bore down on him. Whatever future he had was

cold and bleak without Emily's light to guide his way out of the darkness that held his soul prisoner. He had never been so happy as when he had been with her. He should go back, make her see that they belonged together. He could be strong enough for the both of them.

The idea shocked him even more than the memory of her had. He stood stupidly for a moment, overcome with longing. Wondering why the thought of returning to her seemed so very right.

Lydia took his silence as confirmation that he truly did want her despite his protestations. With a small, knowing smile she repeated, "You lie. And I will prove it." So saying, she grasped his arm and, before he knew what she was planning, yanked him out the garden doors and into the dark night.

• • •

Emily swayed on her feet, reaching for the wall as she watched Lady Morley pull Malcolm out the French doors and into the garden. She had seen the flirtatious glances the woman had given him, had seen the intimate way Malcolm had bent over the other woman and whispered in her ear. Those things had stunned her immobile, confusion and hurt shocking the breath from her body. Seeing them head out in an undeniable liaison, however, destroyed her.

Though she could discount the episode at Willowhaven as perpetrated by Lady Morley to come between them, how could she discount this? For it gave proof to every fear in her heart as nothing before it had.

She spun about, blindly seeking to escape the scene of her shattered hopes...and ran straight into Caleb and Imogen. Both their eyes were fixed to the spot Malcolm had been with Lady Morley. As one they turned their gazes on her, one mournful, one furious.

"Oh, my poor dear," Imogen murmured, putting an arm about her.

"That stupid, idiotic bastard," Caleb spat. He lurched in Malcolm's direction.

"Wait!" Emily cried, grabbing at his sleeve. "What are you going to do?"

"What do you think? I'm going to put a bullet in that slithering, despicable former friend of mine."

"You most certainly will not."

Caleb stopped and stared at her, frustration and undiluted rage flaming in his eyes.

"Promise me, Caleb," Emily begged in a quick, desperate whisper, "that you will not kill him. He is not worth it. I will not have my brother on the run over a mistake that I made."

His glower returned full force. "It is not your fault."

She ignored his attempts to soothe her guilt. As if she had no fault in the whole heartbreaking debacle. For all the mistakes Malcolm had made, she had made her fair share as well. She should have listened to him, instead of letting her battered heart and her fear guide her.

Though perhaps she had been in the right, after all, for wasn't he running to the very person he had sworn he'd wanted nothing to do with?

"We all knew it was a gamble to come here," she said. "Me more than any of you. I had the proof of his preference for Lady Morley and was fool enough to ignore my better judgment. Besides, Malcolm made no promise to me, no declarations. And—" Her throat closed for a moment, her gaze shifting against her will to where she had last seen Malcolm. "And I am tired," she continued, low and fierce, "of accepting less than I am worth, of believing I'm not worthy of a happy life. As he is more than happy to go on with his life as if nothing happened between us, I will certainly not spend my life pining over him."

With that, she turned and walked out of the ballroom. Away from the rubble that had been the promise of their life together.

• • •

Lydia dragged Malcolm into the shadows of the balcony. Immediately her mouth searched his out, her full breasts pressing into his chest, her slender, perfumed arms dragging him close.

Revulsion ripped through him. With a muttered curse he pushed her away. He took a quick glance about the balcony, thankful at least that they were alone. "Damn it, Lydia, what the hell is wrong with you? How many times do I have to push you away before you understand that I do not desire you?" he demanded.

Her eyes blazed in the moonlight as she glared at him. "You act the eunuch, and you ask what is wrong with me?"

"So I'm a eunuch for refusing your advances?" He let loose a sharp bark of laughter. "I'm glad to see your vanity is still intact after all this time. Why can't you simply believe that I no longer want you in my bed?"

She made a sound of disgust. "You Arborn men, you are all alike. An attractive, desirable woman offers herself to you and you turn frigid. I begin to think, had I not given your brother a healthy dose of liquid courage, he never would have done the deed."

A dark feeling settled in the pit of Malcolm's stomach. The sounds from the ballroom faded away as his focus sharpened on her face. "Liquid courage?" he asked sharply. "What the hell are you taking about?"

Her lips twisted. "Don't tell me he never told you. I swear, Bertram loved you more than anything; I was certain he would have told you all."

"Perhaps you had best explain, madam," he growled.

"No," she said slowly, eyeing him with interest, leaning back against the stone railing and crossing her arms. "No, I don't think I shall."

He took a menacing step toward her. "I warn you, Lydia. Do not play with me, for I have the power to make your life a living hell. You know I do."

She considered him a moment, uncertainty clouding her eyes, before she straightened and shrugged. "Very well. I don't suppose it matters now. Your brother was...hesitant, I believe is the word, to enter into a union with me. He had some medieval notions about honor and brotherly love, it seemed. He knew you cared for me and couldn't stomach taking me for his own. So one night I gave him a little something to help him along."

"You drugged him?" Malcolm demanded furiously.

Her eyes flared in alarm. "Not drugged. Dear me, Malcolm, what kind of monster do you think I am?"

"Do not tempt me to answer that, madam," he growled.

"I merely softened him with alcohol. The man could not hold his liquor." When he continued to stare at her, aghast, she scoffed. "There's no need to look at me like that. He enjoyed it, I assure you, though he did his best at appearing horrified the following morning."

White-hot anger raced through his veins. "I always knew you were an underhanded, conniving spawn of hell. But this is a new low even for you."

"What did I do but help the man get what he wanted? And he did want me. I saw the way he looked at me when he thought no one would notice. But there was always that love for you that stood between us."

"You mean that stood between you and the title." Bertram's face flashed in his mind, so full of regret the morning he'd pulled Malcolm aside and told him he was to marry Lydia. At the time, Malcolm had been unable to see past his grief and rage. Now he looked at it with new eyes. Bertram had been a man tricked into a marriage he never wanted, forced to do his duty and hurt his only brother. Too honorable to put the blame where it had truly belonged, squarely on Lydia's shoulders.

"You destroyed his life," he rasped. "You destroyed mine. All for a title and a fortune. How can you live with yourself?"

"Very well, thank you."

He gaped at her.

"What would have happened to us if I had married you instead, Malcolm?" she went on blithely. "How would you have supported us? We were both of us so young. You had no skills, no income, no property. We would have lived on your brother's charity to get by. No, it was much better this way."

Unable to stomach her a moment more, he turned away.

"You cannot mean to leave," she demanded.

"I do," he bit out.

She rushed to plant herself in front of him. "Very well, I admit it must be upsetting to you, learning all that."

He let out a disbelieving laugh. "Upsetting? Madam, you have no idea."

She had the gall to roll her eyes. "Please, Malcolm. You are being dramatic. That is all in the past. It has no bearing on the present."

"It has *everything* to do with it."

"Come now," she said. "Yes, I may have made mistakes in the past. But the fact remains that we are both here, we are both available for a dalliance. I have always wanted you, Malcolm, though I chose security instead of lust. And you are so much more than you used to be." Her voice lowered to a purr, her hands finding and stroking over his jacket lapels. "There's no reason on earth that we cannot continue where we left off."

His hand shot out, gripping her fingers, removing them forcibly from his chest. Her mouth opened in a surprised oval.

"You will keep your hands from my person," he said with deadly calm. "You disgust me more than you ever have. What you did to my brother, and the damage you did to my relationship with him, can never be forgiven. Never."

He went around her, determined to leave her with all haste. But she was not done with him.

"And where will you go?" she lashed out, her voice gone harsh with her outrage. "Will you return to the insipid, weak Lady Emily? For I'm sure she won't have you back. Not now."

Nothing else she could have said could have stopped him. He whirled on her. "What have you done?"

She seemed at once to realize her mistake. Her eyes widened, and she backed up a step. "Nothing. I've done nothing."

"You lie," he snarled. He stormed forward, until she backed up against the stone balustrade. "I repeat, madam, what have you done?" When she made no answer, merely glared mutinously up at him, a horrible sinking feeling settled in the pit of his stomach.

How had he not seen it before? Had he been so focused on what he perceived as Emily's betrayal that he'd been unable to see the forest for the trees? "It was you, wasn't it?" he rasped. "You made certain Emily knew about our past." And then, even worse, a memory of Lydia sneaking into the study after him, kissing him. "Damn it, she followed you, didn't she? That night at Willowhaven, you got her to follow you when you cornered me in the study. That was why you kissed me. It was all to destroy Emily's confidence in me."

Lydia pressed her lips closed in defiance. Even so, he saw the flash of real fear in her eyes. Without a doubt it had been Lydia. This had all the markings of her cruel mischief.

And he had been a fool—to believe Emily would have been swayed by something so minor as a past infatuation.

Damn it, he had to get back to her.

But his silence seemed to give Lydia courage. "If her confidence was shattered, do not blame me. If I loved someone, I would not allow something like that to come between us."

The word took him aback. "Love?" He had known Emily cared deeply for him. But he had never believed she might love him. Did Emily truly love him, then?

Once again Lydia saw her mistake. "I meant that she must not love you or she would not have been swayed."

He turned on her in an instant. "How could you have done it, Lydia? Was it not enough that you took my brother from me? You had to take Emily as well?"

Her face twisted in disgust, transforming to something ugly. "And you think you would have been happy with her? That sad, scarred thing? So sweet, so understanding, filling your head with silly stories of chickens of all things. How you could have fallen for *that* is beyond me."

He took an abrupt step toward her, making her gasp. "You followed us," he snarled. "You listened in on a private moment, you defiled her confidence in me. All for your jealousies, your disgusting vanities."

He turned away before he did something he regretted. "You have done enough damage. It is over, Lydia. And if you contact me or Emily ever again, I swear you shall pay."

Not allowing her to respond, he stalked through the ballroom doors and into the brilliance within. All the while his head spun.

He was furious with himself. He'd thought that Emily had not had the faith in him to fight for what they'd had. Instead Lydia had gotten to her, had poisoned her. He well knew her skills in manipulation. He had been victim to them himself. And Emily, who had just begun to find confidence in herself, would have been defenseless against Lydia's machinations.

No, Emily was not at fault for falling prey to such cruelties. *He* was. He had thought he was protecting her by keeping his distance. Instead it had been like offering up a lamb on a platter to a wolf.

But that was not the only revelation that had the power to unmoor him this night. Now that his soul was free of her influence, he could see that it had not been Lydia's betrayal all those years ago that had affected him so deeply. Oh, it had hurt him, certainly. It had fractured his very heart.

But it had been Bertram that had shattered it beyond repair.

His brother had been the one person there for him throughout the entirety of his life. His rock, his anchor, whatever trite drivel people liked to associate with those that were the most important to them. From birth on, through their childhood, their parents' deaths, the hell that had been their uncle's house, they had never let the other forget that they were loved. That they were wanted.

Then had come Lydia.

When Bertram had announced his intent to wed her, something in Malcolm had shriveled and died. If Bertram could betray him, could hurt him, anyone could.

Now he was faced with the debilitating truth that Bertram had never willingly betrayed him. That he had been coerced into something he had never wanted.

The knowledge burned him down to a cinder.

Though a thousand candles shone brightly over his head, he felt charred inside, the darkness of it all-consuming. No light, no matter how radiant, would ever be able to reach it, to vanquish it.

Except for Emily, his heart whispered.

He stumbled at the vivid thought. Ignoring the tide of humanity surging around him, he grasped onto the memory of her for all he was worth. As he focused on her sweet face, on the way she felt in his arms and the incredible passion she had unselfishly given to him, he felt the scorched bits of himself fall away, the useless pile of rubble he had become realigning into something new and full of hope. And love.

Damn it, but he loved her.

He had already determined that he had been a fool to leave her. Now he knew, he would return to Willowhaven that very night. And would not leave again until Emily was his.

"Lord Morley."

Lady Beezleton's voice brought him up short. He smiled and bowed to his hostess, though inside he was seething with impatience to be off. "My lady."

She peered at him through her lorgnette. "You look as if you are determined to get somewhere important."

"I'm afraid I must be off for the evening."

"We are sorry to lose you."

He nodded and made to step past her. Until she spoke again.

"Did you see Lord Willbridge?"

Every nerve in his body surged with energy as he stared down at the woman. She must be deluded. "Willbridge?" he asked carefully.

"I know the two of you are thick as thieves; I thought he would have sought you out. He was here with his bride, though they did not stay for long." She shrugged. "No matter, for even a few minutes of their presence was enough to make my little ball the fête of the year." She chuckled delightedly.

The news that his friend had been there left him stunned. When last he'd seen Willbridge and Imogen, they had been back at

Willowhaven. How—and for that matter, *why*—would they have come to London?

He peered at Lady Beezleton. She was elderly, to be sure, but her eyes were clear and sharp. She wasn't confused in the least. Which meant Willbridge truly had been there.

"I don't understand," he muttered. "What were they doing here?"

Lady Beezleton raised one gray eyebrow. "I've no idea. It seemed they were looking for someone."

Looking for someone? A thought hit him then, leaving him ice cold. Mayhap there was something wrong with Emily. Perhaps she was ill, had asked for him.

He shook his head. They would not have traveled all the way to London for something of that kind. Even if Emily were failing, Willbridge wouldn't know what she meant to him. That she was the most important person in his life.

"If you do see them," Lady Beezleton went on, oblivious to his mental torture, "please give them my regards. And that lovely young woman they had with them."

His every sense sharpened. "What young woman?" he demanded.

Lady Beezleton blinked at his tone but was too well-bred to comment on it. "The lady they had with them. Willbridge's sister, I believe."

"Lady Daphne?" But no, surely they would not have brought her to London ahead of her come-out.

"Oh, I am horrid with names. I cannot recall."

He barely stopped the frustrated growl that clawed inside his chest. "Perhaps," he managed through clenched teeth, "if you could describe her?"

"Certainly. She was wearing a lovely pale blue silk gown that had the most cunning little puffed sleeves. There were small seed pearls in her hair, a brilliant addition, as they contrasted nicely with the color."

A growl rose up in Malcolm's throat. He had just determined to go to Willbridge's town house and see for himself when she said it.

"Oh, and the scar, of course."

Elation filled him. Taking the woman's hand up for a quick kiss, he spun about and raced from the ballroom.

She had come. She had traveled all the way to London, had braved a ball, had done the very thing she had dreaded most in the world. And there was no doubt in his mind why.

She had done it for him.

Though the question remained, why had she left before finding him? As he sprinted out the mansion and called for his carriage, he thought of where he had been in the past half hour. Dread settled under his skin. Had she seen him with Lydia? After the devastation that woman had caused between them at Willowhaven, he could imagine what Emily must have assumed if she had. Damn Lydia all to hell. Even now she was turning his life upside down.

No matter, he thought as his carriage rolled up. He barked his direction to the driver and vaulted inside. For within the hour she would know the truth of his feelings for her.

She would finally be his.

Chapter 27

Heart pounding like mad in his chest, Malcolm sprinted up the front steps to the Masters town home. He hammered on the solid front door before his feet had even found purchase on the top step. As he stood waiting impatiently to be let in, he recalled all the times he had entered this house in the past, in preparation for a night of debauchery or drunk and stinking at the completion of one. His visit today was for another purpose entirely. And he would hopefully leave with a fuller heart and a brighter future.

The door swung open. The butler bowed, stepping aside. "Lord Morley. Lord Willbridge is in his study."

As Malcolm was wont to do here, he hurried past the butler in the direction indicated. He had the mad desire to forego seeking Willbridge out first, to find Emily instead. His entire body tingled with the awareness that she was here somewhere, within these walls. So close he could sense her.

But Willbridge deserved the respect of hearing Malcolm's intentions first. He had been one of his closest friends since childhood. And how did Malcolm repay him? By taking advantage of the promise he had given, kissing the man's sister senseless, pursuing her, then inadvertently breaking her heart. Though Willbridge had brought Emily to London to find him, what were his true feelings on the matter? It was a big man, indeed, that would not be upset in some way that his friend wanted his little sister.

Coming up on the study, Malcolm's steps slowed. Unaccountably nervous, he took a deep breath and knocked.

"Enter." Willbridge's voice was neutral, giving away nothing.

Straightening his shoulders, Malcolm stepped over the threshold. And was immediately met by a very large fist.

It was luck and luck alone that kept Malcolm on his feet. The force of the punch had him stumbling back, crashing into the door frame. He cleared the stars from his eyes. Cradling his throbbing jaw, he looked up.

Willbridge stood with feet planted in a fighter's stance, his fists white-knuckled and raised before him. There was no softness in his expression, no forgiveness. Pure fury pulsated from his tightly wound form.

"So I was right," Malcolm muttered with a sinking heart. "You did see me with Lydia."

Willbridge's eyes narrowed. "You deserve much more from me than a bruised jaw. But I promised Emily I would not kill you, and so this was my one option. Damn it, I trusted you, Morley. With someone infinitely precious to me."

The pain in his friend's voice was like a dagger in Malcolm's chest. "That moment with Lydia—it isn't what it looked like. I feel nothing for her any longer. Nothing."

His friend was deaf to any excuses. "You broke my sister's heart."

"I swear, I never meant to hurt her."

"Yet you did."

A vision of Emily's face when last they'd been together at the river's edge sliced through his thoughts. The pain in her eyes. So what if Lydia had been the puppeteer in the whole mess. He had been equally guilty for not seeing what Lydia was up to, for leaving Emily to her mercy.

"I did," he whispered, overcome with his idiocy, and what it had cost him. "I can never make up for it."

"You can make up for it by leaving and never returning."

"I can't do that. I need to see Emily."

Willbridge's brows lowered further over his blazing gray eyes. "I don't know the details of your association with her during my absence. I cringe with shame when I think how I entrusted her to you. It was against my better judgment to bring her here after you. You who were my friend, who would prey on my sister. If you think I will allow you to even breathe in her presence again, you are sorely mistaken."

"Please, Willbridge," Malcolm begged, holding his hands out before him when his friend would have moved forward, no doubt to throw him bodily from the room, "for what we were to one another."

"You deserve nothing from me," Willbridge growled. "When you broke my sister's heart, you forfeited any right to favors from me. If it were up to me, I would beat you to a bloody pulp, and smile while doing it."

Malcolm lowered his hand, raising his chin a fraction. "Do it then," he said quietly. "I won't stop you."

If anything, Willbridge looked angrier. "Don't you dare," he spat. "You will not play a victim now, not after what you've done."

"I am the furthest thing from a victim there is," Malcolm said, self-loathing coating every word until he could taste the bitterness on his tongue. "What I have allowed to happen to Emily is reprehensible. Do your worst. I give you free rein."

Willbridge's fists shook, his eyes darkening. Malcolm forced himself to look his friend in the face. He had wronged him as much as he had Emily, had broken the sacred trust that had been given to him. He waited for the blows to come.

They never did.

Willbridge seemed to deflate. He ran a hand over his face, looking a decade older. "Leave, Morley," he rasped. "I never want to see your face darkening my door again."

Malcolm's heart, which had begun to beat again with Emily's help, fractured.

"Caleb, what's going on here?"

The quiet, feminine voice broke over the tense cloud of rage and grief that pulsed throughout the room. Malcolm's stomach flipped. But when he turned it was to find not Emily, but Imogen.

Instantly Willbridge's face softened. No, not just his face. His entire body changed, his posture relaxing visibly. He held out a hand and his wife went to him. "Nothing, love. Morley was just leaving." He shot Malcolm a warning look over her head.

"He doesn't appear ready to leave," she commented, directing her steady gaze to Malcolm. There was a mildly censorious glint in her eyes. No, not quite censorious. More disappointed. It was more potent than any of Willbridge's ragings, and hit him harder than the fist to his jaw. He squirmed with guilt.

"I trust, Lord Morley," she said in her soft voice, "you are here to make things right?"

"I am," Malcolm answered without hesitation.

A look of understanding passed between them. Willbridge glanced at them both in turn, mounting disbelief twisting his features. "To hell he will!" he roared.

Imogen turned her patient gaze to her husband. "If he's come here to undo the damage that has been done, I believe it wise to hear him out."

"I don't want to hear a damn thing to come out of his mouth," he snarled.

Imogen didn't so much as flinch at the outrage pouring off of Willbridge. Despite the despair clawing at him, Malcolm was impressed at her unflinching poise.

"It isn't for either of us to decide that," she said softly.

"You think I'll put this on Emily's shoulders?"

"She is not made of porcelain, Caleb," Imogen said. "She's stronger than you suppose. And besides, she's a grown woman. It's her future happiness on the line. She must make this decision on her own."

"She's been hurt enough," Willbridge countered hotly. "I won't give her any undue pain by forcing her into company with this bastard."

"You will not be forcing her into anything. You will be giving her a choice."

Malcolm, having stood by silently during this volley of words, finally had enough. He stepped forward, holding up a hand. "Do I have any say in this?" he asked, his voice tight.

Willbridge turned on him. "No," he snapped. "This isn't about you."

"This has everything to do with me," Malcolm said quietly. "Emily is my life. Please, Willbridge." When his friend made to turn dismissively from him, he swallowed hard and whispered, the words broken, "I love her."

Imogen's sharply indrawn breath was the only sound in the heavy quiet of the room. Malcolm heard it as if from a distance. His entire being was focused on his friend. If he could still call him friend after all was said and done. His chest ached at the thought. But, though it pained him, it was faint compared to the all-encompassing panic he'd experienced before.

That was because of Emily, he knew. She had healed that in him.

Willbridge stared back at him, his eyes wide and stunned, before looking down at his wife. She gazed back at him, her own eyes shining, a small, encouraging smile on her face. "I will let her decide," he finally said, his voice gruff.

Malcolm's heart leapt in his chest, hope rising up in him like a floodwater. It must have showed on his face, for his friend frowned again.

"Tomorrow," Willbridge stated firmly. "You can come back tomorrow and not a moment sooner. We've just got her settled in her room, and I will not disturb her now."

Malcolm bit back the argument that leapt to his lips. He finally knew the future he wanted, realized the truth in his heart. He wanted that future, with Emily beside him, to start as soon as possible.

But it would not help his case one bit to fight Willbridge's decree. As much as it would pain him to do so, he would leave this house, with Emily only a floor above him. And use the time between now and morning to dream and plan that brightening future.

Morning could not come soon enough.

"Thank you, Willbridge," he said with feeling.

His friend flushed slightly, straightening his spine and nodding briskly.

Malcolm turned to Imogen. He took up her hand, pressing it between his own warmly. But the words he wanted to say to her wouldn't come. How could he explain what was in his heart, how much it meant to him that she had come to his defense, that she was giving him a chance that he never would have had, nor deserved. "Thank you," was all he could manage.

The words were woefully inadequate. But Imogen seemed to hear the deeper meaning in them. She smiled, a true smile, and Malcolm could see in that moment what had bewitched his friend.

"Until morning, my lord," she said softly.

Ignoring the pull in his gut to sprint to the upper floors and seek Emily out, Malcolm walked with purposeful steps to the front door and to his carriage. Tomorrow, he told himself. He would return tomorrow and see if Emily could find it in her heart to forgive him.

Barking quick directions to the waiting groom, he vaulted up into the coach, slamming the door behind him. Even before he settled into his seat, he felt the other presence within. As the subtle scents of vanilla and roses assailed his senses, he realized with a thudding heart that he would not have to wait till morning for Emily's decision over his fate, after all.

• • •

Emily knew the moment Malcolm sensed her presence. He went still, every line of his body, backlit by the street lamps outside the carriage window, taut and thrumming. She felt her resolve falter for a moment. But she would not—or could not—back down now.

Her too new and extremely fragile confidence had taken a severe beating upon seeing him with Lady Morley. But his unexpected appearance at her brother's town house had sparked a furious fire in her belly that had momentarily smothered her better judgment. Nothing would do but for her to tell him, then and there, exactly what she thought of him.

How she had managed to get down to the street, much less enter the carriage, without being detected, she would never know.

Perhaps it was all those years of moving unobtrusively through life, all that practice in remaining unseen. Whatever the reason, she was here now, trying desperately to find the words she needed.

The carriage started off, the sudden jolt of it pulling on her already frayed nerves. She waited, watching him. He peered back, his eyes dark, gleaming like jet beads in the faint light. She cursed the shadows. While she had been happy enough to hide in them before, they hindered her ability to read his expression.

"Emily."

The sound of his voice, so low, rumbling through the confines of the carriage with heartbreaking familiarity, sent a jolt of need tearing through her nerves. She nearly gasped from the pain of it. It told her more than anything that, no matter her wishes on the matter, no matter how she would harden her emotions against him, her heart still belonged fully and completely to him. The burn of anger returned then, fueling her outrage, giving voice to the jumbled thoughts crowding her brain.

"You have not treated me fairly, Malcolm," she rasped.

"You are right."

The admission took her aback. As she attempted to right her disarranged thoughts, the carriage made a turn and his face was fully illuminated in the moonlight.

For the first time since he entered the carriage, she could see his eyes. At the sight of them, she sucked in a sharp breath. Never had she seen such an expression, as if he were being burned from the inside out. There was pain and hope, tenderness and despair all wound tightly together like tangled threads. She had the sudden urge to go to him, to smooth her hand over his brow, to hold him close.

But no, she told herself firmly, she could not be soft now. She had to be stronger than she ever had been if she was to get through this.

"I was fine before you came along," she began, her voice soft but growing stronger with each word. "I know you must have thought me a pathetic thing, frightened of my own shadow, with no hope for a future of my own. I know how you must have laughed at me, poor Lady Emily Masters and her ruined face and sad life."

If anything, the fire behind his eyes blazed even hotter. "Don't—" he started, his voice breaking.

She held up a hand in desperation, knowing if he stopped her she would never get the words out. "You may have thought that of me, but I was at least happy. Or, if not particularly happy, I was content." She realized then with a sharp stab that she could never return to that life with even a semblance of happiness. She would forever be discontent with her lot, for she would always want him in it. The fury that had begun a slow burn in her flared hot for all she used to have, and all she had lost, and all she wanted now but would never have. In a burst of grief she reached across the space between them and, balling up her fist, hit him in the shoulder. Hard.

"How dare you," she cried, sending her fists flying with each word. "How dare you make me love you. You have ruined my life!"

He sat still beneath her onslaught, taking every hit. Her words turned to sobs that broke over her in waves, stealing her words away. His arms came about her then, pulling her to his chest. For a second her spirit rallied and she struggled against his hold. But his arms were too strong, the pull of the comfort she could claim from them too potent. The anger drained from her, leaving heartache in its wake. She collapsed against his chest, spent, hating herself for her weakness.

For long minutes she lay exhausted and insensible, aware only of the warmth of his embrace and the steady beat of his heart under her cheek. Soon, however, other truths began to intrude: the sway of the carriage, his breath stirring the hair at the top of her head, his voice rumbling beneath her ear. She forced herself to focus on his words.

"I'm so sorry. I cannot begin to say how sorry I am. If I could go back, to do it all again, I would."

She struggled upright, pushing herself away from him. "Well, you cannot," she rasped. She felt weary to her very bones. "I know you came to my brother's home tonight to see me. But after what

I witnessed at that ball, I think you can understand I would prefer it if you did not attempt to contact me again. Now, I have had my say, and so cannot have further reason to subject myself to your company. Please turn the carriage around and return me to my brother's house."

"No."

Emily attempted to dredge up her outrage again at his effrontery. It was a pitiful thing at best. Exhausted almost beyond bearing, she looked him full in the eye and said, her voice broken, "Please, Malcolm. If you ever cared for me at all, you will leave me with my family and never try to see me again."

"I will not because I cannot let you go without having my say as well."

"You can have nothing to say to me that I have not already seen proof of in your actions."

"My actions in the past were those of a fool."

The harshness of his voice, the self-hatred that seemed to saturate it, took her aback. He must have taken her stunned silence for acquiescence, for he continued.

"When I first saw you again, what seems a lifetime ago on that first day at Willowhaven, I was a different man. There was nothing I wanted less than an emotional entanglement. I was more than happy to live the rest of my life with my heart cut off from the rest of humanity. In doing so, I need never worry that I would be betrayed again."

Despite herself, Emily's heart gave a twist at his words. Words that seemed as if they were being ripped from the very depths of his soul.

"But you did something to me from the first moment our eyes met." His lips twisted ruefully. "You touched something inside me I thought long dead. Reawakened me to feelings I thought gone forever."

He reached across the space separating them and took up her hand. His fingers were warm, surrounding her chill ones. Filling her with warmth. "You broke down every barrier I had erected," he said gruffly, his gloved thumb rubbing over her knuckles. "And I am so very glad you did. You have given me a reason to live. And more joy than I have any right to."

His words were wrapping around her heart, weaving and tangling until she feared she would never be able to free herself. Ah, but she wanted to believe him. More than anything in this world. With effort she thought of Lady Morley leaving him in the study at Willowhaven, both of them looking rumpled from an amorous embrace. And then tonight, of him with Lady Morley, the way his body had bent so intimately over her, the heated longing in that woman's eyes. It mattered not that such a union could never be. What mattered were the feelings he no doubt still held for his former lover.

With a woman Emily could never hope to compete against.

"You must think me simple indeed. You cannot know that I have recently seen that your heart belongs elsewhere, my lord. Please do not attempt to fool me with your half-truths and deceits. This evening you proved that every word you spoke to me at Willowhaven was a lie, that you have never stopped wanting Lady Morley."

In a moment he was kneeling before her. He took her arms in his hands, forcing her startled gaze to his. "Listen to me, and listen well. Yes, I once loved Lydia. But that was long ago. Once she betrayed me with my own brother, she lost my heart and any claim to it."

"Is that why you told her the story I confided in you of Jonathan?" She laughed harshly, the sound ripping from her chest. "The poor pathetic girl, so infatuated with you, telling you stories of chickens, of all things. How you must have laughed over that."

"I never told her, I swear it. She listened in on us, admitted as much to me tonight."

"But I saw you," Emily whispered. "You and her, at Willowhaven. And again tonight at Lady Beezleton's ball. I saw you lean over her, saw you go off together..." Her voice trailed off, the pain in the memory snagging on the words like a burr.

He shook his head. "What you saw was Lydia attempting to

renew what we once had. And me turning her down. On both occasions."

She stared at him. "You expect me to believe you would turn down the overtures of such a woman, a woman you admit you once loved?"

"Yes." The word came out without hesitation.

"Why?"

"Because," he murmured, pulling her closer, his eyes achingly warm even in the cold moonlight, "my heart belongs, completely and forevermore, to another."

Emily's mouth went dry as she stared up at him. Surely he didn't mean her. He couldn't possibly love her.

His next words proved her wrong.

"I love you, Emily." He smiled faintly, his gaze scouring her upturned face.

Emily shook her head, the dim image of his face blurring as her eyes filled with tears.

"I have no reason to hope you can ever forgive me. I took things into my own hands, made decisions for you I thought were best but that in the end drove us apart. I stayed away from you in the hopes that it would protect you from Lydia but only managed to keep you in the dark, leaving you vulnerable to her cruelties. And I thought your faith in me faltered, when in reality it was my own faith that did so. I love you, Emily," he repeated. "So very much, and so much more than I ever thought it possible to love another. You have given my heart reason to beat again."

Certainly she was in bed dreaming this whole thing. She had fallen asleep after Imogen had left her and was even now curled up in bed, fast asleep.

"Pinch me," she whispered.

The corners of his eyes crinkled in amusement before his face transformed to something infinitely tender. "I will do better than that to convince you," he murmured before his head bent to hers.

Chapter 28

The first touch of Malcolm's lips to hers was unlike anything she had ever experienced. In all the times they had kissed, never had there been this deep-seated knowledge that he loved her. It wrapped around her heart and, as unbelievable as it seemed, she recognized it immediately for the truth it was. A calling of one heart to another, as if they had been predestined for one another since the beginning of time.

She opened to him without reservation. Her arms came about him, dragging him close, her mouth opening beneath the onslaught of his kiss. He tasted like champagne and spice, sweet and sultry and thoroughly male. His tongue twined with hers, its bold strokes sending heat to the most private core of her. He dragged her closer, pushing between the cradle of her thighs, and the heat turned to moist need. She wanted him there, she knew. Pressing against her, inside her, until she could not tell where one of them ended and the other began.

He broke the kiss, his lips moving over her scarred cheek, caressing it tenderly, before moving to her ear. "You are beautiful," he whispered. "The most beautiful creature in the world. What you do to me, Emily. I have never felt this in my life."

Tears stung her eyes. These were not mere words, she knew. She felt their source, the deep place in him they had come from, and wanted to weep for the joy they brought her. That this man could think her beautiful—but, more than that, could make her *feel* beautiful—touched her deeply.

He paid homage to the column of her throat, his mouth lathing kisses lower and lower. With nimble fingers he undid the tie of her cloak, pulled the fabric aside.

And froze.

By instinct Emily froze as well, her eyes flying open. Had he seen something to disgust him? Mariah's gown was more revealing than anything she had worn before. It would show, without a doubt, that she was not buxom in the least, was not curvaceous or voluptuous. Perhaps he would find her wanting.

When she looked at his face, it told a different story entirely. It was as if he were devouring her, the hunger in his expression was so great.

"This is not your gown," he remarked hoarsely.

"No," she whispered. She licked suddenly dry lips. "It's Mariah's. Imogen let me borrow it. For the ball." She plucked at the shimmering silk. "We had to take it in. I don't fill it out well. I know I am not built in the way most men prefer—"

"Shh." Malcolm placed a finger against her lips. Emily's cheeks grew warm as he continued to take her in. She wished she could cover herself, could hide from his too-intense gaze.

Then his hands came up to cup her breasts. And Emily forgot her embarrassment.

"I have never hated Lydia more than I do now."

"What are you talking about?" she blurted.

His eyes met hers, and she felt her soul was branded by the fiery possession in them. "She prevented me from seeing you thus in the light of a thousand candles, from asking you to dance, from taking you in my arms in front of all of Society and showing them that the most stunning creature there at that damnable ball was mine and mine alone."

Emily leaped across the small space separating them, her mouth finding his, her hands pulling ineffectively at his evening clothes. His hands were much more skilled, making short work of his cravat, removing his coat and waistcoat. As they moved to her clothing, however, the coach slowed to a gentle stop.

He raised his head, peering down at her in the gloom. "It appears we're home."

Just then the door to the carriage began to open. Quick as a shot Malcolm's hand gripped tight to the handle. "A moment more, if you please, Daniel," he called through the door.

"Very good, my lord," the driver's voice answered.

Malcolm looked at her with unfathomable eyes. "I will have him turn the coach around, will have you back in your brother's house shortly."

Regret speared through her. "I would that we had more time."

"Yes," he said, and that one word held a world of meaning, all of it reflected in her heart. "Though," he continued, "I must say I should be glad for it. I would not want to make love for the first time to my future wife in a carriage."

"Your future wife," she said, dazed.

He smiled gently, cupping her cheek in his palm. "Did you think I would declare myself heart and soul to you and not want to spend the rest of my life with you? But I should ask you first. I would not take away that choice from you, Emily. I want you to be happy."

She blinked up at him, overcome. "So ask me," she whispered.

His smile widened. Pushing her back in her seat, he knelt properly in front of her on one knee—as well as he could manage in the cramped confines of the coach—and said clearly and steadily, "Lady Emily Masters, I love you with all of my heart. Will you do me the very great honor of marrying me—"

"Yes!" she squealed, launching herself into his arms.

He chuckled into her shoulder. Soon, however, the chuckles subsided and his lips began to do wonderful things to the side of her neck.

"I don't suppose," she managed unsteadily, "that you would mind showing me your home? I have only seen the inside from the doorway, after all."

He stilled. "You wish to come inside?"

"More than anything," she breathed.

Malcolm pulled back to look at her. Love and longing, all tempered by that stubborn will of his, filled his face. "You know what will happen if you do, Emily."

She didn't hesitate. "I know, Malcolm."

He gripped her hand in his, bringing it to his mouth for a hard kiss before he flung the door to the carriage wide. "You see nothing," he ordered before, taking her hand in his, he pulled Emily from the carriage and up the front steps. She had a quick view of the startled face of the driver before Malcolm unlocked the door and hauled her inside.

Emily let loose a startled laugh. "He'll think you're a magician, pulling unexpected women from carriages like that…"

Her words trailed off as he dragged her into his arms. "Only one woman," he declared hotly. "Only ever you."

With that he lifted her in his arms and strode through the house. There was not a light to be seen, the only illumination the pale moonlight bleaching everything of color. Yet his steps were sure and swift as he climbed the staircase, even more certain as he made his way down a hallway that no doubt led to private apartments. He flung open one particular door, slamming it closed behind him. Emily's feet found purchase on the floor, though her world went spinning as Malcolm dragged her body to his.

There was no one to stop them, no reason to leave the pleasure of one another's arms. That knowledge, along with the promise of their future together, should have slowed their hands. Instead, a frenzy took over them. Emily could not get him undressed fast enough, could not wait to feel him over her, in her.

Malcolm must have felt the same. Her dress quickly found its way to the floor, her undergarments soon after. He stepped back several feet, his eyes raking her nude body. Emily thought vaguely that she should cover herself. She had never been thus before a man, never so exposed.

Yet the molten fire in his eyes had her feeling like one of the sirens of old.

Feeling powerful that she could so affect him, she stood straighter. The position thrust her breasts out. His dark eyes widened in appreciation.

"You are mine," he growled. He pulled his shirt over his head, went to work on unfastening his breeches next. Emily's eyes fastened greedily to the sculpted contours of his chest, the faint dusting of black hair that tapered down beyond her sight. He pushed his breeches and smalls down and stood gloriously naked before her view. His manhood thrust toward her, erect and proud. She should have been frightened. Instead wonder washed over her, heat and moisture blooming anew between her legs as she imagined it entering her, filling her.

"I am yours," she whispered fiercely. "And you are mine."

Satisfaction bloomed in his smile. "Yes," he answered a moment before he took her in his arms.

The feel of his bare skin against hers, the contrast of smooth warmth and rough hair, made her almost wild with wanting. Lips latching hungrily to hers, he wrapped his arms tight about her, lifting her feet from the ground. Soon she was falling, the softness of blankets and pillows catching her. His hard body quickly followed, pushing her deeper into the bedding.

His hands and mouth were everywhere at once, pushing her to the brink. Of what, she didn't know, though her body arched, searching for it. Desperate for it. When his mouth found her nipple, drawing it eagerly into his hot mouth, she moaned. His fingers found the core of her, pushing through the thatch of curls there to stroke over that most sensitive place. She very nearly screamed.

"You're so wet," he rasped. "Emily, love, I need you. Now."

He moved over her, pushing between her thighs. She opened fully, trembling as he pressed into her. When he paused, she wanted to cry.

"Emily," he grated between clenched teeth, "if you wish me to stop I will. But after this, there is no turning back."

Warmth filled her, making her heart feel as if it would burst from her chest. Smiling, she took his face tenderly between her hands. "There was no turning back the moment you came back into my life, Malcolm. I loved the perfect idea of you all those years. Now I love even more fully the man you are."

His eyes seemed to fill before he lowered his forehead to hers.

"God, but I love you," he whispered thickly. With a steady thrust, he surged forward, seating himself to the hilt within her. Filling her body and soul.

Her body pulsed around him, welcoming him, the sharp pain of his entrance quickly fading until all that was left was a low burning flame. He stayed perfectly still above her, waiting patiently as she adjusted to him, his arms trembling as he held his weight from her slight form. And she didn't think she could have loved him more. She smiled up at him. "I love you, Malcolm," she whispered.

Relief and wonder filled his eyes. He took her lips in a gentle kiss, even as he began to move slowly within her. Each thrust was an exquisite torture, rising her to where she had been and beyond. Never did she think such heights of pleasure existed, that two people could be so completely connected. Their breaths mingled, her gasp followed by his low moan, their hips moving in perfect synchronization.

His thrusts became quicker, the tension in her building. She lifted her legs about his slender flanks, tilting her hips. Bringing him in even deeper than before. His mouth found her neck, bit gently as a low growl escaped him. That sound shuddered through her. Carrying her to the brink.

Sending her over its edge.

Emily exploded in sensation, her body clenching and trembling as waves of pleasure washed over her. Above her Malcolm's thrusts became frantic before, with one wild shout, he went ridged. He fell beside her, pulling her into his side. She laid her head on his chest, listening to the steady beat of his heart, a heart that belonged to her, as fully as hers belonged to him. She drifted off with a smile on her face, for the first time in a long while looking forward to the coming day—the coming years.

With Malcolm at her side.

Epilogue

Mere hours after smuggling Emily back inside her brother's town house, Malcolm hurried up the front steps. He had kissed her sweet lips, had held her close just that morning, yet it felt like a lifetime ago. He would have much preferred to run off to Gretna Green with her. As one, however, they had agreed that Willbridge, for all he was to them, deserved much more than a hasty union done under cover of night.

If truth be told, Malcolm wanted more as well. He wanted to claim her as his wife in broad daylight, shouting it from the rooftops, laying his heart out for all the world to see. As much as he could not believe his good fortune, Emily had somehow chosen to look on his scarred, battered soul, and had fallen in love with him regardless.

He was a lucky bastard indeed.

Willbridge himself opened the door to his knock, his face a hard, unforgiving mask. Yes, he was a lucky bastard. *If* he could survive getting past Willbridge.

"Morley," Willbridge said, his voice cold.

"Willbridge."

"You're here bloody early."

"Yes." Malcolm shifted from foot to foot, his fingers tightening about the bouquet of tulips he held.

Willbridge eyed the flowers beneath a lowered brow, then grunted. "Just as well. She's waiting for you in the drawing room."

Malcolm could not keep the smile from his face.

A low growl rumbled from Willbridge. "I would not be too

confident if I were you." When Malcolm said nothing, he scowled. "Come along, then."

Malcolm followed his friend up to the drawing room. Every step, every inch closer, he felt the invisible connection between him and Emily pulsing with golden light. Soon, he thought, anticipation burning bright. Soon he would see her. It had seemed an eternity since he had left her side. After today, he would not be forced so far from her again.

She sat perched on a pale gray couch, a stream of sunlight illuminating her. She looked a veritable angel. The copper of her hair shone brilliant, her porcelain skin seeming the finest alabaster. She looked up from the book she was reading at his entrance and a faint pink stained the curve of her cheeks. She didn't smile; they had agreed that it would be best if they made it appear they had never met the evening before, had never come to an understanding. For love of her brother.

Even so, her pewter eyes shone with her joy. It took everything in Malcolm not to go to her, to take her in his arms, and kiss her senseless.

"Get on with it then," Willbridge grumbled. "We haven't got all day."

Malcolm didn't give his friend a second glance. He hurried forward, bowing first to Imogen, who sat in a separate high-backed chair, before he returned his attention to Emily.

"Lady Emily." He took up her hand, pressing his lips to her fingers, before he handed her the bouquet.

"Thank you, my lord. They are lovely," she murmured. Her eyes never left his.

They stared at one another for several long moments before Imogen came forward. She took the flowers from Emily's hand. "I'll have the housekeeper put these in water for you, dear. Why don't you take a seat, Lord Morley. I do believe there's room beside Emily."

Malcolm didn't need further urging. As he settled in, he saw Imogen and Willbridge talking in low tones near the drawing room door. "I certainly will not leave them alone," Willbridge said, leveling a glower on Malcolm before he crossed his arms over his chest and planted his feet wide.

So Willbridge would not leave, would he? Malcolm's lips quirked. Just as well, for he and Emily had planned a script for this little farce. All to appease her brother.

He turned to her. Her eyes were wide and patient. And filled with such love he thought his heart would burst from his chest then and there from the happiness filling him. Suddenly the script, the theatrics they had planned, didn't mean a damn thing. All that mattered was this woman, and that the world knew she was his.

He dropped to his knees before her. Her eyes flared in surprise. Behind him he heard Imogen's faint gasp, heard Caleb's low growl. Not giving a damn, he took Emily's hands in his.

"In the space of weeks, you have turned my very world on its head. So many small things happened to lead me to you. I thank God that Willbridge married, that I made that asinine promise to him to watch over you. Without those things, I would never have seen the true jewel you are, would not have found the partner of my life. The other half of my soul."

"So this is my fault, is it?" Willbridge grumbled before Imogen's loud shush quieted him.

Malcolm hardly heard a bit of it, so focused was he on the woman before him. Her face shone with her happiness, her eyes alight with love. His throat grew tight, and he swallowed hard past the sudden lump there.

"If you entrust your heart to me," he rasped, "I promise you I will spend the rest of my existence making your happiness my priority. I vow, here and now, to never knowingly give you a moment's pain, to make certain every minute is filled with as much joy as you give me right now. I love you, with everything I was, everything I am, and everything I ever will be. Lady Emily Masters, will you marry me?"

Before the words were out of his mouth, Emily launched herself forward. Her sweet arms came about him, her lips met his. He vaguely heard the faint sound of a door closing, and then all else faded.

Some time later he raised his head to look down on her smiling face. Tears tracked down her cheeks like crystals. He tenderly wiped them away. "Is that a yes, then?"

She laughed shakily. "I do believe you know the answer to that, as I gave it to you last night. And now that you have given me your promises," she continued, her voice growing husky, "I have some of my own to give to you."

To his shock, she slid off the couch to kneel in front of him. Taking up his hand in hers, bringing it to her lips, she said, her voice solemn and thick with emotion, "I promise that you will never have reason to doubt my love for you. That I will take the heart you have entrusted me with and cherish it forever. That you will never again have to walk this life alone."

It had been a lifetime since Malcolm had cried. He did now, without embarrassment or shame, letting the tears fall freely down his face. Emily gazed up at him, her own eyes shining. She gently wiped away the moisture from his cheeks.

"That wasn't fair," he said softly, his voice hoarse with emotion. "It's the woman who's supposed to cry at these things."

"It's your own fault, you silly man," she said with a small smile. "I was quite content with the promises we made to one another last night. Though I admit," she continued huskily, "I'm very glad you went off script."

He pulled her close. "Seeing as we've been left blessedly alone, do you think you'd be willing to go off script again?"

She happily obliged, dragging his mouth back to hers. Sealing their promises with a kiss.

Acknowledgments

I am incredibly blessed to have so many supportive people in my corner. From cheering me on, to lending an ear, to offering a shoulder, you all keep me going, every single day.

Thank you to my agent, Kim Lionetti, and to my editor, Kayla Park, and the entire team at EverAfter Romance, for loving Emily and Malcolm as much as I do.

Thank you to SVRWA, to my amazing RWA 2017 Golden Heart Rebelles, to my fellow Drawing Room Patronesses, to my fantastic Le Bou Crew, and to my writing tribe. I wish I could give every one of you a hug.

Thank you to my fabulous critique and plotting partners and beta readers for this book: Addie, Cathy, Maria, Silvi, Julie, Joni, and Debbie L. Your advice was invaluable.

Thank you to my family and friends who have cheered for me and supported me. I am grateful for each and every one of you.

Thank you to my amazing readers; you make my heart happy. And a special thanks to those who asked for Emily's story!

And, of course, a huge thank-you to my husband and children. You are my everything. I hope I've made you proud. (Even though, Mr. Britton, I still haven't put that sword with the secret compartment in the hilt in my book...) I love you so very much.

CHRISTINA BRITTON developed a passion for writing romance novels shortly after buying her first at the tender age of thirteen. Though for several years she turned to art and put brush instead of pen to paper, she has returned to her first love and is now writing full-time. She spends her days dreaming of corsets and cravats and noblemen with tortured souls.

She lives with her husband and two children in the San Francisco Bay Area. A member of Romance Writers of America, she also belongs to her local chapter, Silicon Valley RWA, and is a 2017 RWA® Golden Heart® Winner. You can find her on the web at **www.christinabritton.com**, Twitter as **@cbrittonauthor**, or **facebook.com/ChristinaBrittonAuthor**.